THE
FORBIDDEN
DOOR

Dean Koontz is the author of more than a dozen *New York Times* No.1 bestsellers. His books have sold over 500 million copies worldwide, and his work is published in 38 languages.

He was born and raised in Pennsylvania and lives with his wife Gerda and their dog Elsa in southern California.

🐦 @DeanKoontz
📘 Facebook.com/deankoontzofficial
www.deankoontz.com

BY DEAN KOONTZ

DEAN KOONTZ
THE
FORBIDDEN
DOOR

HarperCollins*Publishers*

HarperCollins*Publishers*
1 London Bridge Street,
London SE1 9GF

www.harpercollins.co.uk

This paperback edition 2019
1

First published in Great Britain by HarperCollins*Publishers* 2018

First published in the USA in 2018 by Bantam Books,
an imprint of Random House,
A division of Penguin Random House LLC, New York.

A catalogue record for this book
is available from the British Library

ISBN: 978-0-00-829145-7 (PB B-format)
ISBN: 978-0-00-829148-8 (PB A-format)

Text design by Virginia Norey

Printed and bound in Great Britain by
CPI Group (UK) Ltd, Croydon, CR0 4YY

MIX
Paper from
responsible sources
FSC™ C007454

This book is produced from independently certified FSC™ paper
to ensure responsible forest management.

For more information visit: www.harpercollins.co.uk/green

This book is dedicated to Leason and Marlene Pomeroy,
affectionately known as the fireball and the firecracker,
who are a wondrous delight.

For all we have and are,
For all our children's fate . . .
—RUDYARD KIPLING, "For All We Have and Are"

✳

Staccato signals of constant information
A loose affiliation of millionaires
And billionaires and, baby,
These are the days of miracle and wonder.
—PAUL SIMON, "The Boy in the Bubble"

✳

Creating a neural [brain] lace is the thing that really matters
for humanity to achieve symbiosis with machines.
—ELON MUSK

THE
FORBIDDEN
DOOR

PART ONE

Desperate Heart

1

At FIRST THE BREEZE WAS NO MORE THAN A LONG sigh, breathing through the Texas high country as though expressing some sadness attendant to Nature herself.

They were sitting in the fresh air, in the late-afternoon light, because they assumed that the house was bugged, that anything they said within its rooms would be monitored in real time.

Likewise, they trusted neither the porches nor the barn, nor the horse stables.

When they had something important to discuss, they retreated to the redwood lawn chairs under the massive oak tree in the backyard, facing a flatness of grassland that rolled on to the distant horizon and, for all that the eye could tell, continued to eternity.

As Sunday afternoon became evening, Ancel and Clare Hawk sat in those chairs, she with a martini, he with Macallan Scotch over ice, steeling themselves for an upcoming television program they didn't want to watch but that might change their lives.

"What bombshell can they be talking about?" Clare wondered.

"It's TV news," Ancel said. "They pitch most every story like it'll shake the foundations of the world. It's how they sell soap."

Clare watched him as he stared out at the deep, trembling grass and the vastness of sky as if he never tired of them and saw some new meaning in them every time he gave them his attention. A big man with a weathered face and work-scarred hands, he looked as if his heart might be as hard as bone, though she'd never known one more tender.

After thirty-four years of marriage, they had endured hardships and shared many successes. But now—and perhaps for as long as they yet might have together—their lives were defined by one blessing and one unbearable loss, the birth of their only child, Nick, and his death at the age of thirty-two, the previous November.

Clare said, "I'm feeling like it's more than selling soap, like it's some vicious damn twist of the knife."

Ancel reached out with his left hand, which she held tightly. "We thought it all out, Clare. We have plans. We're ready for whatever."

"I'm not ready to lose Jane, too. I'll never be ready."

"It won't happen. They're who they are, she's who she is, and I'd put my money on her every time."

Just when the faded-denim sky began to darkle toward sapphire overhead and took upon itself a glossy sheen, the breeze quickened and set the oak tree to whispering.

Their daughter-in-law, Jane Hawk, who was as close to them as any real daughter might have been, had recently been indicted for espionage, treason, and seven counts of murder, crimes that she hadn't committed. She would be the sole subject of this evening's *Sunday Magazine,* a one-hour TV program that rarely devoted more than ten minutes to a profile of anyone, either president or pop singer. The most-wanted fugitive in America and a media sensation, Jane was labeled "the beautiful monster" by the tabloids, a cognomen used in promos for the forthcoming special edition of *Sunday Magazine.*

Ancel said, "Her indictment by some misled grand jury, now this TV show, all the noise about it . . . you realize what it must mean?"

"Nothing good."

"Well, but I think she's got evidence that'll destroy the sons of bitches, and they know she's got it. They're desperate. If she finds a reporter or someone in the Bureau who maybe she can trust—"

"She tried before. The bigger the story, the fewer people she can trust. And this is as big as a story gets."

"They're desperate," Ancel insisted. "They're throwin' all they got at her, tryin' to turn the whole country against her, make her a monster no one'll ever believe."

"And what then?" Clare worried. "How does she have any hope if the whole country's against her?"

"Because it won't be."

"I don't know how you can be so sure."

"The way they demonize her, this hysteria they ginned up in the media—it's too much piled on top of too much. People sense it."

"Those who know her, but that's not a world."

"People all over, they're talkin' about what the real story might be, whether maybe she's bein' set up."

"What people? All over where?"

"All over the Internet."

"Since when do you spend five minutes on the Internet?"

"Since this latest with her."

The sun appeared to roll below the horizon, although in fact the horizon rolled away from the sun. In the instant when all the remaining light of day was indirect across the red western sky, the breeze quickened again and became a wind aborning, as if all were a clockwork.

As the looser leaves of the live oak were shaken down, Clare let go of Ancel's hand and covered her glass, and he shielded his.

There was no privacy in the house, and they weren't finished counseling each other in matters of grief and hope, preparing for the affront that would be the TV program. The wind brought the dark, and the dark brought a chill, but the sea of stars was a work of wonder and a source of solace.

2

TEN MILES FROM HAWK RANCH, EGON GOTTFREY heads the operation to take Ancel and Clare Hawk into custody and ensure their fullest cooperation in the search for their daughter-in-law.

Well, *custody* is too formal a word. Each member of Gottfrey's team carries valid Department of Homeland Security credentials. They also possess valid ID for the NSA and the FBI, though they work at those two agencies only on paper. They receive three salaries and earn three pensions, ostensibly to preserve and defend the United States, while in fact working for the revolution. The leaders of the revolution make sure that their foot soldiers are well rewarded by the very system they are intent on overthrowing.

Because of Egon Gottfrey's successful career in Homeland, he was approached to join the Techno Arcadians, the visionaries who conduct the secret revolution. He is now one of them. And why not? He doesn't believe in the United States anyway.

The Techno Arcadians will change the world. They will pacify contentious humanity, end poverty, create Utopia through technology.

Or so the Unknown Playwright would have us believe.

The Hawks will not be arrested. Gottfrey and his crew will take possession of them. Neither attorneys nor courts will be involved.

Having arrived in Worstead, Texas, shortly after four o'clock in the afternoon, Egon Gottfrey is bored by the town within half an hour of checking into the Holiday Inn.

In 1896, when this jerkwater became a center through which the region's farms and ranches shipped their products to market, it had been called Sheepshear Station, because of the amount of baled wool that passed through on the way to textile mills.

That's the story, and there's no point in questioning it.

By 1901, when the town was incorporated, the founders felt that the name Sheepshear Station wasn't sophisticated enough to match their vision of the future. Besides, snarky types routinely called it Sheepshit Station. It was then named Worstead, after Worstede, the parish in Norfolk, England, where worsted wool was first made.

Anyway, that's what Gottfrey is supposed to believe.

More than fourteen thousand rustic citizens now call it home.

Whatever they call it, Egon Gottfrey finds it to be a thin vision of a place, incomplete in its detail, much like an artist's pencil study done before proceeding to oil paints. But every place feels like that to him.

The streets aren't shaded. The only trees are in the park in the town square, as if there is a limited budget for stage dressing.

Near sunset, he walks the downtown area, where the buildings mostly have flat roofs with parapets, the kind behind which villains and sheriffs alike crouch to fire on each other in a thousand old movies. Many structures are of locally quarried limestone or rust-colored sand-struck brick. The sameness and plainness don't allow the chamber of commerce to call the architecture *quaint*.

At Julio's Steakhouse, where the bar extends onto an elevated and roofed patio overlooking the street, Paloma Sutherland and Sally Jones, two of the agents under Gottfrey's command, having come in from Dallas, are precisely where they are supposed to be, enjoying a drink at a street-side table. They make eye contact as he passes.

And in the park, on a bench, Rupert Baldwin is studying a news-paper. Wearing Hush Puppies and a roomy corduroy suit and a beige shirt and a bolo tie with an ornamental turquoise clasp, he looks like some nerdy high school biology teacher, but he is tough and ruthless.

As Gottfrey walks past, Rupert only clears his throat.

On another bench sits Vince Penn, half as wide as he is tall, with a flat face and the big hands of a natural-born strangler.

Vince holds a handful of pebbles. Now and then, he throws one of the stones with wicked accuracy, targeting the unwary squirrels that have been conditioned by Worstead locals to trust people.

South of the park stands a two-star mom-and-pop motel, Purple Sage Inn, as unconvincing as any location in town.

Parked in front of Room 12 is a bespoke Range Rover created by Overfinch North America, a vehicle with major performance upgrades, a carbon-fiber styling package, and a dual-valve titanium exhaust system; it's a recent perk for certain members of the revolution. The Range Rover means Gottfrey's two most senior agents—Christopher Roberts and Janis Dern—have checked in.

Counting Egon Gottfrey and the two men who are at this moment conducting surveillance of the entrance to Hawk Ranch, ten miles east of Worstead, the team of nine is complete.

In this operation, they are not using burner phones, not even Midland GXT walkie-talkies, which are often useful. In some parts of the country, Texas being one, there are too many paranoid fools who think elements of the government and certain industries conspire in wicked schemes; some are in law enforcement or were in the military, and they spend countless hours monitoring microwave transmissions for evidence to confirm their wild suspicions.

Or so the Unknown Playwright would have us believe.

As Gottfrey continues his walk through town, no longer to confirm the presence of his team, merely to pass time, the sinking sun floods the streets with crimson light. The once-pale limestone buildings are now radiant by reflection, but they appear to be built of translucent onyx lit from within. The very air is aglow, as if all the light in the invisible spectrum—infrared and other—is beginning to manifest to the eye, as though the illusion that is the world will burst and reveal what lies under this so-called reality.

Egon Gottfrey is not merely a nihilist who believes there is no meaning in life. He's a *radical philosophical* nihilist who contends that there is no possibility of an objective basis for truth, and therefore no such thing as truth, but also that the entire world and his existence—everyone's existence—are a fantasy, a vivid delusion.

The world is as ephemeral as a dream, each moment of the day but a mirage within an infinite honeycomb of mirages. The only thing about himself that he can say exists, with certainty, is his mind wrapped in the illusion of his physical body. He thinks; therefore, he is. But his body, his life, his country, and his world are all illusion.

On embracing this view of the human condition, a lesser mind might have gone mad, surrendering to despair. Gottfrey has remained sane by playing along with the illusion that is the world, as if it is a stage production for an unknowable audience, as if he is an actor in a drama for which he's never seen a script. It's marionette theater. He is a marionette, and he's okay with that.

He's okay with it for two reasons, the first of which is that he has a sharply honed curiosity. He is his own fanboy, eager to see what will happen to him next.

Second, Gottfrey likes his role as a figure of authority with power over others. Even though it all means nothing, even though he has no control over events, just goes along to get along, it is far better to be one through whom the Unknown Playwright wields power rather than to be one on whom that power is brought to bear.

3

THE ROOM ILLUMINED ONLY BY THE NETHERWORLD glow of the TV, the vaguest reflections of moving figures on the screen throbbing across the walls like spectral presences . . .

Ancel sitting stiffly in his armchair, stone-faced in response to *Sunday Magazine*'s lies and distortions, the program mirrored in his gray eyes . . .

Clare couldn't stay in her chair, couldn't just watch and listen and do nothing. She got up and paced, talking back to the screen: "Bullshit" and "Liar" and "You hateful bastard."

This was nothing like any previous edition of *Sunday Magazine*. Always before it had avoided both puff pieces and vitriolic attacks, striving for balance, at times almost highbrow. But *this*. This was the worst kind of tabloid exploitation and alarmism. This special, "The Beautiful Monster," had one intention—to paint Jane as an evil angel, a traitor to her country, who wasn't only capable of horrific violence but who also perhaps took pleasure in wanton murder.

At the half-hour break, the program host teased the blockbuster revelation that they had been selling in the promos for days. In a portentous voice, he promised to feature it in the next segment.

As the first commercial played, Clare perched on a footstool and closed her eyes and wrapped her arms around herself, chilled. "What is this, Ancel? This isn't journalism, not one iota of it."

"Character assassination. Propaganda. These people she's up against, they're veins of rot runnin' through government and tech companies, hell-bent to destroy her before she can tell her story."

"You think people are still going to defend her after this?"

"I do, Clare. These fools are hammerin' too hard, makin' her out to be some girl version of Dracula and Charles Manson and Benedict Arnold rolled into one."

"A lot of stupid people will believe it," Clare worried.

"Some stupid. Some gullible. Not everyone. Maybe not most."

She said, "I don't want to watch any more of this."

"Neither do I. But that's not a choice, is it? We're one with Jane. They blow up her life, they blow up ours. We've got to see what's left of us when this show is done."

After the break, *Sunday Magazine* harked back to Jane's photo taken on completion of her Bureau training at Quantico, where she'd met Nick when he was assigned to Corps Combat Development Command at the same base. There were wedding photographs: Nick in his Marine dress uniform, Jane in a simple white bridal gown. Such a stunning couple.

Seeing her lost son and his bride so happy, so vibrant, Clare was overcome with emotion.

The narration moved to film of Nick receiving the Navy Cross, which was one step below the Medal of Honor, Jane looking on with such love and pride.

Clare got up from the footstool and went to Ancel and sat on the arm of his chair and put a hand on his shoulder, and he put a hand on her knee and squeezed and said, "I know."

The narrator began to talk of Nick's suicide the previous November.

He and Jane had been at home in Alexandria, Virginia, preparing dinner, having a little wine. Their boy, Travis, was on a sleepover with another five-year-old in the neighborhood, so that his parents might have a romantic evening. Nick went to the bathroom . . . and didn't return. Jane found him clothed, sitting in the bathtub. With his Marine-issue combat knife, he'd cut his neck deeply enough to sever a carotid artery. He left a note, the first sentence in his neat cursive, which deteriorated thereafter: *Something is wrong with me. I need. I very much need. I very much need to be dead.*

More than four months had passed since that devastating call from Jane. Clare's tears now were as hot as her tears then.

"That," the narrator solemnly intoned, "was Jane Hawk's story, and the investigation by the Alexandria police confirmed every detail. In the days following Nick's death, friends say Jane became obsessed with what she believed was an inexplicable rise in suicides nationwide. She discovered that thousands of happy, accomplished people like her husband, none with a history of depression, were taking their lives for no apparent reason. On leave from the FBI, so deep in grief that friends worried for her mental health, she began to research this disturbing trend, which soon consumed her."

Suddenly it seemed that the tenor of the show might change, that all the terrible things said about Jane in the first half hour might be considered from a more sympathetic perspective, raising doubts about the official portrayal of her as traitorous and cruel.

The program turned to a university professor, an expert in suicide prevention. He claimed that nothing was unusual about the increase in suicides over the past two years, that the rate always fluctuated. He claimed that the percentage of affluent, apparently happy people killing themselves was still within normal parameters.

"That can't be right," Clare said.

Next came an expert in criminal psychology, a woman with hair pulled tightly back in a chignon, as lean as a whippet, eyes owlish behind black-framed round lenses, wearing a severely tailored suit that matched the severity of her manner as she discussed what was known of the subject's difficult childhood.

Jane. A piano prodigy from the age of four. Daughter of the famous pianist Martin Duroc. Some said Duroc was demanding, distant. Jane was estranged from him. Her mother, also a talented pianist, had committed suicide. Nine-year-old Jane had discovered the bloody body in a bathtub. A year later, Duroc remarried in spite of his daughter's objection. A decade thereafter, Jane declined a full scholarship to Oberlin, rejected a music career, finished four years of college in three, and sought a life in law enforcement.

"And it's intriguing to consider her six years at the FBI," the psychologist said. As the camera moved close on her face to capture the pale solemnity of her expression, she lowered her voice as if imparting a confidence. "During her time in the Bureau, Jane was assigned to cases under the purview of Behavioral Analysis Units Three and Four, which deal with mass murderers and serial killers. She participated in ten investigations with eight resolutions. For a young woman who might have a long-harbored grudge against men, being immersed in the world of murderous male sociopaths, required to *think like them* in order to find and apprehend them, the experience could have had profound traumatic effects on her psychology."

Clare shuddered with a sense of some abomination coming. She rose from the arm of Ancel's chair. "What the *hell* does that mean?"

On the screen now: J. J. Crutchfield. The narrator recounted the sordid story of this killer who had kept the eyes of his women victims in jars of preservative. Jane had wounded and captured him.

And now: narration over video of the isolated farm where two vicious men had raped and murdered twenty-two girls. Here the agent working the case with Jane had been shot to death, and it had fallen to her, alone in the night, to counter-stalk the two murderers who were stalking her. She had taken out both of them, killing the second in the cellar rape room where the victims had been killed, before they were buried in the former hog pen.

More video from that night, outside the farmhouse, after the police arrived. Jane conferring with officers in the crosslight of patrol cars, strikingly beautiful, like an avenging goddess, but hair wild, her uplit face made subtly ominous by a mascara of shadows.

Sunday Magazine froze the video on a close-up that did not deny her beauty but that suggested . . . What? A disturbing hardness about her? A potential for cruelty? Madness?

Walking along a street in Alexandria, the town where Nick and Jane had lived, the program host addressed the camera. "How thin is the line between heroism and villainy?"

"Don't be stupid," Clare said. "They aren't separated by a thin line. They're different countries, an ocean apart."

Ancel sat silent and grim-faced.

"When a good person," the host said, "badly damaged by profound childhood trauma, for too long is immersed in the dark world of serial killers . . . might she lose her way?"

He stopped in front of the Alexandria police headquarters.

"After the events of recent weeks that have made Jane Hawk front-page news, the police department that originally certified her husband's death a suicide has quietly reopened the case. The body has been exhumed. A subsequent autopsy and extensive toxicological tests reveal that Nicholas Hawk had a powerful sedative in his system and that the angle and nature of the lethal cut in his neck are not consistent with a self-administered knife wound."

Clare felt cold in heart and blood and bone. Such a world of deceit. Such bold, shameless lies. Nick's remains had been cremated. Only his ashes were buried in Arlington National Cemetery. There was no body to exhume.

4

SUNDAY MAGAZINE WAS NOT ON JANE'S RADAR.

Hours earlier, she had survived an ordeal near Lake Tahoe that had almost been the end of her, leaving her shaken and desolate. She had obtained evidence of murder that might help her break open the conspiracy that had taken Nick's life and so many others, but she'd gotten it at considerable emotional, psychological, and moral cost.

Through a cold day darkened by storm clouds, blinded by torrents of snow, she drove south, then west, out of the Sierra Nevada, out of the blizzard—and, after many miles, out of that darkness of spirit, into grace and gratitude for her survival.

In Placerville, she paid cash for one night at a generic motel, using her Elizabeth Bennet driver's license as ID, because she was wearing the chopped-everywhichway black wig and excess makeup and blue lipstick that made her Liz.

She bought deli sandwiches and a pint of vodka at a nearby market and got Coca-Cola and ice from the motel vending alcove and took a shower as hot as she could tolerate and ate the sandwiches while sitting in bed, listening to Mariah Carey on the radio. She drank a vodka-and-Coke and was finishing her second drink, grateful to be alive, when her burner phone rang.

She intended to call Gavin and Jessica Washington down in eastern Orange County, the friends with whom she had secreted her son, Travis, the only place in the world where he was not likely to be found. If the boy fell into the hands of her enemies, they would kill him because they knew that his death would at last break her. When the disposable phone rang, she thought it must be Gavin or Jessie; no one else had the number.

But it was Travis. "Mommy? Uncle Gavin and Aunt Jessie went for groceries, and they never came back."

Jane swung her legs off the bed, stood, and felt as if she were standing for the attention of a hangman, a noose tight around her neck and a trapdoor under her feet. At once she sat down, dizzy with dread.

He had been with Gavin and Jessie for more than two months. If something happened to them, he was alone. Five years old and alone.

Her heart as loud as a cortege drum, but much faster than the meter of mourning, reverberating in blood and bone . . .

Travis was a little toughie, being strong like he knew his dad would have been, scared but self-controlled. Jane was able to get the situation from him. Gavin and Jessie had realized they were under surveillance, had somehow been connected to Jane. In their Land Rover, with Travis and their two German shepherds, they'd escaped from their house into the dark desert hills. They were pursued— "This crazy-big truck and like even a helicopter, Mom, a helicopter that could see us in the dark"—but they avoided capture. They drove to a bolt-hole, long ago approved by Jane, in the Borrego Valley, south of Borrego Springs. After settling in a small house on acreage owned by a man named Cornell Jasperson, Gavin shaved his head and Jessie changed her appearance with a wig and makeup, and they went into town to buy supplies. They meant to be back in two hours. Eight had now passed.

They must be dead. They would not have allowed themselves to be captured, and they would never have shirked their responsibility to look after Travis. Gavin and Jessie were ex-Army, two of the best and most reliable people Jane had ever known.

She'd loved them like a brother and sister before she'd left her child in their care, and she loved them yet more for their unfailing commitment to Travis. Even in these dark times of so much terror and death, when each day brought new threats and sorrows, new shocks to mind and heart, she had not become inured to loss. This one pierced her, a psychic bullet that would have dropped her into tears and numbing grief if her child had not been in such jeopardy.

She didn't tell Travis they were dead. She could discern by the catch in his voice that he suspected as much, but there was nothing to be gained by confirming his fear. She needed to project calm and confidence, to give him reason for courage.

"Where are you, sweetheart? In the house where they left you?"

If he was still in the house where Gavin and Jessie had meant to hole up with him, he was more likely to be found sooner.

"No. Me and the dogs, we walked over to Cornell's place like we were supposed to if there was trouble."

Cornell lived off the grid. He was not likely to be linked to Gavin and Jessie soon. Travis might be safe there for two or three days, though not much longer. The word *might* was a gut punch.

"Honey, you'll be safe with the dogs and Cornell until I can come for you. I *will* come for you, sweetie. Nothing can stop me."

"I know. I know you will."

"Are you all right with Cornell?"

"He's kind of weird, but he's nice."

Cornell was a brilliant eccentric whose eccentricities were complicated by a mild form of autism.

"There's no reason to be afraid of Cornell. You do what he tells you, sweetie, and I'll come for you just as soon as I can."

"Okay. I can't wait, but I will."

"We can't talk even on burner phones again. It's too dangerous now. But I'll come for you." She got to her feet and was steady this time. "Nobody ever loved anyone more than I love you, Travis."

"Me, too. I miss you all the time a lot. Do you have the lady I gave you?"

The lady was a cameo, the face of a broken locket that he had found and that he thought important because, to his mind if not to hers, the profile carved in soapstone resembled Jane.

It was on the nightstand with other objects—switchblade, butane lighter, penlight, small canister of Sabre 5.0 pepper spray, four zipties each held in tight coils by a rubber band—the tools and simple weapons and instruments of restraint that she had cleaned out of the pockets of her sport coat before hanging it up. Plucking the cameo off the nightstand, she said, "It's in my hand right now."

"It's good luck. It's like everything is gonna be all right if you just always have the lady."

"I know, baby. I have her. I'll never lose her. Everything will be all right."

5

BEFORE DINNER, EGON GOTTFREY RETURNS TO HIS motel to see if the courier has arrived from the laboratory in Menlo Park, California.

Waiting for him at the front desk is a large white Styrofoam chest of the kind that might contain mail-order steaks or a dozen pints of gelato in exotic flavors.

This marionette theater in which he has a role is well managed, and the necessary props never fail to appear where they are needed.

He carries the insulated box to his room, where he uses his switchblade to slit the tape sealing the lid in place. Clouds of pale, cold vapor issue from perforated packets of dry ice that coddle a Medexpress container twice the size of a lunch box.

In a compartment without dry ice are hypodermic syringes, cannulas, and other items related to intravenous injections.

In the bathroom, Gottfrey places the Medexpress container on the counter beside the sink. The digital readout reports an interior temperature of thirty-eight degrees Fahrenheit. He swings back the lid and counts twelve insulated sleeves of quilted, silvery material about an inch in diameter and seven inches long, each containing a glass ampule of cloudy amber fluid.

Three ampules for each person residing at Hawk Ranch. The ranch manager, Juan Saba, and his wife, Marie. And Ancel and Clare Hawk.

Each set of three ampules contains a nanotech brain implant. A control mechanism. Hundreds of thousands of parts, maybe millions, each comprising just a few molecules. Inert until injected, warmed by the subject's blood, they become brain-tropic.

The concept intrigues Gottfrey. Although he has not received such an implant, he considers himself to be a marionette controlled by unknown forces. And when he injects people with these mechanisms, to some extent he becomes their puppeteer, a marionette who controls marionettes of his own. His mind controls their minds.

The incredibly tiny nanoconstructs migrate through veins to the heart, then through arteries to the brain, where they penetrate the blood-brain barrier and pass through the walls of capillaries just as do vital substances that the brain needs. They enter the tissue of the brain and self-assemble into a complex weblike structure.

The injected people are programmed to be obedient. They are made to forget they have been injected. They don't know they are enslaved. They become "adjusted people." The control is so complete that they will commit suicide if told to do so.

Indeed, Clare and Ancel Hawk's son, Nick, had been in a special class of adjusted people, those on the Hamlet list. The Arcadians have developed a computer model that identifies men and women who excel in their fields of endeavor and who possess certain traits that suggest they will become leaders with considerable influence in the culture; if those individuals hold positions on key issues that conflict with Arcadian philosophy and goals, they are injected and controlled. To doubly ensure they don't influence others with their dangerous ideas and don't pass their unique genomes on to a lot of children, they are instructed to kill themselves.

This control mechanism might terrify Gottfrey if he didn't believe that the brain and the body it controls are both illusions, as is everything else in so-called reality. His disembodied mind is the only thing that exists. When nothing is real, there is nothing to fear. You need only surrender to the Unknown Playwright who crafts the narrative and go where the play takes you; it's like being in a fascinating dream from which you never wake.

He closes the Medexpress container and returns with it to the bedroom, where he places it in the Styrofoam chest with the dry ice.

When he goes out for dinner, he leaves the lights on and hangs the DO NOT DISTURB sign from the doorknob.

6

THE SHADOWY ROOM, THE LIGHT OF THE TV THAT illuminated nothing, the dark at the windows, the moral darkness of *Sunday Magazine* . . .

Clare's chest felt tight, each breath constrained, as she stood watching a homicide detective, someone *said to be* a detective, a fortyish man who looked as clean-cut as any father on a family-friendly 1950s sitcom, but who must be dirtier than any drug dealer or pimp. He spoke of an exhumed body that didn't exist, that had been ashes since the previous November, of toxicological tests that couldn't have been conducted on *ashes*. He claimed to have evidence that Nick Hawk was *murdered* with his Marine-issue knife. It was known, he said, that Jane had been selling national-defense secrets to enemies of the country even then, and he speculated that Nick, a true American hero who had received the Navy Cross, might have grown suspicious of her, might have confronted her with his suspicions.

Ancel rose from his chair. By nature he wasn't an angry soul. He gave everyone the benefit of the doubt, rarely raised his voice, and dealt with difficult people by avoiding them. Clare had never seen him so incensed, though his rage might have gone unnoticed by anyone but her, for it manifested only as a pulse in his temple, in the clenching of his jaws, in the set of his shoulders.

With the program near its end, they stood in silent sentinel to outrageous deceit, as Jane's father, Martin Duroc, was interviewed in his home, with a piano in the background to remind everyone of his renown. "Jane was a sweet but emotionally fragile child. And so young when she found her mother after the suicide." He seemed to choke with emotion. "I'm afraid something snapped in her then. She became withdrawn. No amount of counseling or therapy helped. I felt as if I'd lost a wife *and* a daughter. Yet I never imagined she would become . . . what she is now. I pray she'll turn herself in."

Jane *knew* that he'd killed her mother to marry another woman. He had supposedly been hundreds of miles from home that night, but in fact he'd been in the house, though she couldn't prove his guilt.

Now the program ended as Duroc took a display handkerchief from the breast pocket of his suit to dab at his eyes, and Clare said, "My God, what do we do? What *can* we do?"

"I intend to get fall-down drunk," Ancel said. "No other way I'll be able to sleep tonight. And there's nothin' we can do for Jane. Damn the whole crooked lot of them."

Never in Clare's experience had Ancel been drunk, and she doubted that he meant to lose himself in a bottle this time.

He confirmed her doubt by turning to her and fluttering the fingers of one hand as if they were the pinions of a bird's wing, a prearranged signal that meant *time to fly*.

She couldn't disagree. Jane had warned that the conspirators might become so frustrated by their inability to find her that they would come after her in-laws, hoping to use them to get her. Now that these vicious shits had pulled this stunt with *Sunday Magazine*, they would expect Clare and Ancel to make a statement to the press tomorrow. So they would come before dawn.

The telephone rang.

Ancel said, "It's one friend or another, knows Jane, saw the show, wants to say they're with us. Let it go to voicemail. It won't be the last. I'm not in the mood tonight. Call 'em back tomorrow. I'm gettin' that damn bottle of Scotch. What about you?"

"This . . . it sickens me," Clare said. "I'm furious and scared for her and . . . and I feel so helpless."

"What can I do, honey? What do you want to do?"

"Can't do a damn thing. This is so rotten. I'm going to bed."

"You won't sleep. Not after this."

"I'll take an Ambien. I can't handle whisky like you, I'd be throwing up all night." She was amazed at how convincingly she delivered her lines. They had never practiced a scene like this.

They spoke no more as they prepared to leave before sunrise.

Clare loved this house, their first and only, where they'd begun their marriage, where they'd raised Nick, where they'd learned from Nick and Jane, during a visit, that she was pregnant with their first—and now only—grandchild. Clare wondered when they would be able to return. She wondered *if*.

7

Because the revolution is everything to him, Ivan Petro works seven days a week, and on this first Sunday in April, he seems destined also to work around the clock.

He is based in Sacramento, where Techno Arcadians maintain a significant network in the state government, which is as corrupt as any, more so than most.

He's having dinner in his favorite Italian restaurant when he, like thousands of other Arcadians, starts receiving text messages about the incident involving Jane Hawk in Lake Tahoe, including a photograph taken there, showing her current appearance.

No hit team has been dispatched to nail her, because a late-season blizzard in the Sierra Nevada has grounded all helicopters.

Although the highways in that territory are treacherous, they are passable. No one knows what she's driving or in which direction she's gone; but she probably will want to get out of the Tahoe area, all the way out of the storm, before going to ground for the night.

If she flees west on U.S. Highway 50, she'll be coming straight toward Ivan Petro.

As he finishes a plate of saltimbocca, he checks the weather report and learns that snow is falling only as far as Riverton. In the twenty miles west of Riverton, there is no town of any size until Placerville, which has a population of maybe ten thousand.

Ivan finishes a second glass of Chianti. He doesn't order the two servings of cannoli that he was anticipating with such pleasure.

An hour after nightfall, he's in Placerville, stalking the so-called beautiful monster, on what is shaping up to be perhaps the most important night of his life.

Ivan Petro appears to have a molecular density greater than that of mere flesh and bone, as though the substance of which he's constituted was first made molten in a coke-fired oven before being poured into a man shape. Teeth as blunt and white as those of a horse, face broad and flushed as if he has spent his entire life in a stinging wind that has left this permanent coloration. People have called him "Big Guy" since he was eleven years old.

Ivan is a hit team all by himself.

It has been assumed that Jane must be staying in motels, paying cash and using forged ID, remaining nowhere more than a night or two. The national chains in the hospitality industry will accept cash in advance from someone without a credit card, but it is far from a common practice. To avoid raising an eyebrow and attracting undue attention, she most likely prefers mom-and-pop operations, one- and two-star motels more accustomed to cash transactions.

Placerville is not so large that it offers scores of mom-and-pop motels. With his Department of Homeland Security credentials and his authoritative demeanor, using a description of Tahoe Jane but not her name, he receives cooperation from the clerks at the front desks of the establishments most likely to interest the fugitive.

In any endeavor like this, luck plays a role. If Jane chose to continue through Placerville to Sacramento and points beyond, Ivan is wasting his time. But luck strikes after his second stop. He is in his Range Rover, a third motel address entered in his navigator, stopped at a red traffic light, when he sees a woman of interest come out of a supermarket.

Carrying what appears to be a deli bag, she passes the Range Rover and crosses the street to the motel on the northwest corner. She resembles the photo of Jane incognita taken in Tahoe: stylish chopped-shaggy black hair, a little Goth makeup around the eyes.

He can't see if she is wearing a nose ring or if her lipstick is blue, as in the photograph, but she's a looker, wearing a sport coat that's maybe cut for concealed-carry. And she has attitude, moves with grace and confidence that people often mention when talking about Jane Hawk.

She walks past the motel office and along the covered walkway serving the rooms.

The light changes to green, and Ivan eases through the intersection, timing it so that he is gliding past when she lets herself into Room 8.

Most of the motel's rooms are evidently not yet booked for the night, because only four vehicles stand in the parking lot. Only one of the four is anywhere near Room 8, and it is parked directly in front of that door: a metallic-gray Ford Explorer Sport.

Ivan hangs a U-turn at the next intersection and pulls off the street into an apartment complex across from the motel.

The apartments are in an arrangement of bland stucco boxes tricked up with decorative iron stair railings and faux shutters in a sad attempt at style. In front of the buildings is a long pergola that, during the day, shades the vehicles of residents as well as those of visitors. It now provides moonshade for the Range Rover.

The Explorer Sport is parked between lampposts, and with binoculars Ivan glasses the rear license plates. Using the computer terminal in the console of the customized Rover, he back-doors the California DMV and inputs the number. The vehicle is registered to Leonard Borland at an address in San Francisco.

Ivan switches to Google Street and looks at what stands at that address: a ten-story apartment building. He suspects that if he visited the place, no tenant named Leonard Borland would live there.

Rather than go to that trouble, he returns to the DMV system and seeks driver's licenses issued to men named Leonard Borland, of which there are several with various middle names. None of them shares the address to which the Explorer Sport is registered.

This might mean only that another Leonard Borland owns the Sport but does not drive it himself, does not drive at all.

But what it *might* mean isn't in this case worth considering.

It's been known for some time that Jane Hawk has a source for forged documents so well crafted that the forger is able to insert them undetected into government records, ensuring they will withstand scrutiny if she is stopped by the highway patrol.

Minutes after checking out the various Leonard Borlands, Ivan Petro receives an electrifying phone call. The guardians with whom Travis Hawk's mother entrusted him have been found in Borrego Springs, where they have been killed in an exchange of gunfire. The boy has yet to be located. A major search is being organized to comb every inch of the town and the surrounding Borrego Valley.

Almost an hour later, following much fevered calculation, Ivan arrives at a course of action. He isn't going to call for backup and allow the credit for the capture of Jane Hawk to go to those Arcadians above him in the revolution, many of whom are in the habit of adding to their résumés accomplishments that aren't theirs.

He calls them poachers, though never to their face. They are dangerous people, such vipers that it's amazing they aren't poisoned by the potency of their own venom. He treats them with unfailing respect, though he despises them.

However, he is self-aware enough to know that were he to rise into their ranks and be accepted, he would no longer despise them, would find them ideal company. He despises the insiders only because he isn't one of them; being excluded is what feeds his hatred.

Since childhood, he's been a superb hater. He hated his father for the many beatings and hated his indifferent mother for raising no objection to them. His hatred had festered into pure black rancor until, at fifteen, he was big enough and furious enough to pay his old man back with interest and knock some remorse into his mother as well, before walking out on them forever.

Because they had no interest in teaching him anything at all, other than fearful obedience, they no doubt still have no awareness that by their cruelty they taught him the most important of all life lessons: Happiness depends on acquiring as much power as possible, power in all its forms—physical strength, superior knowledge, money and more money, political control over others.

His parents are ignorant alcoholics full of class resentment, but in essence they are alike to the Arcadian poachers who have thus far thwarted Ivan's ascent in the revolution. He hates them all.

Anyway, he has a plan, and it's a good one that could elevate him into the hierarchy where he belongs.

The motel is not a place where he can surprise her, overpower her, take custody of her, and put her through a hard interrogation without drawing unwanted attention. If he is patient, a better opportunity will present itself.

If he can break her on his own, learn where the boy is . . . he can present *both* mother and child to the revolution as a single package and in such a way that credit is given where it is due.

The cargo area of the Range Rover is stocked with surveillance gear, from which he selects a transponder with a lithium battery. It's the size of a pack of cigarettes. After programming the unit's identifier code into his GPS, he crosses the street to the motel.

The best way to accomplish a task like this is boldly, as though it's the most natural thing in the world to stoop beside a stranger's car and attach a transponder. The back of this particular unit features a plastic bubble containing a powerful epoxy. With a penknife, Ivan slits the bubble, reaches between the tire and the rear quarter panel, and presses the transponder to the wheel well. The epoxy sets in ten seconds. Because it is an adhesive used to attach heat-dispersing tiles to space shuttles, there is no chance it will be dislodged by any patch of rough road or in a collision.

If people in the passing vehicles notice Ivan at work, they aren't curious. He crosses the street and returns to the Range Rover without incident.

However, fewer than ten minutes pass before the door of Room 8 opens and the woman exits, carrying luggage. She needs two trips to load the Sport. She is clearly agitated and in a hurry.

He is sure, now beyond all doubt, that she is Jane Hawk.

He suspects she has somehow learned what has happened to Gavin and Jessica Washington, the two guardians of her boy, who have been killed in Borrego Springs.

He watches her drive away from the motel and does not at once pursue her. He doesn't need to keep her in sight in order to tail her. The transponder that he attached to her Explorer is represented as a blinking red signifier on the screen of the Range Rover GPS.

Ivan waits a few minutes before reversing out of the pergola. He turns left onto the street. Jane Hawk is headed west on Highway 50, toward Sacramento and points beyond, and so is Ivan Petro.

8

FEAR FOR HER LOVELY BOY CONTESTED WITH SHARP grief for Gavin and Jessie. They had known the danger of committing to help Jane and Travis. But they had seen their own freedom threatened by the cabal and its Orwellian technology against which Jane had taken up arms. They had accepted the risk. They were now part of her forever.

If Gavin and Jessie had been found by the Arcadians, those agents had intended either to torture them or enslave them with nano-implants to learn where Jane's child was hidden. And now the people who murdered them would scour Borrego Springs and the Borrego Valley in search of Travis.

She could not let fear paralyze her, but neither could she allow it to hurry her into reckless action. During her six years with the Bureau, she'd endured harrowing encounters with serial killers and mass murderers, and during the past few months, with a world of totalitarian sociopaths in pursuit of her, she had faced and escaped more lethal threats than in her entire FBI career. She survived because she could stay cool in the hottest circumstances.

There was no emotion hotter than the terror that blazed in a mother when her child was in peril. Losing her boy would burn her to the ground emotionally. Nevertheless, if she hoped to save him, she must be prudent and coldly calculating, must act strategically and with tactics proven through hard experience.

She would need most of the night to get to Borrego Valley. Her enemies would be expecting her. They would surely staff the valley in daunting numbers. She would be exhausted, easy to take down. She needed to delay until she had a plan and was at her full strength.

She couldn't sleep. So drive till sleep was possible. Wherever she stopped, she'd be that much closer to her boy when morning came.

After dressing again as Elizabeth Bennet, she put her luggage in the car. She drove west toward Sacramento. Mile by mile, she told herself that the world on its metaled tracks was not engineered with malevolence, that there was mercy in the mechanism, that her child, who was the very image of his father, would not be taken from her as had been her husband, as had been her mother so many years ago. And yet her fear was great.

9

Egon Gottfrey dines alone in Cathy's Café in downtown Worstead. Although he takes most meals without company, he is never troubled by loneliness. Were he to have dinner with two or twenty others, he would still be alone, for his own mind is the only thing that he can prove is real. If the café, the town, and the world are illusions, then so might be the minds of other people who occupy the phantom physical bodies with which he interacts.

Only the Unknown Playwright knows for sure.

For whatever reason, the Unknown Playwright wants the food in Cathy's Café to taste good, and so it does. Gottfrey can't explain how a disembodied mind divorced from sensory organs can taste and smell and see and hear and feel, but he does all those things.

He might suppose his situation is like that of Keanu Reeves in *The Matrix:* his paralyzed body suspended in a tank, the illusion of this life nothing more than a digital feed piped into his brain. To embrace that explanation, he'd have to abandon radical philosophical nihilism, which he has embraced since his sophomore year in college, prior to which he'd been deeply confused about life and his purpose. He cannot prove the existence of the tank, the paralyzed body, the digital feed, and neither can he prove that movies exist or that there is an entity named Keanu Reeves.

So he will hold fast to the philosophy that has for so long guided him. Nothing is real. All experience is an illusion provided by a mysterious source. He's just along for the ride, so to speak.

After dinner, Gottfrey walks through nearby neighborhoods. Worstead is an even less convincing place at night than in daylight. As early as nine o'clock, at least twelve thousand of the town's supposed fourteen thousand residents must already be in bed.

Of the few places with any action, the busiest seems to be a bar featuring country music, which is surrounded by pickups and SUVs. The roof-mounted sign names the place NASHVILLE WEST, and under that, in smaller lettering, are the words EAT—DRINK—MUSIC.

If the Unknown Playwright wants Egon to believe this world is real, there are instances like this when he or she—or it—makes mistakes that reveal the falsity of the scene. The sign would make sense if all three words were nouns: FOOD—DRINK—MUSIC. Or if all were verbs: EAT—DRINK—LISTEN. But as it now reads, the customer is invited to eat and drink the music, which makes no sense.

Sometimes it seems that Egon is smarter than the Unknown Playwright: a strange idea on which he doesn't care to dwell.

In his motel room again, at ten o'clock, he changes from street shoes to lace-up hiking boots.

For twenty minutes, he sits staring at the bedside clock.

He trades his sport coat for a warmer jacket that nonetheless conceals his shoulder rig and pistol.

He removes the Medexpress container from the dry-ice chest and carries it out to his Rhino GX. This is the largest luxury SUV made in America, a product of U.S. Specialty Vehicles. It looks like a hardened military transport but with high style, including a matte-black finish. The Rhino is a symbol of his value to the revolution, or so he is supposed to believe.

During the nine-mile drive to Hawk Ranch, even someone far less enlightened than Egon Gottfrey ought to realize that the world is not real, because large areas remain unfinished. These vast plains are often dark to the horizon. Here and there, tiny clusters of distant lights suggest isolated habitats. It's like stepping behind an intricately assembled stage setting of a bustling city street and discovering a cavernous backstage with counterweight pulleys and fly lines and painted drops, all of it deserted and quiet, belying the metropolis visible from the audience.

Eight miles from Worstead, he goes off-road, guided now by GPS, homing on a locater in the Ford Explorer driven by Pedro Lobo, one of the two youngest members of the team. Pedro and his twin brother, Alejandro, have been maintaining surveillance of the entrance to Hawk Ranch for the past thirty-six hours.

Half a mile from Pedro's location, Gottfrey switches off his headlamps. If he follows a direct line to Pedro, as shown on the dashboard screen, he'll supposedly encounter no treacherous terrain.

The enormous meadow is in places runneled, and the grass stands eighteen inches high. Even in this cool night, from time to time, feeble swarms of winged insects, too dimly glimpsed to be identified in the moonlight, are disturbed out of the land, clicking their brittle wings and body shells ineffectively against the Rhino GX.

Pedro has established his surveillance post within a grove of cottonwoods. In the pale moonlight, the trees loom blacker than the star-shot sky.

Gottfrey is the last to arrive. Among the trees, in addition to the Explorer, stands the 800-horsepower Cadillac Escalade customized by Specialty Vehicle Engineering, assigned to Paloma Sutherland and Sally Jones. Here also are a Jeep Wrangler with the Poison Spyder Package from 4 Wheel Parts, an aftermarket builder, which is shared by Rupert Baldwin and Vince Penn, as well as the bespoke Range Rover by Overfinch assigned to Christopher Roberts and Janis Dern.

In an operation like this, undertaken in a small town, it's important to split the team among various vehicles, so that they don't appear to be related and are less likely to call attention to themselves than would a group of outsiders traveling together.

The five men and three women are gathered at the Explorer, half-seen shadows within the deep moonshadows of the cottonwoods, conversing softly, when Gottfrey leaves the Rhino GX and joins them.

The grove of trees stands thirty yards from the county road and directly across from the entrance to Ancel and Clare Hawk's ranch.

Gottfrey has seen film of the ranch. At its entrance, the private access road is flanked by stone posts supporting an arch of wrought iron incorporating the name HAWK. A single lane of blacktop, bordered by ranch fencing and overhung by live oaks, proceeds 150 yards through rich grassland to the ranch buildings.

From this distance, in daylight, the main residence, stables, barn, and manager's house can't be seen beyond the screening oaks. During the day, with binoculars, Pedro and Alejandro took turns watching the sole entrance to—and exit from—the ranch.

Now they monitor the place with ATN PVS7-3 night-vision goggles, MIL-SPEC Generation 4 gear, which gather in all available light across the spectrum and magnify it eighty thousand times.

"At seven-thirty this morning," Pedro tells Gottfrey, "Ancel and Clare left for church in their Ford F-550. Three minutes later, Juan and Marie Saba followed in their pickup."

"Are you sure they were just going to church?"

"We have a portable satellite dish. Even out here, it links us to the Internet. Then we back-door NSA audio feed from both houses."

Gottfrey has to admit the Unknown Playwright deserves praise for a quaint detail like church, which adds verisimilitude to this Texas setting that has otherwise at times seemed thinly sketched.

Alejandro Lobo says, "Juan and Marie returned from church at nine twenty-six. After church, Ancel and Clare remained in town to have breakfast. They returned to the ranch at ten thirty-five."

"They've been there ever since," Pedro added.

"What's the situation now?"

"Quiet in both houses," Alejandro reports. "The Sabas went to bed early. The Hawks watched *Sunday Magazine*."

"What was their reaction?"

"Infuriated, sickened, helpless. He said he was going to get good and drunk. She took an Ambien. As far as we can tell, they both knocked themselves out for the night, one way or the other."

"As far as you can tell, evidently, supposedly, as we are asked and expected to believe," Gottfrey replies.

"Sir?" Alejandro says in puzzlement, and his twin asks, "You think we missed something?"

"No, no," Gottfrey assures them. He turns to the other six half-seen figures that might be only spirits in a Shakespearean drama, the black cottonwood shapes like some grove of yew trees where the sorrowing dead gather to lament their passing. "Let's gear up, people. No engine noise to alert them. We're going on foot."

In the cargo space of the Explorer are Kevlar vests and bullet-resistant helmets. They strip off their jackets and shoulder rigs to put on the vests and then rearm themselves.

Although Ancel and Clare Hawk are gunned up, Gottfrey and his crew do not want to kill anyone, merely enslave them with nanotech.

10

SHORTLY BEFORE MIDNIGHT, WEIGHED DOWN WITH weariness, vision blurring from lack of sleep, Jane paid cash for a motel room in Lathrop, California.

She always wanted a king-size bed, not because she tossed and turned in her sleep, which she didn't, and not because she liked to keep a pistol within easy reach under a pillow adjacent to her own, which she did. For six years, she and Nick had slept in a king-size bed. Whenever she had come half awake in the night, she had reached out to find him; on touching him, she had always felt safe from the storms of life and quickly fell back into sleep. He wasn't there to be touched anymore. But as long as she left a space for him, when she reached out in the dark, his pillow and his share of the sheets were waiting for him; if drowsy enough, she could believe that he'd gotten up for a moment and would soon come back to warm the bed beside her, whereupon dreams returned to her soft and easy. But if even sleep-sodden she realized that he was gone from her world forever, this provision of mattress consoled her with the thought that on some inconceivable shore beyond this life, he remained her Nick, his love undiminished, and saved a space for her.

Although exhausted, she feared that she would lie awake for so long that she might have to get up and dress and drive on. But when her head touched the pillow, sleep instantly claimed her.

On this difficult night, she expected sleep to be filled with scenes of her child in peril, but instead she dreamed of ships at sea and buses and trains. On the ship, her fellow passengers were the sinister strangers of anxiety dreams. On the train, they were Gavin Washington; his wife, Jessie; Nathan Silverman—Jane's former mentor at the Bureau—and her mother, all dead in the world of the waking, but here journeying together toward . . . *"No, not yet,"* Jane told her mother. *"Not yet, not even for you."* She disembarked from the train to board a bus on which other passengers included the two serial killers she killed on a lonely farm, a Dark Web entrepreneur she'd killed in self-defense, and J. J. Crutchfield, the collector of women's eyes whom she had wounded and captured, who died in prison.

More than once, she reached out to the empty side of the bed, and each time she fell back to sleep, but always there was another bus, a train, a ship at sea.

11

THE HIGH MOON A SILVER COIN IN THE SEQUINED purse of the night, the shabby Lathrop motel poorly lighted in recognition of the fact that a swirl of neon and a declaration of vacancy, at this late hour, will not induce a single additional traveler to make his bed there . . .

Parked across the street from those grim lodgings, Ivan Petro does the math for murder but isn't able to make it work.

The motel has fifteen units. The number of vehicles suggests that only six rooms are rented. Considering that Jane Hawk is in one room, there are as few as five other guests or as many as ten. In an apartment above the motel office, one or two owner-operators of the establishment lie in uneasy sleep, troubled by dreams of bankruptcy. As few as six people other than Jane—or as many as twelve.

If it was six or even seven, he might start in the apartment and kill his way to her room, eliminating potential witnesses. With a lock-release device, he can slip through any door without much noise. If he wears night-vision goggles, the gloom of bedrooms will not render him blind. He can kill fast and quietly with a knife. As skilled as the Hawk bitch is at self-defense, capturing *her* will involve some struggle, some noise, so that he can't move against her while other motel guests, on hearing an altercation, might call 911.

There are four reasons why Ivan excels at what he does. First, he is much smarter than other Arcadians in his cell of the cabal. Second, he possesses not merely a passion but also an intellectual basis for the destruction of the historic order and the imposition of a utopia run by a ruling elite; he has read all of Nietzsche, Max Weber, and Freud, so he understands how efficient and stable society would be if all the delusions of meaning and illusions of free will were stripped from the confused masses. Third, he detests those Arcadians who have thus far kept him out of the highest circles of the revolution, and he hates himself for his failure to ascend; and all this anger is jet fuel for his ambition, ensuring that he works harder than anyone else. Fourth, he has great patience. He is not a hot-headed rebel, not a wild-eyed anarchist whose ideology is so tightly wound that he rushes into action with a war cry.

Under these conditions, the risk of trying to take Jane Hawk is too great. He can wait. A better moment will come.

His wristwatch has an alarm function. He sets it for 5:00 A.M. There are no streetlamps where he is parked. He powers his seat into a reclining position. He closes his eyes and, because he is a man who cares about no one but himself and is too certain of his future to worry about himself, he falls asleep in seconds.

12

PEDRO AND ALEJANDRO REMAIN BEHIND WITH THE vehicles in the grove of cottonwoods.

Vince Penn, an army tank on legs, wearing night-vision goggles, leads the way through the meadow, as insects sing to the moon.

Carrying the Medexpress container, Paloma Sutherland is second in the procession. Egon Gottfrey is third, and the remaining four members of the team follow single-file behind him.

At this late hour, the road is so devoid of traffic that it seems no longer to lead anywhere that man or machine still exists. Broken lane-dividing lines glow softly like some coded message to be deciphered.

The team doesn't approach the house on the private lane, which might invite discovery. They climb the fence and continue overland.

The wind that sprang up at sundown has blown away to the west, leaving a stillness in its wake.

The two-story white-clapboard main residence stands under old, canopied oaks. Lights glow at downstairs and upstairs windows.

The Hawks are evidently up late in spite of Ambien and Scotch.

Ancel's Ford F-550 truck stands in a graveled parking area.

The stables and barn are dark, as is the residence of the ranch manager, a barely visible geometric form three hundred yards to the northwest.

The silence is deeper than elsewhere, bereft of insect song.

They take positions all around the house, except for Paloma, who stands aside with the Medexpress container.

Rupert and Chris climb the back porch steps, while Vince and Gottfrey move on the front. They have LockAid lock-release guns that defeat the deadbolts with little noise.

There is no alarm, for the Hawks believe themselves to be self-sufficient in matters of self-defense. They are Texans, after all, and they are ranchers; if they weren't born with full knowledge of fire-arms, they were born with a predisposition to learn. Any of Gott-frey's team could be shot dead, including Egon himself.

Guns drawn, Egon and Vince venture into the lighted foyer as Rupert and Chris enter by the kitchen door.

Earlier, they memorized the layout of the house from plans imported to their laptops.

Rupert and Chris will clear the ground floor. Vince and Gottfrey move directly to the stairs and ascend.

The house is solidly constructed, but they make some noise. Yet they arrive in the upstairs hallway without encountering anyone.

Every open door is a danger, every closed door yet a greater threat, if you believe you are a physical being and can therefore die. Vince has a fine sweat on his brow. Egon Gottfrey remains dry. They clear the second floor room by room, but they find no one.

Returning to the stairs, Gottfrey sees Rupert and Chris in the foyer below. Chris shrugs, and Rupert looks disgusted.

Then to the enormous barn. Click on the lights. Dust motes like galaxies spiraling. The scent of hay. In one corner, the Hawks keep two other vehicles, a Chevy sedan and a Ford SUV; both are here.

Vince Penn is big and powerful and stalwart, but the Unknown Playwright has chosen to make him the slowest intellect on the team. He blathers his way to a conclusion that is instantly obvious to everyone else: "Hey, you think maybe they left on horseback? Could be, huh? If they went on horseback, you know, they could escape overland. Then Pedro and Alejandro wouldn't know they slipped out."

Onward to the stables. As light blooms, horses swing their heads over stall doors and nicker. Eight stalls. Just three horses.

"How damn many horses do they have?" Gottfrey wonders. "If they rode out on horseback, the ranch manager will know where they went."

The manager's residence is reached by a single lane of blacktop cracked by weather and crumbling along the edges.

Dark without and within, the Craftsman-style bungalow shelters under another oak.

Gottfrey intends to invade it as they did the previous house. However, when they are still about fifteen yards from the place, every window brightens, and exterior lamps shed cones of light as well. They halt as the front door opens.

Recognizable from the photographs in the NSA's Jane Hawk file, Juan and Maria Saba step out of the bungalow. He is holding what might be a .22 rifle, and she grips a long-bladed machete.

Gottfrey is familiar with the concept of humor, though he doesn't find much that is humorous in his scripted existence. He's amused, however, by this couple's intention to stand off seven heavily armed professionals with these pathetic weapons.

From the door behind the Sabas appear two, four . . . *eight* other men and women, all with more impressive weaponry.

And from around each side of the bungalow come others, male and female, a few teenagers, all bearing firearms, some also outfitted with machetes in scabbards. About half of them seem to be Hispanic.

Among this solemn little army of citizen soldiers, none appears to be amused, and in fact Gottfrey can't maintain his own smile.

How long has this crowd gathered in silence, so that Pedro and his brother, monitoring the premises, have heard not a word spoken?

"We want no trouble," Juan Saba says. "Leave now."

"FBI," Gottfrey declares, rather than flashing his Homeland credentials. FBI has more history, more glamour, and is taken more seriously than Homeland Security. "We're here with arrest warrants."

They possess no warrants, but a lie is not a lie when there's no such thing as truth. Words are merely words, used like tools.

He holds his ID high for them to see. "Put down your weapons."

"FBI," Saba says. "Yes, FBI, we are supposed to believe."

Interesting. Saba seems to be expressing the doubt of one who, like Gottfrey, embraces radical philosophical nihilism. This would appear to suggest that his mind is as real as Egon's.

"Some here are brave uncles, aunts, cousins," Juan Saba says. "Some are neighbors, brave friends of Mr. and Mrs. Hawk—and friends of Jane."

"Jane Hawk," Gottfrey declares, "is guilty of multiple murders and treason. Anyone who assists her now is an accessory after the fact and will be charged and brought to trial."

There are maybe thirty people arrayed in front of the house, not one face clouded with either anger or fear, all expressionless, as if they mean to convey that their resistance isn't driven by emotion, which might wane under pressure, that it is motivated by loyalty or justice or some equally noble virtue.

Into their challenging silence, Gottfrey says, "If you insist on standing with a traitor and murderer, if you won't help us find Ancel and Clare, I'll call for backup. You can't outlast a federally imposed siege of this property. Get real, Mr. Saba."

After half a minute of silence perhaps intended to establish that he is unmoved by this threat, Juan Saba says, "You don't want a big, loud thing here. You come with your needles to make slaves of Ancel and Clare. Such devil's work can be done only in the quiet dark. They aren't here anymore. You can't force us to help you find them. We'll make much noise and shine the light of justice on you."

This is a twist that Egon Gottfrey hasn't seen coming. Jane has told her in-laws about the brain implants, and they have shared this with Juan Saba, who shared it with these others. And they are all credulous enough to believe this mind-control story to be a fact.

Rupert Baldwin has little patience for the pretensions of common folk like this, who believe in the myth of constitutional rights. Loud enough for Saba to hear, he says, "We're not going to allow this bunch of shitkickers to push us around, are we?"

Gottfrey has no objection to a shootout. His physical existence is an illusion; he can't be killed. It would be interesting to see how such a close-quarters pitched battle might turn out.

However, just as he can somehow see, hear, feel, taste, and smell with this illusion of a physical body, he can also experience pain.

Gottfrey has no copy of the script. It always seems that the Unknown Playwright trusts him to *intuit* what he is expected to say and do. Gottfrey has come to believe that when his intuition isn't keen enough to discern what is wanted of him, the Unknown Playwright inflicts pain, in one form or another, to encourage him to try harder to be true to the narrative in the future.

Gottfrey and his crew are not clad head to foot in Kevlar. A lot of pain can be inflicted with a leg wound, with an arm wound.

In Gottfrey's experience, clandestine action is what is usually expected. He isn't likely to be rewarded for instigating a shootout.

Saba says, "These friends will be with Maria and me while we do chores and oversee the day workers, and while we sleep. We won't be taken by surprise. We won't be easy."

"Even if they went on horseback," Gottfrey says, "we have ways of tracking them, ways of finding them."

"Then go to your ways," Saba advises.

"You'll live to regret this."

"There is no regret in doing right. Go to your ways."

"Arrogant shitkicker," Rupert Baldwin snarls.

Before the situation might spiral out of control, Gottfrey orders his people to concede and return to the grove of cottonwoods.

When they are with Pedro and Alejandro, wrapped in the fabric of cottonwood shadows threaded by moonlight, he takes the Medexpress container from Paloma and sends his people back to their motels.

Only Rupert Baldwin is given a task, which it is hoped he can complete before noon. Rupert is brilliant at tracking quarry through the millions of tearless, blinkless eyes that monitor the country's buildings and streets, that observe from security cameras in reeking alleyways and from satellites in airless orbit. Furthermore, Rupert is reliably quick and vicious in the face of any threat.

They will find Ancel and Clare soon enough. And in time the Sabas, Juan and Maria, will be humbled and cruelly used.

And why not? Like everyone else, the Sabas are merely concepts that can't be proven real. Symbols that can never be deciphered, figments, meaningless distortions of light.

13

CORNELL JASPERSON KNEW MANY THINGS. SUCH as, he knew thousands of books, because he had devoted his life to reading.

On his five-acre property stood a shabby little blue stucco house with a white metal roof shaded by unkempt queen palms. Set back from the house, a forbidding ramshackle barn seemed to tremble on the verge of collapse.

Cornell Jasperson knew, as few people did, that the barn was structurally sound and that within it, accessible only through steel doors with electronic locks, was a library for the end of the world.

As he walked through that library now, he knew it remained as precious as he had intended it to be when he had it built, but he also knew it was no longer as safe a refuge as it had seemed before.

The hidden, windowless forty-foot-square library was lined with thirteen hundred linear feet of bookshelves on three walls and part of the fourth. Four intricately figured Persian carpets warmed the polished-concrete floor. Many seating options: chairs and recliners, no two of the same style or period. He knew the layout so well that, when reading, he could move from one sitting place to another that better suited his mood, without taking his eyes from the page. Side tables and footstools. Lamps, lamps, lamps. Table lamps, floor lamps. Shades of stained glass by Tiffany, blown glass, etched glass, colored-and-cut crystal. Cornell loved light filtered and softened by color and texture, and this library lay bejeweled with light.

Cornell knew that civilization was a shaky construct, that many civilizations had collapsed throughout world history. He knew—or at least believed—that the current civilization would collapse. He was what they called a prepper, prepared for the end, ready to ride out thirty months of chaos and violence during which a new civilization might rise out of the ruins of the current one.

Within the six hundred thousand forbidding acres of the Anza-Borrego Desert State Park, little Borrego Springs was the only town. And at this southern end of Borrego Valley, the residences were few. When the distant cities lost power, water, and access to gasoline, when the food-distribution network collapsed, millions would perish. The desperate survivors might seek fertile, defendable land, but they would have no reason to trek all the way to the parched and barren wastes of the Anza-Borrego. Here, at least, there would be no need to stave off savage hordes.

Anyway, the library was not where he would hunker down during the days of blood and terror. This treasury of books served as his waiting place, hidden away from the world but not as grim as the underground bunker where, at the penultimate moment, he would take refuge via a well-concealed secret passageway, living under the world like the Phantom of the Opera or some troll.

Cornell knew that most people thought he was strange, even creepy. He'd been diagnosed with Asperger's disorder and various forms of autism. Maybe all those diagnoses were correct or maybe none were. His IQ was very high, and he'd made a lot of money while sitting alone in a room, developing apps that had proved enormously popular. When he was rich, no less than when he'd been poor, people thought he was strange, even creepy.

Six foot nine, long-boned, knob-jointed, with large and ill-set shoulder blades that he thought were reminiscent of the plates on the backs of certain dinosaurs, with strong hands large enough to juggle honeydew melons—or human heads—Cornell knew that over the years he had frightened many people who entered his presence unexpectedly. A few had been unable to fully repress a startled cry of fear.

His cousin Gavin and Gavin's wife, Jessica, insisted that he had a sweet, round face, like a milk-chocolate-brown baby Jesus, and a few other people told him similar things, but they were probably just being kind. When Cornell looked at himself in a mirror, he couldn't tell if his reflection might be pleasant or fearsome. His face was his face, so he was too familiar with it to reach a final conclusion. Sometimes he thought he looked like that black actor Denzel Washington, but at other times he thought *Frankenstein*.

Cornell knew that women would never chase after him like they probably chased Denzel. He would forever be a target of snarky teenage boys and drunkards with something to prove. But that was okay. As part of his personality disorder, or whatever it was, he couldn't tolerate being touched, anyway; he was happiest alone with a book.

As Mr. Paul Simon had sung, *I am a rock, I am an island.*

Anyway, Cornell knew all that and a great deal more, but he did *not* know what he should do about the boy.

He stopped beside the recliner where Travis was lying curled upon himself, sleeping in the golden light of a Tiffany lamp.

Five years old.

Cornell could hardly believe that he had ever been as small as this child. Travis was scarily little, like he could break apart if he just rolled off the recliner.

Now that Gavin and Jessica had gone away and not come back, the boy had no one to take care of him except a shambling, misassembled man who didn't know how to take care of anyone except himself.

Gavin and Jessica's dogs, big dangerous-looking dogs, German shepherds, had come with Travis. Now they padded through the library to stand on the farther side of the recliner, watching Cornell as Cornell watched the boy. As if they thought he might try to harm Travis.

Cornell said, "Don't bite or claw me, please and thank you."

The dogs said nothing, though their eyes seemed to speak volumes, mostly regarding their distrust for this big, strange man.

"I never had dogs," he told them. "I never had a son. Can't have a son if I can't tolerate being touched, even a woman's touch."

The dogs cocked their heads as if considering this revelation.

"I like to be alone."

The boy murmured in his sleep.

"Or I thought I did," Cornell said.

14

E GON GOTTFREY BEHIND THE WHEEL OF THE HUGE
Rhino GX, headlights cleaving the prairie dark ahead, infinite blackness to both sides of the county road, the soft glow of the instrument panel and the hum of tires on blacktop so convincing that he
can almost believe the car and the road and the night are real . . .

In time, Worstead again, as barely sketched as some town in a
low-budget Western, the buildings mere façades, no citizens afoot
after midnight, a lone and bold coyote slinking past the dark drug-
store, eyes radiant in the headlights . . .

Gottfrey is neither angry nor even disappointed about the turn of
events at Hawk Ranch. In this honeycomb of illusions that is his
existence, nothing matters enough to warrant strong emotions.

Having passed his motel, Gottfrey doesn't know where he is
going. He is only along for the ride.

He is not surprised, however, when he passes Nashville West,
pulls to the curb half a block from the roadhouse, switches off the
lights, and kills the engine.

Although closing time must be approaching, several vehicles remain in the parking lot.

When he gets out of the Rhino GX, Gottfrey hears country music,
a live band, not a jukebox.

EAT—DRINK—MUSIC.

He moves to a corner of the roadhouse where a burned-out light
welcomes shadows and those who need them.

The wait is not a long one. A weather-bitten man in cowboy
boots, faded jeans, a checkered flannel shirt, and a white Stetson
exits Nashville West. He is singing with a slur the song that the
band just finished playing.

Even someone who believes in the reality of all things as they appear might think this man is too much of a walking cliché to be real.

He approaches—what else—a Ford pickup on which is fixed a bumper sticker that declares TEXAS TRUE.

"Hey, cowpoke," says Gottfrey, stepping close behind the man.

He thumbs the button on the handle of a collapsible baton. The instrument instantly telescopes out to twenty inches, and he raises it high. When Wyatt Earp turns to favor him with a loose smile, Gottfrey hammers the steel knob at the end of the baton into his whiskey-flushed face.

The crunch of bone crush, the rush of freed blood, the shock of sudden sobriety in the widening eyes, the Stetson spinning up as the cowpoke folds down, denim and flannel to blacktop . . .

Gottfrey hammers the arms raised in defense, fingers snapping like breadsticks, and knocks out of the man the feeble cry for help that is more of a wretched gagging than it is a shout.

Five blows later, the task complete, Egon Gottfrey thumbs the button, which collapses the baton.

He returns to the Rhino and drives away. His heart rate is maybe sixty beats per minute. He isn't breathing hard. What he's done required little effort and no anger or other strong emotion.

The cowboy—like everyone and everything else—means nothing to him. Gottfrey isn't angered by the turn of events at Hawk Ranch, and he harbors no spite—certainly no rage—against the stranger in the roadhouse parking lot. As always, he merely intuits what the script requires of him. He is not an independent agent.

There is no objective basis from which to determine what is true or real. Consequently, nothing is true or real except his mind. He is only along for the ride.

15

A DEPARTING GUEST SLAMMED A DOOR. JANE HALF woke in the motel room in Lathrop, after five hours of sack time.

She lay for a while in the dark, in a slowly dissolving web of sleep, trying to imagine that she had only dreamed the death of her husband and the danger to her child, that she had herewith awakened into a world where she and Nick and Travis still lived in Virginia, facing a future filled with the promise of peace and grace.

She possessed an ability to adapt quickly to change and threat, though not by resorting to denial, at which she was no good at all. She threw aside the blanket, swung her legs out of bed, and knew this was still a world of murder, slander, envy, theft, deceit, and implacable evil, where peace must be won each day, where legions didn't know grace or, perceiving it, thought it mere weakness.

Having showered the previous evening, she dressed and made herself up to look like the photo on another of the forged driver's licenses she possessed, this one in the name of Elinor Dashwood.

When all this began, she had shoulder-length blond hair, which was now cut short. She pulled on a pixie-cut chestnut-brown wig. Nonprescription contact lenses morphed her blue eyes brown. Stage-prop glasses with black frames gave her a studious appearance.

A successful disguise was a simple one. The reflection in the bathroom mirror wouldn't fool her son, but she didn't look enough like the traitor in the news to be recognized on the street.

No casual disguise could deceive the facial-recognition software married to security systems in airports, train stations, and bus depots, which was why she could travel only by car.

She loaded her luggage into her Explorer Sport, a stolen and remade vehicle, without GPS, purchased with cash from an off-market dealer in Arizona. She drove out of Lathrop, south on Interstate 5.

Hours later, she left the interstate for a truck stop, filled the SUV's tank, and bought takeout—ham sandwiches, black coffee. She ate in the Explorer, in a remote corner of the parking lot, far from easy observation by all the drivers coming and going.

She was still more than an hour north of Los Angeles, in this busy plot of commerce aswarm with trucks and other vehicles, the magnificent and sparsely populated San Joaquin Valley all around, and the blue sky as serene as the world under it could never be.

She used one of her burner phones to call another disposable that she'd left with a friend who had lost his wife and one of his two daughters in this secret civil war. He was now hiding out in Texas. His name had been linked to hers in the news. When Luther Tillman answered on the third ring, she said, "Just me."

"Best two words I've heard in days, knowing you're out there."

"Good to hear your voice, too."

In metropolitan areas, the National Security Agency had planes that could be launched to scoop telecom signals from those carrier waves reserved for disposable cellphones and apply track-to-source technology to locate terrorists communicating in the run-up to an attack. Neither Jane nor Luther was in a metro area. There was no chance this conversation would be monitored in real time by anyone.

Nevertheless, they used no names and spoke discreetly. What was impossible yesterday might have become possible today.

Referring to Luther's daughter Jolie, who had almost been injected with a control mechanism, whose sister and mother were now enslaved and lost to her, Jane said, "How's the girl?"

"Angry. But not angry with me anymore for getting involved in this. She knows I really had no choice. She's smart, resilient."

"So how are you?"

"Not good. Feeling lost. But hanging in there."

Jane took a breath to speak, hesitated, shuddered, and took another breath. "Man, I so hate what I'm about to do."

"If there's any way I can help, tell me. I'm going a little crazy here. Being off duty, it's not me."

"Jolie needs you there."

"She wants them crushed for what happened to her mom and sister. She wants that real bad. I want to give her that."

"And if she loses you, too?"

"If we don't blow this wide open, she not only loses me. She loses herself, her future, her freedom."

Jane sat in silence for a moment, watching a large motor home negotiate the parking lot. Then she said, "You know what's the most important thing in the world to me?"

"Yeah. You showed me the cameo."

"Now I need to go into a very tight place and get him out of there before they find him. I'm not able to do it alone."

"Oh, shit."

"Yeah. Neck deep."

"Where are you? Where do you need me to be?"

"My friends, where you are now, they'll fly you to Palm Springs tomorrow morning, then drive you to Indio." She gave him an address.

"What do I need to bring?"

"What you used to carry every day to work," she said.

He'd been a sheriff in Minnesota, and whatever else he might have brought to work every day, he always carried a gun.

She said, "First thing after we hang up, have someone there take a photo of you, a head shot." She gave him an email address. "On the subject line, put 'Emergency.' The only message should be 'You're expecting the attached photo.'"

Luther read the email address, and she confirmed it.

"You better believe we'll do this," he said, "no matter what it takes."

"I believe. I have to, or otherwise fall apart," she said. "With you, I believe we will, we'll do it."

He said, "I owe you for what I have left, for Jolie. I love you for that."

"You're the best. Just stay cool."

"Hell, I've had ice in my veins for days now."

16

IN THE DISTANT SOUTHEAST, TILLED FIELDS MOIST from irrigation, issuing a thin mist from the respiring earth . . . Much nearer and to the south, a weedy field leading to an open grove of live oaks . . .

In the truck-stop parking lot, Jane reviewed her options one more time, the people from whom she might seek help. She needed someone in addition to Luther Tillman. Her preference among the possibilities was an unlikely choice, but she kept returning to him.

A week earlier, in Texas, she had been driving the desert night in a black Ford Escape when a Texas Highway Patrol officer pulled her over. She'd left him cuffed to her vehicle, which had been hot once it had been connected to her, and made off with his cruiser, a black-and-white Dodge Charger. Certain that she couldn't outrun the roadblocks, she'd used the patrol car's lightbar to pull over a Mercedes E350, intending to take the car and use the driver as cover, because the police would be looking for a woman alone. She hadn't expected that she and the eighty-one-year-old widower who owned the E350, Bernie Riggowitz, would spend more than twelve hours together or that they would bond so completely.

Now she took from her wallet a photo of his late wife that he'd given her, with whom he'd driven all over the country on extended road trips. Miriam was lovely, her face a portrait of kindness.

Jane called Bernie's cell number. When he answered, she said, "I'm looking at this picture of Miriam you gave me, and I can't help asking myself, how did a guy like you win over a doll like her?"

"I'm no *plosher*, so I won't say I was a double for Cary Grant back then. But I was sweet as halva. Halva and chutzpa can take a guy a long way, plus I could dance a little. How's by you, Alice?"

She had told him that her name was Alice Liddell. Because he never followed the news—*Feh! It's all lies or depressing*—he hadn't known she was the most-wanted fugitive in America, only that she was "mixed up in something you need to mix yourself out of."

"Maybe by now," Jane said, "you know more about me."

"Oh, you're everywhere. I know all kinds of *shmontses* about you now. I might believe one percent of it if I was stupid. But anyone wants me to spill anything about you, they can go talk to the wall."

"You're a peach. Where are you, Bernie?"

"I'm here in Scottsdale with Nasia and Segev making over me, everything ipsy-pipsy. But . . ."

Nasia was his daughter, Segev his son-in-law.

"But?" she said.

"But they want me to stop traveling, move in here, be pampered to death. They think Miriam's in that grave. They won't understand she's out there everywhere we ever went together all those years of driving. I'm not lonely on the road, 'cause she's always with me."

"Nasia is your only child, isn't she?"

"My best blessing now that Miriam's gone. So I have to pretend maybe I'll give up the road, which I won't."

"You know I have such a blessing, too."

"*Do I know?* Since I found out, I can't sleep for worry. You never mentioned when we had our little drive together."

"You didn't know who I was then. My kid is suddenly in a very bad jam. I can't get him . . ." Speaking about her helplessness brought a tightness to her chest, a knot of emotion that made it hard to speak for a moment. "I can't get him out of this jam alone."

"The way you talk, a person would think I'm a stranger. You can't just tell me what I should do?"

"It's going to be damn dangerous. I have no right—"

"Are we *mishpokhe* or what?"

"I don't know what that means."

"What it means is, it means *family*."

"That's very sweet. But in fact we aren't family."

"I know my own family, *bubeleh*—who is and who's not. Didn't you call me Grandpa one day in Texas? And didn't I tell that nice policeman you were my granddaughter? So then it's settled. Tell me what, when, where."

Under that serene blue sky, on the tumultuous surface of the earth, as long as there were Bernies and Luthers, there was hope.

Jane said, "You and Miriam traveled sometimes in a motor home."

"We took most trips by car, some in a Fleetwood Southwind. It's a different country one way from the other, but always beautiful."

"You could still drive a motor home?"

"Can I walk, can I talk, can I twiddle my thumbs? I could drive you coast to coast without a bump."

"What size was that Fleetwood of yours?"

"Thirty-two feet, but I can do longer. Gas is better than diesel. A diesel pusher—engine in back—will be a lot heavier and harder to turn. Where are we going?"

"Tell you tomorrow. Let's meet in Indio, near Palm Springs." She gave him the address. "Can you be there tomorrow afternoon?"

"Indio's five hours from here. I could be there and back and there again, with time to stop for a nosh. You got a motor home?"

"I'll have one. From Enrique, the guy we visited in Nogales that time. Meanwhile, have someone take a photo of you, a head shot." She gave him the email address that she'd given to Luther.

"Don't you worry," Bernie said. "Whatever we need to do, we'll do it twice."

"There's no way I can ever thank you enough, Bernie."

"So before you hang up, say the word for me."

"What word?"

"What we are and always will be."

Her voice caught again in her throat. *"Mishpokhe."*

"Pretty good. You should let that *kh* rattle against the roof of your mouth a little better, but not bad for a first try, *bubeleh.*"

17

GOTTFREY NEVER SLEEPS MORE THAN A FEW HOURS. He doesn't know why he needs *any* sleep. Sleep is a requirement of the body, and his body isn't real. A disembodied mind should function without sleep.

But he isn't the author of this drama, isn't responsible for the conflicting details that suggest a careless playwright.

He is only along for the ride.

After a late breakfast in the Holiday Inn coffee shop, he walks two blocks to the Best Western, where Rupert Baldwin is staying.

The sky over Worstead is wooly and gray. The air pools in stillness; but a predawn breeze earlier smoothed a layer of pale dust along the gutter, in and out of which wander paw prints laid down by a dog or by the coyote that he saw the previous night.

At the Best Western, when Gottfrey knocks on the door to Room 16, Rupert calls out, "It's not locked."

In the same Hush Puppies and rumpled corduroy suit and beige shirt and bolo tie that he was wearing for the operation at Hawk

Ranch, Rupert sits at a small table with two chairs. Through reading glasses, he squints at one of two laptops that are open and in use.

The bedspread has not been turned back, though it is slightly rumpled, as if Rupert had rested sleeplessly atop it for a short while before getting on with the search for Ancel and Clare Hawk.

Closing the door behind him, Gottfrey says, "Couldn't sleep?"

"Didn't need to."

Intrigued, Gottfrey asks, "Do you ever?"

Without looking up, Rupert asks, "Do I ever what?"

"Need to sleep."

"Not when I have Hershey's Special Dark and can wash down some crank with Red Bull." He taps a can of the high-caffeine energy drink, beside which is a bag of miniature dark-chocolate candy bars.

" 'Crank'? You're using methamphetamine?"

"Not often. Only since this case. I hate this slut. I want her dead sooner than now. I want her in-laws injected and licking my boots, and then I want them dead."

"There's another one," Gottfrey says. "A conflicting detail. You never wear boots."

Rupert finally looks up from the laptop, frowning, his stare as sharp as the prongs of a meat fork. "Something wrong with you?"

Gottfrey shrugs. "Things should've gone better last night."

"Better? Hell, it couldn't have gone *worse*." Rupert returns his attention to the laptop. "When *all* the Hawks are dead, including her brat, I'm going to surprise that shitkicker Juan Saba, cut off his package, and feed it to his wife before I blow her brains out."

"You sure are passionate about this. Dedicated to the mission."

"In case you haven't thought it through, it's us or them. And it's damn well not going to be *me*. One rogue bitch Bureau agent and her bumpkin in-laws can't get the better of us. We're an ass-kicking head-busting *machine*, never been anything like us."

Stepping behind Rupert, Gottfrey considers the laptop screen. An analytic program is assessing and enhancing an image taken from orbit. Changes occur with such speed that he can't understand what is before him. "Find anything? Where maybe they went on horseback?"

"I back-doored our satellites—government, commercial—couldn't get shit on this part of Texas after sunset yesterday."

"What about China?"

China is all about weaponizing space and orbital surveillance, so NSA has seeded a rootkit in their military's computer network. A hacker like Rupert can dive in and float through the Chinese system at such a low level they don't know anybody's swimming there.

"I finally found some relevant Chicom video," Rupert confirms.

Although it is as dark as Satan's colon on those plains at night, the Chinese are even more interested in what America does in the dark than in the day. They fear the U.S. has mobile missile platforms that are shifted around at night. The Chicoms have highly sensitive look-down capability in infrared, and Rupert is working with a segment of streamed video that he cloned from their archives.

"In that meadowland, after a cool day when the ground didn't soak up heat, there's not much background infrared to filter out."

"But there's wildlife," Gottfrey says.

"Most too small to matter, except deer. And deer travel in small families, usually more than two. It's largely federal land not licensed for grazing, so we don't have to sort out a lot of cattle."

Pointing to the constantly melting and solidifying image on the screen, Gottfrey says, "What am I going to see when this clarifies?"

"Horses are big—fifteen or sixteen hundred pounds for Clare Hawk's mare, two thousand for Ancel's stallion. They put out strong heat signatures, especially carrying riders and exerting themselves. I've processed this once, just now giving it a final cleanup."

When a scene resolves and freezes, it isn't like the raw image captured by satellite. It's been analyzed and enhanced—translated—to make sense to the human eye. The straight-down angle on the meadowland is rendered in shades of gray, faint whorling-feathering patterns that represent the effect of a fitful breeze in the grass. Here and there, faint reddish hazes represent ground-source heat, and scattered small hot-red points might be the issue of wildlife.

The most prominent features in the image are two ruby-red heat signatures brighter and larger than the others.

As Rupert works the keyboard, the static image evolves into a video stream. The red signifiers move through the gray featherings toward a bisecting band without pattern near which are clustered reddish geometric shapes representing six or eight buildings.

"By the time the Chicom satellite passed over here, the Hawks had already gone almost twenty miles from their ranch."

"How do you know those aren't a couple deer?"

"A female deer tends to follow a male, behind and a little off to one side. And deer won't travel as directly as this. They wander. These are horses under the guidance of riders."

"But we can't know this is Clare and Ancel Hawk."

"The satellite captured them at two-ten A.M. There's not likely to be a pair of other riders out at that hour."

"What're those buildings?"

"Another ranch. The band of gray without pattern is the state route that passes through Worstead before it gets to this place."

When the video ends, Egon Gottfrey says, "That's all you have?"

"Satellite's moving damn fast. You don't get a feature-length film of anything."

"What if they didn't stop at that other ranch? They might have passed it by, crossed the road, and gone somewhere else."

Rupert turns to the second laptop and calls up a file. "Just finished putting this together before you knocked."

The first photo, captured from Google Street View, shows a gated entrance to a property and a sign that reads LONGRIN STABLES.

Rupert clicks away the first photo and splits the screen for two Texas DMV images of driver's licenses, one for Chase Longrin, one for Alexis Longrin. They appear to be in their early thirties, good-looking in spite of the poor quality of DMV photography.

"Husband and wife," Rupert says. "We recently became suspicious of them. Maybe they're a conduit for messages from Jane to her in-laws. Nick Hawk and Chase Longrin were best friends in high school."

Gottfrey considers the two faces. Chase still looks like a high-school jock. Alexis is a pretty woman.

It's noon. Almost ten hours since the two riders on horseback—if they were riders and horses—had been captured by the satellite.

Gottfrey says, "Let's go have a chat with the Longrins."

18

THE WOMAN IN RESEDA, KNOWN AS JUDY WHITE but also as Lois Jones, neither of which was her real name, claimed to be a Syrian refugee, though her accent sounded sometimes like Eastern European Slavic, at other times flat-out Russian. She didn't answer her phone in any traditional manner. "You have wrong number, go away."

From experience, Jane knew neither Judy nor Lois would hang up.

"We've done business before."

"I not in business. Read palms. Tell fortunes. My gift. Is life mission, not business."

"Enrique introduced us."

"You have wrong number, go away."

"When I saw you a week or so ago, the last thing you said to me was, 'Go. Go where you go. You want to die, so go die.'"

"Was nothing personal. Just opinion. Observation. My gift."

"You're going to get two photos by email." Jane explained what she needed. "I want to stop by and get everything in three hours."

"Want, want, want. Everybody want. Is impossible, three hours."

"I'll pay triple the usual."

"Don't die on way here, nobody to pay us."

"I'll do my best to get there alive."

"So you say." Judy and Lois terminated the call.

19

THIS GUY SAID HE KNEW A GUY WHO BOUGHT CARS from Enrique de Soto, reworked wheels to outrun anything a cop might jack around in. This guy who knew a guy, he swaggered like some TV-wrestling star.

Enrique's product started out stolen and went for a makeover in Nogales, Mexico, where its identifiers were removed and the GPS was stripped out. The vehicle was either given a new engine compatible to the Batmobile or otherwise supercharged. Anything you purchased from Enrique came with a valid California DMV registration or with one from a DMV of your choice in any Canadian province.

This guy who knew a guy also knew what sweet prices Enrique charged for his merchandise, and he was dumb enough to think that Enrique kept a bank's worth of cash on the premises.

Ricky de Soto worked out of several weathered barns on a former horse ranch near Nogales, Arizona, directly across the border from Nogales, Mexico. The front barn held no vehicles, but was stocked with junk furniture and other items to provide Ricky with cover as an antiques dealer.

So that morning, this guy who knew a guy came into Ricky's

office without an appointment, smelling of some pussy-boy cologne. Obviously a bodybuilder. Shaved and waxed bullet head. Tattoo of a snake around his throat. Wearing a loose black raincoat in a warm rainless morning. He was accompanied by a nervous dude who resembled Mick Jagger but even skinnier, with the bad teeth of a methhead.

They evidently didn't think they looked like what they were. The one with the tattoo mentioned a good customer of Enrique's and started talking cars, a lot of shit picked up from bad movies. The methhead thought he was casual, easing around the office, pretending to admire the cheap vases and the mantel clocks that passed for collectibles, but he was moving away from his buddy and into a backup shooting position.

Bullet Head's raincoat didn't hang right, because there was no weight on the left side to balance the concealed sawed-off shotgun in a sling under the right-side panel of fabric.

Ricky didn't worry that he might have misjudged his visitors. In the event that he was mistaken, he would have no regrets.

When the guy in the raincoat asked if he could smoke, just to explain why he was reaching into the right-hand pocket of his coat, Ricky stepped hard on the pedal in the knee space of his desk. A 12-gauge shotgun was mounted to the center rail that supported the desktop. The pedal drew taut a wire that pulled the trigger. The skirt on the front of the desk was a mere quarter-inch panel of Masonite. At such close range, the blast chopped Raincoat Guy mostly in the crotch and lower abdomen, and blew him down.

Skinny Mick had a gun in, of all places, an ankle holster. As the fool bent and fumbled for it, Ricky drew a pistol from a holster attached to the side of his office chair and stood and shot the meth addict twice. He stepped around the desk and shot the screaming guy in the raincoat, who wasn't long for this world, anyway.

All the gunfire in close quarters left Ricky de Soto half deaf. He stepped around the bodies, left his office, pulled the door shut.

The would-be heist artists had arrived in a Cadillac Escalade, possibly stolen, in any case now hot. It would have to be boxed over to Mexico, given a new identity. Because he hadn't paid some punk to boost it, there would be a good profit when it was ready for sale.

He didn't work the operation alone, of course, but the other guys were in the barns farthest back from the highway. By the time he walked there, with grasshoppers springing out of the tall grass alongside the oiled-dirt driveway as if to celebrate him, his hearing slowly returned, though he would have tinnitus for a while.

He told Danny and Tio what had happened. They knew what to do without being instructed, and they headed directly for his office.

One of the benefits of having major acreage was that you had numerous places where graves could be dug discreetly with a back-hoe.

Ricky didn't immediately follow Danny and Tio, but stood yawn-ing elaborately, trying to pop the tinnitus out of his ears.

His iPhone rang, and as usual there was no caller ID, because his clientele preferred anonymity. He took the call. "Yeah?"

She said, "Hardly more than a week since I saw you. I must be the best customer you have."

Sexy as she was, he knew her voice as much from dreams as from the times she'd done business with him face-to-face.

He said, "You're so big now, maybe I shouldn't risk doing any more business with you."

"Like I'm going to believe your balls fell off. I'm only a few hun-dred miles away, I'd have heard them hit the ground."

He laughed. "*Bonita chica*, maybe yours are bigger than mine."

"I need a motor home. I'm sure you've fitted them out before with cute little hard-to-find compartments."

"Could be I got a couple right now."

"Gas, not a diesel pusher. Thirty-six to forty feet."

"I got a Tiffin Allegro thirty-six. Total refit, custom paint. Nobody ever knew her would know her now, she's so pretty."

She told him the size of the custom storage spaces she needed.

She also specified a pistol that she required.

He said, "Doable on both counts."

"I need everything by late tomorrow morning."

"Shit, no."

"I'll pay a premium."

"Tiffin Allegro thirty-six-footer, new off the showroom floor, would cost you a hundred eighty thousand."

"Like you bought it right off the showroom floor. What was your wholesale price—four thousand to some booster?"

"Plus there's the work you want done overnight."

"Ricky, Ricky, Ricky. Will you pretend you have to charge sales tax? Listen, one thing you *do* need to add to the total is delivery."

"You think I'm Amazon or somethin'?"

"You know the address near Palm Springs. You once recommended the man there to me, but I never needed him until now."

Enrique's nephew, Ferrante, operated a legit business in Indio, customizing limousines, high-end SUVs, and other vehicles, not only making them more luxurious than the original manufacturers had made them, but also armoring them and installing bullet-resistant glass and run-flat tires for wealthy people who watched the world grow darker and heard lethal violence justified from podium to pulpit.

In addition, as insurance against another government screwup that would sink the economy yet again and devastate his customizing business, Ferrante dealt in illegal arms from a secret basement under one of his factories. Because his mother, Josefina, Enrique's sister, had for some reason raised the boy in the Church, he would not sell weapons to criminals, only to the upstanding citizens who purchased his armored vehicles, titans of industry and banking and social-media companies—and probably to a rogue FBI agent who was maybe more righteous than the people who accused her of treason.

"I assume," Jane Hawk said, "your contact there will let your vehicle on his lot and let me prepare for a trip I have to make."

"We're tight. But I have to say he's a weird duck. He does Mass daily, always saying his rosary like some old *abuela* who wears a mantilla even in the shower. He's got this blood obsession."

" 'Blood obsession'?"

"You meet him, you'll see. But he's not *loco*. He's smart. He knows how the world works. I guarantee you can do your meet there."

"I'm assuming the Tiffin Allegro can tow an SUV."

"What SUV you want it to tow?"

She told him. "So how much will you rob me for?"

He stood thinking, watching the insects leap, watching a sudden flock of crows cackle down out of the sun, snaring the bugs in mid jump, glossy black wings thrashing the golden grass and fireweed, the singing of the grasshoppers now like thin screams.

"A hundred twenty thousand on delivery. You got that much?"

"Yeah. But you're a true bandit, Ricky."

"There's a way I could let you have it for seventy."

"What way is that?"

"Take a break from what you're doin', stay a month with me."

"A month with you, Ricky, I'd be used up, worn out, no good for anything anymore."

"I'd be gentle. You'd be surprised."

"I know you'd be gentle. You're chivalrous. But I'm a widow, you know, and figuratively speaking I'm wearing black."

"I forgot the whole widow thing for a minute. My apologies."

"Accepted. And don't worry about the hundred twenty, it's all in clean bills. Nobody's looking for it."

"I don't worry about you," he said. "I know you won't screw me, not that way, and I guess not any other way."

"Business and romance never mix, anyway," she said.

"Guy who had this operation before me," Enrique said, "hooked up with this lady customer, ended up with his head cut off."

"There you go. Let's keep our heads, Ricky."

She terminated the call.

Up there at the barn in which Enrique had his office, at a door that couldn't be seen from the highway, Danny and Tio were dumping a dead guy in the open cargo bed of a Mule, a nice little electric vehicle that was useful for a variety of tasks.

20

THE SHADOWS OF THE PARKING LOT LAMPPOSTS, sheathed at noon, now slowly extending west across the truck-stop blacktop, like swords drawn to defend against the dragon growl of diesel engines . . .

Enrique de Soto had come to Jane Hawk's attention when she had tracked down Marcus Paul Headsman, a serial killer who'd stolen a car from Enrique. The FBI had too few agents and too many cases to care about the small-beer de Soto operation. Headsman was the game. Likewise, over in the Department of Justice, prosecutorial overload required a triage approach to selecting which criminals to proceed against. Jane had first purchased a Ford Escape from Ricky, shortly after she went on the run. She'd given him the impression that the law had never bothered him because she'd shredded the file on him, which was neither true nor necessary. Ricky was macho enough to convince himself that a good-looking FBI agent would be so drawn to him that she'd cut off the hands of justice to keep them from seizing him.

One of the most dispiriting things about her current situation was the need to work with criminals whom she would have liked to put behind bars. There were degrees of evil, however, and in these dark times, which seemed to darkle deeper every day, absolute purity of action ensured defeat. The armies of virtue were either too few in number or too cowed by the volume of political hatred to be counted upon. When bargaining with lesser evils to obtain what was necessary to wage war against Evil in the uppercase, she'd keep her footing if she was always alert to the stain it left on her, if she remained aware of the need for contrition, and if she would—supposing that she lived—eventually bring to justice those like Ricky de Soto with whom she'd had to traffic.

Now, in a remote corner of the big parking lot, with the Explorer Sport shielding her from observation by those coming and going from the truck stop, she knelt on the blacktop and used a hammer to pound a screwdriver into the charging port of the burner phone, destroying the battery and, with it, the identifier by which the phone might be tracked. She smashed the screen and broke open the casing, intending to cross the fifty yards of weedy field and throw the debris into the ravine toward which the land sloped.

In this age when every phone and computer and laptop and every car with a GPS and even every high-tech wristwatch was a beacon by which you could be tracked, measured paranoia was essential to survival. If the first call she made was to any person who might conceivably be a target of law enforcement, she discarded her burner after a single use. Luther Tillman's location was unknown to all authorities, and Bernie Riggowitz was a most unlikely subject for surveillance; however, once she had spoken to Enrique de Soto, she needed to dispose of the phone, lest someone monitoring him might learn its identifier code and even now be committing the nation's every resource to locate and apprehend her.

Recently she had destroyed a lot of disposable phones.

Of course, if these days Enrique was in fact a hot target of one law-enforcement agency or another, simply placing the order for the motor home had all but ensured Jane's destruction. When the Tiffin Allegro 36 showed up in Indio, driven by one of Ricky's people, soon thereafter a demon horde of SWAT-geared Arcadians would storm the place. However, she had no choice but to trust that Ricky had taken adequate steps to mask his true identity when he'd bought the smartphone and contracted with a telecom company.

She picked up the broken burner and rose to her feet and saw the guy first from the corner of her eye. He was coming through the bristled field, from the direction of the oaks and ravine, moving fast, a shotgun raised and ready.

21

FROM HIS ROVER, THROUGH BINOCULARS, IVAN Petro watches Jane Hawk exit the truck-stop diner with a bag of takeout and a tall drink container. Spine straight, shoulders back, with the grace and confidence of a born athlete, she exhibits none of the furtiveness or wariness that might mark her as a fugitive. The pixie-cut wig is different from the shaggy black number she wore the previous night, but neither the hair nor the horn-rimmed glasses can conceal her essential Janeness.

She returns to the Explorer and drives as far from the bustling business as the pavement allows and parks next to an open field.

After Ivan repositions his SUV, he uses the binoculars again, pulls her close, and sees that she is eating lunch. She has put down the window. A soft breeze stirs her hair, suggesting that she has also put down the front window on the passenger side.

He watches her, thinking. When she seems to be talking on a cellphone, he decides he better seize this opportunity.

His all-wheel-drive vehicle has a special GPS, developed by the NSA, which offers displays not only of highways, roads, and streets, but also off-road topography in considerable detail. Because Jane has chosen to have lunch in the most remote corner of the property, Ivan realizes that a way exists to get close to her without calling attention to his Range Rover or himself.

He leaves the truck stop not by its exit lane, but overland. Her Explorer faces due east. He passes behind her, a hundred yards to the west. She can see him, if at all, only in the rearview mirror.

He crosses the fifty yards of open land and drives between two live oaks, under massive anaconda limbs of hardened sinuosity. He negotiates a long slope—a carpet of beetle-shaped leaves crunching under the tires, scaring squirrels up tree trunks—and descends into a realm of Gothic shadows, the dark ground patterned by a scattering of sunlight configured by the branches and leaves overhead.

At the bottom of the glen, he drives east until the blinking indicators on the GPS display—red for the Explorer, green for his Rover—are parallel, whereupon he stops and switches off the engine.

The slope to the north is maybe two hundred feet long but not too steep to climb. When he gets to the top, there will be about a fifty-yard length of open ground between him and the Explorer.

The pistol he's carrying is a Colt .45, but he doesn't want to take her down with that. He needs to capture her, not kill her, if he's going to learn where to find her child and where she's stashed the evidence that might convict some Arcadians.

He gets out of the Rover and lifts the tailgate. He zippers open a shotgun case and removes a wireless Taser XREP 12-gauge. This pump-action weapon provides a five-round magazine and fires an extended-range electronic projectile that weighs less than an ounce but delivers a twenty-second, five-hundred-volt shock.

A classic Taser arcs up to fifty thousand volts, but this slug does more with less, because the waveform is precisely shaped to match the electric signals in the human nervous system. The four barbed electrodes on the nose of the slug hook to skin or clothes, causing intense pain and muscle paralysis, incapacitating the target with little chance of permanent injury and hardly any risk of death.

With her vehicle screening the assault from those at the truck stop, he needs to disable her only long enough to cuff her wrists and ankles, and then administer chloroform with an inhaler.

Ivan is at least a hundred pounds heavier than she is, slabs of muscle. He can easily carry her into the trees, and then either continue carrying her or drag her down the slope to the Range Rover.

He ascends through crackling drifts of dead leaves. The ground is blanketed in a camouflage of oak shadows and glimmering shapes of sunlight. It would be easy to put a foot wrong and sprain an ankle. He takes longer to reach the crest than he expected.

The delay works to his advantage. When he arrives at the rim of the glen and shelters among the last trees, he sees that he needn't worry about the passenger-side window being open to allow a clear shot at Jane in the driver's seat. She's out of the SUV, kneeling on the blacktop, hammering what might be a disposable phone.

Although a standard Taser with wires can disable a target up to thirty-five feet, the XREP 12-gauge has an effective range of one hundred feet. He's about half again that distance from the woman and needs to close the gap before he fires.

When he steps out of the cover of the trees, there is a danger that she will see him, even as distracted as she is by the phone. The field before him bristles with weeds and parched ribbon grass; but he will make little noise forging through it.

He moves fast, holding the gun with both hands, a few inches above his waist, ready to bring it up and halt and tag her with the laser sight before he fires. The powder in an XREP round is less than in a standard shell; the slug, which is comparatively light, never achieves a velocity that will kill or seriously injure.

The slug is a wonder of miniaturization: three fins that deploy when it leaves the muzzle of the shotgun, enabling it to spin to stay on target; circuitry nestled inside shock-absorbing plastic; a microprocessor that commands a voltage capacitor to fire while also modulating the shape, intensity, and duration of the current; two tiny lithium batteries to power the microprocessor and provide the disabling electrical charge; a transformer to convert battery energy to stunning effect.

He is maybe 120 feet from her, hasn't yet drawn her attention, and decides to close to eighty, just to be sure to drop her with the first round.

Then she sees him.

22

Upon glimpsing the man in her peripheral vision, Jane might have dropped the hammer and gone for the Heckler in her shoulder rig. But intuition inspired her instead to throw the hammer as she pivoted toward her assailant.

He wasn't holding the weapon as if he expected a hard recoil. The sound of the shot wasn't as loud as it ought to be, and Jane knew at once that this was a Taser XREP.

Fractions of a second mattered now.

When she moved to throw the hammer, the laser dot on her breast had been displaced to her left arm, but the shooter had squeezed the trigger just then, as the hammer left her hand.

Instantly she began to shrug off the sport coat.

On impact, four electrified barbs on the nose of the projectile hooked the coat sleeve, near the shoulder, instead of piercing her thin T-shirt over her breasts, where it would have administered a disabling shock.

Even as the projectile's chassis separated from its nose to dangle on a copper wire, exactly as it was designed to do, Jane cried out at the initial—and smaller—localized shock to her left biceps, conveyed through her clothing. But the satin-lined sleeves were already sliding off her arms.

Nearly all people, when hit, instinctively grabbed the dangling wire—which was called the "hand trap"—to tear out the barbs that were delivering the painful localized shock. But if she grasped the live wire, her hand would contract involuntarily. Clenching the wire tightly, unable to let go, she would receive a much bigger shock as electricity flowed through her body. She would spasm, fall, lie paralyzed for twenty seconds, and be disoriented thereafter.

If she didn't grip the wire, six longer barbs would pop through the fabric of her sleeve and deliver the disabling shock anyway.

Half a second after the nose barbs hooked her coat, even as the chassis of the projectile was separating from the nose to offer the live wire, her right arm was free. As her left arm slipped out of that sleeve, a brief hellish current stung her fingers, but the garment puddled to the ground, sparing her from the full power of the initial shock.

Although she couldn't feel the laser dot on her body, she knew her assailant must be squeezing off another round. She dropped as she drew the Heckler, the second projectile shattered against the Explorer, and she rolled toward the front bumper.

23

THIS HATEFUL BITCH, THIS SELF-RIGHTEOUS SELF-appointed save-the-world *bitch*, this counterrevolutionary *pig*, has the reflexes of a cat, a damn *hyperactive* cat.

She's twisting away from the laser dot and shrugging out of the coat even as Ivan is pulling the trigger, so just for insurance he at once fires again.

He's not thinking about the hammer; it's a wild pitch meant to distract him, and Ivan Petro won't be distracted, hell if he will, he's focused on her, he squeezes off a third round.

Her aim is almost as good as her reflexes. The tumbling hammer, like some instrument in an Olympic event, arcs high and spins down to strike him just as he fires for the third time. It clips his left hand, with which he holds the slide handle that chambers each round.

The pain brings with it an instant numbness, so that he can't keep a grip on the shotgun with his left hand. And he can't operate it with only his right.

Two rounds remain in the Taser, useless to him for the moment. The bitch is on the ground, a difficult—almost impossible—target from this distance, when he has only one good hand. She rolls and then squirms along the blacktop toward the front of the Explorer, seeking partial cover from which she can rise into a genuflection and open fire; she's seconds from using him for target practice. He has no prospect of cover in this open field, only below-the-knee weeds and ribbon grass. Instead of drawing his pistol, he throws down the Taser 12-gauge and runs in a crouch toward the oaks.

24

A CLOUD OF MIDGES BESTIRRED FROM THE GRASS, circling around her head like some crown of damnation predictive of imminent death, the sun seeming much hotter than it was a moment earlier, and yet a thin cold sweat on the nape of her neck . . .

The low-velocity rounds from the Taser 12-gauge wouldn't have drawn the attention of anyone at the distant truck stop, not with the growl of half a dozen eighteen-wheelers coming and going at any one time. The crack of the Heckler, however, might penetrate the truck drone and alert someone.

Anyway, she didn't dare risk killing the bastard. She needed to take him down, get some answers from him. How did he find her? Was there a transponder on her Explorer? If so, who else knew about it? How many others were coming?

Holstering the pistol, she scrambled to her feet, stomped on the chassis of the Taser projectile that was attached to her sport coat and trailing at the end of the copper wire. She crushed it and stomped again, separating the nose from the wire, protected by the rubber soles of her sneakers. She snatched up the coat, shook it, casting off the debris, and sprinted after her attacker.

He was a big bull on two feet, a minotaur without a labyrinth. She needed to avoid getting close-up physical with him and take him by surprise instead.

She thought the hammer had struck him, might have done some damage, which was why he'd cast aside the Taser 12-gauge and fled.

Fast for his size, with a substantial head start, he would reach the cover of the trees well before she did. If she plunged into the woodlet in his wake, she'd likely plunge as well into a bullet.

She hesitated at the dropped Taser shotgun but then snatched it up to be sure he didn't return for it. She angled west of him and demanded more speed of herself and hoped that she made the tree line before he dared to stop, turn, and see where she had gone.

After the bright sun, the sudden shadows pooling in the broad glen seemed to have substance, a palpable darkness that was cool on her skin and a pressure on her eyes, its weight imposing a stillness in the oak grove and stifling all sound except her breathing.

She put down the Taser 12-gauge and slipped her arms into the sleeves of her coat and stood with her back to a massive tree trunk. She drew the Heckler and held it in both hands, arms close to her breast, muzzle directed toward the crosswork of layered limbs above, her stalker somewhere behind her, fifty or sixty feet to the east.

Waiting for her wide-open eyes to become dark adapted, striving to quiet her breathing, she listened intently but still heard only the distant Peterbilts and Macks, nothing nearby. The trucks were so far away that, instead of growling, they made a throaty, threatening purr, as if they were massive saber-toothed tigers that had crossed a gulf of time to hunt long after the extinction of their species.

Alert for any sound from her stalker, she knew that he likewise listened for the smallest revelation of her position. Cautiously she leaned away from the tree and turned her head to look around it.

If the canopy of oaks hadn't allowed a brace of sun spears to stab down on the black Range Rover, she might not have seen it at the bottom of the glen, about sixty feet to the east and south of where she'd parked her Explorer. The vehicle waited, glossy-dark and as ominous as a hearse, shapes of sunlight in its windows like the pale, luminous faces of the long departed.

The lower half of the south wall of the glen, rising beyond the Range Rover, lay under a heavy thatching of branches. Those shadows were unrelieved. She liked those shadows, the cover they offered.

He would avoid the vehicle, figuring that she'd expect him to make for it and would then draw down on him while he was exposed. For the same reason, he wouldn't imagine that she would go near it.

Moving anywhere was tricky, because the ground lay strewn with dead leaves that announced her when she stepped on them and with loose stones that would clatter out from underfoot.

The big man's silence suggested that patience was one of his virtues. Evidently he was content to wait her out.

She couldn't afford patience. If he had called for backup, a small army of these Arcadian creeps might be en route.

She put her back to the tree again and thought about the Range Rover and the dark slope beyond it. She looked downhill to study the frequency of trees and patted her sport-coat pockets to check where everything was stowed.

She holstered her pistol and sat on the ground and quietly removed her sneakers and pulled off her socks and slipped her bare feet into the shoes and tied the laces tight. With her switchblade, she cut a hole in the ribbed top of one sock. Working quickly, she knotted the toes of the socks together, extracted one of her plastic zipties from a coat pocket, freed it from the rubber band that kept it tightly coiled, put the zip-tie through the hole she'd made, and cinched it tightly to that sock. She coiled the plastic once more and stuffed it, with the socks, down the front of her jeans.

She got to her feet and stood with her back against the tree once more and took slow deep breaths and tried to think of another plan. There wasn't one.

25

Egon Gottfrey AND HIS CREW OF EIGHT DESCEND on Longrin Stables in five vehicles, fast along the approach lane, clouds of dust roiling in their wake, as if they have ignited a prairie fire.

This once-failed property is now a thriving horse-breeding business built on sweat equity, producing standardbreds for harness racing, show-quality Tennessee walking horses, and the National Show Horse, a breed that combines the Arabian and the American saddlebred.

Gottfrey doesn't care about the Longrins' hard work or about the beauty of the horses, or about the dust that shrouds him and his crew as they slide to a stop in the receiving yard and pile out of their vehicles, a few of them sneezing.

He cares only about discerning what the Unknown Playwright's script requires of him next. He's pretty sure they're here to find Ancel and Clare Hawk *at any cost,* and they must knock heads and break knees if necessary.

They are not wearing Kevlar because the law-abiding Longrins aren't likely to instigate violence. Each of them wears a hands-free earpiece walkie-talkie, and each knows what he or she needs to do.

The last vehicle in the procession, the Cadillac Escalade driven by Paloma Sutherland, parks across the lane, barring exit. She and Sally Jones bail out and take up positions, pistols drawn.

Chris Roberts and Janis Dern park at the Victorian-style house and move fast to mount the porch steps, he at the back, she at the front of the residence. She pounds hard on the door. "FBI! FBI!"

Pedro and Alejandro set out to locate the stable hands and corral them in the fenced exercise yard outside Stable 5.

Gottfrey, accompanied by Vince Penn and Rupert Baldwin, makes his way quickly to Stable 3, where Chase Longrin has an office at one end of the building, opposite the tack room.

Vince is sneezing, and Rupert is cursing between violent fits of coughing. Gottfrey keeps trying to spit out the taste of dust.

The yellowish clouds drift with them; they aren't able to walk into fresh air. The persistent aggravation of the dust might make a lesser man than Gottfrey concede its reality. However, he's annoyed not with the dust, which is no more real than the stables, but with the Unknown Playwright who suddenly seems intent on furnishing the scene with more realistic detail than has lately been his style.

When they enter Stable 3, with stalls to both sides and curious horses attendant to their visitors, the smells of manure and straw and horseflesh form a fragrance divine compared to the dust outside. They breathe deeply as they stride toward the end of the structure, and Gottfrey calls out, "Chase Longrin? FBI! FBI, Mr. Longrin."

Chase Longrin—six feet two, sun-bleached hair, sun-bronzed face—stands at the desk in his office, facing the open door, his expression as hard as that of a defender of the Alamo.

Entering the room, with Vince and Rupert close behind him, Gottfrey says, "Egon Gottfrey. FBI," as he holds up his ID.

"Yes," says Longrin, "so I heard. You sure did make a splashy entrance. Mr. J. Edgar Hoover would be proud."

"We have a warrant for the arrest of Ancel and Clare Hawk."

"You've got the wrong ranch. They live on the other side of Worstead, about nineteen miles by the state route."

"They came here by horseback after two o'clock this morning. Before you deny that, Mr. Longrin, I must advise you that it's a crime to lie to an FBI agent even if you're not under oath."

Looking Rupert Baldwin up and down, Longrin says, "Didn't the FBI used to have a dress code?"

"We've found satellite video, infrared that tracks them all the way from their place to yours," Gottfrey lies.

"I'd like to see your warrant, Agent Gottfrey."

"The arrest warrant is for Ancel and Clare Hawk, not you."

"I mean the warrant to search my property."

"We are in active and urgent pursuit of suspects in a matter of national security, with reason to believe those we seek are on these premises. We're operating under a broad FISA court order. A post hoc copy of the warrant is the best you'll get."

Rupert Baldwin, pinch-faced perhaps because he's taken offense at the dress code remark, taps Gottfrey on the shoulder. He draws his boss's attention to the computer screen on Longrin's desk.

The screen is quartered into four images, each a security-camera view of part of the property, including the receiving yard where the dust has settled around the Rhino GX and other vehicles.

"Mr. Longrin," says Gottfrey, "keeping in mind it's a felony to lie to an FBI agent—where is your security-system video archived? We need to review Ancel and Clare Hawk's arrival last night, so that we can determine if—and in what vehicle—they left here."

26

IVAN PETRO DOWN ON ONE KNEE BEHIND A TREE, maintaining a low profile, possessed of a Zen master's patience, passionate about the revolution, his fierce ambition fueled by bitter envy of those fools above him in the Arcadian ranks, smarter than them, able to quote long passages of Nietzsche and Weber and Freud word for word . . .

In spite of his superior qualities and advantages, he wonders if he should call for assistance after all, let others know that he has found Jane Hawk. He is uneasy when he recalls with what alacrity she escaped the 12-gauge Taser.

No, she's just a woman, a former FBI agent trained at Quantico, all right, but still only a woman. Ivan is not one of those men who has no use for women. He has a use for them, one use, and he often uses them well, until they beg for surcease. He's not going to back away from this golden opportunity, not back away for backup. She is his ticket to the top. She belongs to him. She and her boy are his.

He waits and listens.

His left hand aches from the hammer blow, two skinned knuckles oozing a thin bloody serum, fingers beginning to swell and grow stiff. His pistol is in his right hand.

Twenty feet east of him, Jane is betrayed by a clatter and prolonged rustle, loose stones and dry leaves sliding downhill.

He turns toward the noise.

27

THE LIVE OAKS WERE OLD, ROOTED IN CENTURIES, and most of their lowest limbs hung well above her head. The trick was to throw the stones hard and far, as high as possible to gain distance, but not so high that they were dropped short by an intervening limb. She stepped out from shelter, hoping he wasn't looking this way. She threw one stone, the second, grabbed the Taser XREP, and plummeted downhill in long, wild strides, making some noise that perhaps was covered by whatever racket her two missiles produced, fearful of a bullet but exhilarated because action was better than paralysis.

She passed one tree and skidded to a halt behind the next. A foot in front of her, an inpour of sunshine pooled on a drift of dead leaves. She stooped and, with her butane lighter, set the leaves ablaze.

There was no danger of a catastrophic forest fire; only an isolated grove of thirty or forty trees leafed through the glen. They were old, magnificent. It would be sad if they burned beyond recovery. But if she had to devastate the entire woodlet to save herself and her son, she would have no regret.

She rose, pocketed the lighter, and drew her pistol. With Taser in her left hand and Heckler in her right, she moved fast through the shrouding gloom, before the fire could flare bright enough to reveal her. Running, she squeezed off four rounds, counting on the reports and their echoes to cover what other sounds she made, aiming west, at nothing, so the muzzle flare wouldn't be evident to him where he waited to the east of her. The crack of gunfire echoed off the walls of the glen, off the trees, making it hard to determine from which direction the shots issued, encouraging him to believe that she'd spotted him and that he needed to keep his head down.

At the foot of the slope, on the floor of the glen, Jane looked back and saw reflections of the flames fluttering among the trees, pulsing shadows interleaved with those wings of light. The blaze was already bright enough to draw her enemy's attention and distract him if he raised his head.

She hurried east, avoiding shafts of incoming sunshine, glad that she was wearing dark colors, staying low as she raced toward the Range Rover, firing another six rounds to the west.

28

SOMEWHERE EAST OF IVAN PETRO, THE CLATTER OF dislodged stones carries with it a rustling mass of dead oak leaves.

He steps out from the tree where he's been sheltering and scans the shaded glen. In the direction from which the sound arose, the bosky murk is deep, pierced by a few thin golden stalks of sunlight illuminating little, like the stems of radiant flowers that rise through the oak canopy to bloom out of sight above the trees.

The crack of a pistol reminds him that Jane was at the top of her class in marksmanship at Quantico. He drops to the ground in a crackle of dried weeds, a disturbance of gnats swarming his nose and teasing from him a single, regretted sneeze. He lies flat through three more shots, the sounds ricocheting from glen wall to glen wall, the sound suppressed and diffused by the trees.

After a silence, Ivan is about to lift his head to reconnoiter when she starts shooting again. Six rounds in rapid succession. The large number of shots convinces him that he isn't the target, that she doesn't have a fix on his position. Supposing she prefers a pistol with a standard ten-round capacity, she has just emptied the magazine without a target in sight, which means her purpose must be to keep his head down while she moves from one place to another.

She has spare magazines.

Spare magazines and a plan.

As he rises to his knees, his attention is drawn at once to the fire. Fifty or sixty feet to the west. Midway between the bottom of the glen and its north rim. A low, bright riffle of flames spreads not because of a breeze, for the air is still, but because it feeds on the rich fuel of dead leaves and weeds. Suddenly the fire leaps as high as two feet, flailing the nearby trees with orange light, and a snake of pale smoke uncoils like a cobra swaying to a flute.

This is a distraction, just as were the ten shots she fired. Just as were the rattling stones and the slithering leafslide that had for a moment drawn his attention eastward.

Distraction from what?

29

AT THE BOTTOM OF THE GLEN, JANE CROUCHED ON the south side of the Range Rover, screened from her adversary, wherever he might be on the north slope. She put down the Taser XREP. She ejected the depleted magazine from the Heckler and snapped a fresh one into place and holstered the gun.

Success now depended on speed, disconcerting the big man with another development while he was still trying to decide what to make of the first fire and the gunshots, before he committed to some course of action that she didn't want him to take.

She flipped open the small port on the rear quarter panel of the Rover and twisted the cap off the fuel tank. She withdrew the knotted socks from the front of her jeans and stuffed them into the gas tank filler neck, using the stiff plastic zip-tie to work them into the tank itself. When the gasoline began to travel by exosmosis through the socks, she could smell the fumes swelling in strength.

She waited until the fabric ought to be saturated. Gripping the dry end of the stiff plastic zip-tie, she pulled the makeshift torch out of the tank, being careful to avoid dripping fuel on herself, taking care not to get any whatsoever on her right hand. Shut the tank cap. Closed the flip door.

Turning away from the Rover, she peered into the darkest portion of the glen: the nearby section of the south slope leading upward under a dense thatching of limbs and leaves. The land seemed less steep here than on the north wall of the glen, but the footing could still be treacherous.

With the rim of the glen defined by a narrow, ragged band of light far ahead, with blackness close on all sides, she ascended, dangling the dripping mass of cotton socks at arm's length, to her left side. There seemed to be no grass or weeds here where the sun seldom penetrated. Oak-tree sheddings crunched underfoot, but she thought her would-be captor must be too far away to hear. Although surface roots caused her to stumble, she kept her balance, quickly venturing forty or fifty feet.

She dropped the fuel-sodden socks in dry leaves and retreated ten feet and, with her right hand, touched the butane flame to yet more leaves downslope from the crude incendiary device. When this new fuel kindled, before the light could swell bright enough to reveal her, she hurried to the Rover and crouched there once more.

She watched this second fire quicken low and at first fitfully until it found the drizzle of gasoline that she had left when making her way up the hill, whereupon it flared into a bright zipper and sizzled directly to the source. Flames leaped high, like a demonic manifestation, and fell back, but then surged again, bits of burning leaves spiraling up on rising thermals, carried into darkness where they quivered like a swarm of fireflies.

She looked west and saw that the first fire was spreading toward the north rim but also downhill toward the floor of the glen, not yet climbing into the trees, though some limbs were festooned with smoke like beards of Spanish moss.

He was patient, certain that if he hunkered down and waited, she would make a mistake and reveal herself. His patience had given her time to upend the situation, rattle his expectations.

He was a very big man, and big men in his line of work tended to be overconfident, to have an unconscious belief that they were all but invincible. Some also had a tendency to conflate strength with wit, attributing to themselves greater intelligence and cunning than they possessed.

If he was one such, he would be frustrated by his failure to rise in the ranks to a position he thought commensurate with his value to the cause. She had seen such men in the FBI and elsewhere.

This frustration would explain why, once he found her, he had come after her alone instead of waiting for backup, as any clear-thinking Arcadian would have done. She was the prize of prizes, the cure for his frustration, and he must be loath to share the credit for her capture.

When she'd thwarted the Taser attack, especially if the hammer injured him, his confidence would have been rattled. Now, within a few minutes, she'd moved aggressively through the shadows, shooting ten rounds and setting two fires, counting on chaos to un-settle him further. When a man who rarely entertained much self-doubt began to wonder if he might be vulnerable after all, then what virtues he possessed—such as patience—frequently deserted him.

Fire could create its own draft. The heat from this second blaze drew toward it the cool air in the glen, a breeze that hugged the ground and chased the flames toward the top of the slope. But there were countercurrents, and when flaming debris was cast high enough by the lower draft, it was spun back into this little valley, some of it descending as harmless ashes, some still burning when it fell upon combustible material.

Maybe she'd misjudged him. Maybe the chaos she'd sown would grow out of control and consume her with him. Maybe playing with fire, as she had been doing for many weeks, figuratively and now literally, had drawn the devil to her or she to him, and this was now the fire of her final judgment.

She wriggled under the Range Rover.

30

At THE LONGRIN HOUSE, JANIS DERN'S INSISTENT knocking and loud proclamation of her status as FBI bring to the door a freckle-faced girl of about twelve, a tomboy type in sneakers and worn blue jeans and a T-shirt emblazoned with the words SEM-PER FI.

The kid says, "Good gracious, lady, we're not deaf."

"Who're you?" Janis demands.

"Laurie Longrin. If you'd like to have a seat on the porch, I can bring you some iced tea or lemonade, whichever you prefer."

"Where's your mother, your father?"

"Dad's over in his office at Stable Three. Mom is out in the potato patch, plantin' seeds."

"Where would that be?"

The girl gestures more or less northwest, then steps across the threshold, pulls the door shut, and squeezes past Janis. "Come on, I'll show you the way."

Janis is the youngest of four sisters. As a consequence of that experience, she has determined never to have children, and in fact never to trust a child.

She says, "Hey, hey, wait a second," halting Laurie at the porch steps. "This isn't a farm. It's a horse-breeding operation."

"We're versatile," Laurie says. "We make horses *and* potatoes. Carrots, too, onions and radishes. And we sew really nice quilts."

"I know your type," Janis says. "You're a conniving little shit, aren't you?"

Before the girl can respond, Janis turns to the door, opens it, shouts, "FBI, FBI," and enters the house.

The noxious child forces her way past Janis, into the foyer, sees Chris Roberts following the hall forward from the kitchen, and sprints up the stairs. "Here they come, Mom, and they aren't the freakin' FBI!"

Janis races after the kid, reaches the top of the stairs in time to see her disappear into a room near the end of the hall. A door slams. By the time Janis gets there, the door is locked.

If she were an FBI agent in reality and not just on paper, this situation would present Janis Dern with a problem regarding illegal searches and seizures. However, because she's in no danger of having to answer to anyone at the Bureau or Homeland, only to her Techno Arcadian superiors, who expect results by any means necessary, she draws her pistol and kicks the door hard and kicks it again.

There is no deadbolt, only a simple privacy latch, which comes apart on the second kick, and the door rackets open.

Pistol in both hands, though expecting no serious resistance let alone a firefight, Janis enters the room low and so fast that the rebounding door misses her.

A home office. Laurie to the left, looking too damn pleased with herself. *Devious little bitch.* Her mother, Alexis, sitting at the desk, working so intently on a computer that she doesn't even look up when the door crashes open.

"What're you doing?" Janis demands of the mother. "Get away from the computer."

Chris Roberts crosses the room in a few long strides, seizes the wheeled office chair, and shoves the woman away from the desk.

"Too late!" cries the infuriating brat.

In Chase Longrin's office in Stable 3, a sudden tumult issues from the speaker in the twelve-line phone on the desk, followed by Janis Dern's voice: *"What're you doing? Get away from the computer."*

Egon Gottfrey hadn't previously noticed the red indicator light glowing above the word INTERCOM. As they had arrived in the stable and announced themselves, before they even found this office, Longrin must have opened a line between here and somewhere in the house.

A young girl's voice comes over the intercom: *"Too late!"*

Gottfrey looks up at Chase Longrin, who is smiling.

Studying the computer screen, Chris Roberts says, "I think she just deleted the security-system video archives."

Ancel and Clare Hawk came here in the night, on horseback, and they left in one vehicle or another, which would have been captured by the security cameras.

Janis looms over the smug child, glaring down at her, wanting to grab a fistful of her hair and pull hard and knock her down. "I know your type, oh, I know your type, you smartass little puke."

Undaunted, the girl says, "What kind of numbnuts would believe potatoes grow from seeds?"

Raising the pistol as if to slash the barrel across Laurie's face, Janis doesn't intend to strike the girl, only to scare the exasperating self-satisfied look off that freckled countenance. It's a patented Francine look. Exactly like Janis's sister Francine.

The mother pulls a gun from under her chair and fires a round into the ceiling, bringing down a rain of plaster chips.

Janis pivots toward the mother, and here they are, each with a pistol in a two-hand grip, each a trigger pull away from blood and maybe death.

"Whoa, whoa, whoa! Nobody wants this," says Chris, having been careful not to draw his weapon.

"Maybe I want this," Janis disagrees.

"This isn't like you," Chris says. "What's got you so pissed?"

"Little Miss *Semper Fi*, this ugly freckled gash, thinks the rules don't apply to her."

"I'm not ugly," the girl declares. "I know that for a fact."

"It's you," the mother accuses Janis, "who thinks the rules don't apply to her. You and these other bastards. Get out of my house."

"It's *our* house," Janis says, "until we give it back to you."

Chris Roberts needs two tense minutes to negotiate an end to the standoff in Alexis Longrin's home office.

31

NEAR THE TOP OF THE NORTH SLOPE, IVAN PETRO stands in shadow, watching firelight colonize the darkness, the thin smoke growing thicker. The acrid scent burns in his nostrils.

He now knows the meaning of *disquiet* as never before. He has long taken pride in being above all fear, being the bearer of fear who brings it to others. Being a learned man, even although self-taught, he can define *disquiet*: the mildest state of fear, a general uneasiness threaded with doubt. Knowing the definition and being gripped by disquiet are, however, different things, for in fact those threads of doubt are more like wires vibrating in his veins.

There are some in the revolution who embrace a disturbing explanation for why Jane Hawk is so elusive and so successful at bringing down everyone she targets. They think it's not just her Bureau training and her natural talents that make her a singular threat. They say she is also empowered by insanity, a special kind of mad rage because of her husband's murder and the threat to her child. Some serial killers carve their way through a long list of victims, active for years before being apprehended, because their madness is strangely coupled with reason rather than being divorced from it, and they have as well a heightened sense of intuition, so that they not only think outside the box, but also outside the box that the first box came in.

Ivan has thought this Insane Jane explanation is fanciful at best, but in truth ridiculous. He has secretly scorned those who find the idea compelling.

He's no longer sure what to think of her, though at the moment no theory exists that he would scorn.

There is no way to spot her in this shadowed valley where spreading fire dances and, in its dancing, throws off a thousand phantom figures of shadow, light, and smoke. Its many voices— some sibilant, some full of croak and crackle—provide cover for any sounds she makes.

His injured hand throbs, stiff and all but useless. The thin haze of smoke makes his eyes itch and water. Although he is standing still, he finds himself breathing as fast as if he were running.

The Range Rover is not at this moment threatened by the blaze, but suddenly he is sure that her intention is to disable it, so he can't drive out of the woods. She means to strand him and then stalk him through the bewildering, shifting shapes of fire and shadow.

He is a man of reason, self-taught but highly learned, a man who lives by facts and numbers and sharp calculations, with a seldom exercised imagination, with no taste for fantasy in literature or films. He is likewise proudly free of all superstition. Brains and brute strength are all he's ever needed. Yet a previously unknown sensation crawls his spine, prickles his nerves, and in spite of the growing heat in the glen, a coldness arises within his chest.

Furious that some primitive belief in the uncanny is embedded in him and waiting for the right circumstances to conjure it, Ivan is determined to repress it and assert himself as a man of reason, fearless action, and unstoppable force.

There are two threats to the Range Rover—the spreading fire and the woman who set the fire. If he must kill her, rather than capture her, in order to drive the vehicle out of the glen before the fire consumes it, then he will.

And when he presents Jane Hawk's bloody, broken body to his smug superiors, maybe he'll shoot them, too, if they don't promote him as he has long deserved.

Pistol in his right hand, arm straight out in front of him, he strides down the shadowed slope, as fearless as a terminator robot from the future, turning his head left and right, scanning the woods for a target, periodically glancing back, moving fast because she would expect him to come slowly if he came at all.

32

SUCH WAS THE CLEARANCE UNDER THE RANGE Rover that Jane had to lie with her head turned to the side, one cheek flat to the earth.

He might assume that she had taken up a position on the level bottom of the glen, behind one tree or another, where shadows hadn't been faded by firelight. Or he might think she'd gotten into the Rover, intending to ambush him as he reached to open the driver's door.

She didn't believe he would give any credit to the possibility that she was lying concealed *under* the vehicle.

For one thing, because of his size, he could never squirm beneath the SUV; and so he'd assume that the space wouldn't accommodate her, either. In chaotic moments, a hunter of people had a strong tendency to calculate the options available to his target based on his own limitations if he'd been the hunted one.

Furthermore, it seemed reckless of her to commit herself to such a confining space. Given her reputation and her success taking down people at the top of the conspiracy, he wouldn't expect her to be so imprudent.

What seemed like a rash act to a man like him, however, was simple necessity to a mother whose child remained a couple hundred miles away, in peril and arguably the *second*-most-wanted fugitive in America.

If she'd meant to kill the man, she would have done this a different way. But there were questions for which she urgently needed answers.

With bright appetite, the second fire grazed across the south slope, hungry but not yet ravenous. Unless a stronger breeze sprang up, the flames weren't likely to reach the Rover before Jane's quarry appeared.

Most of the smoke rose through the trees, drawn toward cooler air, but a thin haze drifted under the Rover. Although the growing conflagration had many voices, the cover it would give her when she moved wasn't sufficient to mask a cough. She breathed into the crook of her elbow, the sleeve of her sport coat against her nose, peering over her forearm at the floor of the glen where perhaps the big man would appear.

She cursed him silently, willed him to arrive, *commanded* his attendance as if she had the power over him that he would have over the "adjusted people" who had been injected with nanomechanisms, prayed for his deliverance into her hands. Suddenly there he was, visible to her only from the ankles down, evidently committed to boldness, moving fast, heading directly for the Range Rover.

Then he did something she had not expected.

33

LESS THAN FIVE MINUTES SINCE THE FIRST FIRE flared, but in that brief time, this transformation from Thoreau to

Poe, from a tranquil sylvan retreat into a Halloween-night scene, the previously noble trees now grotesque black shapes backdropped by veins of fire that bleed out in a steadily greater flood . . .

Ivan Petro has nothing to gain by caution. The glen is a stage, and the bitch controls it as if she's both author and director. She has set the scene, designed the visuals, put the Rover in the center of the proscenium arch, and she's given him only one entrance to the play—down the path he's taken and straight to the driver's door. If she hasn't used these distractions to flee, if she's watching, she sees him approach and chooses to let him get closer to the vehicle.

Every ancient, moss-mottled tree trunk offers an assassin cover, and Ivan worries that the bitch might even have climbed into one of these long-enduring oaks to lie upon a sturdy limb and stare down at him through a filigree of leaves.

He has been transformed no less than has the glen. He can smell his own sour sweat, and his stomach feels as if a knot has been tied in it. For the first time in maybe eighteen years, since he repaid his father's violence with some of his own and freed himself from the hell that is family, he suffers a surge of acid reflux so strong that a bitter taste arises in the back of his mouth.

If the bitch is hiding in the Rover, she isn't in the cargo area, because even lying flat in that space, she'd be only an inch or two below the windows, too easily seen. She isn't in the front seat, either, because there would be too many obstacles in her way—steering wheel, pedals, console—nowhere to get low except in the footwell that serves the passenger seat, where she would be too visible in spite of the darkness gathered in the vehicle.

So if she's in there, she must be on the floor behind the front passenger seat, with her back pressed to the door, her feet braced against the transmission hump, her gun in a two-hand grip, waiting for him to appear, fire-lit, in one of the side windows.

If she's crouched against the farther flank of the vehicle, rather than inside it, that's all right, too, because what he's about to do is likely to move her to act and, by acting, make a target of herself.

Approaching the driver's side, before there's a chance she can see him from in there, he squeezes off three quick shots, shattering the window into the rear seat, blowing out the window on the farther side. He's a little jumpy and in pain and totally pissed off, so one round is off the mark and shatters the glass in the driver's door.

If she's in there, she should have been startled into returning fire. Nor does she rise from the farther side of the Rover to cut him down.

Ivan scans the witchy trees, the shadowy north slope, the south slope beribboned with fire, but there is no sign of her.

Expecting a bullet in the back of the head or straight on in the face, using his throbbing left hand, he fumbles with the handle and opens the driver's door. The interior light comes on. He can see into both the front and back seats, and Jane isn't in either.

He sits behind the wheel and, wincing in pain, pulls the door shut. All it's about now is getting out of here faster than fast.

The electronic key is in his pocket. The Range Rover has a push-button ignition. He doesn't put down the pistol, but holds it ready, using his bad hand to start the engine.

Born off the sloped south wall of the glen, phantom snakes of smoke serpentine through the shot-out back window on the passenger side, and a fit of coughing racks Ivan. For a moment, he forgets how to release the emergency brake, fumbling for a lever that he recalls from a previous vehicle.

Fire is seething close on the south slope. Burning debris has ignited the layers of leaves on the floor of the glen directly ahead of him. Suddenly he's more concerned about being trapped by fire than he is about Jane Hawk.

Which is a mistake.

When he looks away from the south slope to remind himself where the brake release can be found, he is at once aware of a presence rising beyond the imploded window in the driver's door.

It's her.

She's got the Taser XREP 12-gauge. Before Ivan can bring his Colt .45 around and kill her, she fires point-blank.

The four electrodes on the nose of the cartridge hook the side of his bare neck, and the first charge, the localized charge, stings as though he's thrust his head into a wasp nest. He's aware of the pistol falling out of his hand. When the chassis separates from the nose of the Taser projectile, he doesn't grasp the wire by which it dangles, but then a second set of longer electrodes deploys. He's slammed by the primary charge, vision dazzled into brief blindness by internal fireworks as colorful as any Independence Day display, his teeth chattering until his jaws lock, pain coursing from his scalp to the soles of his feet, every fascicle of nerve fibers short-circuiting. Paralysis.

34

For a moment, Ivan Petro is a child again, shaking with pain, cowering in the shadow of his father, gagging on the refluxed acid that burns up his throat and forms a bitter pool in his mouth, as it had so often during those years lived in nervous expectation of the old man's violence. Ivan is too weak to run, too confused to hide, clenching his jaws to keep from expressing the raw ferocity of his hatred, which will only earn him more hard slaps, more punches, more cruel pinches.

He tries to swallow, but he can't, so he hangs his head and lets the acid drool from his mouth into his lap. When he raises his head, he thinks their house is on fire, and he is bewildered as to the cause of this disaster. Then he realizes that he's a grown man who has put the things of childhood far behind him. He is sitting in a vehicle, his wrists zip-tied to the steering wheel, and the truth of time and place returns to him.

He turns his head to his left. She's standing a few feet from the missing window, her face reflecting the firelight from the south slope, that perfect face radiant like the face of a goddess, one eye brown, the other blue.

His speech is thick at first. "Your eyes are two colors. You lost a contact. I know which is true. Blue is true. Jane Hawk's eyes are blue."

"And you're Ivan Petro."

"You took my wallet."

She tosses the wallet through the open window. It strikes his face and falls into the stomach acid on his pants.

The air smells of smoke. There's a haze of it in the Rover. Leaf fires and weed fires burn low throughout the glen.

"Where did you first make me?" she asks.

Because his mind isn't yet as clear as it needs to be, he says, "Placerville. You came out of some market with a deli bag."

"Where is it?" she asks.

"Placerville? You know where it is. You've been there."

"Don't jerk me around. Time's running out. Where did you plant the transponder?"

He shouldn't have mentioned Placerville. "You were sleeping, so I put it up your pretty ass."

She raises a pistol, a Heckler, and points it at his face.

He smiles scornfully. "You think I buy that crap about how you're a cold-blooded killer? Spare me your evil eye."

"I'll kill a hundred of you to save my boy."

"He's dead already. They filmed it for you. Slit his belly open and let him scream to death."

She only stares at Ivan. One blue, one brown, plus the round black eye of the gun muzzle.

A bead of sweat passes between his eyes and down his nose.

She lowers the pistol. "You're parked in dead leaves. Fire under the gas tank soon. Maybe it'll do the job for me."

The engine isn't running. She switched it off. Ivan can drive with his hands bound to the steering wheel, but even if she didn't take the electronic key, he can't reach the push-button ignition or the emergency-brake release.

His pistol is still on the passenger seat, where he dropped it.

He wheezes as if the smoke has gathered in his lungs. He fakes a coughing fit while he strains to strip the teeth of the zip-tie on his right wrist, which is cinched low on the steering wheel, not in her line of sight. It's a ratchet latch; straining against it draws it tighter; it can't be loosened once snug; it can only be cut. He coughs and strains nonetheless, because his wrists are as thick as ankles, and he is 275 pounds of hard-trained muscle and bone, and his hatred for this bitch is more intense than ever it was for his father. No power on Earth is greater than hatred, for it can destroy nations and fuel genocides in which millions die. He is empowered by hatred so virulent and implacable that no binding can restrain him.

She moves back a step or two. "The transponder. Quick now. Or I'll go search for it myself, leave you to burn."

He can't pretend to be racked by coughing forever. Continuing to strain against the zip-tie, he buys time by telling her what she wants to know. "The kid hasn't been killed, not even been found yet."

"Then maybe you have a chance."

"Transponder's attached with epoxy. Can't remove it."

"If you want to live, tell me true."

"True. You've got to hammer. Hammer it apart."

The white-hot pain in his right hand now exceeds that in his left, the plastic tie cutting into his flesh, his fingers slick with blood. But he thrives on pain, eats it and is nourished by it; he has grown from child to man on a diet of pain.

"It's in the back wheel well. Passenger side."

"Who've you told about my Explorer, the license number?"

"No one. Those bastard poachers would take you, take all the credit, and keep me down."

He can smell his hot blood dripping from his hand. A blackness pulses around the perimeter of his vision. The pain is so terrible that it brings into his throat another flood of bitter acid, which he swallows hard to repress.

"What's wrong with you?" she wonders.

"You twisted, crazy bitch. *You*. You're what's wrong with me."

"You're sweating more than it's hot."

"Makes me sweat bullets, telling me I'll be left to burn."

"You're doing something there." Having backed away, she approaches again. "What're you doing?"

He chokes on another rush of acid, and it foams from his nose, and his breath stinks as if it is the exhalation of a corpse.

35

SITTING BEHIND THE STEERING WHEEL, IVAN PETRO reminded Jane of a realistically detailed special-effects mannequin like those that had sometimes been used in old horror movies made before computer animation became ever better and cheaper, when the script called for the head to explode. The cords of muscle in his neck were as taut as winch cables. His skull almost seemed to inflate: flushed face swollen and streaming sweat, nostrils flared, eyes protuberant, the arterioles in his temples prominent and throbbing. Yellowish foam suddenly gushed from his nostrils, and he let out a cry that seemed to be an expression equally of rage and despair, and following that cry came a stream of vicious obscenities in a spray of foul spittle, as if he meant to kill her with the intensity of his hatred.

When she stepped close to the broken-out window in the driver's door, she saw his right hand against the steering wheel, like the carved-stone fist of some wrathful god who could cleave the planet with a single blow; the zip-tie embedded in the flesh of his wrist, blood oozing as black as tar in the half-light, his shirt sleeve saturated to the elbow.

That band of hard, binding plastic was a quarter of an inch thick, and the angled teeth of the one-way ratcheted clasp was a marvel of design. The zip-tie had proved far more reliable than handcuffs. She had never known anyone to be able to free himself after being properly manacled. It simply wasn't possible.

Ivan Petro surely realized the futility of this struggle. Yet his fury escalated, his hatred intensified, his effort increased, as though this brief imprisonment had driven him into raving madness, so that he'd strive to break free until a cerebral artery ruptured and death flooded through his brain.

The zip-tie snapped.

His sledgehammer fist flew from the steering wheel, braceleted in bloody plastic, a volley of blood drops spattering the dashboard, the windshield, even as the damaged hand dropped toward the pistol on the passenger seat. Cut muscle, sprained tendons, injured nerves didn't affect him, as if some mystical entity had taken possession of him, some dark spirit not constrained by the laws of nature.

Jane said, "No," and he said, "*Yes*," and she shot him twice in the neck as his hand came off the passenger seat with the pistol.

Stunned, Jane backed away a few steps, feeling as if she had crossed from the waking world into a manic dream without the need to fall asleep. If he'd snapped the zip-tie, then maybe anything could happen. Maybe the ravaged flesh of his bullet-torn throat could mend before her eyes and the bullets whistle backward through the smoky air and into the barrel of her Heckler and return to the magazine, as if they had never been fired.

Ivan Petro remained slumped in the driver's seat, however, and the dreamlike horror began to relent—until, as fire flared through the leaves around the Rover, she recognized something chilling about the angle of the dead man's head. It was tipped slightly forward and toward his right shoulder. The posture of Petro, behind the wheel of the Rover, was similar to that of her Nick when she had found him sitting in the bathtub, dead by his own hand. No, not just similar. The same. The angle of the head, the bloody throat.

For a day after her beautiful Nick removed himself from this world, she had been in a state of shock. Before her muddled thinking cleared, before she grew certain he hadn't been capable of suicide under any circumstances, those first twenty-four hours were like a century in Purgatory. In confusion and grief, she searched her heart for what guilt might be hers. What might she have done to turn him away from self-destruction? What could she have been for him that she had not been? Why hadn't she recognized his precarious state of mind?

She had known him too well, however, to accept for long that he had taken his own life. They were not just lovers, not just husband and wife, not just creators of their lovely boy; their souls were so precisely configured to fit together that she and Nick were a two-piece puzzle, a puzzle solved when they took their marriage vows, the meaning of life made pellucid to them when they became as one.

Now the angle of Ivan Petro's head and his gruesome throat wound put her back in Virginia on that terrible evening just days before Thanksgiving. For a moment, the world seemed so strange that she couldn't hope ever to make her way through it to a place of peace—but only for a moment.

Part of Nick remained alive, their boy, and she could not fail Travis. To fail him would also be to fail Nick for real this time.

"Screw that," she said.

She turned her back on Ivan Petro and sprinted across the glen, up the north slope, where thin strata of pale smoke moved west to east, layered ghosts swimming toward a different haunt. Shadow-robed trees loomed in solemn threat, like the unforgiving judges in some final court.

As she ascended, her eyes stung and her nostrils burned and her chest ached. When she drew near the crest, concussion waves trembled through her from the explosion of the Range Rover's fuel tank, but she did not look back.

She broke from the trees into the field of weeds and ribbon grass, greedily inhaling clean air, blowing out the smell of smoke.

Passing the hammer that she had thrown at Petro, she plucked it off the ground. At the Explorer, she snatched up the screwdriver and the pieces of the shattered burner phone, threw everything onto the passenger seat.

When she went around to the driver's door, she saw a dark and churning column just now emerging through the tree tops in the glen, a few tendrils of lighter smoke rising elsewhere.

She drove around the perimeter of the parking lot, toward the exit lane. It seemed that people at the truck stop had become aware of the fire in the woodlet only after the explosion and the sudden greater rush of smoke that followed it. As far as she could tell, no one associated her with those events.

Out of the truck stop, quick onto Interstate 5, southbound. Sirens in the distance. The wailing rose, rose higher, but then faded, and she never saw the sources or was able to deduce from where they came.

Fewer than ten minutes had passed in the glen. She was an hour north of Los Angeles, early enough to beat the rush-hour traffic that would clog every artery in and out of the city.

She thought of the dead man in the woods. The shakes took her.

Others might have hoped for good luck tomorrow in Indio and later in Borrego Valley, but in times as troubled as these, she placed no hope in the cruel gods of fortune. She trusted only in her own preparations and actions, in the power of love to inspire her to do the wisest thing to the best of her ability.

She pulled into a rest stop before the Tejon Pass, waited until she had the place to herself, located the transponder in the wheel well of her Explorer, and used her hammer to render it inoperative. The backplate of the device couldn't be loosened from the epoxy that fixed it to the car. But when she examined the fragments that fell to the pavement, she was confident that the SUV was not trackable.

Once more racing south on I-5, she wanted music, a song written out of profound love. She chose pianist David Benoit playing "Kei's Song," which he'd written for his wife. She turned up the volume.

Piano chords and notes are known not only to her ears, but also are felt in her fingertips, weave through her heart, nourish her soul as milk makes strong the bones.

36

THE GRIEVING BOY, WHO'D TAKEN MOST OF THE night to fall asleep, still slept and slept. The dogs needed to be toileted and fed, but leaving the boy alone seemed wrong. Cornell ought to do something—what?—to be prepared for when the mother came to collect her child.

Like Mr. Paul Simon had sung, *The mother and child reunion is only a motion away.*

This was more responsibility than Cornell usually shouldered. When he tried to sit near the boy and read, he couldn't concentrate on the prose. He worried that he was going to do something—or fail to do something—that would endanger Travis.

Now he stood over the La-Z-Boy recliner again, watching the child. Travis breathed so softly, maybe he wasn't breathing at all. Cornell wanted to touch him, see if he was alive, but dared not.

All night the German shepherds had patrolled the library, taking turns sleeping, sniffing Cornell, trying to induce him to pet them, which he couldn't do, because it might be like touching a person.

Any place where another person touched him was a wound that

didn't bleed blood, that bled the very essence of him, his mind and soul. By a touch, another person could drain Cornell out of himself and leave his body a mindless husk.

This was a false fear related to his personality disorder. But knowing it was a false fear didn't make him less fearful. Strange. Otherwise, he respected reason. But this streak of unreason was baked into him like a vein of cinnamon in a morning roll, though cinnamon was a good thing and unreason was not good.

The dogs were agitated. They needed to potty.

Cornell didn't want the dogs to potty on his Persian carpets.

If he tried to put the dogs' leashes on their collars, they might touch him. *No good, no good, no good.*

The dogs might be trained not to run away. But what if they did? The boy loved them. He'd be devastated if the dogs ran away.

Here was what responsibility meant. It meant making decisions that affected someone other than Cornell himself.

When the dogs started whining, he said, "All right, I'll take you out. But don't run away from me, please and thank you."

Outside, the day was warm and bright, with none of the soft colors of the library lamplight that he loved so much.

The dogs ran a few yards from the door before they peed. Then they sniffed around for a minute, and finally both squatted to poop.

Cornell was embarrassed, watching the dogs toilet, but he was also fascinated because they seemed self-conscious, glancing at him sheepishly, maybe because he hadn't watched them do this before.

When they had pooped, they stood staring at him expectantly, ears pricked forward. After a minute of confusion, he realized they expected him to pick up the poop in plastic bags, like people did.

He didn't have plastic bags. Besides, except for the graveled area around the blue house, in which cacti and succulents were the only landscaping, the rest of this acreage, including that in the vicinity of the barn, was a mess of dead grass, sage, long-stemmed buckwheat, assorted weeds, and bare earth. Leaving poop wasn't as offensive as it would have been on a golf course or a church lawn.

As Cornell moved toward the house, his hulking freak-show shadow preceding him, the dogs watched. When he called them, they glanced at the poop and regarded him with puzzlement, maybe wondering why he was so poorly trained. But at last they came to the house with him.

The large bag of kibble stood in the kitchen where the boy had said it would be. His suitcase of spare clothes and other items was in the smaller of the two bedrooms.

After locking the door, Cornell returned to the barn, carrying the kibble in one hand and the suitcase in the other.

"Come along, please and thank you," he said to the dogs, and it delighted him that they trotted at his side, one to his left, one to his right, as if they cared for him the way they cared for the boy.

The electronic key in his pants pocket automatically unlocked what appeared to be a flimsy man-size barn door that was in fact steel behind its rotten-plank façade. He and the dogs stepped into a white vestibule. He closed the door behind him. After a few seconds, its lock engaged with a hard *clack*. The electronic lock on the door before him responded to his hand on the knob and unlocked itself, so he could push through into the library.

To the left of the door through which Cornell entered, another door led to the bathroom. To the right lay the part of the fourth wall that wasn't lined with books, but instead featured a kitchen counter, cabinets, a double sink, two large Sub-Zero refrigerators, two microwaves, and an oven.

The boy stood peering in one of the Sub-Zeros.

The dogs whined with pleasure and hurried to the boy.

Travis turned to Cornell. "Mr. Jasperson, can I ask something?"

"Can you? Yes. Of course. And call me Cornell."

"What runs the 'frigerators?"

Cornell blinked at him. He put down the kibble and suitcase. "Umm. Runs? Well, the power company."

"What happens after the world ends?"

"The world won't end. Just civilization." When the boy frowned,

Cornell explained, "Just cities and stuff, not the planet. Not the planet. Not the planet."

"So what runs the 'frigerators then?"

"A generator. A big tank of propane buried out there. It'll run library and bunker fourteen months, or just the bunker for thirty."

"What then?" the boy asked.

"Maybe a new civilization will start up."

"What if nothing starts?"

"Umm. Umm. Then I'll probably be dead."

"Probably," Travis agreed. "I thought you never go into town."

"I don't ever go to town anymore. Hardly ever did, even when I lived in the little blue house. I don't want to scare people."

"So where do you get chocolate milk and stuff if you never go into town?"

"Gavin comes down here once every month like clockwork. He stocks the refrigerators."

"Maybe he will. If he's not . . ."

"Umm. If he's not dead. If he's not dead. If he's not dead."

The boy closed the refrigerator and regarded Cornell solemnly, as did the dogs. "Mr. Jasperson, why do you say things three times?"

"You can call me Cornell. I don't say everything three times."

"But you say some things three times."

"Umm. Things I don't want to happen or wish weren't true. Or sometimes things I think aren't true but wish they were."

"Does that work?"

"No. But I feel a little better. Do you want something to eat?"

"I'm kind of hungry."

"I can make eggs scrambled or fried, cheese or not, or eggs all other ways. With toast. I can make baloney sandwiches. Mustard or mayonnaise or both. I can make many kinds of meals."

"Are you hungry?" the boy asked.

"I am. I'm hungry."

"Then I'll have what you're having," the boy said.

The dogs padded to the bag of kibble, sniffing with excitement.

"I should feed the dogs." Cornell bent to the bag. "They're nice dogs so far. They don't bite so far. Not so far."

"They like you a lot," Travis said.

Cornell froze. Hunched over the bag, he turned his head to stare at the boy. "How do you know?"

"Can't you see? They like you."

"I don't see. I don't know how to see that."

"Well, they do. They like you."

Cornell looked at one dog, at the other. They wagged their tails. "Umm. Maybe it's just because I have the food."

"No, they really like you."

Around other people, Cornell always felt too big and awkward and strange, even around his cousin Gavin, and he felt no less so around animals. Before this, dogs barked at him. Cats hissed, bared their teeth, and fled. "Umm. Maybe, maybe not. But that would be something. That would be something. That sure would be something."

37

IF HE BELIEVED THEY WERE REAL, EGON GOTTFREY would hate Texans, and if he believed Texas was a real place rather than a concept, he would never go there again.

Chase and Alexis Longrin, with their three daughters—Laurie, Daphne, and Artemis—are being temporarily detained in the living room.

When Chris Roberts and Janis Dern attempt to interrogate the family, all five detainees act as though they are gathered here by their own choice. They pretend to be unaware of any intruders, and speak only to one another, mostly about television shows they have seen recently. They are certain that Gottfrey and his crew aren't legitimate authorities—or at least that they aren't loyal to either the Bureau or the country. Clearly, through her in-laws, Jane Hawk has poisoned the minds of these people.

Egon Gottfrey observes this impudence until it bores him. Then he goes to the fenced exercise yard at Stable 5, where Pedro and Alejandro have corralled all the employees, eight men and two women. Nine of those ten are day workers and can claim not to have been on the property at 2:00 A.M., when Ancel and Clare Hawk arrived on horseback—and perhaps soon thereafter left by a more comfortable form of transportation.

Only one of them, Bodie Houston, a lean-muscled sun-seared thirtysomething guy with jet-black hair, has been here all night, in a small ranch-manager's house. He claims to so admire the FBI, its history and its high standards and its incorruptible agents, that he bitterly regrets having slept too soundly to have seen anything. *Bitterly* regrets it. "As a kid, see, all I ever did want to be was FBI. What an honor if I could help you fellas. Damn, but don't I feel as useless as a fifth leg on a horse."

Gottfrey regards him in silence after that speech, trying to decide whether the Unknown Playwright wants him to handcuff Bodie Houston, drive him to a remote location, and throw him off a cliff—or walk away.

He chooses to walk away.

38

CORNELL'S LIBRARY FOR THE END OF THE WORLD. Windowless. Quiet. A fortress of books. In one of the reading areas, four mismatched—but beautiful—armchairs faced one another in a circle. Between the chairs were antique tables, each of a different period. Stained-glass lamps on the tables. The colored light so soft and pretty. Chairs and everything standing on a late-nineteenth-century Tabriz carpet in shades of red and gold.

Cornell had tried to make the library match his idea of what Heaven would be like, except he hoped that he wouldn't be alone in Heaven and that he wouldn't look scary to people there and that he would know what to say to the other people he met.

Now he had company, and it seemed like this was a test to see if he might be ready for an afterlife in which he wouldn't be alone.

The two big dogs were lying on the carpet, each with its tail tucked between its legs, one of them snoring. Cornell had quickly grown more comfortable with the dogs than he'd thought possible on first encountering them. For one thing, there was no need to carry on a conversation with the dogs.

Cornell sat in a wingback chair. The boy was lost in a big club chair. By contrast with the child, Cornell felt like a pterodactyl folded onto a perch meant for a sparrow. Feet on footstools, they faced each other from the north and south points of the reading circle. The dining trays were hooked over their chair arms.

"Sandwiches are real good," the boy said.

Cornell wasn't sure what to say, though it seemed safe just to describe the sandwich. "Buttered bread, two slices of baloney, two slices of cheese, one Velveeta and one provolone, sliced tomatoes, a little mayonnaise, put in a sandwich press and toasted." That seemed to go over well, so he added, "Two sweet pickles on the side and a little bag of potato chips for each of us."

"The cola is good with the sandwiches," the boy said.

Having read everything on the soda can, having an eidetic memory, Cornell decided not to list the contents of the beverage, but he did quote a fact he found interesting: " 'Canned under the authority of the Coca-Cola Company, Atlanta, Georgia, 30313, by a member of the Coca-Cola Bottlers' Association, Atlanta, Georgia, 30327.' "

The boy said, "I've never been to Atlanta."

"Neither have I," said Cornell.

"We should go someday."

"No, that's a scary idea."

"Scary why?"

"Too far. Too big," Cornell said.

"I guess it is if you say so."

This conversation thing with a new person was easier for Cornell than it had often been before.

After a silence, the boy said, "You're Uncle Gavin's cousin."

"My mother, Shamira, was his mother's sister. But the family disowned her and she disowned them when she was sixteen, before I was born. The family never knew about me."

"How do you . . . disown somebody?"

"You push them out, close the door, and never see them again."

"Wow. That's mean. Why'd they do that?"

"My mother was a terrible angry drug addict and a prostitute."

"What's a prositoot?"

"She sold sex. Oh. You didn't hear that. You didn't hear it. You didn't hear. She . . . she . . . she made love for money."

This conversation thing had broken Cornell into a sweat.

The boy said, "Making love is making babies. She made babies?"

"Just me. I was a baby once."

"So who's your dad?"

"Nobody knows. It's a big mystery."

"Doesn't your mom remember? You should ask her."

"My mother died when I was eighteen."

The boy put down his sandwich. "That's really sad."

"It was a long time ago. Go ahead and eat. See, I'm eating. She died of a drug overdose, she couldn't help herself. We have to eat, we can't help ourselves."

The boy sat looking at his sandwich. Then he said, "It isn't right, people having to die."

"No. No, it isn't. It isn't right. It isn't right. But that's the way it is. And we have to eat."

"So if the family never knew about you, how does Uncle Gavin know?"

"When I got rich, I hired a detective to find my family and tell me about them. Gavin was the one I thought I might like. And I do. I like him . . . or liked him. He's the only one I let know about me. Which is why maybe you're still safe here. You're still safe here. You're safe here."

"I sort of feel safe."

"That's good. That's nice. Now eat your sandwich, please and thank you."

The boy took a bite of the sandwich and chewed thoughtfully and swallowed and said, "How rich are you?"

"About three hundred million."

"Wow. I can't count that high."

"It's scary," Cornell said. Thinking about all that money was so frightening that he almost put down his sandwich. But he needed to be a positive role model for the boy, so he continued eating.

"How'd you *make* all that money?"

"I invented several very popular apps."

"I heard of apps, but I don't know any."

"You will one day. Anyway, by the time I was twenty-four, I made so much money it scared the bejesus out of me."

"Why would money scare you?"

"I started out with ten dollars. Four years later, after taxes, I had three hundred million. That can't happen unless a civilization— unless all of this, the way we live—is a mouse of cards."

"A what?"

"I apologize, please and thank you. Sometimes the wrong word comes out of me. *House.* Our civilization must be a house of cards. So I decided to get ready for Apocageddon."

"And so you built this secret library."

"And the even more secret bunker. Do you think I'm crazy?"

"No, you aren't crazy. You're real smart."

Pleased by the boy's praise, Cornell said, "I wouldn't have been able to do it and keep it secret without all the Filipino workers who couldn't speak a word of English."

39

BEGINNING TO WONDER IF THE SCRIPT CALLS FOR him to be stymied by a bunch of muleheaded Texas horse traders, Egon Gottfrey checks in with Rupert Baldwin, who is busy in Chase Longrin's office in Stable 3.

Rupert has gone through the contents of the desk and the filing cabinet without finding anything of interest, and he has scattered those papers on the floor, perhaps as payback for Chase's comment about the Bureau's dress code. Rupert considers himself a sartorial rebel; he is fond of his corduroy suits and bolo ties.

Using Longrin's computer, he has back-doored the DMV to search state records for vehicles registered to the Longrins or to Longrin Stables. Pickup trucks, horse vans, two SUVs, a Ford sedan . . .

Rupert says, "I gave the list to Vince. He's checking to see if there's a set of wheels that should be here but isn't."

The Unknown Playwright is in a mood for dramatic efficiency, because even as Rupert finishes speaking, Vince Penn bursts into the room like the burly star of a former circus act featuring a bear. "All the vehicles are here except for the Mercury Mountaineer. I checked the garage, all the stables, the hay barn. I went into the house and checked under the beds, but it's nowhere." He looks from Gottfrey to Rupert Baldwin to Gottfrey again. "That last part about the beds, see, that was just a joke."

In the interest of moving things along, Egon Gottfrey doesn't get into a conversation with Vince.

On learning that the Mountaineer is their search target, Rupert uses its DMV registration to consult a cross-referenced National Security Agency directory that contains the unique GPS transponder code of every vehicle in the country. He obtains the one by which this particular Mountaineer can be tracked by satellite.

Gottfrey watches as a map appears on the screen and a blinking red indicator signifies the location of the vehicle.

"It's not moving. Maybe parked," says Rupert.

"Parked where?"

"Downtown Killeen, Texas."

"How far from here is that?"

"Not far," says Vince Penn. "I was in Killeen for a few weeks once. Met this girl there. She wasn't beautiful or nothing, but she was pretty enough so I thought I might marry her. Then it turned out she was a whore, and it wasn't marriage she wanted."

Somewhat more helpful than Vince, Rupert says, "It looks like about a hundred thirty-some miles. Nearest helicopter we could use is in Austin. By the time it came here and picked us up and flew us to Killeen, it'd be quicker by car. We have to drive through Austin, which will slow us down, but we can still make it to Killeen in two hours, maybe two hours fifteen."

40

CORNELL JASPERSON KEPT THINKING THAT SOMEthing very bad was about to happen. He and the boy were getting along so well, and the dogs had not attacked him. Nevertheless, every now and then Cornell stiffened and lifted his head and listened intently, in expectation of a sudden threat. Not the collapse of civilization, not yet, but something not good.

For dessert, they enjoyed pineapple-coconut muffins, which they tore apart and ate with their fingers, still sitting in the circle of lamp-lit chairs.

"While I lived over there in the little blue house, I did all the construction drawings myself."

"You said fipaleen workers. What're they?" the boy wondered.

"Filipino. From the Republic of the Philippines, half a world away. Seven thousand islands, though most people live on eleven."

"Gee, couldn't you find workers closer than half a world?"

"Not highly skilled construction workers who spoke only Tagalog and couldn't tell anyone in Borrego Valley that they were building a secret library and bunker, please and thank you."

"*Tagalog* is a funny word."

"Umm. It sort of is."

A crawly feeling quivered down the nape of Cornell's neck, between his misshapen shoulder blades, along his spine. For no good reason, he looked at the ceiling in expectation of . . . something.

"What's wrong?" the boy asked.

"Umm. Umm. Nothing. Anyway, by the time I made three hundred million, I also made a lot of connections with powerful people. I located the workers, got them visas and green cards, brought them from the Philippines. They were nice. They worked hard. Sometimes they sang at night. Their singing was very pretty."

"What did they sing?"

"Mostly about Malaysian legends and the sea and the stars and Buddha and Jesus. Sometimes Elvis Costello in Tagalog."

Cornell sang a few lines in Tagalog, amazed to be so relaxed. He sang without feeling silly. He looked at the boy when they were talking, though he didn't usually look so directly at other people.

"These muffins are really good," the boy said.

Cornell licked sweet icing from his fingers. "Very kind of you to say so."

"How'd you talk to the fipaleens without them knowing English?"

"Before I hired them, I learned Tagalog. They lived in trailers on the property and never went into town, and by the time they flew back home, I'd made millionaires of them all."

"That's humongous! Twelve millionaires."

"Umm. It cost a lot more than that. Counting materials and all the donations, it cost an arm and an egg."

"You mean leg?"

"Leg. I don't know why that happens, that word thing. Anyway, it cost a farm and a leg. Oh, there it happened again."

The boy laughed.

So did Cornell, though a moment later he was frowning at the cluster of four security monitors that hung from the ceiling. When a warm-blooded moving creature, larger than a coyote, drew within ten feet of the building, a soft alarm would sound, and an image of the visitor would appear on each screen; from any point in the library, he could see what was happening outside. The screens were blank.

"Donations to what?" the boy asked. "To like Wounded Warriors? Uncle Gavin and Aunt Jessie give to them and others like them."

"These were donations to some officials, to let us have a high construction fence, to build without getting plans approved, without inspections. A secret bunker isn't much good if it's not secret."

"You mean payoffs, bribes."

"How does a five-year-old boy know payoffs and bribes?"

"I'm going on six. And, anyway, my mom's FBI. I'm an FBI kid."

"Yes, of course. An FBI kid."

"These are the best muffins ever," the boy said.

"Umm. I got the recipe from one of the construction workers. They grow a lot of pineapples and coconuts in the Philippines. Would you like me to get you another muffin?"

"Sure, you bet. That would be great, please and thank you."

When Cornell lifted his tray and scooted forward in the chair and put the tray on the footstool, the two dogs raised their heads to consider the unfinished muffin.

"Nothing of that belongs to you," Cornell said. The good dogs lowered their heads. And he regretted having spoken sharply.

At the kitchenette, as he took a muffin from a Tupperware container and put it on a small plate, he glanced at the security monitors a couple times, though no alarm had sounded.

He supposed that he was just Cornell being Cornell: too smart for his own good—as his mother had often said—plagued by a weird developmental disability, afraid civilization was going to collapse, but even more afraid that someone might touch him and drain the soul out of his body. He was maybe a little too obsessed with death.

As Mr. Paul Simon had sung, *We come and we go. That's a thing that I keep in the back of my head.*

41

EGON GOTTFREY LEAVES SIX OF HIS PEOPLE TO KEEP the Longrin family and their employees in custody, at gunpoint, until they hear from him. The detainees must not be allowed to place an unsupervised phone call during that time, which would surely be a call to Ancel and Clare Hawk to warn them that they have been traced to Killeen.

Rupert Baldwin and Vince Penn will accompany Gottfrey. As they climb into their Jeep Wrangler and as he approaches his Rhino GX, Janis Dern, who followed him from the house, calls out, "Hey, Egon. Can I have a minute?"

Janis is a dedicated revolutionary and an effective agent, but she seems too tightly wound, as if one of these days an escalating series of dire sounds—gears stripped, springs sprung, flywheels fractured—will arise within her, culminating in a glittering, smoking ejectamenta of clockwork fragments bursting from her ears, nostrils, mouth, and other orifices.

She stands too close to Egon, as though she has no concept of personal space, and she makes insistent eye contact, as she always does. "You've got to leave me the ampules and a hypodermic needle and everything else I need to inject a control mechanism."

"Inject who?"

"Laurie Longrin."

"One of the children?"

"See, then we'll have someone in the family to report to us."

"The brain has to reach a certain stage of development before the implant can assemble and function properly. Sixteen. You know we only inject after the sixteenth birthday."

"Oh, please, that's such a steaming pile of horseshit. Just theory."

"It's fact," Egon says, though in truth, like so much else, this is only what the Unknown Playwright wants them to believe.

As Paloma Sutherland moves the customized Cadillac Escalade that blocks the driveway and as Sally Jones waves them through, Rupert and Vince leave in the Jeep Wrangler.

"Only after their sixteenth birthday," Gottfrey repeats.

Janis Dern draws a deep breath, blows it out in exasperation. "They didn't try enough kids to be sure the problem is universal."

"Nine," Egon says. "Every one had a psychological crack-up within three months. Physical collapse, too. Had to be terminated."

"Nine is too damn small a sample to prove anything. It's worth a try with Laurie. *This family can lead us to Jane Hawk.* If the brat goes bat-shit crazy and bleeds from the eyes, so what? Why do you care?"

"I don't. I'm along for the ride. I just do what he wants."

She frowns. "He who?"

"The Unknown . . ." Egon looks away from her yellowish-brown flypaper eyes, but they remain stuck to him as he reconsiders his reply. "My Arcadian operator. You answer to me. I answer to him."

"So ask him for permission to inject Laurie Longrin. The worst he can do is say no."

He meets her stare again. "We're wasting time here. I need to get to Killeen."

Janis Dern is quite attractive if you don't look into her eyes for too long. They are eyes less suited to a woman of her physical charms than to a miscreant come forth from a toxic womb, malformed and insane at birth, to whom value and pleasure are to be found only in hatred.

"Janis, I can't give you a control mechanism for the girl. It's not what the script calls for."

Tears well in those eyes that previously have been as dry as cinders. She doesn't shed them, but the tears shimmer and glimmer.

She puts one hand to his face, tenderly pressing it against his right cheek. Leaning even closer, she whispers, "If you can't do this for me . . . then could you instead think of Laurie the next time you need to let off some steam?"

Genuinely bewildered, he says, "Let off some steam?"

"You've never shown an interest in me, but I've always been so intensely drawn to you. My desire is unrequited, and I've resigned myself to that. But next time things go so wrong you need to relieve the tension, instead of wasting some drunken cowboy with a TEXAS TRUE bumper sticker, think of that snarky little bitch Laurie."

This twist in the script leaves him speechless. The Unknown Playwright's wicked imagination has at last thwarted Egon's usually reliable intuition. He never saw this coming.

Assuming that his silence means he fears her disapproval, Janis slides her fingers along his cheek to his mouth and presses them to his lips. "No need to explain yourself. And please don't think that I've declared my feelings in the hope that we might have something together. I'm resigned to your disinterest. But I've loved you from afar, and I'll continue to love you. You're so strong. You do what you want, take what you want, always with such certainty that you'll triumph. The cowboy could've had a gun. And the others . . .

the ones I know about, anyway . . . in each case something could've gone very wrong, but you were *fearless*. I watched. I saw."

When she takes her fingers from his lips, he remains so amazed that he can't help saying, "No reason to fear them. None of them was real. Nothing is real."

"They're all just plebs, plodders, rabble, two-legged cattle," she says, under the misconception that they are both talking about the unwashed masses who will eventually come under the rule of the Arcadians, unaware that he is expressing his philosophy of life, his radical nihilism. "Do you have siblings, Egon?"

"No. There's no one but me. No one real."

"How fortunate. I had three older sisters. You hate children?"

"I don't allow myself such strong emotions. What's the point if nothing's real?"

"Well, I have enough hate for both of us. Think about it, Egon. You don't have to love me in return. But maybe someday, when you're stressed out and you need relief, maybe you can come back here and do this one thing for me, just out of the goodness of your heart."

She walks away from him and returns to the Longrins' house.

Egon gets behind the wheel of the Rhino GX. He drives out to the end of the private lane that serves Longrin Stables, where Rupert and Vince are waiting for him in the Jeep Wrangler.

They turn right onto the highway, east toward distant Austin.

The afternoon sky is vast and empty. The fields dwindle to every horizon, as if they have become the sole feature of a world that has been shorn of its mountains and drained of its seas.

Egon Gottfrey wonders what the script requires of him aside from this trip to Killeen. His usually reliable intuition regarding the author's intent fails him for the moment. He has no feeling for whether he's supposed to kill Laurie Longrin or Janis Dern—or both. Mile by mile, indecision plagues him, and his tension grows.

42

THE GREEN PLAQUE ON THE GATE ANNOUNCED GRANDPA AND GRANDMA'S PLACE. Behind the white picket fence, on the manicured lawn, three gnomes sat on tree stumps, two smoking pipes and one playing what might have been a lute. Three other gnomes danced in delight. The blades on the four-foot-high windmill turned in the mild breeze. There was an ornate birdbath, too, but no feathered bathers; perhaps some avian instinct warned them not to dare it.

The sign above the front door read BLESS THIS HOUSE.

Jane rang the bell.

Judy White and Lois Jones, one and the same, yet neither, opened the door. Fifty-something. Buxom, well-rounded. Jet-black hair. Egg-yolk-yellow fingernail polish. Blue toenails. She wore flip-flops, a too-tight leopard-pattern sweat suit, seven diamond rings, numerous gold-and-diamond bracelets, and a necklace of matched sapphires.

She took the cigarette from between her lips and let smoke drift out of her mouth rather than blow it, and then she said, "So you look like something happen."

"Something did. But I'm here."

"You have three times usual money?"

Jane held up the paper bag that had contained her truck-stop sandwiches.

"Come in, darling. Sit. I see if Pete have everything ready."

The house reeked of cigarette smoke that would have dropped little grandchildren like malathion felled mosquitoes, had there been any grandchildren, which there weren't. The interior—darkish, with far too much heavy antique furniture and brocade draperies and Persian carpets—offered none of the kitsch that fancified the front yard and served as a disguise.

The woman went to her husband's large workroom at the back of the house, leaving Jane alone with the two white cats as big as bobcats. One was lying on a sofa, the other on a La-Z-Boy recliner. They watched her as if she were prey.

Jane moved toward a leather armchair, but the yellow-eyed cat leaped off the sofa and sprang onto that seat before she could occupy it.

As she turned toward the now-empty sofa, the green-eyed cat abandoned the recliner and took the first cat's original perch.

When Jane looked at the La-Z-Boy, both cats hissed.

She said, "I'll just stand," which stopped the hissing.

At the back of the rambling house, where visitors were rarely wanted, Pete Jones—who was also John White and perhaps numerous other people—worked with several antique presses, laser printers, laminating machines, and so much other, more exotic equipment that the place had a Frankenstein air. Instead of reanimating the dead, however, he produced impeccably forged documents of all kinds.

The vision in leopard sweats reappeared in the archway between the living room and dining room, carrying something like a dress box that contained Jane's order. "I put on table. You look, darling." She set the box on the table and removed the lid.

In the center of the dining-room table stood a crystal ball on a silver plinth. Beside it lay a deck of Tarot cards fanned out and ready for shuffling.

Jane examined everything in the box. "Very good. Very nice. My compliments to Pete."

"Better than nice."

"Yes, you're right. It's all excellent."

The woman accepted the sandwich bag and took from it the two bricks of hundred-dollar bills held by rubber bands. She riffled the edges of the bills across her thumb, twice with each brick, cocking her head toward the sound.

"No need count, you always honest," she said, though she had probably done an accurate count with her devilishly sensitive thumb and hearing.

"It's so nice to be trusted," Jane said.

"You want to know?"

"Know what?"

Judy Lois White Jones nodded her head at the crystal ball and the cards. Her smile was humorless, feline. Her eyes were as black and her stare as viscid as pools of tar.

Jane said, "I don't believe in all that."

"Don't have to believe to be true. Will be rich, will be poor? Will be happy, will be sad? Will live, will die? Just have to ask."

At the front door, as she stepped outside, Jane turned and met the woman's eyes. "I make my own future. So do you."

"But what is future? Crystal and cards could tell."

"Have a nice day, Mrs. White-Jones. I know I will."

"Maybe, maybe not," the woman said, and closed the door.

43

THE JEEP WRANGLER AND THE RHINO GX ARE MAK-ing good time until, north of Austin and south of Georgetown, they come upon an eighteen-wheeler that, minutes earlier, jackknifed on Interstate 35. The thin-skinned cargo trailer has split open, spilling a load of colorful athletic shoes designed by the nation's current number one rap star. Maybe a hundred large cartons have tumbled onto the roadway, and most of these have burst open, casting forth uncountable shoeboxes emblazoned with the rapper's face, and in turn the lids have flown off these smaller containers. A Day-Glo rainbow of expensive footwear is drifted across what little of the roadway the overturned vehicle itself does not block, and in fact the sudden avalanche of high-priced gotta-have sneakers seems to have overwhelmed a less-than-substantial Mini Cooper, smashing it into the guardrail. Two Texas Highway Patrol officers have recently arrived on scene, and beyond the barricade of truck and shoes, a southbound ambulance is flashing its way along the shoulder of the road.

Traffic backs up so quickly in Egon Gottfrey's wake that before he quite knows what has happened, he's locked in, bumper to bumper, with the vehicles behind and in front of him.

He sits for a minute, wondering what the Unknown Playwright expects of him. Then he gets out of the Rhino to assess whether he might be able to maneuver out of his lane, onto the shoulder of the highway, and then reverse southward to the nearest exit.

Just then a third highway patrol officer comes along, putting down flares along the outer edge of the lane, to keep the shoulder open for emergency vehicles inbound from the south.

Gottfrey halts the trooper, presents his Bureau ID, and says, "You'll have to help us here. I—and my men in that Jeep Wrangler—urgently need to get past this mess."

The trooper is maybe six feet four, built like a pro wrestler. He stares down at Gottfrey in silence for a moment, frowning as though he has been addressed in a language known only by people on another planet. Then he says, "Sir, in these circumstances, your D.C. badge means about as much to me as your library card. We got people hurt and a road to open."

As the officer turns away, Gottfrey says, "I want your full name and badge number. There will be grave consequences if we don't get to Killeen within an hour."

The trooper seems to swell two inches taller as he turns on Gottfrey. "Sir, with all due respect, if you've just got to be in Killeen inside an hour, may I suggest you best stick a propeller in your ass and fart your way there."

Gottfrey does not know what to say to that, and perhaps wisely he chooses to say nothing.

After going forward three vehicles to the Jeep Wrangler and conferring with Rupert, he walks back to the Rhino and gets behind the wheel. He turns on the engine and powers down the windows and switches off the engine and tells himself that this delay doesn't matter.

None of this has any meaning, anyway. The overturned truck is not real. The shoes are not real. The rude highway patrol officer is not real. Killeen is not real.

Gottfrey is only along for the ride. The delay means nothing to him. So . . . it's curious, then, that he has the urge to get out of the Rhino and draw his pistol and shoot the trooper in the back.

He is reasonably sure, however, that if he did such a thing, he would be going off script to such an extent that he would inevitably be punished for misinterpreting the playwright's work.

As Egon Gottfrey strives to be only a disembodied mind with no stake in these events, other drivers and their passengers in some of the surrounding vehicles realize the nature of the treasure that has spilled out of the overturned Peterbilt. Doors are flung open and people spring out. They dash forward into the heaps of ruptured cardboard containers, snatching up three-, four-, and five-hundred-dollar Day-Glo sneakers, some still in their boxes, others loose and surely mismatched as to size. In a kind of ecstasy, they hurry back to their cars and SUVs with armfuls of celebrity footwear, only to return to the melee for more, while those people who remain in their vehicles look on with shocked and fearful expressions, as if they find themselves trapped in a traffic jam during a zombie apocalypse.

The shoe shoppers are not real. The sneakers are not real. It all has no meaning.

Egon Gottfrey is only along for the ride. But when he thinks of Killeen, where perhaps Ancel and Clare can yet be found, he looks at the collapsible baton lying on the passenger seat, and he remem-

bers the drunken cowboy outside Nashville West, and he is over-
come with the urge to use that effective weapon on a few of these
greedy shoe collectors, an urge that must be resisted.

44

PALM SPRINGS. THE SANTA ROSA AND SAN JACINTO
Mountains stark and mostly barren, plunging dramatically to the
idyllic valley floor, palm trees stirring gently in the warm currents
of the day, glittering shops and restaurants lining Palm Canyon
Drive, all sun-splashed and palm-shaded, with an air of unhurried
living . . .

Places like this—built with tradition as much as with wood,
stone, nails, and mortar—had once made Jane feel safe, places
where the storied past flowed through the present, where a way of
life was largely preserved, evolving but slowly and with grace.

These days, perhaps such impressions were illusions. Maybe no
place could long sustain against whatever new theory and collec-
tive madness was championed by the lords of the electronic and
social media that saturated life. As their highest principle, those
shapers of the future believed that the past was in all ways unspeak-
ably primitive, that all change was for the better.

A block back from Palm Canyon Drive, she found a modest motel
charging immodest prices, even on a weekday in April when the
in-season rates slowly began to phase toward the off. The afternoon
temperature was eighty-four degrees. A month from now, it might
be a hundred and ten, and nearly as hot at midnight as at noon. The
clerk took her cash, xeroxed her driver's license, gave her a key
card.

The luggage she carried from the Explorer to Room 17 included a titanium-alloy attaché case containing $210,000, about half of what she had taken from a creep named Simon Yegg three days earlier.

All the higher-echelon Arcadians squirreled away large sums of cash, getaway money that, in a crisis, would see them through to new lives under different names in distant countries. In spite of their arrogant confidence that they could establish Utopia, they couldn't rid themselves of a tumor of doubt that prickled in their brains.

Flanking a small table were a pair of skirted armchairs. Jane lifted part of one skirt and slid the attaché case under the chair.

She hung out the DO NOT DISTURB sign and engaged the deadbolt.

She parted the draperies enough to see the Explorer and watched for ten minutes, but no one showed an unusual interest in the SUV.

For a while, she sat on the edge of the bed, holding the burner phone that Travis had called last night. She pressed it to her chest, as if it were some magical object that would compel her boy to pick up *his* phone down there in Borrego Valley, as if the mere fact of holding their phones at the same time would conjoin their hearts and minds so that she would feel him close and know that he was safe.

She dared not call him. Her enemies, who were legion, had surely by now established continual surveillance of Borrego Valley by aircraft equipped to fish from the air those carrier waves that were reserved for cellphones. The latest technology even allowed them to focus on transmissions from disposable phones within a fifty-mile radius. An analytical scanning program, customized for this operation, would search the transmissions for key words like *mom* and *love* and *dad* and *sweetheart* and *Travis*.

As she'd warned her boy when he called the previous night, it was now too dangerous to use even disposable phones.

Reluctantly, she returned the phone to one of her suitcases.

45

Above the flatness of the city of Killeen, the sky appears likewise flat as it shades toward sapphire prior to twilight, and not only flat but also heavy, as if it is a massive descending slab that might crush everything on the earth under it.

Arriving less than five minutes after Rupert and Vince, but woefully late, Egon Gottfrey parks on the north side of the street. When he steps out of the Rhino GX, he feels oppressed under that too-solid-looking sky.

The historic district of Killeen, Texas, dating to the 1880s, features one- and two-story buildings with common walls, so it appears as if many enterprises occupy one long construct. The squat structures are mostly brick, painted brick, and stone. Substantial iron railings separate the sidewalks from the street. It's as if the locals are aware the sky is descending with tremendous weight and therefore build low and solid as a defense against calamity.

The meterless parking is vertical to the sidewalk, and the Longrins' white Mercury Mountaineer is angled nose to the curb in front of a Realtor's office, across the street from Egon's Rhino GX.

For a city of more than 140,000, there is little traffic on East C Street at this hour, perhaps because some businesses closed at five o'clock—a loan company, law offices—and because others are evangelical operations like Friends of Jesus Apostolic Ministries and the Upper Room Deliverance Center. Some storefronts with heavily tinted windows are unidentified, maybe occupied or maybe not.

Gottfrey interprets the light traffic and the lack of business signage as just more evidence of the Unknown Playwright's periodic laziness when it comes to sketching in the details of a scene.

There are also a karaoke bar and a Mexican restaurant with bar, however, so things might be livelier after night has fully fallen.

As if the Unknown Playwright is aware of Gottfrey's criticism and wishes to tweak him, the crosswalk at the end of the block is a swath of highly detailed brick in an intricate diagonal basket-weave pattern that only a master mason could have executed so precisely.

Eight or nine pedestrians are afoot, half in Army uniforms, no doubt stationed at Fort Hood, which is adjacent to Killeen and nearly surrounds it. On his journey to the Mountaineer, where Rupert and Vince wait, Gottfrey passes three soldiers, each of whom greets him—"Howdy" and "How're y'all?" and "Evenin', sir." He takes this as further tweaking, and he replies, "Yeah, yeah" and "Right back at ya" and "Yada-yada."

"Vehicle's unlocked," Rupert reports to Gottfrey. "We've combed through it. Nothing. Except the key was left under the front seat."

"We think that means they're not coming back for it," Vince adds. "Abandoned it. Just walked away. Maybe hiding in Killeen or maybe got some other wheels somehow. Seems like a dead end."

"There's no such thing as a dead end," Gottfrey says.

However, he has noticed there are no traffic cams in this area and no evident security cameras over entrances to these businesses. This fact, more than the historic buildings, makes him feel as though he has been thrown back in time to the Wild West when, to keep tabs on the population, authorities were limited to just their own eyes.

A tall, white-haired, distinguished-looking man is watching them through the glass door of the nearby real-estate agency.

Because Gottfrey is highly attuned to the rhythms of the role he is expected to play, he recognizes that this man is an important walk-on character who might have information that will swing the pursuit of Ancel and Clare in a new and more fruitful direction.

"Wait here," he tells Rupert and Vince.

When Gottfrey approaches the door of the real-estate agency, it opens, and the white-haired man steps outside. "Unless I've lost my nose for righteousness, you gentlemen have the look of the law."

"FBI," says Gottfrey, and presents that ID.

The man insists on a handshake. "Jim Lee Cassidy. I'm honored,

Agent Gottfrey." He nods at the Mountaineer. "That handsome vehicle was driven by a down-home church-clean shoulders-back couple who couldn't have been nicer if'n you held a gun to their heads. But bein' a suspicious old fart, I felt somethin' wasn't right about 'em."

"They wanted to rent a property or something?"

"No, sir. As they get out of that Mountaineer, it just happens I'm goin' from my car to my office, carryin' a valise not latched right. It comes open, spillin' an embarrassment of private papers on the sidewalk here. A mischievous breeze scatters stuff every which a way, so those two go scramblin' after everythin' as if'n the wind is takin' their own admission papers to Heaven. They hadn't helped, I would've lost some things of considerable consequence."

From an inner coat pocket, Gottfrey produces a photograph of Ancel and Clare.

"That's the very pair," Jim Lee Cassidy confirms.

The Hawks have striven to keep as low a profile as possible, and the Arcadians have used their influence with the media to keep Jane's in-laws out of the story, hoping to foster in them the false idea that they are not being intensely observed.

He says, "What was it about them that made you suspicious?"

"Well, sir, once the papers was gathered up, me and him fell into conversation, just two minutes or three, but the woman kept tuggin' his sleeve and remindin' him they had reservations. Plus it seemed every passin' vehicle worried her, the way she looked after it. And when a police car cruised by, it made 'em both jumpy."

"When was this?" Gottfrey asks.

"I was comin' back from showin' a house to this young couple as sweet as two dill pickles. Had an appointment with a good client in my office at ten-thirty, so it was maybe five minutes past the hour."

"This morning? These reservations she was worried about—they wouldn't have been for lunch in some restaurant, not at that hour. Did you see where they went from here?"

Jim Lee Cassidy taps the side of his head with a forefinger as if to say he is always thinking. "I contrived to linger till I saw 'em go all the way to Second Street and turn right. From there, it's not another block to the bus station. Maybe a bus reservation?"

"If they wanted a bus, why not park nearer the station?"

"You're just askin' to be polite. I figure they didn't want it known they left Killeen by bus. Wanted to look like they was still here somewhere. Could you tell a helpful fella what they done?"

"Child pornography," Gottfrey lies.

Cassidy's face tightens with righteous anger. "I'd known that, they'd never made it to the bus station." He shakes his head. "They looked clean-cut as if'n they was baptized every day of their lives. You just never know about people anymore, who they really are."

"Nobody's real," Gottfrey says. "It's all like one big video game, virtual reality. You just never know."

46

WHAT A NICE DAY IT HAD BEEN.

Maybe it shouldn't have been such a nice day with Gavin and Jessica probably dead and with so much trouble about the boy.

But good and bad came at you with no rhyme or reason. One moment it was raining money; the next moment it was a shitstorm.

Cornell needed to take things as they came, not get too happy or too upset. If he got too happy or too upset, he felt oppressed, as though his feelings had weight and were crushing him, and his skin grew so tight it seemed like it might split, and his nerves crackled, and a buzzing rose in his bones, as if tiny bees had built a hive in his skeleton. Then he had to lie down in the dark and the quiet, and he had to think of a pool of water in some deep cavern, a stillness of water with no shapes of light quivering on it, nothing swimming in it; he had to let the black water soothe his tight skin, let the silent water quiet his nerves, let the cool water drown the bees in his bones, let the water buoy him, so that the weight of big emotions was lifted from him.

Anyway, after their lunch, Cornell had thought the boy would watch TV. He believed that ordinary children mostly watched TV and played video games and tormented one another relentlessly; that is, "ordinary" as compared to the abnormal child that Cornell had been.

A little satellite dish hidden on the roof of the barn fed the TV in Cornell's library. He never watched any programs or the news, which was all depressing or lies. He turned the TV on only for a minute every day to check that the regular shows were still being aired, because that meant the end of civilization hadn't yet begun.

This boy didn't care about TV, either. He just wanted to see his mother, and he mostly sat on the carpet, cuddling with the dogs.

The boy would have to wait for his mother to get there, and getting there wouldn't be easy considering that, according to Gavin, every law-enforcement agency was looking for her. She would not arrive sooner than tomorrow, maybe even later than that.

Suddenly it had occurred to Cornell that Travis's mother might not get to them at all. She might die. Mothers died. His own mother had died of a drug overdose.

If the boy's mother died . . . where would the boy go? His father had died months earlier. If Gavin and Jessica were dead and if the mother died, would the boy have anywhere to go?

The mother must not die. She must not die. She must not die.

A terrible sadness had come over Cornell as he watched his three visitors and thought how the boy might have nowhere to go.

Although Cornell was good at math and coding and designing popular apps, he wasn't good with big emotions. Big emotions made him grow heavy and tighten up and crackle and buzz.

He had to put this terrible sadness away before it grew so heavy it weighed him down, before it forced him to leave the boy alone and go to the bunker and lie in the quiet darkness for hours.

He pictured the sadness as a gray brick of lead weighing on his heart. He pictured putting it into a FedEx box and addressing it to someone who really needed to be weighed down by sadness, like some terrorist bomber who killed people. He pictured the FedEx truck driving away, dwindling into the distance . . . gone from sight.

Although this made Cornell feel better, if he just sat there watching the boy cuddling with the dogs and waiting for his mother, he would get sad again. So he would have to do what he had always done to keep himself balanced and steady. He said, "I have to read."

The boy looked up from the dogs. "What are you going to read?"

"Not Ralph Waldo Emerson. No, no, no. Not ever again. And not Sigmund Freud. He was crazier than any of his patients. I like to read novels, short stories. Fiction makes me feel better."

"I can read a little," the boy said.

"That's very good. Being able to read a little at your age, that is very good," Cornell said as he got up from his armchair.

"Would you read to me, Mr. Jasperson?"

Halfway out of the chair, Cornell froze. He was in an awkward posture, one hand on a chair arm, still pushing himself up, one foot on the floor, one leg in the air to swing it over the footstool, but nevertheless he locked in that configuration, as if his joints had fused. He blinked at the boy and opened his mouth to speak, but he had been struck speechless.

Reading was a personal matter to Cornell, more personal than anything else. When drawn into a story, he was free. He could become the central character—male or female, child or adult—and live a different life from his own, no longer abnormal in either appearance or behavior. No one ever read aloud to him; he was an autodidact. He had never conceived of the possibility of reading aloud to another person. It seemed to be a dangerous sharing of himself—and a rude intrusion into the interior life of the listener.

"My mother sometimes reads to me," the boy said.

Supported by one hand and one leg, still with one leg in the air, Cornell said, "Really?"

"My dad used to read to me, too. And Uncle Gavin."

"How very strange," Cornell said.

The boy frowned. "It's not strange at all."

"It isn't?"

"No. It's nice. Parents read to kids all the time."

"Not my parents."

"I'd read to you if I could read better."

Cornell's raised leg came down to the floor, and whatever the cause of his paralysis, it passed. He stood thinking for a while and then said, "We wouldn't be on a sofa? We'd be in separate chairs? At a distance?"

"Sure. Whatever. Can I sit in the La-Z-Boy and can the dogs get in the chair with me when they want?"

"They have not attacked me," Cornell said. "They have not attacked me. They have not attacked. They're good dogs. They can have their own chair or share yours."

"Great! So what are you going to read?"

"Give me a moment to decide, please and thank you."

Intrigued by the novelty of reading aloud, Cornell went off to prowl the shelves.

The boy was smart, though maybe not yet ready for Dostoyevsky. Cornell hadn't been ready for Dostoyevsky until he was thirteen. Dickens? Maybe. He moved along the shelves, reading titles, and finally selected one.

He settled his considerable frame into his armchair and said, "I've read this one four times. You'll like this one." He opened the book and began to read: " 'First of all, it was October, a rare month for boys. Not that all months aren't rare. But there be bad and good, as the pirates say.' "

"What book is it?" the boy asked.

Cornell held up the novel so that the boy could see the jacket and the author's name. "*Something Wicked This Way Comes* by Mr. Ray Bradbury. It sounds very scary, but it's not really. It's magic."

"Scary is okay," the boy said. "Scary is just the way things are sometimes."

And in this manner they had passed the long afternoon: Cornell reading and the boy listening and the dogs—sometimes one, sometimes both—sharing the La-Z-Boy with their young master. At first reading aloud to someone was the strangest thing, though after a while it wasn't strange at all.

What a nice day it had been.

Now night fell on Borrego Valley.

47

AFTER STRIPPING OUT OF HER CLOTHES AND RE-moving the wig, she took her pistol into the bathroom and put it on the vanity. Although the shower was gloriously hot, she didn't linger in the spray.

She dressed in fresh clothes. The pixie-cut wig smelled less of smoke than did the garments she'd shed. New contact lenses made her blue eyes brown. She put on stage-prop glasses with dark frames.

After washing her underwear and T-shirt in the bathroom sink, she hung them to dry on the shower-curtain rod.

She paged through an issue of *Palm Springs Life* magazine and found an ad for a dry cleaner. She drove there and paid an express charge to be able to pick up her sport coat and jeans the next morning.

She thought it darkly amusing: the most-wanted fugitive in

America tending to such mundane tasks. In the movies, a protagonist on the run never took a break from the chase to buy toothpaste.

In a restaurant, she ordered a twelve-ounce filet mignon. Hold the baked potato. Double vegetables. A glass of Caymus cabernet.

After ordering dinner, she took a pill from a bottle of acid reducer and chased it with water. From a pocket, she retrieved the cameo that Travis had given her. Waiting for the wine, she worked the soapstone carving between thumb and forefinger, as a penitent might caress the beads of a rosary while petitioning for mercy.

48

THE TRAILWAYS BUS STATION IN KILLEEN, TEXAS, IS so thinly sketched that only a fool would believe it's real. A single-story white metal building with a minimum-pitch roof. Not even a pretense of style. There is no landscaping whatsoever, unless you are of the opinion that half an acre of medium-gray asphalt paving mottled with darker oil stains is the equivalent of greenery, predicated on the fact that blacktop and plants are both carbon-based.

Garage bays—where buses are parked, cleaned, serviced, and repaired—occupy most of the structure, and the public area is cramped and drab, but tidy.

Although the space is clean, the twentysomething woman at the ticket counter is immaculate and more detailed than her environment. Pleasant to look at, she wears her lustrous blond hair in a ponytail tied with white ribbon. No makeup, no eye shadow, no lipstick. Her well-scrubbed skin is smooth, with a slight pink flush. When she smiles, her teeth look as if they have never made contact with food or drink to sully them, and the whites of her eyes are as clear as purified milk. She wears a spotless white dress with a Peter

Pan collar, and as Egon Gottfrey approaches the counter, the woman's hands glisten with sanitizing gel as she works them together.

He flashes his FBI photo ID. "I need to talk to whoever worked this counter this morning."

She is Sue Ann McMaster, who never before met an FBI person, who can't imagine what she could tell him about anything that would be worth his time, who is near the end of her *second* shift today because Lureen Klaven took a bad fall this morning and couldn't work the afternoon. She says she loves the smell of Purell hands, and as the last of the gel evaporates, she asks what he needs to know.

When she sees the photo of Ancel and Clare, she smiles broadly. "Oh, yes, they were lovely people, going to Houston for the birth of their first grandchild. Just bubbling with excitement about it."

"What time did their bus leave?"

"It was supposed to depart at ten twenty-five, and maybe it was five minutes late. We have three buses a day going to Houston, and our on-time departure performance is over ninety percent."

"What time do they arrive in Houston?"

"Oh, hours ago. Three o'clock is the ETA." She checks her computer. "Pretty close perfect. They docked in Houston at nine minutes past three."

"Can you give me the address of the terminal in Houston?"

When Gottfrey comes out of the bus station, Rupert and Vince are leaning against their Jeep Wrangler, staring at the sky. The darkness and the wealth of stars should create a perception of the immensity of the universe and the emptiness between its infinite suns, but it feels no less heavy than before and still seems to be coming down on him—in spite of the fact that it's only an illusion.

He is beginning to think that this perception of a looming, crushing weight arises from an intuitive sense that somehow he is screwing up, that Ancel and Clare are slipping away in spite of all the resources at his disposal, that he no longer understands the script and is in the process of displeasing the Unknown Playwright.

The Killeen Police Department is within a block of the bus station. The watch commander is pleased to provide three FBI agents with a private office and computer.

Houston is one of the increasing number of cities from which the NSA now receives real-time input of video from airports, train stations, and bus depots.

While Rupert Baldwin back-doors the NSA Data Center in Utah and swims through the immense ocean of digital data, seeking archived video from the Houston terminal to which the passengers from Killeen were delivered hours earlier, Gottfrey bounces some questions off Vince Penn. He expects no useful answers, but this helps him frame his own theory of what Ancel and Clare's intentions might be.

"At the hour they left the Longrin ranch, say two-thirty in the morning, with hardly any traffic on the roads, they should have been here in Killeen by four-thirty, if not sooner. According to Jim Lee Cassidy they had just parked their Mercury Mountaineer outside his real-estate office at a few minutes after ten o'clock. That leaves five and a half missing hours. Where were they all that time?"

"Maybe a motel. Getting some shut-eye," Vince suggests.

"After that TV show, they figure they're targeted, they'll be injected, so they go on the run—only to stop for some shut-eye?"

"Everybody's got to sleep. Even Dracula sleeps, and he's the living dead."

"When you go on the run, don't you take essentials, a few changes of clothes, toiletries? Cash?"

"I never been on the run."

"Jim Lee Cassidy didn't say anything about them having luggage. If they'd had bags of any kind, when he saw them go two blocks and turn right at the corner, he would have *known* they were going to the bus depot. He wouldn't have had to guess."

"Well, he's a Realtor," says Vince.

Gottfrey knows he shouldn't ask. "What does that mean?"

"They're like surgeons. They work with real things, so if they can't be certain, they won't say they are. They'll only guess."

"Surgeons and Realtors, huh?"

"And astronauts," Vince adds.

"Here we go," Rupert Baldwin says. "Their bus, pulling into the terminal in Houston earlier today."

The three of them huddle before the computer, watching as one by one the travelers disembark. The camera provides a clearer image than is sometimes the case. Ancel and Clare are not on the bus.

49

THE NIGHT FEATHERED BY PALMS AND FERNS, PER-fumed by jasmine, now by burgers on a barbecue . . . the blood-red blooms of a trumpet vine in a lighted arbor . . . young women's laughter so innocent that it seems to come from another world in which no degradation of any kind exists . . . and one block later Glenn Miller's softly swinging "String of Pearls" issuing from the open window of a house . . .

After dinner, Jane walked residential streets. In the velvet shadows and subdued lighting, she gazed at a diamonded sky as mysterious as always it would be.

Every ordinary thing was in this moment extraordinary and precious beyond valuation, rich with meaning, but the meaning ineffable, all of it endangered in these darkening times.

Eventually, in a pocket park, she stood watching the motel across the street, where she'd taken a room. A few people came and went, but none concerned her. She focused on the window of her room, where she'd left the lights on, waiting to see the drapery panels part slightly or tremble as someone moved against them. Nothing.

She crossed the street and let herself into the room. She was alone. Wherever death might come for her, it wasn't here or now.

50

THE WATCH COMMANDER AT THE KILLEEN POLICE Department happens to know the manager of the bus station, Dennis van Horn. He calls him at home and introduces Egon Gottfrey, who then takes the phone.

According to van Horn, the bus driver from Killeen, Lonnie John Bricker, has finished his day by driving another coach that departed Houston at 4:00 P.M., scheduled to arrive in San Antonio at 7:10. Now at 7:26, it is likely that Bricker is still at the terminal in San Antonio, filling out his trip report.

At 7:39, again in the office provided by the watch commander, Gottfrey sits at the computer—Vince standing to his left, Rupert to his right—and conducts a Skype interview with Lonnie John Bricker.

The bus driver is a burly, balding man of about fifty. His round and rubbery face has a perpetual look of sweet bewilderment that underlies his every other expression. It is a face that makes him likable on sight and no doubt is comically expressive when he tells jokes to his buddies at the local bar.

Bricker frowns and leans warily toward the screen out there in San Antonio, as though Gottfrey might be a tiny man hiding inside that distant computer. "Well, no offense intended, but I still can't know for sure you're in Killeen. And when you held your badge thing to the camera, I couldn't see it clear enough to know was it real FBI or from some Junior G-Man play set."

In instances like this, Skype is a time-saving convenience; however, it's harder to intimidate the hell out of the subject of an interview when you are not in the same city with him. You can't loom over the guy or accidentally knock a mug of hot coffee into his lap.

Gottfrey says, "The head of security at the terminal there, Mr. Titus, has confirmed my identity to you."

"No offense intended to him, either, but he's near as much a stranger to me as you are. Don't I need myself a lawyer here?"

"You're not a suspect, Mr. Bricker. You're a witness who might have seen something in regards to a case of national importance."

"What I've been doin' all day is hump one bus to Houston and hump another bus to San Antone, so all I've seen is highway and some asshole drivers. The true FBI isn't after speeders and tailgaters."

According to the laws of physics established by the Unknown Playwright, when the urge to pistol-whip some idiot overcomes you, that is also not possible via Skype.

"I'm just stating for the record," says Bricker, "you told me I'm not a suspect and I don't need to lawyer up. So whatever I say here, it can't be used against me in a court of law"—he raises one hand in a pledge—"so help me, God."

Lonnie John Bricker has opened his own law practice.

"All right then," says Gottfrey. "I sent Mr. Titus two photos, and he printed them out for you."

Bricker glances at the photographs lying on the desk beside him, and then he squints at the screen again. "What about them?"

"Do you remember that man and woman being passengers on the bus you drove from Killeen to Houston earlier today?"

"Why wouldn't I remember them? Or at least her. She's maybe almost sixty, but she's still a looker, and she sure had an eye for me. A lot of the ladies think us bus drivers are romantic figures, always off to some far place."

"What do you mean, she had an eye for you?" According to what Gottfrey knows about Clare Hawk, this doesn't sound like her. "How could you tell she had an eye for you?"

Leaning back in his chair, Bricker smiles smugly and shakes his head. "No offense intended, but if by your age you haven't learned to see the love light shining in some beauty's eyes, you probably can't never be taught how."

When Vince Penn snickers at this statement, Gottfrey restrains himself from putting the bus driver in his place with a sharp rebuke and from shooting Vince dead, thereby removing him from the script.

"Mr. Bricker, can you tell me where they got off the bus?"

"It was a full-booked run, door-to-door, no in-betweeners. They got off in Houston."

"You remember seeing them get off?"

Bricker broods for a moment. "They could've got off while I was at the exterior luggage compartments, getting people's bags."

"Did this man and woman have luggage?"

"I think . . . maybe just carry-on . . . maybe none."

"Well, the problem is, we've reviewed the security video in Houston. They never disembarked there."

The look of bewilderment underlying Bricker's other expressions takes command of his rubbery face. "I don't know what that means."

"When all the passengers have received their luggage, do you return to the bus to be sure everyone has gotten off?"

"I generally walk the aisle, take a look around. Wasn't anyone there."

"Is there a lavatory on board the bus?"

"That's right."

"Do you always check the lavatory at the end of a trip?"

"Sometimes."

"Why not always, routinely?"

Getting defensive, Bricker says, "I don't clean toilets. Only reason to check the lav is if there's a couple passengers you think might have a habit, one of them might go in there to shoot up, so you find a junkie dead of an overdose."

"Has that ever happened to you?"

"No. But I heard of it."

"So you didn't check the lavatory this time?"

"There wasn't any obvious freak aboard. They were a straight-arrow bunch, nice and quiet from Killeen to Houston."

"What happens to the bus after you've off-loaded the luggage and all the passengers are gone?"

"I drove a different bus to San Antone. The one from Killeen, it was cleaned, fueled, serviced as needed, got ready for its next leg. I don't know maintenance routine. You'll have to ask somebody else about maintenance routine. Can I go now or am I in trouble?"

"Why would you be in trouble, Mr. Bricker?"

"No good reason. But the law does get it wrong sometimes."

After a silence, Gottfrey says, "You aren't in trouble. But I would be remiss if I didn't make sure you understood that lying to an agent of the FBI is a crime."

After a silence of his own, Bricker says, "I didn't lie. What would I have to lie about? I just drove from Killeen to Houston."

"I'm happy for you, Mr. Bricker. I'm happy you didn't lie. When people do lie, we always find out sooner or later."

51

THE FRECKLE-FACED LITTLE BITCH KEEPS SMIRKING at Janis Dern. She's been told to keep her smart mouth shut or it'll be taped shut, so she doesn't speak. But the kid can mock and insult with a look as well as with a word.

If Francine, the eldest of the four Dern sisters, wasn't still alive,

Janis would need to consider that this tomboy bitch is the very reincarnation of the other.

To discourage rebellion against this illegal detention, the ten employees have been locked in Stable 2. The exits from the long building are being guarded by Pedro and Alejandro Lobo.

Some of the detainees have spouses or others who expect them to return home at a certain time. They have made carefully monitored phone calls to explain that they will be working late. Very late.

The family poses a different problem. They draw strength and confidence from one another. As a unit, they're dangerous. To better manage them and to prevent them from conspiring to do something reckless, they have been separated.

Here at the house, Alexis Longrin is shackled to a chair at the kitchen table, watched over by Chris Roberts. Chase Longrin has been locked in a windowless half bath off the downstairs hall, sitting on the toilet, cuffed ankle to ankle and wrist to wrist, with a trammeling line that links the cuffs and prevents him from standing.

Paloma Sutherland, who has left Sally Jones alone to block the driveway with the Cadillac Escalade, is with the two younger girls—eight-year-old Daphne and six-year-old Artemis—in the bedroom that they share. Paloma has a way with younger children. They might even like being imprisoned by her. Anyway, Daphne and Artemis are too young to have been fully corrupted by twelve-year-old Laurie, though Daphne earlier exhibited moments of spirited resistance.

Janis has assigned herself to the oldest of the Longrin girls.

Posters decorate Laurie's room. Horses standing proud. Horses galloping. Airborne skateboarders performing ollies and flips. A solemn Marine in the Corps' most formal dress mess uniform, right arm across his chest, hand on the hilt of his Mameluke sword.

Laurie's ankles are zip-tied to the front stretcher bar of her desk chair, preventing her from getting to her feet. Her left hand is likewise bound to an arm of the chair.

Janis leaves the girl's right hand free, as an insult. "You need one hand to pick your nose. You look like a girl who picks her nose a lot. Do you eat your boogers? You sure look like a geek girl who eats her boogers. You want to give me the screw-you finger, don't you? That's the kind of crude, rude girl you are, so I left your hand free for that, too. But you know what? If you give me the finger, I'll use the butt of my pistol on it, like a hammer, break all three knuckles. You're done giving me shit. I won't take any more."

Laurie neither sulks nor cringes timidly. She sits in stoic indifference, though she is alert to everything Janis does.

A bookcase contains perhaps a hundred volumes, paperbacks and hardcovers, all young-adult novels. Janis has never read any of the books, has never heard of any of the authors. But she spends a few minutes examining the collection, making little sounds of derisive amusement or sighing or shaking her head, conveying contempt for the girl's puerile taste in literature.

She searches the dresser drawers as well, disarranging the contents. She withdraws some garments for a closer look and then drops them on the floor, treading carelessly on them when she suspects the items are ones the girl particularly likes.

Finally she picks up a side chair and carries it to the desk and sits, facing Laurie. Janis says nothing, but only stares at her prisoner's profile.

After a while, Laurie glances at her, expressionless, and then turns her head forward once more to contemplate the desk.

"What's all this shit on the walls?" Janis asks.

Laurie says nothing.

"It's okay, you can talk. I won't tape your mouth shut. What kind of girl's room is this, anyway?"

"It's stuff I like."

"I don't see any *girl* things."

"Horses are girl things. Lots of girls love horses."

"Okay, but what I don't see is any *girly* things."

Laurie says nothing.

"When will you turn thirteen?"

"Next month. What's it to you?"

"Do you skateboard?"

"Yeah."

"What's with the *semper fi* T-shirt and the poster? You want to be a Marine someday?"

"I could be if I wanted."

From a distance of maybe two feet, Janis stares at the girl's profile in silence. Finally she says, "So are you a lesbo?"

"No. Of course not."

"Other girls, real girls, they'd have posters of boy bands."

"Boy bands and actors—that's not who's cool," Laurie says.

"So who do you think is cool? *Girl* bands, actresses with long smooth legs and wet mouths you could kiss?"

Laurie faces Janis again and glares at her. "You're disgusting. Crude and stupid."

Janis smiles knowingly. "So who do you think is cool?"

"People who do what's right but tough to do, what takes guts, what takes a spine."

"Well, you know, it takes a spine for a lesbo to out herself," Janis taunts.

"Maybe you didn't notice, but the Marine in the poster is a guy. He's a *hunk*. All by himself, he could wade through an army of boy-band types and knock them all flat."

They're eye to eye now, and face-offs are something Janis does well. She has an intimidating stare that disturbs people; they meet it, and they're afraid, but they're often even more afraid to look away. One of the men she's taken up with and later dropped told her that she has ax-murderer eyes. Another said that during sex her yellow-brown eyes were as wild as those of some jungle animal, some fierce predator, which turned him on, except eventually he realized that her stare was predatory when sex *wasn't* on the agenda, even in moments that he thought were tender. She receives such insults as compliments. She uses her stare as though it is a stiletto, piercing people with it, some of them being people into whom she would enjoy sliding a *real* blade.

When the girl doesn't soon look away, Janis leans closer, until their faces are a foot apart, and she lowers her voice almost to a whisper. "Did Jane Hawk tell you about the brain implants? Or maybe she told your daddy and you overheard it?"

"I don't know what you're talking about."

"No, even if your daddy knows, he wouldn't have scared you by sharing it. But I will."

Maintaining eye contact, Janis touches a forefinger to the crook of the girl's left arm.

Laurie twitches but says nothing and doesn't look away.

"That's where they find a vein and inject you. With three big ampules holding maybe millions of tiny machines suspended in liquid, each just a few molecules. Nanoconstructs. They swim through your blood, into your head, assemble themselves into a web, a control mechanism powered by the electrical current in your brain. Then you're told to forget it happened, and you forget. For the rest of your life, we *own* you, but you don't know it. For the rest of your life, you do exactly what you're told, and you're happy to do it. If we say kill your sisters, you will. If we tell you to kill yourself, you will. No more snark from Laurie Longrin. No more smirking, no cheeky backtalk, no *attitude*. Just obedient little Laurie, so eager to please, eager to kiss my ass if I want it kissed."

Janis reads desperation in her captive's eyes and knows that she isn't *mis*reading this.

The girl can't keep a faint tremor out of her voice. "If you had such a thing, you'd already be injecting me."

"I would, yes. Oh, I'd love it. I'd keep you for a pet. But my boss decides who and when—or maybe someone above him decides. My boss says the script requires us to be discreet, to be selective in who we choose to enslave with injections. The script doesn't call for us to do millions of you overnight."

Frowning, the girl says, "What script?"

"It's just the way he talks. But you listen to me, Little Miss Attitude. If I get my hands on those ampules, whether it's a week from now or a year, I'll come back for you and inject you. I don't care what the script says, what my boss says. You'll spend the rest of your miserable life looking over your shoulder, but you won't see me coming. Then you'll be my bootlicker, Little Miss Lickspittle."

Intimidated, the girl breaks eye contact. But then gathers her courage and says, "Heck, you're just a walking, talking pile of horseshit, that's all you are." She meets her captor's eyes again and smiles. "What kind of numbnuts thinks potatoes grow from seeds?"

Janis sometimes has a problem with temper. It's not as though she needs counseling or therapy. Screw that. She's not a chronic sorehead. She certainly doesn't have a psychological *condition*. She is just a hard-charging achiever who sees how the world works and who knows how it *should* work and who gets damn impatient when she encounters people like this freckled smart-mouth brat who is all attitude, who'll never be anything but sand in the gears.

There is no danger that Janis will beat Laurie Longrin to death the way Egon beat that drunken cowboy to death.

How beautiful Egon was in his cold, efficient rage, a maître de ballet bringing the grace of dance to brutal violence.

Janis isn't going to pull her pistol, isn't going to shoot this kid in her smug, smirky face. There's no danger of that whatsoever.

Her response to the mockery about the potato seeds is measured, exactly the degree of corporal punishment required to teach this insolent child some manners. She raises her arm and slaps Laurie's face hard—there has to be some pain, after all, if a lesson is to be learned—and then backhands her with equal vigor.

The girl gasps in shock but doesn't cry out.

Janis gets up and goes into the adjacent bathroom. For a while, she runs cold water over her stinging hand.

When she returns to the bedroom, the girl sits stone-faced. She doesn't in any way acknowledge her captor's presence. A thread of blood sews its way from the right corner of her mouth, down her chin, along her slender throat.

Janis doesn't return to the chair that earlier she put near the girl, but she doesn't take the chair back to the place from which she moved it, either. Let the little bitch dread the resumption of their chat. Let her wonder when the conversation will begin again, where it might lead, what consequences it might have.

Instead, Janis goes to the bookcases. She tears the print blocks out of the boards of the hardcovers and rips apart the paperbacks. It is most likely from books that this wayward child acquired her *attitude.* That was certainly the case with Francine, Janis's childhood tormentor, who would have treated Cinderella far worse than Cindy's hateful stepsisters had treated her.

52

THE DEPARTMENT OF HOMELAND SECURITY HAS RE-cently opened an office in a wing of the Killeen–Fort Hood Regional Airport.

Egon Gottfrey and his men possess Homeland Security ID as genuine as their FBI credentials. Before they leave the Killeen Police Department for the airport, Gottfrey calls the deputy director of Homeland and requests that he instruct the on-duty personnel at the airport office to welcome him and his men as VIPs.

The deputy director is an Arcadian.

This is another advantage of conducting a secret revolution from inside the existing government rather than mounting an armed rebellion from outside. The authorities you will one day exterminate or convert with nanomachine implants are pleased to assist you; there is no resistance. And they have ready for your use just about any expensive piece of equipment you might require.

When Gottfrey arrives, carrying the Medexpress cooler with the control mechanisms meant for Ancel and Clare, this Killeen outpost of Homeland has readied a twin-engine helicopter. Fully equipped for night flight. Nine-passenger capacity. The pilot is on-site to take them to Houston, where they will put down in the vicinity of the bus terminal before 10:00 P.M.

The Rhino GX and the Jeep Wrangler will be driven by Homeland agents stationed in Killeen, though they won't reach Houston until midnight. They will deliver the vehicles to the Hyatt Regency Hotel, downtown, where Gottfrey, Baldwin, and Penn will spend the night.

The Rhino and the Jeep appear on the vehicle-inventory lists of Homeland, the FBI, and the NSA. But none of those organizations shares such data; so no question will be raised as to why Egon and his men, ostensibly Homeland agents, are driving FBI vehicles.

And so it is: A helo that can't be proven to exist lifts off from Killeen, a city that can't be proven to exist, carrying three men whose bodies are only concepts and whose minds, except in Gottfrey's case, might also be nothing more than concepts, ferrying them to Houston, another city that can't be proven to exist, through a night sky that had earlier seemed as solid as stone but that, of course, is no more verifiably real than anything else.

Because Gottfrey and his associates haven't had dinner and won't have time to eat in Houston, a selection of sandwiches from Subway is provided aboard the helo.

Although the sandwiches are no more real than anything else, they are tasty, aromatic, filling, vividly detailed in their appeal to all five senses. *So real.* This isn't the first time something as ordinary as food has briefly shaken Egon's belief system.

Sometimes when he is weary and tense and frustrated, radical philosophical nihilism is a most difficult faith by which to live.

He doesn't doubt the truth of it, however, because he recalls how lost he was as a young man, how self-destructive and afraid, before taking the class in which he learned there is no objective basis for truth, that nothing can be proved either by science or math, or by religion. All is illusion.

If he were a *better* radical nihilist, he would be neither tense nor frustrated. He should just let himself be carried along by the script, enjoy the ride, go with the flow.

※

Like some huge nocturnal dragonfly, the helo passes over the Houston sprawl, descends into it, and puts down in an empty lot across the street from the bus station. The wind from the churning blades stirs up ghostly winged figures of dust that fly away into the lamp-lit streets. Gottfrey and his men wait until the blades cease whisking the air and the dust settles before they disembark and walk to the nearby terminal.

The head of vehicle maintenance is Louis Calloway. Off duty at this hour, he has returned from his home to walk them through what happened with the bus from Killeen when Lonnie John Bricker signed over possession of it and drove another coach to San Antonio.

What it boils down to is this:

The garage has a number of high-ceiling bays in which buses are parked between trips. Here the interiors are cleaned and a mechanic inspects the vehicle's engine, drive train, and other systems, using a checklist of items to be confirmed. There are no walls between the bays. It's a cavernous space, shadowy in places. If Ancel and Clare failed to disembark on arrival from Killeen, if they hid in the tiny lavatory, they might have gotten out of the bus once it arrived in one of these bays and might have entered another bus that had been serviced. They could have hidden in the second coach's recently cleaned lavatory, waiting to be on the road before stepping out of the cramped lavatory to take seats for which they never purchased tickets.

Although this scenario is possible, there are problems with it, most of which even Vince Penn is able to identify. For one thing, no passengers are allowed here. Ancel and Clare would have needed to be as schooled and skilled as covert agents, as well as supernaturally lucky, to slip out of the Killeen bus and into another one without being seen by the workers in the garage.

Furthermore, they would have needed to exit the first coach quickly, before someone came to clean it, and within seconds board another bus *on which service had been completed*, there to hide in the lav. But how would they know which vehicles were serviced and which were not? And what would they do if the new vehicle in which they hid was fully booked and later proved to have no open seats when they emerged from its lavatory?

Perhaps they took the risk. If so, it has paid off. No driver in midtrip has reported an excess of passengers.

But would they commit to a bus without knowing its destination? Maybe. Because of their daughter-in-law, they know surveillance of travelers is ubiquitous these days. To disappear during a trip via any form of public transportation, they need some ruse like this.

From Louis Calloway, head of vehicle maintenance, Gottfrey requests a list identifying the buses that were in the service bays when the coach from Killeen was there, the cities to which those buses were next dispatched, the addresses of the terminals that were ultimate destinations, an ETA for each, and other scheduled stops between Houston and the end-of-trip terminals, if any.

Following up on these leads and reviewing the archived video from all these terminals in search of Jane Hawk's in-laws will be a huge amount of work. After a long and eventful day, Gottfrey and his men are too tired to take on this task.

As it seems the script requires, he emails his immediate Arcadian superior and attaches the list that Calloway provides. He asks for support staff to follow these leads while he, Rupert, and Vince catch a few hours of sleep.

✳

In the back of the taxi, for the trip to the Hyatt Regency Hotel, Rupert takes the hump seat, with Gottfrey to his left and Vince to his right, to spare his boss the ordeal of sitting beside the ever-chatty Agent Penn. The Medexpress carrier is on the floor between Gottfrey's feet, the readout showing forty-one degrees, still plenty cool enough to keep the nanomechanisms in stasis.

They aren't a block from the bus station when Gottfrey receives a call from the leader of their cell, Sheila Draper-Cruxton, a court of appeals judge. Their smartphones share an NSA-devised encryption program guaranteeing a private conversation. She has received the Calloway list and is assigning people to follow up on it.

Like revolutionary political movements since time immemorial, the Techno Arcadians are organized into cells, with a limited number of people in each. If one Arcadian goes rogue, he won't know enough names to betray a significant portion of the conspiracy and destroy it. Those at the top of each cell receive instructions through a regional commander who is known to them only by a nom de guerre, and all the regional commanders get their orders from the members of a mysterious central committee who, through surrogates, recruited them.

The Unknown Playwright seems to love all this hugger-muggery, though Gottfrey could do with less of it.

Anyway, Judge Draper-Cruxton has received word from her regional commander that the people with whom Jane Hawk secreted her child were killed Sunday afternoon in Borrego Springs, California. The boy is surely hidden somewhere in Borrego Valley.

In the past twenty-four hours, Arcadians from various agencies have quietly established observation posts at every road entering the valley. A substantial contingent of agents has infiltrated the territory, not merely to search for the boy but also to be ready for the mother, because it is believed she will come for her child.

In fact, according to Judge Draper-Cruxton, earlier today an Arcadian attached to the Department of Homeland Security was shot to death in an oak woods north of Los Angeles. A fire was set to cover the crime. There is reason to believe that the dead man crossed paths with Jane Hawk and that she is *already* on her way to the boy.

The elegant Sheila Draper-Cruxton is a deeply cultured woman, a paragon of refinement, and Egon likes to listen to her feminine and mannerly yet very direct voice as she says, "These developments make the search for the in-laws more urgent by the hour."

"We're doing all we can," Gottfrey assures her, keeping his voice low enough that the cab driver can't hear. "I'm trying my best to follow the script."

"I assure you I did not intend those to be words of criticism. I have every confidence in your ability and dedication. However, if the in-laws know *anything* about where the unfortunate child might be hidden in Borrego Valley, we must extract the information from them posthaste. When Jane goes there for the boy, we should already be waiting with him. We can play the spider and she the buzzing fly."

"What do you want me to do?"

"You should get some sleep, but be prepared to jump at a moment's notice if the Calloway list should lead us to the in-laws somewhere there in Texas."

"I can do that, I can jump, you know I can jump," Gottfrey says. Listening to himself, he realizes he is mentally fuzzy.

"Are you quite all right?" Judge Draper-Cruxton asks.

"Just tired. Been a lot of busy scenes in the script lately."

"How very true," says the judge. "We are forcing Hawk into a corner. This little drama is accelerating to an endgame. Another thing—those control mechanisms that were sent to you in Worstead. Did you leave them with your people there?"

"No. I've kept them with me. They were meant for the in-laws."

"Very well, then. I will send six agents to support your people at the Longrin ranch. They will bring more control mechanisms. Just in case we are unable to find the in-laws, it has been decided that we must inject Chase and Alexis Longrin on the off chance they know Ancel and Clare's ultimate destination."

"I doubt the in-laws shared that with them."

"I doubt it, as well," says the judge. "However, Chase and Alexis have fucked us over. I have no patience for coddling such human debris. We'll zombify these ignorant shitkickers and peel their brains for what they know."

Never before has Gottfrey heard such dialogue coming from his poised and cultivated cell leader. He wonders what the Unknown Playwright means to signify by her descent into crudity. Is the intention to convey that perhaps in spite of the judge's expressed certainty, she isn't really sure they can bring down Jane Hawk?

53

THE ROOM IN DARKNESS BUT FOR THE DRAPERY-filtered light from the window opposite the foot of the bed, a soft and spectral glow ribbed with thin shadows marking the folds of fabric, like an X-ray of some alien species with strange bone structure . . .

The motel stood on a quiet street, but Jane couldn't rest.

Lying in bed, head raised on pillows, she wasn't able to keep her eyes closed. Faces foiled sleep, materializing in her interior darkness. Gavin and Jessie Washington. Nathan Silverman, her mentor at the Bureau. Nick. Repeatedly, Nick. Her mother, lost these many years. Most disturbing of all, Travis. Disturbing because her unconscious chose to include him among the gallery of those other faces, all of which belonged to people who had gone to graves.

She turned on a bedside lamp.

She went into the bathroom. On the vanity stood a motel ice bucket, a can of Coke, and a half-full pint bottle of Belvedere.

Too often, she needed vodka to sleep. She was determined not to make a habit of it. But she had to be rested tomorrow for the ordeal in Borrego Valley. Anyway, it wouldn't be vodka that killed her.

For something to do while she finished a Belvedere and Coke, she retrieved the titanium-alloy attaché case from under the skirted chair. She took it to the bed and opened it and considered the twenty-one banded packets of hundred-dollar bills. $210,000.

She'd stolen it from a thief, though such street justice didn't make the money clean. This was war, however. Wars were expensive.

She took twelve packets from the case and set them aside: the money she owed Enrique de Soto for the motor home and the vehicle it would be towing when it arrived in Indio.

A white plastic bag lined the little waste can in the bathroom. With a pair of scissors that she carried in one of two suitcases, she cut the bag into a flat sheet and used it to wrap the brick of money. She sealed the folded ends with Scotch tape that she also carried in a suitcase.

She was a well-prepared traveler. Scissors, tape, antacid, vodka, .45 Compact with sound suppressor, switchblade, zip-ties, spray bottle of chloroform that she had made herself from art-store acetone by the action of chloride of lime . . .

"Damn if I'm not a regular Girl Scout."

She went to bed, turned off the lamp, and slept.

54

CHRIS ROBERTS OPENS THE DOOR TO LAURIE LON-grin's room, and Janis Dern looks up from the pile of books that she has torn apart.

"See you a minute?" Chris asks.

Leaving the chastened girl to lick the blood from the corner of her mouth, Janis steps into the hall and shuts the door behind her.

Chris says, "I just got a call from Egon. They don't have the in-laws yet, but they're still in the chase."

"Damn, Chris, we can't hold all these people indefinitely."

"Won't have to. A support team of six is already on the road from Austin, be here in maybe half an hour. They'll do sharp-elbow one-on-one interviews with all the employees being held in Stable Two, threaten them with prosecution for aiding and abetting Jane Hawk, scare the spunk out of them, and then send them home."

"What about the Longrins?"

"Injections."

"Shit, yeah!" Janis high-fives Chris. "Maybe we'll get Ancel and Clare before Egon does. Chase and Nick were best friends in high school. If the sonofabitch doesn't know where the in-laws went, if he hasn't been the contact between Jane and them, I'll tongue-kiss a rattlesnake."

Chris grins. "Probably wouldn't be your first."

"The quality of men these days, I'm either giving tongue to a rattlesnake or a gerbil. How many injection sets are we gonna have?"

"Egon didn't say what they're bringing. All we need is two."

"If there's extra, I have a use for one."

He looks at the closed door to Laurie's room. "But she's only twelve, brain still growing. Inject before they're sixteen . . . you know what'll happen."

"I know what happened to a few. The sample was too small. It doesn't mean anything. Besides, after we convert the parents, the kids will know. Kids always know. They detect the difference. We'll have to do something with all three of the kids, anyway."

Chris is uneasy, but after the work they've done together, he wants to be a good partner. "All right, but I won't be there when you do it . . . or through the wait."

Earlier generations of the nanomechanism took eight to twelve hours from the time of injection to the moment when control of the subject was established and he—or she—became an adjusted person. The newest generation of control mechanism requires only four hours.

Janis says, "If they bring just two injection sets, we could do Chase first, squeeze him for what he knows. If he gives us Ancel and Clare, we don't want wifey. I'll use the second set"—she gestures toward the bedroom door—"with the smart-mouth tomboy in there."

She doesn't need a translator to know the meaning of the look Chris gives her, but he's forthright about his desire. "Nobody can get a hate-on faster or harder than you. You're so damn intense, I'd give just about anything to know what you're like in bed."

"More than you could ever handle, sweet thing. We've been here before, and you know how it is. Partners don't do each other. Not if they want to stay sharp on the job."

He sighs. "When the revolution's over, I'm going to want to be totally in you."

She likes Chris, she really does, but his vision is limited to the short term, while she takes the long view. "A good revolution," she says, "is never over. It's a way of life."

55

In THE LIBRARY OF MANY CHAIRS, THERE WERE ALSO two deep, long, comfortable sofas facing each other from opposite ends of a gold-blue-maroon Persian carpet. Cornell often slept in one or the other. When he spent the night in the library instead of in the bunker, he was more likely to have pleasant sleep, as if his favorite authors were writing his dreams.

This night, he put plump pillows and a blanket on each sofa. He placed small, chilled bottles of water on coasters, on the tables that served the sofas. Beside each coaster, in a small plastic bag, he set a lemon cookie with chocolate chips in case either of them should wake in the night and want a convenient snack before going back to sleep.

Travis used the bathroom first and brushed his teeth and put on white-and-black pajamas like a karate costume. Both sofas were big, but he took the smaller of the two.

When Cornell entered the bathroom and saw what the boy had left there, his heart raced and his stomach turned over, and he needed to leave the room at once.

The boy was lying on the sofa, arranging the blanket around himself, one dog up there with him, the other dog on the floor next to its master's slippers.

Cornell said, "Umm. Umm. Umm. You left a thing in there so I can't use the sink."

"I flushed," the boy assured him.

"Yes, yes, yes. You did flush, please and thank you. But beside the sink you left a little plastic glass. Umm. Umm. Umm. And in the glass you left a little tube of toothpaste and . . . and . . . and your toothbrush, left it in the little glass, in the little glass. In the little glass."

"Where should I leave it?"

"Not in the bathroom. Leave it with your things. On the table there with your water and your cookie would be okay. That would be okay. That would be good."

The boy folded back the blanket and sat up. "Okay, sure. Sorry I left it there. But why?"

Cornell stood fidgeting, shifting from foot to foot, wondering if the dogs would decide to attack him, after all. "Umm. Umm. Well, it's a toothbrush, and a toothbrush is a very personal thing, very, and when there's a toothbrush not mine standing by the sink where I'm going to brush my own teeth . . . it's like being gouged, no, I mean like being touched, and I can never be touched."

"Uncle Gavin explained how that is." The boy stepped into his slippers. "But I guess I didn't know about the toothbrush thing."

"Neither did I." Cornell shuddered. "Umm. It's a surprise."

The boy got the plastic glass with the toothbrush and brought it back to his sofa and put it on the table beside his cookie. "I'm sorry, Mr. Jasperson."

"No need to be sorry, no need, no need. You didn't know, I didn't know, nobody knew."

Cornell went into the bathroom and brushed his teeth and changed into his pajamas, which were soft and blue like the sky. He could sleep well only in soft and blue.

In the library once more, he turned out all the lights except for a blown-glass lamp at the end of the sofa farthest from his head. A soft peach-color glow issued from it.

"I always leave on one lamp," Cornell said. "Is that okay?"

"Sure. Even though there aren't boogeymen or nothing, it's still nice not to sleep in the dark."

Cornell settled on his sofa. Pulled the blanket over himself. He turned on his side and looked across the Persian carpet to the boy with his dogs. "Are you okay?"

"Yeah. I guess. Are you okay?"

"I'm okay. Umm. Umm. Umm."

"What do you want to say?" the boy asked.

Cornell pointed behind his head to the table that stood beside the sofa. "Do you see the iPod there?"

"Yeah. I see it."

"Sometimes at night if I wake up and I'm scared, I play music that makes me feel better. Is that okay? I'll play it low."

"It won't bother me. My mom's a musician. She plays the piano. She's really good."

"I'm looking forward to meeting your mother."

"You'll like her. Everyone likes her. Except all the bad guys she puts in prison. She's the best."

Cornell says, "She'll be here soon."

"She promised," the boy said. "She always keeps promises."

Both dogs yawned extravagantly, as if the conversation bored them. Cornell didn't want to offend the dogs, so he said no more.

Soon the boy was softly snoring.

Cornell lay watching the boy and the big dogs, amazed that they were here, that his guest had liked the lunch sandwiches, also the different sandwiches for dinner. He was amazed that he had read most of the Bradbury novel aloud to the boy.

Always before, Cornell had liked everything to be just the same today as it had been yesterday, and he had hoped tomorrow would be the same as today.

Now everything was different, and he wanted tomorrow to be the same kind of different as today.

On the other hand, if things could get so different from one day to the next, they could get different all over again and maybe the next time in not such a nice way.

PART TWO

While Jane Sleeps

1

Laurie Longrin was a strong and happy girl because her family was strong and happy. She had figured that out long ago.

If your family was a mess, your dad a sex-crazed tail chaser and your mom one of those who floated her breakfast cornflakes in booze, well, then your chances of being strong and happy weren't promising. But if your dad and mom loved each other and worked hard—especially when their work brought beautiful horses into your life every day—you were more than halfway to being strong and happy. The rest was up to you.

Of course Laurie could still screw up, like when she zoned out or even fell asleep during nearly every Sunday sermon. Or like when she used the word *horseshit* more often than the average almost-thirteen-year-old girl.

If you were strong and happy, you were able to recognize those qualities in others. And if you could admit to your own evils, like the overuse of the word *horseshit* or a tendency to get snarky with ignorant people, just to name two, then you were better able to see evil in others and know them for what they were.

For instance, Agent Janis Dern, who was an FBI bad apple if she was FBI at all, who wasn't just psycho-sick but also as pure evil as Cruella De Vil. Except if given the chance, Janis Dern wouldn't make a fancy coat from Dalmatian-puppy skins but instead from little-girl skins.

When she stepped out of the room to talk with the guy named Chris, Janis closed the door, but they didn't lower their voices. Laurie could still hear them. She was pretty sure Janis *wanted* her to hear them. When Janis had first talked about the injections that would make Laurie a zombie, it had sounded half true and half like, well, horseshit. But she and Chris talked about six more of their kind coming here as backup, talked about injecting Daddy and maybe Mom and maybe Laurie herself, and the more they talked, the more real it sounded, *too real* by the time they were talking about sex and doing each other.

Laurie wasn't just sitting there, zip-tied to her desk chair, hysterical about the danger she was in, hoping Ethan Stackpool would miraculously appear and rescue her from death and worse than death. Ethan Stackpool was amazing to look at, sweet, smart, strong for his age, but he was in the seventh grade, like Laurie, so he was still a few years away from being an action hero able to knock the plumbing out of a dozen bad guys. Although she couldn't help thinking about Ethan Stackpool at times like this—and lots of other times—Laurie was busy saving herself the minute Janis stepped into the upstairs hallway and closed the door behind her.

Evil is stupid. Doing evil might get you what you wanted in the short term, but it never worked in the long term. Laurie had learned this from books, from some movies, and just from general observation of life.

For instance, in the general-observation category, Janis Dern was evil and stupid. She'd bound each of Laurie's ankles to the front stretcher bar of the desk chair and her left hand to the left arm of the chair, but let the right hand remain free so she could make that idiotic nasty crack about nose picking and booger eating. Janis probably also didn't cuff that hand because, when the two of them were face-to-face and she was ragging Laurie, she *wanted* to be given the finger and *really would have* used the butt of her pistol like a hammer, as she had promised, to shatter all three knuckles in the offending digit. But Janis Dern, agent of the FBEI, Federal Bureau of Evil Idiots, had apparently given no thought to what might be in the drawers of a schoolgirl's desk besides bubblegum and barrettes. Among other things, Laurie's desk contained a pair of scissors.

The moment the door closed, while Laurie listened to the crazy-sick talk of the two agents and thought about Ethan Stackpool, she opened the pencil drawer in the desk and took out the scissors. She cut through the thick plastic tie that restrained her left hand. She bent forward in the chair and cut the tie on her left ankle, then the tie on her right.

With her left hand, she presented the middle finger to the hall-way door, and she kept the scissors in her right hand because they were the only weapon she had.

Only a day earlier, she would not have thought she could stab anyone, not in a million years. But now that the choice was between stabbing someone or being turned into a zombie slave, she could be a stabbing *machine* if it came to that.

Waiting for Janis to return and trying to surprise her was a bad idea. Janis was strong, crazy, and evil.

Better to raise the bottom sash of the double-hung windows, raise the bug screen, and slip out onto the roof of the veranda that encircled the house.

She was on the north side of the house, where she couldn't be seen from the stables, though she was looking down on the Cadillac Escalade that blocked the private lane leading in from the state route. The Cadillac stood under a lamppost. A woman leaned against the farther side of the big SUV, smoking a cigarette, her back to Laurie.

Because the veranda wrapped the entire residence, Laurie was able to move along the shingled roof, around the corner to the back, the west side, where she was not visible from either the driveway or any of the stables.

To the west lay a fenced meadow, beyond that open grassland and a lot of darkness. Lights at two other spreads—one to the north, one to the south—were so far away they looked not like ranches but like distant ships on a vast, dark sea.

She could jump down to the backyard and try to make her way to Stable 5, far from where they were holding the employees in Stable 2. She could find a suitable mare and ride out for help.

But in a minute or two, Janis would discover her prisoner had escaped, and in three minutes every FBEI agent on the property would be hunting her. There wouldn't be time to saddle the mare. Laurie would have to ride bareback, which she could do, though there might not even be time for that.

Besides, these people were big-time bad hats, rotten enough to kill people, so they might shoot a horse out from under her if given the chance. She couldn't live with herself if she was responsible for the death of a horse.

The other alternative was to enter the house by a window of a different room and then go to a place that these invaders might not know about, where there was a phone that she could use. Her parents' bedroom was here at the back of the house. At this time of year, the upstairs windows were never locked because they were often opened for fresh air.

The bedroom was dark beyond the glass. She quietly slid up a bug screen and then the lower sash of a window.

2

Several MILES SOUTH OF THE TOWN OF BORREGO Springs, the Anza-Borrego Desert, Monday fading into Tuesday, the temperature still at seventy-nine degrees almost six hours after nightfall . . .

The valley floor in this area stubbled with mesquite and sage and nameless brush, but nonetheless ashen under a paling moon, as eerie as some dreamscape where alien terrors wait below to ascend through sandy soil as easily as sharks through water . . .

Along this lonely stretch of Borrego Springs Road, the sign stands where it was erected Monday afternoon: U.S. DEPARTMENT OF THE INTERIOR / DESERT FLORA STUDY GROUP / TRESPASSERS WILL BE PROSECUTED.

There is no desert-flora study group. Trespassers will, however, be prosecuted, though prosecution might be the least that will be done to them.

Beyond the sign is a tent forty feet on a side and ten feet high, with seven or eight people busy therein. The tent contains a communications hub through which a task force of eighty agents—already in the valley—is being organized, instructed, and tracked in the search for young Travis Hawk and his mother. Four computer workstations, manned around the clock, enable field operatives to call in the names of locals whom they determine suspicious, license-plate numbers, and other inquiries that can then be expeditiously researched through the numerous law-enforcement and government-intelligence-agency data troves to which Arcadians have access. A freezer full of pizzas and sandwiches, two microwave ovens, and a refrigerator containing bottled water and sodas provide minimum amenities, though most agents in the search party will get their meals from fast-food outlets in Borrego Springs.

Behind the tent are three large trucks. One contains tanks of propane and the generator that powers this temporary installation; on its roof, a satellite dish is canted toward the stars. The second truck provides six spacious portable toilets with sinks and running water. The third is fitted out as a dormitory offering beds for ten, though most of the agents will sleep in their vehicles as the need for rest overcomes them.

The most reasonable projection of the task-force commander and his advisers is that the boy will be found and his mother captured or killed within the next twenty-four hours.

Carter Jergen stands just outside the open zippered-flap door of the tent, in the outfall of light, staring across the highway at more pale wasteland and then dark mountains rising like a wall that make him feel as if he's in an ancient crater where a frightful mass impacted millennia ago. When he looks at the sky, the stars and moon seem menacing, as though the universe is a mechanism with a million-year cycle that, in its current repetition, is shortly to arrive at the fateful moment when an asteroid slams into this same ground, instantly pulverizing him so that no scrap of flesh or bit of bone will remain to prove he ever existed.

Of course it's not an incoming asteroid he fears. Irrationally, it's a human being, a mere hundred-twenty-five-pound woman with the looks of a supermodel.

She has proved so difficult to kill that it seems as though, while still an infant, she must have been dipped in the water of immortality, like the Trojan War hero Achilles, except that even the entire foot by which she'd been held had been submerged, leaving her without a vulnerable Achilles' heel.

After the shootout in the market, where they killed Gavin and Jessica Washington on Sunday afternoon, Carter Jergen and Radley Dubose, acting as agents of the National Security Agency but in fact serving the Techno Arcadian agenda, had called in backup to assist in the search for Travis Hawk and to prepare for what seems to be an inevitable attempt by his mother to get to her son first and spirit him out of the area to a new safe haven.

Jergen wishes they had taken the two guardians of the boy by surprise, so they could either have tortured them or injected them with control mechanisms to learn the child's whereabouts. If they have the boy, they'll have Jane. Better yet . . . kill him and thereby break her spirit beyond recovery.

Homeland has run a psychological profile of Jane Hawk. They predict a 90 percent chance that, if they catch and kill the boy, she will be so shattered by her failure to protect him, she'll kill herself, sparing them from having to face off against her.

Jergen might take more solace from the conclusions of that report if Homeland's profiles of potential foreign and domestic terrorists had not usually been woefully poor predictors of those individuals' true intentions, behavior, and prospects.

The outfall of light in which Jergen stands now abruptly diminishes to such an extent that he can be pretty sure Radley Dubose has followed him out of the tent. Dubose, the pride of Crap County, West Virginia, had been accepted into Princeton, perhaps by a chronically intoxicated dean of admissions, and had graduated no doubt by delivering, in person, a threat to disembowel the president of the university if denied a diploma. He stands about six feet five and weighs around 230 pounds, and Jergen thinks it's a sure bet that Dubose's DNA traces back to 40,000 B.C., to an early Cro-Magnon generation and an ancestor who was the first hired thug in service to the first petty dictator in human history.

Although he fills a doorway with his physical bulk and can paralyze a rabid wolf with his glower, Dubose moves with the grace of a dancer and perfect stealth. Only the occlusion of light from within the tent is a clue to his presence. Jergen can't even hear his partner breathing.

Still staring at the sky, Jergen says, "I know the valley isn't a crater, but it feels like one. Do you ever wonder if something big and fast is coming out of all those stars, some asteroid that'll make us as extinct as the dinosaurs?"

Dubose says, "The only asteroid coming down right now is me, and the only shit I'm going to make extinct is that tight-ass Hawk bitch and the little brat that popped out of her twat five years ago."

Jergen sighs. "Princeton certainly imparts to its graduates a flair for colorful expression."

"What is it with your fixation on where we went to school? You're thirty-seven. I'm thirty-five. Princeton was just a stupid thing I had to get through to go where I wanted. Do you have some kind of weird sentimental attachment to Harvard?"

As Dubose looms at his side, Jergen says, "Generations of my family's men have graduated from Harvard. It's a matter of family pride, achievement, tradition."

"There it is again, that freaky Boston Brahmin way of looking at the world. Going to classes, playing lacrosse, pledging a fraternity—none of that involves risk. And the only reward is the status you have in the eyes of the ever-fewer number of people who think Harvard is special. That's not an achievement."

"I suppose you'll tell me what is."

"Generations of my family have distilled whiskey, grown pot, sold capsules of speed and ecstasy, and never got caught. Now there you have a truly awesome tradition and achievement."

"Selling drugs to children might be a tradition, but it's not an achievement."

"My old man and uncle never sold younger than middle school. A fourteen-year-old isn't a child. Hell, that's the age of consent."

"It isn't the age of consent, not even in the darkest hollers of West Virginia."

"It used to be," Dubose says.

"Yeah, and if you go back a century or two, most places didn't even bother having an age of consent."

Dubose puts an arm around Jergen's shoulders in a gesture of unwelcome camaraderie. "Those were the days, huh? Too bad we don't have a time machine." He pats Jergen's shoulder. "We've had four hours of sleep, some terrific pizza, and enough caffeine to make a sloth hyperactive. Let's get on the hunt."

THE FORBIDDEN DOOR 167

Like the fearsome, rough beast in Yeats's poem that slouches toward Bethlehem to be born, Dubose moves toward a row of vehicles parked in darkness on the south side of the tent.

Jergen follows. "It wasn't terrific pizza. It sucked."

"Because you had that pizza for pussies, nothing on the cheese but black olives, mushrooms, some kind of fairy grass."

"It was cilantro."

"If you'd had the five-meat pizza, you'd feel fortified."

Carter Jergen winces at the memory of the gross slabs of meat and cheese Dubose consumed. In time, that festival of flesh is going to inspire a butt-horn serenade, and Jergen lacks a gas mask.

Because the masters of this revolution believe in granting perks to the agents who carry out their orders, especially as the cost of doing so is borne by taxpayers, they provide cool wheels. The pure-jazz vehicle recently assigned to Jergen and Dubose is a Hennessey VelociRaptor 6 × 6, an 800-horsepower bespoke version of the four-door Ford F-150 Raptor with new axles, two additional wheels, kick-ass off-road tires, and a long list of other upgrades. It is big, black, glossy, and fabulous.

Dubose is in possession of the keys, as he has been since they received the VelociRaptor the previous Friday evening.

"I'll take the wheel this time," says Jergen.

"What wheel is that?" Dubose wonders as he climbs into the driver's seat and pulls the door shut.

Jergen rides shotgun.

3

LAURIE LONGRIN IN THE MYSTERY OF HER PARENTS' bedroom, the faintest thread of light under the door to the hallway, draperies closed at one of the three windows, the other two offering only swaths of the black Texas-prairie night, the stars too far away to aid her vision . . .

She helped with housework and sometimes cleaned here, so she knew the layout well enough to feel along the bed, past the bench at the foot of it, on which the quilted spread was folded at day's end, and across an open area to a dresser.

Magically, the oval mirror in the dresser seemed to gather what feeble light the room contained, presenting less like a mirror than like a window into a deeply shadowed room in a parallel world, where everything had a subtle gloss and where a figure that might have been a girl or the ghost of a girl stood featureless and fearful.

What Laurie feared was failing to get out of there and up to safety before Janis Dern and Chris Whoever stopped talking about sex and death in the upstairs hall. When the vicious Dern beast returned to Laurie's bedroom, that horrible creature would realize she had stupidly allowed her captive to escape, and she'd sound an alarm. A search of the house might begin simultaneously with a search of the immediate grounds.

To the left of the dresser was a door to the master bathroom. To the right, a closet door. In the blinding dark, her trembling fingers found the lever handle on the closet door, which would make a ratcheting noise if operated too fast. She eased the handle down from horizontal. The door, if swollen, sometimes stuttered against the jamb, so she pulled carefully on it.

In the walk-in closet, she closed the door and dared to switch on the light.

Standing tiptoe, she could barely reach the loop on the end of the cord that allowed her to pull down the trapdoor in the ceiling, to the back of which was fixed a folded ladder. The heavy springs on the trap protested, but she doubted that the sound could be heard through two closed doors and as far away as the hallway. The ladder automatically unfolded its three segments as the trapdoor opened.

She clicked the wall switch and, in blackness purified of light, climbed monkeylike on all fours. She scampered into the attic, felt blindly for the recall lever in the trapdoor frame, found it, and grimaced as the three sections of rungs accordioned upward with more noise than they had made when descending to the closet floor, although perhaps still not making enough racket to draw anyone's attention. The ladder-loaded trap returned to its frame with a soft thump.

The attic had a finished floor of plywood. In this raftered darkness, which was high enough for her father to stand erect, boxes were stacked in rows: all of Christmas—except the tree—sealed in cardboard; excess books displaced from shelves downstairs; souvenirs of times and places that were too distant to be of current interest but too important to be discarded; Mother's glorious wedding dress in a zippered vinyl bag inside a cedar-lined chest. . . .

With her arms held out to the left and right, her fingertips sliding along palisades of cardboard, Laurie inched blindly forward. Her father had installed this flooring when the house was remodeled, not long before her birth; he used the best materials and secured the plywood to the joists with screws instead of nails, but here and there between the plies were small voids that squeaked underfoot.

This center aisle pretty much aligned with the second-floor hall, where Janis Dern and Chris Hornydude might still be discussing his inexplicable lust for her and her cool indifference. If enough squeaking arose in the ceiling above them, they might decide that the cause was something more than mice.

The attic received a cleaning twice a year, but dust gathered there in the interim, and Laurie disturbed it in her passage. An unspent sneeze teased her nose, and she paused to pinch her nostrils shut until the urge passed.

Only she could hear her stampeding heart, though the pounding made it harder to judge how much noise she was making otherwise.

With the sneeze quelled, she began to move again, only to press her face through the silken strands of a spiderweb that masked her from brow to chin. Startled, she paused to wipe off those sticky threads, wondering if the eight-legged architect might even now be crawling through her hair.

Stay cool. Even if a spider was in her hair, it wouldn't bite. If it *did* bite, the bite wouldn't harm her unless the biter was a brown recluse. It wasn't a brown recluse. She just *knew* it wasn't.

Suddenly from below came the voice of the beast at a volume to rattle windows—"The little bitch, the little *shit*, she's gone!"— followed by other voices and slamming doors and swift footfalls on the front stairs.

Confident that what noises she made would now be covered by the hubbub below, Laurie moved more quickly through the high dark, with her left hand still sliding along stacked boxes, but her right arm extended in front of her. She halted when her outthrust hand made contact with cold steel. She felt her way around the tight coil and entered the open spiral stairs.

The treads were padded with rubber, and the handrail kept her steady. She made only a little noise as she climbed into the round room at the very top and center of the house, where the encircling windows admitted the light of moon and stars. This space was ten feet in diameter, like an enclosed widow's walk where the wives of fishermen went to keep a lookout for their menfolk's boats at sea.

The sea in this case was the plain that stretched to every horizon, lush with tall grass, and when anyone climbed up here with dread in his heart, he came to monitor not fishing trawlers but the progress of fire. Some years the rains didn't come but the sun did, and the wind did, and the sun and the wind made dry kindling of the grass across those thousands of acres. Nature nurtured, but it also afflicted. There were times when thunder seemed to announce a storm, but the sky proved to be filled with more bang and flash than with rain, the latter falling in barely enough quantity to chase the birds to their roosts for a few minutes, while the lightning spat fire onto the plain. If the wind was fierce, the vast fields of wild grass could raise walls of flame thirty feet high, even higher, and the fire front moved as fast as a train. Owning a quantity of horses and not enough transports to move them all at once, you wanted to monitor the burning plain from a high vantage point, to know in which direction and at what pace the blaze might be advancing.

The round chamber was mostly glass, but on a shelf between two windows stood one of the eight-line hybrid phones that also served as an intercom, featuring an indicator board with labeled buttons for nearly every room in the house and for each of the stables.

Laurie was pretty sure they would search the house for her but that the search wouldn't extend to the attic. They would expect that she had fled, perhaps to mount a horse or to run out to the state highway in hope of encountering a motorist who might help.

Whatever these people were, they weren't *real* FBI. Real FBI agents didn't want to use brain implants to make slaves out of people, and they didn't tear up a kid's book collection, and they didn't promise to make you over into Little Miss Lickspittle. These FBI imposters wouldn't want the county sheriff's department showing up to check out a report of armed thugs holding hostages. Maybe they would just skedaddle.

As Laurie reached for the phone, she was struck by the thought that perhaps these intruders *were* FBI after all—FBI gone bad like in the movies, wicked and corrupt. If they had real ID and could prove to the sheriff who they were, then maybe the *sheriff* would just go away.

Or what if . . .

If some FBI agents could be so evil, maybe the county sheriff and his deputies couldn't be trusted, either. Maybe they would take her call and listen with concern and promise to come right away with sirens blaring . . . but would instead phone the hideous Dern beast or Chris Sexfiend and say, *The little bitch is in the lookout at the top of the house.* Then the FBI bad hats would come running up here and inject her, and she would have to kiss the Dern monster's ass every time she was ordered to kiss it.

Laurie stood in the dark room, gazing out at the dark plain, and all that darkness seemed to be seeping into her through her eyes and ears and nose. Although rain had fallen this season and the grass was green, she wished for fire and wind and walls of flame to scare away these hateful invaders.

Then she realized who she could trust. Firemen.

The county had several well-equipped fire stations here and there, and a network of volunteer firemen and firewomen who had undergone training. Her dad was one of them. The firemen were all good people, looking out for one another. She knew many of them, because they got together on Memorial Day and Labor Day for a picnic and games, and again for an evening celebration at a rented hall in Worstead each December.

The chief of the volunteers was Mr. Linwood Haney. His wife, Corrine, was a firewoman. They had a daughter—Bonnie Jean, better known as Beejay—who was Laurie's age. Beejay, who liked horses and motorbikes, wanted to be a Marine sniper when she grew up, and the Haneys lived only three miles away, which was just about next door, so it was inevitable, like destiny or something, that she and Laurie were friends. Mr. and Mrs. Haney would for sure believe her, and they would come with other firemen and firewomen.

Until she picked up the handset, Laurie forgot that doing so would cause a green indicator light to appear on the intercom panel beside the label marked FIRE WATCH. In fact, the same green indicator had at that instant lit on every phone in the house and the stables, just to the right of the dark buttons labeled MASTER BED and MASTER BATH.

Maybe none of these intruders had previously noticed the words FIRE WATCH on the phone boards. But if one of the creeps happened to be looking at a phone now, he'd wonder where the fire watch was and who might be using a phone at that location.

She quickly returned the handset to its cradle. The green light winked off.

For a long moment, she stood shaking, trying to think what else she could do.

Nothing. There was nothing to be done but call the Haneys, wake them, and persuade them to marshal the volunteer firemen. Be brief but persuasive. Brief enough so that maybe none of the bad-hat FBI agents would notice the FIRE WATCH light, but convincing enough that Mr. Haney wouldn't think she was pranking him and wouldn't call back to talk to her parents, thereby alerting the Dern beast and her perverted pals.

Laurie couldn't stop shaking.

She didn't like being a scaredy-cat. She *wasn't* a scaredy-cat. Just prudent. Mother said prudence was one of the greater virtues.

Horseshit. This wasn't prudence. This was gutless fear.

What would that cute Ethan Stackpool think of her if he could see her now?

She picked up the handset. Green light. She put the handset down. She picked it up. Green light. She almost put it down again, but then she entered the Haneys' number.

4

THEY CRUISE IN THE JACKED-UP VELOCIRAPTOR, lords of the night, the engine grumbling low, like the voice of some pagan animal god that, in simmering wrath, has stepped out of eternity and into time to hand down hard judgments.

Although he knows the question won't be adequately answered, from his shotgun position Jergen says, "What are we looking for?"

"Indications, signs, manifestations, clues," Dubose replies.

"And how will we know them when we see them?"

"I'm not sure how *you* will know them, my friend, but I'll see them as stains on the fabric of normalcy."

So, as sometimes he does, the hulk is going to pretend to the brilliance of Sherlock Holmes. The five hours till dawn might seem like a hundred before the sun rises at last.

County Highway S3 and Borrego Springs Road are two of the four principal entrances to the valley. Three miles south of the junction of those roads, Dubose slows as he passes a truck bearing the power company's name, which stands just off the pavement along Highway S3, as though loaded with materials and parked in anticipation of some project that will be started in the morning when a crew returns.

In fact, the truck is the property of the NSA and contains a bank of lithium batteries that will power its camera and transmitter for forty-eight hours. The camera is a license-plate scanner that reads the tags on passing vehicles that have turned off California State Highway 78 and come north toward Borrego Springs. The image of every plate will be received in real time at the Desert Flora Study Group tent, where agents keep open back doors to California's and neighboring states' DMVs, ready quickly to identify to whom each vehicle is registered.

A similar truck is parked along Borrego Springs Road, a half mile north of Highway 78. At two strategic points just inside the valley, along County Highway S22, which passes east-west through the town of Borrego Springs, other vehicles are performing the same function under different disguises.

Every car, SUV, van, truck, motor home, and bus entering the valley is scrutinized. Any smallest reason for suspicion triggers an investigation of the people in the suspect vehicle.

If Jane Hawk uses one of several unpaved tracks to enter the valley or if she comes off-road altogether in an all-wheel-drive vehicle, men positioned at key points throughout that rough terrain will surely see her. They will scope her out, report her, and relay the tracking of her from one spotter to another, until she can be intercepted and arrested when she arrives at a paved highway, if not before.

They don't believe she will get here before noon tomorrow. She will not rush in pell-mell. She'll take time to think it through, devise a plan.

Occupying the driver's seat as if it is his birthright, Radley Dubose picks at the scab that hasn't healed over an injustice that frustrates him. "These desk-jockey chickenshits we take orders from, do they have the balls to do what's necessary to take this country and make it ours? They should've let us inject every sheriff's deputy, use them to augment our forces. Then we could lock down the town and the entire valley the moment we think she's here, make it a freakin' concentration camp and grind our way through it, door to door, till we've found the bitch and the kid."

Having long ago taken it upon himself to be the voice of reason in moments when the West Virginia hillbilly wants to do surgery with a chain saw instead of a scalpel, Jergen responds in a low and even tone of voice. "There wasn't time to inject so many."

"Plenty of time," Dubose disagrees. "The new control mechanism takes just four hours to assemble in the brain."

The San Diego County Sheriff's Department maintains a substation in Borrego Springs. Immediately following the shooting of Gavin and Jessica Washington, the watch captain, a man named Foursquare, and some deputies proceeded as if they had authority to investigate. They backed off when Jergen was able to put Captain Foursquare on the phone with the deputy director of the NSA, a former United States senator who was known as a friend of law enforcement and who assured Foursquare that this was a matter of national security, though the name Jane Hawk was not mentioned.

Jergen perseveres. "Trying to overpower and inject deputies who're well armed even off duty, who're suspicious by their very nature and trained to resist aggression . . . we couldn't have taken them all by surprise. It would've gotten messy."

Mistaking his hardball tactics for brilliant strategy, Dubose says, "Yes, all right, a few maybe you can't take by surprise and inject.

Big deal. So you blow their brains out. Then you pin the deaths on Jane after she's either captured or worm food."

"And what if one of the deputies you intend to kill instead kills you?"

Looking away from the road, regarding Jergen as he might a slow-witted child, the big man says, "Like *that* could happen."

"Anyway," Jergen says, "by the time Jane is here, we'll have that little zombie army you want, all of them locals who know the area, a lot more of them than all the deputies at the substation."

Crews have been busy for twenty-four hours, identifying easy targets for injection, approaching them as FBI agents, converting them into adjusted people in the privacy of their homes. More than forty thus far.

Dubose is dismissive. "They're civilians, not in uniform; they can't openly carry guns like the deputies can."

"Not every problem can be settled with a gun," Jergen says.

Dubose favors him with that pitying look again, but before the hulk can reply, Jergen's smartphone rings.

It's from the guy manning the communications hub at the Desert Flora Study Group. Something has gone wrong at one of the houses in which injections are being administered.

5

LAURIE LONGRIN IN THE FIRE-WATCH ROOM, LIKE A bird in a glass cage, unable to fly away, unable to go down below where all the nasty cats were eager to find her and tear off her wings . . .

When Mr. Linwood Haney answered the phone, having surely been awakened from sleep, Laurie said, "It's me, Laurie, Laurie

Longrin, at Longrin Stables, terrible things are happening here, Mr. Haney." By the time she had said that much, she became a motor-mouth, words spinning from her at high speed: "They say FBI, it's a lie, they're rotten, they want Mr. and Mrs. Hawk, where they've gone, Mom and Dad tied up, this crazy woman hit me, she has a gun, all of them guns, six and six more coming, they want to kill us or worse, I'm in the fire watch, they'll find me soon, I don't trust the sheriff, I only trust you."

Mr. Haney calmed her, though she surprised herself when she interrupted him more than once with additional details of what had happened at Longrin Stables. She couldn't quite control herself. She was dismayed at the sharp fear in her voice, because she prided herself on being less of a child than some others her age, on being of sturdy Texas rancher stock.

However, it was only when she started talking to Mr. Haney that she truly realized the full extent of the danger to herself, to her parents and sisters. Oh, she'd known they were in deep shit. She wasn't stupid. But somehow she'd not let herself think clearly about the worst that might happen, maybe because thinking about it would have paralyzed her. When she told Mr. Haney that these vicious, rotten people wanted to kill them or worse, the possibility of such a horror became more real when she heard herself put it into words, *so* real that her fear flashed into fright, hampering her breathing and raising a pain in her chest, as if some demonic angler had cast a line and snared her heart with one of those fishing lures that had multiple wicked hooks.

She took hope when Mr. Haney believed her. He said, "Something like this happened at Ancel and Clare's place Sunday night. Stay calm, Laurie, stay where you are. We're coming. Everything will be okay."

Staring at the phone, at the green light burning beside the words FIRE WATCH, Laurie said, "Hurry. Please, please hurry." And she hung up.

6

FEWER THAN FOUR THOUSAND RESIDENTS LIVE IN Borrego Springs itself, a desert town that Carter Jergen finds offensive to his every sense and sensibility. The place is too warm, too dry, too dusty, the backwater of all backwaters—with only a pittance of water. Many of the palm trees appear stressed, and the only real grass of which he's aware is in Christmas Circle, a park in the center of town. There are acres and acres of concrete and blacktop and more acres of nearly barren desert that reach here and there into the town's precincts, as if the Anza-Borrego Desert is aware of this human encroachment and remains determined to reclaim everything sooner than later. He has seen neither a restaurant serving four-star French cuisine nor one of any kind in which he would want to eat, nor a motel with even half the number of stars in its rating that he would require before staying there, nor a clothing store carrying the finest designer brands. The so-called art gallery contains not one item that resembles any school of art he studied during his university days or since.

Inexplicably, the people who live here seem happy. They are friendly to an annoying extent, saying to him, a total stranger, "Lovely weather!" and "Good morning!" and "Have a nice day!"

He's been in the valley for almost thirty-six hours. If he had to live here the rest of his life, he'd go into the garage and close it up tight and start the car engine and wait to die of carbon-monoxide poisoning; indeed, he'd get down on the garage floor and suck eagerly on the tailpipe to speed up the process.

When this revolution is won, he will spend his time only in the most cosmopolitan of cities and resorts.

Maybe the citizens who live in the desiccated heart of Borrego Springs are happy because they feel greatly superior to those benighted souls who live down-valley in small clusters of residences—or even in isolated single homes—served by crudely paved or dirt roads.

Jergen and Dubose have been summoned to one of these curious neighborhoods that consists of four single-story stucco houses on spacious grassless lots along an unpaved street off Borrego Springs Road. An unmarked black Jeep Grand Cherokee blocks the entrance, manned by two Arcadians in jackets emblazoned with the letters *FBI*.

Because of an orientation meeting that they conducted Monday morning, Jergen and Dubose are known to every operative who has descended on the valley—whether they are FBI, NSA, Homeland, or carry multiple credentials. The VelociRaptor is waved through the roadblock, beyond which four more black Jeep Grand Cherokees are parked along the dead-end street, one in front of each house.

Dubose stops at the address to which they have been summoned, and they step out of the monster Ford.

On an ordinary night, this neighborhood, lacking streetlamps, would lie deep in darkness past 2:00 A.M. Now windows glow in the houses, providing enough ambient light, along with the declining moon, to see large moths capering for the delectation of bats that, with a thrum of membranous wings, swoop low and soar and swoop again, dining in flight.

Instead of a lawn, a thick layer of smooth plum-size stones surrounds the house, as though giant mythical birds, perhaps a flock of Arabian rocs, have stopped here during the night to cough up the contents of their craws. Here and there, specimen cacti rise from the hard landscaping, shadowy shapes like malformed dwarves out of some Tolkien dream.

Following Dubose along a walkway of concrete stepping squares, listening to overhead bats using their sharp little teeth to crunch the crisp bodies of flying-beetle entrées that are being served after the moth appetizers, Jergen feels ever more acutely that he is a stranger in a strange land.

One of the three agents assigned to the conversion of the people in this residence opens the door. "Ahmed al-Adel," he says, for he doesn't expect them to remember his name from the orientation meeting fifteen hours earlier. He is a tall, handsome thirtysomething son of Iraqi immigrants.

Like the others who have invaded this street with Medexpress containers filled with control mechanisms, Ahmed is clean-shaven, neatly barbered, dressed in a black suit and a white shirt and a black tie. He and the other agents came here a little more than four hours previously, at nine o'clock in the evening; but regardless of the hour, it is always easier to elicit quick, complete cooperation from people when FBI agents are dressed and carry themselves as the movies have long portrayed them.

Operating to a degree incognito, Jergen and Dubose avoid the men-in-black cliché. Jergen favors a desert-spa look: a sport coat by Ring Jacket, gray with a white micro-dot pattern; slim-cut white slacks by the same designer; gray-suede, seven-eye lace-up ankle-fit trainers by Axel Arigato. In a spirit of fun, he wears a GraffStar Eclipse ultra-slim lightweight titanium watch with an entirely black face, black hands, and black check marks instead of numbers.

Dubose, reliably a sartorial embarrassment, looks as though he just came in from plowing a cornfield and didn't completely change clothes, but threw on a couple glitzy items to add some flash for a quick trip to Vegas.

"They're in the kitchen," says Ahmed.

In these houses reside eleven people who have received nanoweb control mechanisms; they will soon be enlisted in the valley-wide search for the boy and his mother. The residents of these four homes were selected for injection because none is a child below the age of sixteen. Others have been injected before these people, and still others will be injected in the remaining hours of the night.

Their controls are the latest generation and include a feature known as "the whispering room." While activating the whispering-room feature, they can communicate via microwave transmission, brain to brain, as the celebrated Elon Musk, founder of Tesla automobiles, has predicted will one day be possible and desirable. This makes them highly effective searchers, fifty or more individuals sharing a hive mind, quickly communicating their positions, situations, and discoveries to one another.

This residence is supposed to house two people, Robert and Minette Butterworth, both in their mid-thirties—he a history teacher, she an English teacher. They are seated at the kitchen table, zip-tied to their chairs, mouths covered with duct tape, though not because there is anyone to be alerted by their cries.

Prior to the injections and during the four hours after, while the nanoconstructs foil the blood-brain barrier and assemble within their skulls, those who have been chosen to become adjusted people tend to be tedious. They demand their constitutional rights, ask insistent questions, and in general make an annoyance of themselves. Duct tape is the best cure for their tiresome prattle.

Robert and Minette are pale, wide-eyed with sustained fright, soon to be under the control of their nanowebs, but they are *not* the only residents of the house. A younger woman resembling Minette is also duct-taped and sits at the table in a wheelchair.

The two agents working with Ahmed al-Adel are here as well. Malcolm Kingman is an imposing African American with the face and demeanor of a caring man of the cloth, but the direct and filleting stare of a judge at the Nuremberg trials. Zita Hernandez, a pretty woman of perhaps thirty, rounds out an admirably diverse crew.

Hernandez is of the most interest to Jergen, not just because of her beauty. She wears exquisitely tailored black slacks, a white buttoned-to-the-throat shirt by Michael Kors, a black blazer from Ralph Lauren. The only thing she needs help with is her shoes.

Jergen would like to dress her. After undressing her.

Lovely Zita indicates the pajama-clad woman in the wheelchair. "This is Glynis Gallworth, Minette's sister. She's visiting from Alexandria, Virginia, for a week. She was sleeping in a back bedroom.

We didn't know she was there till things were well along here in the kitchen."

Jergen finds this bit of information perplexing. Alexandria is an upscale, sophisticated town. He is not able to imagine willingly leaving Alexandria to spend a week in a small house with unfortunate décor, on a dead-end dirt street in this desert wasteland.

Zita says, "Glynis is paraplegic ever since a spinal injury when she was a teenager. She works in the State Department in D.C. She's too clueless about the situation to be . . . in the know," by which she means to say, *She's not one of us.*

Glynis appears to be as terrified as her sister and the sister's husband.

"We injected them," says Malcolm Kingman, "but we're not sure if we should inject her."

"This is Arcadian 101," Dubose says.

Kingman and Ahmed al-Adel exchange a look, and then both look at Zita.

Dubose smiles at Glynis. "Ma'am, I'm sure you don't know what your sister and brother-in-law got tangled in. This is an urgent matter of national security, involving a pending act of nuclear terrorism."

The astonished Minette and Robert shake their heads and protest these outrageous charges through the duct tape.

Glynis appears both dubious and frightened, but also confused.

Dubose says, "We have an emergency FISA court order allowing a deposition to be performed with a truth serum," as if even a FISA court could order such a thing. "Your name is *not* in that court order. My associates should have known you couldn't be included in this procedure. But because the nation's survival is at stake and this involves top-secret information, we can't allow you to witness the questioning of your sister and her husband."

With that, the big man steps behind the wheelchair and rolls Glynis out of the kitchen, into the living room, and back to the bedroom where she had been sleeping.

Carter Jergen smiles at Zita Hernandez, and she holds his gaze in what seems like an expression of erotic interest.

Both Ahmed al-Adel and Malcolm Kingman flinch and grimace when the gunshot echoes from the back of the house, which does not speak well of them.

Zita, however, remains impassive even through the second and third shots. Jergen likes her a lot.

7

DEEP IN THE HEART OF TEXAS AND HIGH IN THE windowed fire watch, Laurie Longrin was up far past her usual bedtime, but she wasn't in the least sleepy. Fear affected her like a kind of caffeine, fear for herself and her sisters and her parents.

But there was something else besides fear. She stood in the grip of an exciting expectation, waiting for the firemen to roar into sight, not in a red pumper truck with its deluge gun, but in their many pickups and SUVs, the equivalent of an old-fashioned posse, come in high Lone Star style to chase out the evildoers and save the innocent.

What she felt was in fact more than expectation. Something like exhilaration. Her fear was all mixed up with this crazy wild *thrill*, a reckless confidence that butt was going to be kicked, the bad cast down, the good lifted up, the world made right again.

She wasn't a Pollyanna. She knew good didn't always triumph, not at first try, anyway. There were a megamillion ways things could go wrong. Bad people were often more clever than good people because they spent their entire rotten lives scheming and conniving.

Nonetheless, she wasn't some piss-your-pants pessimist. The fear that now and then shook a shudder from her was tempered by this electrifying current of delight in the prospect of seeing sudden justice done to these hateful thugs.

She hoped this didn't mean that she was going to grow up to be one of those thrill seekers who couldn't be happy unless they were skydiving or walking a tightrope between skyscrapers or wrestling alligators. Laurie wanted to ride horses and become a veterinarian and marry Ethan Stackpool and have maybe four children. Children and alligators were not a good combination.

When two sets of headlights, one close behind the other, turned off the state route and onto the entrance lane to Longrin Stables, the first of a freakin' *parade* of righteous firemen and firewomen, the thrill of delight swelled strong in Laurie and nearly washed away her fear. She licked her split lip, which had earlier been bleeding after the Dern beast slapped her, and she thought, *Kiss your own ass, Janis.*

One thing Laurie didn't need to be told about life was that from time to time everyone was met with disappointments, setbacks that tested your character and made you stronger if you kept your spine stiff and soldiered onward. She knew that, of course, but in her excitement she had forgotten about disappointments and had mistaken this one for triumph.

Neither of the SUVs that raced along the lane was driven by Mr. Linwood Haney or by any of his friends. They were black Suburbans, and the woman standing guard down there—the one named Sally Jones—recognized these newcomers and waved them past the Cadillac Escalade that partially blocked entrance. These were the six additional bad hats who, as Chris Pervert had told Janis in the hallway, were going to do sharp-elbow one-on-one interviews with the employees, scare the spunk out of them before sending them home.

Then no one would be here but Laurie, her sisters, her mom and dad—and twelve of *them* with their guns and their needles and their brain implants.

She stared hard into the darkness, where she knew the state route ran north and south, but there were no other headlights, no rescuers imminent.

Suddenly she realized that she didn't have the scissors with which she'd cut the zip-ties and freed herself. She couldn't remember where she might have put them down on the way from her bedroom to the fire watch. The scissors had been her only weapon.

8

WHEN RADLEY DUBOSE RETURNS TO THE KITCHEN, Minette Butterworth, wrung hard by emotion, is a swollen-faced red-eyed faucet of grief with an apparently inexhaustible reservoir of tears. Behind the duct tape, when she's not making *baaa-baaa* noises like a bleating sheep, she sounds as if she's choking on her grief, swallowing her tongue.

Carter Jergen finds the woman repellent. Excessive displays of emotion are not only undignified but are always, in his opinion, as phony as a politician's promise, a display to draw attention to the wailer and elicit from others either sympathy for her suffering or admiration for the depth of her feeling.

The husband, Robert, is beyond tears and, he would have them believe, beyond fear, as well. His eyes shine with the pure primal hatred of a maddened ape. He shouts his rage to no effect behind the swath of duct tape. He strains against his bonds and rocks the chair in which he sits.

Dubose regards this pair not with disdain, as does Jergen, but as if he is in some zoo, standing before an exhibit of two exotic animals whose droll appearance and antics he would like to have explained to him by a docent.

His interest is short-lived, and he turns to address Ahmed, Malcolm, and the lovely Zita.

"That should have been an easy call, people. In the utopia that technology is making possible for those of us who control it, do you think we ought to encourage continued production of software that's four generations old? Why? For sentimental reasons? Should we maybe keep useless workers on a warehouse payroll just so they can watch the robots do the job more efficiently after the place has been automated?"

Ahmed and Malcolm look abashed, though it's difficult to tell whether they are embarrassed by their own failure to act according to Arcadian principles or are disturbed by Dubose's comparisons of outdated software and displaced workers to Glynis.

Dubose continues. "For those who don't belong with us inside this scientific revolution, utilitarian bioethics must always apply. Society can't waste resources on those millions among the masses who receive far more than they'll ever produce. Such profligate spending has collapsed other civilizations."

The lovely Zita wishes to contribute. "Besides," she says, "it's a matter of compassion. Quality of life. It's cruel to force people who can never be whole to live in diminished circumstances."

"Exactly," Dubose agrees. "We can stop those with diminished capacities from ever being born. But we also have to show the same compassion to those who, born whole, are later broken in one way or another."

Dismayingly, Zita Hernandez is now looking at the hillbilly philosopher with undeniable erotic interest, in fact with greater intensity than that with which earlier she had seemed to regard Carter Jergen.

"For the record," says Dubose, "Jane Hawk attempted to take refuge in this house and, for whatever psychotic reason, she shot Glynis to death."

Ahmed, Malcolm, and Zita all seem to be good with that.

When their control mechanisms are in place, Minette and Robert will forget what they are told to forget and will remember whatever scenario is described to them.

Dubose lifts his chin, striking a noble pose, and says, "Carry on, people," as if he is some great general bucking up the troops or a wise and inspiring statesman equal to Churchill.

He leads Jergen out of the dismal house, into a night of flying beetles and beetle-eating bats, into the astringent smell of coyote urine rising from the surrounding stonescape. In the near distance, the pack of urinators, now on the hunt, issue shrill and eerie cries as if so maddened by the scent of prey that they must spill its blood at once or else, in a frenzy, tear themselves apart.

Dubose drives.

Although Jergen often finds his partner lacking in manners, crude, and a social embarrassment, he admires Dubose's ruthlessness and implacable intent.

"You shot her three times," he says as Dubose wheels the Veloci-Raptor away from the house.

"Yeah."

"One point-blank hollow-point didn't kill her?"

"Put it in her chest, she was stone dead."

"Then why two more?"

"Didn't like her expression."

"What about it?"

"She didn't look dead enough. Just . . . sort of sneering, smug."

"Well, she worked at the State Department," Jergen reminds him.

"Yeah, we know the type."

"So the other two shots . . . ?"

"In the face."

"Do the trick?"

"She looks more dead now."

9

JANIS DERN IS KEEPING HER RAGE IN CHECK. NO need for an anger management class. No need to take a time-out in the corner without speaking privileges. No need to be sent off to bed without dessert while Francine and her two sibling cohorts get extra-large portions of cake—thanks to Daddy's blindness to the meanness with which his precious favorite, Francine, and her two sibling toadies treat their youngest sibling. No need for anything now except a little tough love directed at one freckle-faced smart-mouthed tomboy, a little necessary discipline . . .

The six additional agents have arrived from Austin. They're at Stable 2, giving the detained Longrin employees a few lessons in respect for authority before sending them home.

They have brought a Medexpress carrier containing four control mechanisms. One for Chase Longrin, one for Alexis, and two more just in case. Once the Longrins have been injected, once nanowebs have spun securely across the surfaces and into the crevices of their brains, they'll give up Ancel and Clare's whereabouts.

Let the others worry about Ancel and Clare. Janis has a project of her own.

Although the house and stables have been searched, Laurie Longrin hasn't yet been found. The consensus is that the girl went overland, intending to intersect the state highway and flag down a motorist. The others, who seem swept up in magical thinking, believe she'll either conveniently step on a rattlesnake or be chased down by coyotes before she can get to help.

Janis pities the rattlesnakes and coyotes that try to take a bite of that poisonous little bitch.

Pedro Lobo has come over from Stable 2 and is in the kitchen, guarding Alexis, while Chris Roberts is cruising the state highway, looking for the girl, hoping she'll mistake him for a civilian and seek his aid.

Janis doesn't buy into the consensus.

The brat isn't just smart-mouthed; she's also smart. She would never go blundering into the dark, wild fields without a light, with no better plan than hoping to flag down a motorist on a lonely road long past midnight. Her very nature is to be sand in the gears, a clog in the pipe, a monkey wrench in the machinery. She's likely to hang around the property, as quiet and quick as a rat in shadows, looking for the best way to disrupt things.

The phone-intercom units in the stables have been unplugged and locked away. If the girl fled the house, not just her room, when she went through the window onto the veranda roof, she's probably hoping to sneak back inside just long enough to use a phone.

The doors are locked. The windows are now secured on both the first and second floors.

However, she might know where a spare key is hidden or might have a key of her own.

Or . . .

Or she might have left the house by one window and at once returned to it by another, aware of some hidey-hole where she could wait out a search undiscovered.

No one but Janis takes this theory seriously. Laurie is a *child*, they say. They argue that a frightened *child* would not flee a place of terror only to return to it a moment later.

But the child might do that very thing if she's something of a terror herself, has never been punished for her bad behavior, has never learned there are *negative consequences*, because her scheming and trickery are rewarded by her ignorant, deluded father.

Earlier, Paloma Sutherland, who is guarding Laurie's younger sisters, had searched the upstairs, while Sally Jones and Chris and Janis had hunted for the girl downstairs, around the house, in the garage, and in the stables.

Now Janis explores the ground floor and the second floor as though she's looking for a child half Laurie's size, as if the girl must be a contortionist who can fold herself into the most unlikely spaces. In the very back of every closet. Behind the solid doors in the bottom third of a china cabinet that features glass doors above. Under furniture with even as little as a four-inch clearance. Behind the fire screen, in the inner hearth of a fireplace. Wherever there is paneling on an inner wall, she seeks hidden latch releases that might reveal a safe or other secret space.

In the master bedroom, her attention is drawn to an incongruous object lying on the white quartz top of a mahogany pedestal dresser. Arranged just so are an antique silver tray that holds three Lalique perfume bottles with figured crystal stoppers, an antique silver brush-and-comb set, and three small porcelain figurines of Japanese women in intricately colored kimonos. Lying askew to everything else is a pair of cheap scissors with orange plastic handles.

The girl must have cut the zip-ties with scissors taken from her desk drawer. But no scissors remain in her room. Maybe she took them for self-defense.

Evidently, Paloma Sutherland never noticed the discordant scissors among all the pretties on the dresser.

Janis stares into the mother's dresser mirror as though she possesses the clairvoyant power to see her quarry's reflection when the room was dark and the girl paused here and, for some reason, put down the scissors.

The en suite bathroom offers no hiding place.

When Janis opens the door to the walk-in closet and turns on the light, Laurie isn't crouched in any corner of that space.

From the ceiling dangles a pull cord attached to one end of a trapdoor.

Paloma is the most adamant of those who believe that the girl would not have returned to the house a moment after having fled it. When she searched here, she would not have thought the attic was worth exploring. An only child, Paloma has no understanding whatsoever of the capacity for boldness and deceit of the oldest sister in a family of sisters.

The heavy springs of the ceiling trapdoor briefly groan, but the ladder unfolds to the closet floor with hardly a sound.

10

ALTHOUGH CARTER JERGEN IS GROWING ACCUStomed to grotesque sights, he is taken aback when two large, hairy spiders—he assumes they are tarantulas—shudder out of the dark and into a swath of bare earth illuminated by the headlamps of the VelociRaptor, where it is parked alongside the airstrip.

At first it appears that the hideous arachnids are proceeding in tandem, the second close behind the first, but that's because, in the harsh angled light, it is initially difficult to differentiate between their busy limbs and the elongated twitching shadows of their limbs. In fact, the second spider seems to be climbing onto the first, as if to ride it to whatever work spiders undertake at night. The first tarantula appears displeased and impatient with this impertinence, trying to shrug off the lazy, unwanted passenger. Their legs, each the size of one of Jergen's fingers, jitter and clash, so that they stagger this way and that, proceeding in such a herky-jerky fashion that they make no progress at all, but instead circle back into the darkness out of which they emerged.

On any other night, the Anza Air Park would be closed. It allows only daylight takeoffs and landings. Monday morning, however, the National Security Agency negotiated a rich five-day contract ostensibly to do emergency testing of an unspecified type of airborne day-and-night communications equipment in desert conditions, without interfering with the facility's usual business.

In fact, they will mount continuous visual surveillance of the valley while fishing from the air, within a fifty-mile radius, all conversations conducted on carrier waves assigned to disposable phones. Using an analytic scanning program customized to key words that Jane Hawk might use when speaking to her son or to whoever was currently watching over the boy, a computer aboard the aircraft can "read" conversations almost as fast as they are intercepted. When a suspect conversation is identified, that transmission can be tracked to its source and the location of the phone quickly pinpointed.

The NSA maintains such aircraft in major cities thought to be likely targets of terrorism. One has been flown here from San Diego, another from Los Angeles, and they stand now on a taxiway.

The airplanes are de Havilland DHC-6 Twin Otters with two turboprop engines. The longest runway at this desert airstrip is 2,600 feet, but the Twin Otter needs only 1,200 to take off, even less to land. In a standard configuration, in addition to a crew of two, the craft carries nineteen passengers. Customized for this unique form of surveillance, the passenger compartment provides for only four technicians and their equipment.

A tanker truck stands on a hastily poured pad of quick-cure concrete adjacent to the taxiway where the aircraft wait. It contains sufficient aviation fuel to keep the Twin Otters—which will work in four-hour shifts—in the air around the clock for three days.

Four aircraft mechanics, complete with their equipment, have been brought to the site in a sixty-foot motor home parked adjacent to the Anza Air Park terminal. It is their home for the duration, and it also houses the tanker-truck driver and a pump technician.

In addition, there is an Airbus H120 helicopter with pilot and copilot to provide aerial search and surveillance as needed.

Men are currently placing portable marker lights along both sides of the runway, one every ten feet. The markers are battery powered and can be turned on remotely when one of the de Havillands is coming in for a night landing, then switched off when the plane is safely down.

The proprietors of the air park must be pleased with the value of the contract they received, but they must also be dazzled—or at least surprised—by the size of this operation. Maybe they wonder why such "testing" couldn't have been conducted on one of the many military bases situated in desert terrain.

Wise men and women, however, know what questions should not be asked. And these days, the words *You don't want to know* are an ever more common American catchphrase.

Radley Dubose, who has been talking to the runway lighting crew, returns now to the VelociRaptor.

"They'll be done in three hours. We'll have an Otter in the air by seven in the morning."

As though this desert possesses consciousness, knows how Jergen detests it, and therefore resolves to enflame his disgust at every opportunity, it now sends the two tarantulas skittering out of the shadows once more, but this time locked in more furious combat. The ridden spider stilts erratically on its hairy legs, rushing forward, then circling in place, twitching, furious, frenzied. The bedeviled creature flings itself onto its back, whereupon it and the rider flail their ghastly legs at each other, their repulsive bodies paled by dust as fine as talcum powder. They erupt apart and onto their feet, face-to-face, and strain to their full height, en pointe and legs quivering with tension, so that it seems one or the other will now deliver a lethal bite. Then they relax and, side by side, scurry away into the darkness once more.

"What the hell was that all about?" Jergen wonders.

"Romance," says Dubose. "My friend, if you can't recognize passion when you see it, too damn much time has passed since you were last in the saddle."

11

LIKE SOME COLD HAUNT THAT HAS CROSSED OVER from the world of the dead, Janis Dern drifts through pools of shadow and amber light, under a series of conical lamps attached to the central roof beam, raising not one squeak from the plywood underfoot.

Stacked six to seven feet high, boxes wall the main north-south aisle, except where shadowed passageways intersect from the west and east. In air scented with dust and aging cardboard, the shredded webs of dead spiders hang from the rafters and quiver in a draft, like the gray and tattered flags of forgotten nations, and scattered on the floor are bright flecks of Christmas-ornament glitter sparkling red, green, gold, and silver.

Janis keeps her right hand on the pistol in her belt holster. If the tomboy initially took the scissors with her to use them for self-defense, perhaps she'd left them on the dresser because she had since acquired a better weapon. She might have taken a handgun from one of the nightstands flanking her parents' bed. She is not yet thirteen, a child who should fear firearms and who should certainly have had no training in their use. However, these days there are a great many irresponsible parents, and it is possible that the snarky little bitch knows how to stand, hold, and aim to compensate for recoil.

At first Janis approaches every intersection with exaggerated caution—until she recognizes that ahead of her an open set of steel stairs spirals up to some higher redoubt. She knows at once that the girl has gone there, that this is why the brat *didn't* flee the house for the cover of the night outside. The upper room, whatever it might be, provides something that the brat wants, some advantage, some weapon, some . . .

"Oh, shit," she says, "a phone."

No longer concerned that the tomboy is armed and lying in wait among the stacks of boxes, Janis hurries to the stairs and ascends the tight spirals like a bullet speeding through a rifled barrel.

At the top is a small room of windowed walls offering a 360-degree view of the night, a phone on a shelf between two windows, but no girl.

Suddenly a great turbulence of sound and wind arises, the many panes thrumming and, where loosely fit, rattling in their frames. Dust and chaff and dead leaves and shingle splinters are swept off the surrounding roof of the house to flail the windows as though some pestilential swarm has come out of the deep prairie night. A fierce bright shaft stabs down and sweeps across the glass, flooding the high redoubt with light and with the shadows of mullions and muntins that distort and twist their way around the room as they are harried by the passage of the beam. . . .

Janis stands astonished, pierced by a sense of the uncanny, but this disturbance of the mind and heart lasts only a moment before she realizes that a helicopter has come down fast out of the night. Following her realization, the craft appears behind the searchlight, clearing the roof by no more than twenty feet, to hover above the Escalade that blocks the entry lane. Spotlighted, Sally Jones looks up and waves at the helo, as though she assumes it represents some additional support about which she hasn't been told.

The little bitch tomboy, the deceitful smart-ass sure-to-be-one-day-*whore*, used the phone here, called in someone. Not the county sheriff. There's no law-enforcement designation on the helo. Whoever these bastards are, they believe what bullshit the snot-eating geek told them, so they come roaring in like a brigade of Texas Rangers. This is shaping up to be another version of the fiasco at the Hawks' ranch on Sunday night, when that sonofabitch Juan Saba, the ranch manager, stood them off.

Abruptly Janis remembers that she told Laurie Longrin about the brain implants in some detail. The injections. The nanoconstructs. How they penetrate the blood-brain barrier. How they assemble into a web across and into the tissue of the brain.

All that is something Jane Hawk clearly knows, but it's not something that anyone in the conspiracy is authorized to reveal to others. Janis wanted to terrorize the freckle-faced potato-sucking piglet, and she figured to get hold of a control mechanism later and inject the little rat—or, failing that, to lobby Egon Gottfrey to have the injected parents eventually kill the children and then themselves—so that what she revealed to Laurie wouldn't matter.

Now it matters.

She needs to find the girl. Quick.

12

THE DARK TEXAS PLAIN INFINITE IN APPEARANCE. The sky overhead infinite in fact. Chris Roberts in his radically hot, bespoke Range Rover by Overfinch North America. On top of the world, an insider in the most powerful cabal of insiders in all history, Techno Arcadian fighter for Utopia, one of the rulers of the ruled, destined to live forever—*Infinite! Eternal!*—if medical technology progresses as it has done in recent years. Puff Daddy on the CD deck. *So hard-ass cool!* Chris singing along with Puff Daddy like he did when he was thirteen, so long ago. Puff Daddy and Faith Evans. *So hot, pure sex!* Thinking about shacking up with Janis Dern for a torrid week . . .

He is cruising back and forth on the two-lane state highway, all that lonely blacktop to himself at this late hour. He hopes the Longrin kid will appear on the shoulder of the road, but thus far she remains missing.

His attention is drawn to the running lights of a helicopter approaching from out of the northwest. In even small cities these days, policing is done by air as well as on the streets, and the sight of an airborne patrol spotlighting a fleeing fugitive's car as it races recklessly along a freeway is common stuff on the evening news. In the hinterlands like this, however, the skies are usually quiet at night. Chris intuits trouble in this aerial apparition.

The chopper crosses the highway ahead of him, on a trajectory that will take it directly to Longrin Stables. At an altitude of maybe three hundred feet, in the dark, any identification that might be on the aircraft can't be seen.

When he returns his attention to the road, oncoming headlamps have materialized. They quickly grow larger, brighter, issuing from the direction of Worstead. In a moment, he can see it's not just one vehicle but a caravan. They flash past him like a pack of NASCAR competitors in a tight formation toward the finish line: two, three, five, seven, nine, ten, eleven vehicles, mostly pickups and SUVs, a couple cars.

The timing of the helicopter and the cars isn't coincidental. And there aren't that many places they could be going in this empty country. At this hour, at their speed, the *only* place they can be headed is Longrin Stables.

No more oncoming headlamps appear.

Chris brakes, hangs a hard U-turn, and switches off the music. By the time he reaches the Longrin property, the eleven cars are parked along the private entrance lane, this side of the blocking Escalade, where Sally Jones and a few new agents from Austin engage in a confrontation with a crowd of local men and women. Chris parks athwart the lane to prevent an easy exit by this self-appointed posse. He gets out of the Range Rover and moves toward the crowd, his right hand on the pistol in his belt holster.

13

In THE ATTIC, AT THE END OF ONE OF THE ROWS OF stored goods, Laurie Longrin knelt with her back pressed against the stacked boxes, out of sight of the main aisle.

She'd wanted to remain in the fire watch until Mr. Linwood Haney arrived with other firefighters and the threat posed by the Federal Bureau of Evil Idiots had come to an end. But when the six agents from Austin arrived first, she was kind of spooked. And when she realized that she didn't have the scissors with which to defend herself, a sense of helplessness overcame her. All the windows in the fire watch made her feel naked and vulnerable, though as long as she stayed low, no one on the ground below could see her. Then she realized where she must have put down the scissors: on her mother's dresser, just before moving to the walk-in closet. She decided to go back and get them and return to the fire watch.

Feeling her way in the dark, she'd been almost to the trapdoor when someone pulled it open from below. Closet light rose into the attic, and the ladder unfolded to accommodate whoever might be coming up.

Laurie had hurried back toward the spiral staircase but then realized the fire watch would be a trap. So she came to the end of this row of boxes and knelt there, a narrow aisle to either side of her, but hidden from anyone in the main passageway.

No sooner had she gotten out of sight than the lights had come on. She strained to hear footsteps, detected none. Then the voice of the Janis beast broke the silence—"Oh, shit, a phone!"—and the woman was so close that Laurie almost cried out, for an instant certain that Janis saw her and was speaking directly to her.

Then there were hurried footsteps, and it seemed as though the sulfur-eyed queen of Hell must be climbing the spiral stairs into the fire watch.

Laurie considered easing out of her refuge and hurrying to the trapdoor and down the ladder, to hide somewhere below, where they had already searched. Just as she was about to get off her knees, however, the very skeleton of the big attic—roof sheeting, rafters, collar beams, outriggers, studs—vibrated as hard rhythmic blasts of sound slammed through it. Gusts of wind hissed as they strained through the fine-wire screens over the ventilation cutouts in the eaves, blowing dust off the boxes, tearing the raggedy webs of long-dead spiders from their moorings and billowing them past her like eerie sea anemones. Pinching her nose shut against the tickling dust, breathing through her mouth to avoid sneezing, she stayed on her knees half a minute until she realized that the source of the uproar must be a helicopter, first passing over the house and now hovering near it, whereupon she sprang to her feet in excitement.

Mr. Glenn Alekirk, a local volunteer fireman and once a helo jockey in the navy, owned a four-seat Robinson R44 Raven, with which he surveyed field conditions on his large ranch, made day trips to Austin and San Antonio, and visited in-laws in Uvalde. If this was Mr. Alekirk, the firemen and firewomen were coming with a dramatic display of force, and Laurie was no longer at risk of becoming the puppet and pet of crazy Janis.

She almost stepped into the aisle to her left, but then she realized that her tormentor, having found the fire watch deserted and probably startled by the arrival of the helicopter, would head back to the trapdoor and the ladder. With all the racket, Laurie couldn't be sure where the woman might be. Better to hunker down and wait a few minutes. She sat on the floor with her back to the boxes. The helo kept chugging nearby. She knew that everything would be all right soon. Very soon. Yet her stomach still fluttered. Her heart knocked hard like a fist on a door. The sound of the rotary wing chopping the night air, which had at first been scary and then had been reassuring, began to seem scary again.

14

F*UDDA-FUDDA-FUDDA-FUDDA-FUDDA*, THE CHOP-per noise like the sound made all those years ago when, time and again, Francine had knocked Janis down and knelt on her chest and boxed both her ears with the flat palms of the hands, *fudda-fudda-fudda-fudda-fudda*, until Janis couldn't think straight and the headache came and then tinnitus that continued for hours after the assault concluded . . .

The spiral staircase is like some churning drill bit, so that Janis feels less like she's descending than like she's caught up in the bore and being pulled down, each step like a cutting nub on the shank of a bit, her feet skidding from step to step in spite of the rubber treads, the cold railing vibrating under her hand, the whole construction seeming to turn around her with carnival-ride frenzy.

Fudda-fudda-fudda . . .

At the bottom, feet on the attic floor, she stands for a moment, swaying, dizzy, the chopper noise drilling fear into her, although she had thought herself long past fear.

The unceasing clatter isn't just the sound of this operation at Longrin Stables falling apart, but seems also to be the crack and clatter of her future collapsing. She has screwed up with the little bitch tomboy, let her get away, gave her a chance to call for help, and a mistake of this magnitude does not result in just a slap on the wrist or a boxing of the ears.

Arcadian discipline is swift and severe, which it must be to keep a secret like the nanoimplants from being leaked. If a failure is judged damaging enough to the revolution, then her future will be sealed with a needle, a catheter, and the infusion of three ampules of cloudy amber fluid. Thereafter she will do what she's told to do, be what she is told to be, ever submissive. Perhaps she'll be given to some disgusting Arcadian techno geek to be sexually used and humiliated and physically abused until she ages ten years in one, then strangled and bagged like garbage and thrown away.

Her dizziness doesn't entirely pass, but she begins to move anyway. She's got to find the devious little shit, find her and bind her. There is a way to use the brat to fix this situation. There *must be* a way.

The problem is locating the mocking midget bitch in time. Whatever chaos the helicopter brings with it, if a mob is here in the numbers that came out of Juan Saba's house, the girl can't be allowed to escape among them.

Halfway between the spiral stairs and the trapdoor, several inches within one of the side aisles, lies a spider. Once fat and juicy, it is now deformed in a wet blot of what once had been its internal substance. Recently tramped on.

Janis has never stepped foot in any of the side aisles. She has proceeded to and from the spiral stairs using the main aisle.

It can't be Janis who stepped on the spider.

And the glistening ichor in which it lies attests to the truth that it hasn't been dead for days.

Her attention seems to have been drawn to the squashed spider by some supernatural power, for it is but a dark blot on the light plywood and could be so easily overlooked. She stands transfixed, trembling as the structure around her is trembled by the *fudda-fudda-fudda-fudda-fudda* . . .

15

THE CONFRONTATION AT THE CADILLAC ESCALADE, where Sally Jones and three of the agents from Austin face a crowd of maybe thirty people, is not good. Chris Roberts judges the situation to have a low flashpoint.

The helicopter moves off a little, hovering over the fenced exercise yard, but it is still loud enough to require those engaged in this tense dialogue to raise their voices. They are shouting back and forth. The volume of the conversation only fuels an expectation of violence. The helo's searchlight is trained on the four agents, a crisp white beam that pales them and carves their faces with stark shadows, giving them an ominous aspect that only further unnerves the mob.

Sally and two men from Austin are flashing FBI credentials, making a case for their authority. But the locals—men and women—are not impressed and are in no mood to back down. They want to see arrest warrants, search warrants, which they have no right to see, because this doesn't have anything to do with them.

The most troubling thing is the name they keep citing—*Jane, Jane Hawk, Jane, Jane, Jane Hawk*—because they understand this has something to do with her, with her in-laws, and with the fact that Chase Longrin and the late Nick Hawk were once best friends. They don't speak of Jane Hawk as though she's a traitor to her country and a threat to national security, not as if she's a murderer, but as if she's a victim of slander and libel.

Indeed, more concerning to Chris is that some of these people speak of her not just with the affection that she might earn merely by being one of their own, but with admiration and even veneration. It's as if, by foiling the entire apparatus of the all-powerful state that's been pursuing her for months, she has ascended to the mystical status of a folk hero.

They demand to see Chase and Alexis and the children. They want to know why the employees are being held. They have no right to see anyone or have any questions answered, and they surely know as much. They are intruders here. They are being told they're engaged in the obstruction of justice, but they aren't going to go away. This is quickly becoming a standoff that may go on for days . . . unless it becomes something worse.

The youngest of the Austin agents doesn't bother to shake his badge at the angry crowd. He draws his pistol, holding it against his chest, as if pledging allegiance to it, which is foolish and likely to inflame passions. Some of the people in the crowd are openly armed, but their weapons are in their holsters. Those who don't obviously carry firearms might have them concealed. In this atmosphere, brandishing a gun is like striking a match in the dark to find the source of a gas leak.

Chris Roberts works his way around the mob, toward the wet-behind-the-ears agent to tell him to get a grip and put the gun away. After all, they *are* operating far beyond the limits of the law, by the rules of a thugocracy, the Constitution be damned—and there are risks to that approach. They have friends in high places, yes, and judges who will protect them, yes, and friends in the media who will do their best to bury an embarrassing story, but maybe not if a shootout results in a lot of people dead and others wounded.

16

LAURIE LONGRIN THOUGHT MAYBE IT WAS SAFE TO move. If the Janis monster had not by now gone downstairs and outside to meet whatever contingent of firemen and firewomen had arrived, then surely she'd gone back to the Black Lagoon or Transylvania, or to whatever hole in the ground she called home.

Rising once more to her feet, her back pressed to the stacked cartons at row's end, she took a deep breath, held it, listened. The helicopter moved off a little way, and the attic no longer trembled under it, but the noise from its engine and rotary wing remained loud enough to mask most other sounds.

She didn't want to hide like this. She felt childish and weak. She hadn't been born to hide from trouble. Daddy said you couldn't hide from trouble anyway, that the trouble you were hiding from would find you sooner or later, and while you were hiding from it, the trouble was getting bigger, so that when it finally found you, it was harder to deal with than if you'd just faced up to it in the first place.

So she turned to her left and leaned forward and peered into the aisle. From a distance of less than two feet, she met the eyes of Janis Dern. Even beneath a veil of shadow, something about the woman's face was different from what it had been, distorted by terror or hatred or both, like an early version of the human face before it was refined and the species was put into production. A faint trace of the amber attic light found its way into those fierce eyes, coloring them more yellow than usual, so that they appeared electrified and incandescent.

Her voice was a vicious whisper: "*My little pet.*"

Before Laurie could respond, the yellow-eyed freak jabbed her with something. Even through her T-shirt, she felt the two cold points of pressure. Buzzing, both sound and sensation, filled her from muscle to marrow, and disabling pain crackled across the soles of her feet and across her scalp and everywhere in between. She lost all control of her body and went to the floor as if her bones had melted in an instant. She heard herself making wordless sounds of distress as she spasmed like some fish hooked and reeled in and lying on a riverbank, forever beyond hope of water.

17

F*UDDA-FUDDA-FUDDA.* THE SOUND SOFTER NOW, though still bringing vividly to mind the torture of hands clapping her ears, the pressure of Francine's knees on her chest, her heart compressed as the breast bone bends under the weight . . .

While the little whore is paralyzed, Janis sets aside the handheld Taser and takes a bundle of zip-ties from an inner pocket of her sport coat. She uses one tie to cuff the slut's hands.

"You're gonna get what you deserve," she declares. "You're done, you're finished, you're gonna get just what you've always deserved."

The girl recovers enough to kick out at her, trying for her face, landing a feeble blow on her shoulder.

Infuriated, Janis snatches up the Taser and jolts the little tart again, puts it right on her throat and watches her face convulse and her eyes roll back in her head.

She uses three more zip-ties to fetter the girl's ankles to each other, allowing just enough play in those shackles for the brat to shuffle along but not run.

18

MOTHS ABANDONING THE BORING GLOW OF house windows and driveway lampposts, drawn to the bright shaft, swirling up toward the source as if the searchlight is a tractor beam that levitates them through the night and into some extraterrestrial vessel . . .

As the crowd grows noisier and more insistent, Sally Jones is unable to placate them with reassurances of legal process, and the young agent from Austin doesn't want to put away his gun.

"Hell, look at them," he tells Chris Roberts, "they're not just a bunch of hick farmers. They're roughscuff, rabble with an entire freakin' gun store inventory among them, *and they're photographing us with their phones.*"

"All the more reason not to be photographed breaking Bureau protocol and brandishing a gun."

"If the shit hits the fan and bullets fly, you want *your* face all over the Internet?"

"The Internet isn't the Wild West anymore," Chris says. "We've got laws, we've got a boot on it."

"Yeah, maybe, but we don't have a chokehold on it."

"We've also got high-placed friends on the private side," Chris insists. "Anything gets posted from this tonight, it'll be taken down within the hour, even quicker. They can make it so you google *Longrin Stables* and it's like the place never existed."

The young agent shakes his head, scanning the crowd for the first indication that the worst is about to happen. "I don't like being photographed, not here, not like this, don't like it at all."

19

THE OBNOXIOUS LITTLE SLUT DOESN'T WANT TO GET to her feet. She isn't cool with the way the tables have turned. She acts as though she's still disoriented, too loose-limbed to stand and walk, but it's just an act, pretense, deceit. She *lives* to deceive. She's the bitch queen of deception. Everything she ever says is a lie, and Janis doesn't buy a word of it.

"Get your ass in gear, get on your feet," Janis orders, looming over her. "Get up or I'll Taser your hateful face. I'll make you bite on it, and I'll Taser your lying tongue. You want to take a jolt through that dirty little tongue of yours?"

The threat works. The girl struggles to her feet and stands swaying. There's such contempt graven on her face. But when hasn't there been? That's among the primary identifying qualities of her type: conceit, vanity, arrogance, and the never-ending contempt of one who sees herself above all others.

The shuffling girl weaves along the central aisle, across oval pools of light and bridges of shadow, toward the trapdoor and the ladder, bumping against the walls of boxes, pretending still to be suffering residual effects of the Taserings. By clambering to her feet after claiming that she could not, the little slut has proved her weakness is mere pretense, and yet she can't stop pretending, because guile and trickery are no less components of her blood than is plasma.

"Move, move, damn you," Janis orders, prodding the treacherous little whore.

Backing down the ladder, clutching the side rails, the girl hesitates to place each foot, as though her spatial awareness remains disrupted by the shocks she has taken.

When the cunning little sleaze is halfway down, Janis follows, but she doesn't turn her back on her captive. She knows too well the danger of letting the bitch get behind her. Instead, she faces forward, perches on the trapdoor frame, and then sits from one step of the ladder to the next.

Below Janis, three steps from the bottom, the girl looks up, hair hanging across her face, one eye revealed and bright with calculation.

Before the hateful little weasel can try whatever trick she has conceived, Janis kicks out, booting her in the chest, knocking her backward onto the closet floor.

Off the ladder, Janis grabs a fistful of the brat's T-shirt and yanks on it. "Come on, come on, you little shit, you'll never win an Oscar with a performance like this."

She harries the girl to her feet, out of the closet door, into the master bedroom, and shoves her toward the door to the upstairs hallway.

A girl such as this has a bottomless capacity for treachery, which she proves again when, shuffling past her mother's dresser, she grabs for the scissors that she left there earlier.

Janis anticipates this rebellion. As her captive reaches for the weapon, she boots her in the backside.

The foolish girl staggers forward and, trammeled by the zip-ties, trips herself and falls to her knees.

Janis sweeps the silver brush-and-comb set off the dresser, onto the floor, and then the silver tray with the three small Lalique perfume bottles. She picks up one of the porcelain geishas with its colorful kimono and throws it at the girl. Then the second. The third. She snatches up the scissors.

"Get up, you little sleaze. *Get up, get up!* I'm not going to be injected because of you. I won't be made a slave. Get up or I'll Taser you until you swallow your tongue and choke to death on it."

20

HAVING LOCKED THE EMPLOYEES IN STABLE 2 WITH only Alejandro Lobo to look after them, the other three Austin agents step out of the darkness into the searchlight, bringing the number at the front line of the confrontation to eight, making a show of force that might dissuade the armed posse from pushing this too far.

Chris Roberts hopes that one of the three has had the wit to call for additional backup. Even if more Arcadians are en route, however, the odds are they won't get here in time to stop these rednecks from doing something stupid.

Sally Jones, thus far the only spokesperson for the government in this matter, understands the need to appear equal to the threat of the crowd. She shouts at the restive mob for quiet. "Eight more of us inside the house, four in the stables," she lies. "We came here in serious numbers because this damn well *is* an urgent matter of national security, whether you want to believe us or not. The future of our country is at stake. I know you're all patriots here. I know you want to do the right thing. Think before you do something you'll regret. Many of you probably have children at home. Think about them. You don't want to do anything that leaves those kids without a family. They need you."

"Is that a threat?" shouts a man in the mob. "You mean to shoot us down like we're animals?"

Sally raises both hands in a gesture of placation. "No, no, no. I'm saying we're engaged in legitimate law enforcement here. Anyone who interferes with us will have to be charged according to their offenses and prosecuted to the full extent of the law. There's no way around that. To the full extent of the law. Your babies back home will be without you for a long time. Doing prison, you'll stain yourself *and them,* your family name, their reputation. All for what? All because you've been misinformed."

A man who previously identified himself as Linwood Haney, and who seems to be the leader of this rabble, speaks up. "Bring Chase and Alexis out here, them and their three girls, so we can ask 'em is all this righteous police work like you say."

"We can't do that," Sally says. "You don't understand. Chase and Alexis have agreed to cooperate with us in return for immunity. They're in the middle of giving depositions, under oath. It would compromise the integrity of the deposition process to interrupt the continuity of the recording, and *that* would jeopardize Chase and Alexis's immunity, which is the last thing they would want, believe me, the *last* thing."

Chris winces at this response to Haney. Sally talks down to the crowd, as though she thinks their kind are as ignorant and clueless as the stereotypical hayseeds with which some in the media believe "flyover country" is entirely populated.

Sure enough, a woman shouts an objection. "You sayin' their lawyer is in there with them at this ungodly hour? Hell's bells, woman, their lawyer is Rolly Capshaw. Old Rolly goes to bed eight-thirty every night, sure as the flag has stars and stripes. He won't stay up till three in the mornin' like this even if he knows for a fact it's the night Jesus is comin' back."

Among the crowd, there is considerable agreement with this assessment, and Linwood Haney says, "There won't be a damn thing righteous about any deposition taken without they're allowed a lawyer."

21

THE CLATTER OF THE HELICOPTER IS MORE MUFFLED in the upstairs hallway than it had been in the attic. But as the deceitful little whore pretends that her fettered ankles require slow progress on the front stairs and as Janis prods her to move faster toward the foyer below, the rhythmic pounding of the blades grows louder again.

The sound echoes inside Janis's skull, and a headache grows, and the shells of her ears burn as if abused by the clapping hands of her vicious sister, and though she's standing up, she feels the weight of her long-ago tormentor on her chest.

In the foyer, she jerks the girl around to face her and is satisfied to see stark fear instead of arrogance. "You listen to me, you worthless little slut. Damn if I'm going to have my brain spun up in a control web *because of you*. I'd as soon kill you as spit on you, so the time for trickery is over. *It's over*. I'm going to cut the zip-ties, and I'm taking you out there on the porch, and you're gonna tell these stupid shitkickers you were wrong to call them. Tell them you didn't understand what was really happening here. You're going to give the performance of a lifetime, and don't tell me you can't, because I know your kind. You're just like her. Deceit is woven through your bones. Your tongue is a filthy, licking lie machine. You can be as bratty as you want and get away with it because of what you do for your daddy, like what she did for ours, the sleazy little whore. I know the truth, I saw them that one time, *and I know you.* You're going to stand close to me, lean against me, like you feel safe with me and I'm your best friend ever, stay close so no one can see I'm holding you by the back of your belt. You're going to smile and charm and lie your ass off. You're going to send these shitkickers home, or I swear I'll draw my gun and shoot you in the head, right there on the porch, blow your rotten whore brains all over the damn porch."

22

CHRIS ROBERTS DOESN'T REALIZE THAT JANIS HAS come out of the house with the girl, Laurie, until the helicopter co-pilot sweeps the bright beam away from the line of agents and splashes light across the front veranda.

Disaster.

Whatever the hell Janis thinks she's doing, it's going to end in disaster.

Something's wrong with her. She's always ardent, intense, edgy, but this is not that Janis. This Janis is a human grenade with her pin half pulled. Her shoulders are drawn up, head turtled down. Her alluring body is shorn of curves, by tension shaped into the crossed staves of a scarecrow. Her eyes appear sprung in their sockets like those of some goggle-eyed jack-in-the-box. Her smile is a ghastly slash, and if her face contains any color, the searchlight bleaches it to the pallor of a corpse.

The child beside Janis stares out from among wild tangles of disarranged hair. She stands with hands fisted at her sides. Her posture is that of a shocked ledge walker who missteps and is supported for a microsecond by thin air, who stands in the splinter of an instant between the end of the ledge and the beginning of the plunge.

As one, every member of the crowd falls silent, and there is just the beating of the chopper's blades, like the tolling of a lead bell.

Janis raises her voice. "Laurie Longrin wants to apologize." She punctuates her announcement with a smile like a sickle.

23

FUDDA-FUDDA-FUDDA-FUDDA-FUDDA . . .

With her left hand, Janis Dern grips the little whore's belt, preventing her from making a break for the crowd. The thumb of her other hand is hooked on her own belt, at her right side, so that in an instant she can push her sport coat out of the way and draw the pistol from her hip holster.

The searchlight shouldn't be either hot or cold. It's merely a light. But it makes the painted porch floor glisten like ice, and it chills Janis. It cuts at her eyes. She can't look directly at it.

By the time she and the punk reach the porch steps and stop, the crowd of would-be rescuers falls silent. They stand expectant, some with their mouths open, their faces as dull as those of cattle. They are all as common as dirt, and Janis can never be one of them; never has been, never will be. She has known herself to be above the ruck and rabble since she was nine, since the day she saw Francine on her knees, submissive and servicing that bastard in the way that he preferred, both of them as base as barnyard animals. In that instant, she knows she is not of their blood. The story of their family is a lie. Surely she was born to parents unknown, a husband and wife of the highest station, and soon after birth was kidnapped, sold into this squalid household, for the use and amusement of base and cruel people. Shortly after seeing him with Francine, Janis is alone with their so-called father, and though he doesn't come on to her, she tells him that if she is in line behind her sisters to do what Francine does for him, she will bite it off, bite off what she can and spit it out and bite off more. She doesn't belong in that family. She doesn't belong among these people here tonight, either, and she is too high-born ever to belong among the "adjusted people" who have in their heads a web of a thousand filaments with which their betters manipulate them through the puppet theater of their lives.

Now she smiles at the girl beside her and smiles at these up-turned faces.

This duplicitous little bitch has the skill to deceive the finest lie detector. The brat better con these cretins and send them home to their beds, because if this crisis can't be smoothed away, there is a brain implant with the name *Janis Dern* on it. Janis will not tolerate being injected, reduced to the condition of property. At thirty, she is perhaps too old and not sufficiently beautiful to be stocked in one of the Aspasias, but she will not allow herself to be made property of any kind, for any purpose.

Aspasia is the name of the mistress of some famous mayor of Athens 2,400 years ago, and it is what they call the palatial, highly secret, membership-only brothels in Los Angeles, San Francisco, New York, and D.C. where the Techno Arcadians with the greatest wealth and power go to indulge their most extreme desires. Not common whorehouses. Mansions of exquisite architecture. Decorated with tens of millions of dollars' worth of art, antiques, and furnishings. Palaces of style and refined taste that make it possible for the members of the club to tell themselves that their sickest and most degrading desires are in fact as elevated as the elegant environment. The girls are stunning, each one as beautiful as the most striking supermodels, each one a perfect daughter of Eros. Totally submissive. Ready to satisfy the most extreme desires.

There is no demand they will refuse. Charming, seeming to be happier than angels, they live in Aspasia and never leave, never even have a desire to leave, not one passing impulse to be free. The injections administered to them are different from those used to make "adjusted people." This ultimate nanoimplant deletes every last one of the girl's memories. Deletes her entire personality and installs a new and much simpler one. She becomes a living toy. The process cannot be reversed. Who she was is gone forever.

Janis has been in the Aspasia that is outside Washington, D.C.

Because she is judged to be a fervid revolutionary, beyond all doubt devoted to the cause, she was allowed to go there as a guest of a man who is a member.

The experience haunts her dreams and motivates her to rise in the hierarchy of Techno Arcadia until she is beyond any risk of being punished with injection.

Now she smiles again at the girl beside her and again at the upturned faces of the rescuers, who seem almost to be a different species from her own.

She says, "Laurie Longrin wants to apologize."

The man who took her to the Washington Aspasia is a hugely successful entrepreneur, Gregory, with whom she conducts an intense on-again-off-again affair, which is one way that she ascends the Arcadian ladder. She had heard whispers of the brothels, rumors so vague they weren't credible. Sex with Greg is vigorous, interesting, and . . . edgy. With sly amusement, he sometimes calls himself Jekyll and Hyde, but it turns out there is some truth in this. She had seen only Jekyll, and he wanted her to accompany Hyde to Aspasia, not to participate but only to watch. Among other things, Gregory is an exhibitionist. And he felt that it would be interesting if, when Janis is in the future bedded with Jekyll, she would have in her mind the threat of Hyde. That night at Aspasia, for more than four hours, Gregory indulged in a demonic catalogue of depravities; he subjected the Aspasia girl—who had but a single name, Flavia—to degradations of which Janis never previously conceived. He didn't stab Flavia to death at the moment of his last climax of the night, but later he suggested to Janis that the girl would have received the knife with a smile if he had wished to go that far and pay the charge required to dispose of her remains and install another girl in her quarters.

The revolution must be won, and Janis is determined to be one of those at the apex of this techno utopia, for otherwise there is no refuge for her in this world, no safety, no surcease from fear.

The freckle-faced bitch stands beside her, not immediately responsive to Janis's introduction.

With the hand that is behind the girl, Janis twists Laurie's belt, pinching her waist as a reminder that the little whore's position is precarious.

She repeats, "Laurie Longrin wants to apologize. She called you out here because she misunderstood the situation."

The deceitful slut clears her throat, smiles, and waves at the crowd, which Janis thinks is a clever touch, a convincing gesture.

"This nice lady," says Laurie Longrin, raising her voice to compete with the chopper but letting no quiver of fear taint her words, "this nice lady would like you to leave, and if you leave, she'll kill me."

The stupid bitch has no common sense, no survival instinct. With her last three words, she tries to pull away, but she can't wrench free of her captor's grip.

Janis draws the pistol, jams the muzzle against the girl's temple.

The crowd reacts and some of them start forward.

"Her death's on you!" Janis shouts. "One more step, and I'll blow her brains out. I chambered a round before I came out here, I've got some pull on the trigger, it's a hair away from discharge, her brains'll be all over your stupid faces."

What now, what now? No refuge, no safety, no surcease from fear. Rejection, submission, enslavement, endless degradation. No pleasure left except to kill the hateful little shit.

24

CHRIS AND SALLY AND THE SIX FROM AUSTIN EASE back from their confrontational stance, separating themselves from the mob as well as from Janis Dern. Too many guns, too much emotion. No way this can end in a truce. Every action that Chris and his crew take from now on must be calculated to reduce the number of casualties on their side.

This is not his familiar partner, not the Janis with whom he's worked for more than two years. There has been a dangerous fault line in her, some San Andreas of the mind, waiting for the right kind of stress to quake her. You think that you know a colleague's mind and heart, know her far better than your sister, but maybe no one ever really knows the truth of anyone.

The helicopter's searchlight evidently can be powered higher with the twist of a switch, because abruptly the beam doubles in brightness as it narrows in diameter, leaving a portion of the veranda in soft shadow even as it focuses on Janis and Laurie with such blazing intensity that it seems capable of setting them aflame, and the moths adance within it flicker like sparks rising from some infernal fire under the earth.

The girl shields her eyes with one hand, and Janis shouts at the chopper pilot, who of course can't hear her.

The young Austin agent beside Chris says, "The crazy bastard wants to save her, but he'll get her killed instead."

It's one of those occasions when Death plays games with the living, just to impress upon them that no one is immune from the touch of his fleshless fingers, not even freckled little girls.

Infuriated, driven by emotion rather than reason, with a one-hand grip, Janis takes an unlikely distance shot at the chopper.

The double crack of two guns echo together through the night, which is when Chris Roberts realizes the copilot at the open door must also be a well-trained sniper, perhaps former military.

No one is immune, not even freckled little girls—or those who would kill them.

Before Janis can bring the muzzle of the pistol back to the hostage's head, she receives a bullet of her own, a round of such high caliber and velocity that her skull comes apart like a hollow pumpkin in which Halloween pranksters have put a few cherry bombs, swatches of her hair in flight like strange wet birds borne out of some grim dream. Janis collapses as she's flung backward, and the screaming girl bolts down the steps into the yard, flailing her hands in her hair as if to chase off a swarm of bees, screaming to her knees, and thereafter sobbing.

25

AT 4:10 A.M., IN THE BEDROOM OF HIS SUITE IN THE Hyatt Regency Hotel, Egon Gottfrey is awakened by the ringtone of his smartphone. The script requires him to be at once alert, and he sits up in bed, wide awake after less than four hours of sleep.

From his immediate Arcadian superior, he receives a report of the events at Longrin Stables: Janis Dern dead following a psychotic episode; a tense standoff that could have led to additional deaths but did not; a negotiated exit by all the agents involved, whereby they do not acknowledge wrongdoing of any kind; an agreement by the mob of vigilantes not to question the validity of the agents' FBI credentials as long as they depart at once and permanently; an understanding that there will be no prosecution of the sniper or vengeance of any kind against him; and adequate steps being taken by private-sector Arcadians to prevent Internet distribution of any vigilante account of these events or photographs of the agents involved.

Considering the Unknown Playwright's usual style and narrative tendencies, this is surely not the way he intended this scene to be performed. Consequently, based on past experience, Gottfrey assumes that characters who were supposed to be administrators of pain will find themselves recipients of it, so that they might learn to intuit the intentions of the author more accurately.

Evidently, the Playwright has given up entirely on the learning ability of the Janis Dern character.

However, Gottfrey finds it difficult to believe that he himself will be blamed and made to suffer for this deviation from the script when he wasn't even present for the action. He has been harried from Worstead to Killeen to Houston and has neither failed to follow the leads given him nor complained about the demands that the story has put upon him. *Go with the flow. Nothing is real, anyway.*

Subsequent to the report of the debacle at Longrin Stables, the caller reveals that agents have been following up on the many buses that departed the Houston terminal during the period when Ancel and Clare Hawk might have been stowaways, and that one of them has struck pay dirt. There is video of the fugitives disembarking from a bus that departed Houston at 3:30 P.M. the previous day and arrived in Beaumont less than two hours later, at 5:02. An Uber driver in Beaumont has additional information that will assist in the search.

"From your current location," the caller says, "the drive to Beaumont will take approximately one hour and twenty-seven minutes if you depart prior to morning traffic."

"We'll be there before seven o'clock," Gottfrey says.

"The Medexpress carrier containing the control mechanisms should maintain an appropriate temperature for at least another thirty-six hours."

The carrier is on the nightstand. Gottfrey reports the number on the digital readout. "Forty-two degrees."

"Good. Now, the clothes you were wearing yesterday have been cleaned and pressed. They'll be sent up to you by a bellman when you call the front desk."

"Another conflicting detail," Gottfrey says.

"Excuse me?"

"The hotel's own directory of services doesn't offer four-hour laundry and dry cleaning, certainly not late-night."

"Yes, but of course we made special arrangements."

"A minor rewrite."

"A what?"

"They say it's good to be the king," Gottfrey replies, "but the real power is with the author of the play, who can change details, re-write anything he wants and make it turn out different."

"I hadn't thought of it that way," the caller says. "We're rewriting the play, and the play is this country, the world, the future."

"Well," Gottfrey says, throwing back the bedclothes, "the script calls for me to take a shower."

The caller laughs. "Make it a short one and hit the road. We need to get the in-laws, brain-shag 'em, and find the damn kid. We break Jane's heart, we'll also break the bitch's will."

26

THE SAME NIGHT, THE SAME TEXAS PLAIN INFINITE in appearance, the same sky overhead infinite in fact, the same rad-ically hot, bespoke Range Rover by Overfinch North America . . .

Yet all is different. Chris Roberts marvels at how everything can change so profoundly in one hour. When he was cruising back and forth on this same highway, looking for the runaway Longrin girl, he'd been thinking about shacking up with Janis for a torrid week, picturing her naked, figuring that even at just thirty-five he might need a bottle of Viagra to keep up with her. Now her body and the jigsaw puzzle that is her head are wrapped in a waterproof tarp provided by Longrin Stables, the ends folded and secured with almost an entire roll of strapping tape, resting in the cargo area behind the backseat. Picturing her naked is neither as easy nor as appealing as it was an hour earlier.

This is a sobering journey even for Chris, who is neither a pessimist nor a deep thinker. Pessimism is a waste of time, because you can't forestall disaster by sitting around and brooding about it. Anyway, you can't be a pessimist and also a fun guy; Chris thinks of himself as a major fun guy.

As for deep thinkers . . . Well, the deep thinkers he's known mostly become alcoholics, and if they don't become alcoholics, they kill themselves. The few that have neither killed themselves nor become alcoholics are either in mental institutions or ought to be.

Nevertheless, cruising now through the last hours of the night, on a four-hour drive to the Dallas–Fort Worth metroplex, Chris has what he believes to be a deep thought. It scares him a little: not just the fact that it's deep, but the thought itself.

Because he's the kind of guy who can get people to talk about themselves, he's aware that a significant percentage of the Techno Arcadians he knows have come from dysfunctional families. Janis has said little about her folks, except that she not only renounced her parents and sisters and hadn't seen them in fourteen years, but also wished they would all die of a painful, disfiguring disease. Now, in light of what happened at the Longrin place, Chris wonders if the fact that so many Arcadians come from dysfunctional families might result in the entire Techno Arcadian project becoming dysfunctional in the long run.

Fortunately, he doesn't come from a dysfunctional family, and perhaps this gives him a competitive advantage within the ranks of the revolution. His mother and father love each other and never argue. They ran a prosperous business together, and five years ago—at the age of just fifty-eight—they retired to an ocean-view home in Laguna Beach. They shower him with affection, always have, and he has only excellent memories of his childhood, especially when he reached puberty, whereupon many of the girls in his mom and dad's high-end super-discreet west-side-L.A. escort service thought he was a cute kid, a little blond Tom Cruise, and wanted to please his mother by doing him for free.

Nostalgic reveries aren't enough to take his mind off Janis back there in the cargo area. Each time he hits a bump in the road or takes a sharp turn, the tarp slides around a little, and he imagines—hopes he only imagines—that he hears her making sounds *within* the shroud.

He has a long drive ahead of him before he can deliver Janis to the owner of a construction company, a fellow Techno Arcadian who builds entire communities in the outlying suburbs of Fort Worth and who will find a nice resting place for her under the concrete-slab foundation of one structure or another. They can't very well blame her death on Jane Hawk, considering how many people know otherwise, and in the interest of putting the entire Longrin Stables operation behind them as though it never happened, it is best that Janis just disappear. Her name will be purged from the FBI, Homeland, and NSA personnel records; her pensions have not had time to vest, so they can just evaporate; and because her family, whether slowly dying of a disfiguring disease or healthy, have for fourteen years not known her whereabouts, no relative is going to come looking for her.

That someone as young and hot as Janis should end this way is sad, really sad, *epic sad*, and Chris Roberts doesn't like to be sad. Sad is not who he is. He's a fun guy, and he's driving a radically hot vehicle, and he needs some bitchin' music to chase away the sadness.

Puff Daddy is the right stuff most of the time, but that music doesn't feel right for driving dead Janis to an unmarked grave. He thinks about it for a couple miles, and then he pops some TLC into the system. "Baby-Baby-Baby" starts to improve his mood, and "Red Light Special" and then—*wham!*—"Diggin' on You" hoses away sadness. This was the true wood, back in the day. He was into it even before puberty, cool with the music, sexually precocious, ready for the future yesterday. Tionne Watkins. Lisa Lopes. Rozonda Thomas. *Hot, hot, hot.* And now their big hit "No Scrubs," totally top of the charts. The music gets him up and keeps him up as he races through the predawn Texas dark toward a future that is Arcadian, that is inevitable, that *belongs to him*!

27

No matter how much shampoo she used or how long she stood under the hot water, Laurie Longrin didn't feel clean. Although the water was so stinging hot that she turned a boiled-pink color head to foot, she couldn't melt away the chill in her chest, couldn't stop shivering.

Her mother waited with a bath towel when Laurie at last stepped out of the shower stall. Laurie preferred to dry herself. She'd been drying herself for ages and ages. However, she understood that her mother didn't merely want to do it, but also *needed* to do it, as if reassuring herself that her oldest daughter was alive and unharmed, so Laurie allowed it.

Mother kept telling her—promising her—nothing like this would happen again. They were taking steps to defend themselves against the repetition of such a horror. Every adult on their property would henceforth be armed at all times. From now until Jane Hawk was able to produce evidence to expose these power-mad bastards and clear her name, Laurie and her sisters would be homeschooled, where no one could try to get at them.

Laurie's mom didn't get weepy at every sad movie, didn't get emotional over every little thing, and there were no tears in her eyes now. She was angry, furious, *incensed* at the people who had invaded her home. At the same time, she was tender and loving. *Also* at the same time, she was worried and scared and trying hard to hide those feelings.

Even as rattled as Laurie was, she could recognize all these emotions in her mother because her mom and dad were the two people in the world she most trusted and admired. She was always watching them when they didn't realize it, not watching them from a hiding place or anything creepy like that, just *studying* them to figure out how they were who they were. By watching them, she'd learned who she wanted to be and how to become that person, though she wasn't that person yet; there was a long road ahead.

Mother didn't lie. But she couldn't guarantee that what had happened wouldn't happen again. She and Daddy were people who got things done, didn't take crap, and were confident without being arrogant. What Mother meant was that she would die to stop people coming down on her family the way the thugs had done this time.

Laurie put on pajamas and sat on a vanity bench while her mother brushed and blew dry her hair, and she let herself be tucked in bed because she realized her mother needed to do it. It was also true that Laurie needed to have it done, to have the covers smoothed around her and to be kissed on the brow, the cheek.

But when Mother wanted to sit bedside to watch over her as she slept, Laurie said, "I love you. Really need you. Always will. But Daphne and Artemis are just little kids. They need you even more."

Her mother bent over her and felt her brow, as if Laurie might have a fever. "You're going to be all right."

Those words had not been in the form of a question, but Laurie knew that's what they were. "Yeah, sure, I'll be all right. I've got you and Daddy and Daphne and Artemis and all the horses. I'd be a totally stupid dink if I wasn't going to be all right."

After Mother left, Daddy came to her and sat on the edge of the bed. "I'm so sorry, sweetheart. God, I'm so sorry. But you . . . you were amazing, what you did."

He'd been set upon by a band of vicious goons with guns, maybe FBI, maybe not, but with real-looking FBI badges, and there was nothing he could have done differently and still be law-abiding. Yet he blamed himself for underestimating how wicked even real FBI guys might be if they also were bad hats. He hated having let them get the upper hand to the point that they could do what they wanted, even tie him up. He was a tough guy. She had no doubt her father was a tough guy. But he was also a good guy, and sometimes bad people had an advantage over good guys just because they were good.

She sat up in bed and put her arms around him and hugged him hard, even though she was as tired as if she'd been walking all night through a hurricane, hugged him harder than she had ever hugged him before. He hadn't needed to say anything. And she didn't need to say anything now, because they loved each other and knew the truth of each other—and, besides, being Texans, they didn't indulge in a lot of useless palaver.

Daddy used a dimmer switch to turn her lamp low, but he didn't switch it off. He could have switched it off. She would have been okay in the dark. She wasn't afraid of the dark. No one should be afraid of the dark. It was the wrong kind of people who might kill you, not the dark. But she was glad that he left the lamp on because when he turned at the door and looked back at her, she could see him better. She liked the way he looked—strong and tough, but so very kind. He could see her better, too, so he could see her smile. Laurie figured he needed to see her smile.

When he closed the door behind him, she closed her eyes.

In Laurie's interior darkness, Janis loomed vividly, face distorted and strange, eyes yellow with an infall of attic light, her whisper as vicious as her poisonous stare, *My little pet.*

Laurie opened her eyes.

She had never been so weary, tired in mind and heart and flesh and bone, but she couldn't stop thinking.

Jane Hawk's mother had supposedly killed herself when Jane was a little girl. Her father was a famous pianist, performing all over the world. He'd been on a TV show Sunday evening, saying his only child was mentally ill or some such horseshit. Laurie's parents didn't know, but she'd once overheard them talking about Martin Duroc, how his first wife hadn't really committed suicide, that he had killed her and gotten away with it, how even as a child Jane knew, heard him or something, but had no proof, which was freaky.

Janis and Jane.

How could they both come from basket-case families and turn out so different—one a vicious outlaw, the other doing everything she could to crush the bad hats?

Laurie and her best friend, Bonnie Jean Haney, both came from good families, so probably they would both turn out good. But was it possible, like Janis and Jane, one would turn out to be a psycho bitch and the other a hero Marine or something?

And what about Daphne and Artemis, her sisters? Would maybe one of them grow up to rob banks and blow up churches?

If who you were raised to be and who you most wanted to become didn't matter, if you could become some monster instead . . . That was a scary thing to consider.

If Janis came from a rotten family and didn't want to be a dirtbag herself but became rotten anyway, that was sad.

Whether it was sad or not, however, Janis was dead, and that was good. If Laurie was confused about other things right now, she was not confused about the rightness of Janis being dead. Janis alive— not good. Janis dead—hallelujah.

In spite of being raised right, in spite of wanting to be good, if one day Laurie Longrin became a raging monster, she would *want* someone to kill her.

Finally she closed her eyes. She slept. In one of her dreams, Laurie was all grown up, a rotten crazy bitch, and Janis Dern was an innocent little girl who said *horseshit* too much. They were on the veranda together, trying to encourage the firemen and firewomen to go away so that Laurie could kill little Janis. The sniper in the helicopter shot Laurie, and her head exploded. She kept trying to pick up the pieces and put her head back together, but there was a big chunk of her skull missing and a lot of her brain, and one of her eyes had rolled where she couldn't find it. She was frantically trying to make herself whole again, desperate to live even though she was a monster, and she kept saying, *"I didn't mean it, I was lying, that was all horseshit, I don't want to be killed!"*

When she woke, she wasn't screaming, but she was crying hard. She couldn't stop crying. She buried her face in a pillow to muffle her sobs, so that no one would hear. She cried as though to use a lifetime of tears in this single terrible sadness, and one thing that kept her crying was the new understanding that there was no using up of all tears, that tears would be as much a part of her life, for the rest of her life, as would be laughter and hope.

PART THREE

Reptiles

1

Borrego Valley at Dawn, Fleecy Clouds Blazing bright coral against a turquoise eastern sky paling slowly to blue . . .

Carter Jergen and Radley Dubose are cruising around, looking for stains on the fabric of normalcy, which might turn out to be indications, signs, manifestations—simply put, *clues*—to the whereabouts of Travis Hawk.

More accurately, Dubose is thus engaged, while in the front passenger seat Jergen takes note of a seemingly endless series of things about the desert that disturb him.

Three ungainly vultures describe a narrowing gyre in the dry air above the golf course at the Borrego Springs Resort, perhaps eyeing the pathetic cadaver of an early golfer who has dropped dead of heat stroke on the third green.

"Who would want to play golf in a desert?" Jergen wonders.

"Lots of people," Dubose says. "It's pleasant to play in such low humidity."

"Well, you're never going to find me whacking a golf ball around in hundred-ten-degree heat."

"I would never look for you there, my friend. I would assume your leisure time is full up with polo, croquet, and fox hunts."

Another dig at Jergen's Boston Brahmin roots. The remark has no effect. By now he's immune to such ridicule.

"Anyway," Dubose continues, "it doesn't get a hundred ten for at least another month. Predicted high for today is ninety-two."

Jergen says, "Positively frigid."

Ahead, another denizen of the desert is crossing the highway: a six-foot rattlesnake. In awareness of the VelociRaptor, the serpent raises the first three feet of its length off the pavement and turns its head toward them with eerie fluidity.

Dubose purposefully aims for the viper. The truck hits it at fifty miles an hour, and for a minute or so, the entangled creature slaps noisily against the undercarriage, like a length of cable snared around an axle.

When quiet returns, Jergen says, "What if you didn't kill it? If we get out and it's alive under there somewhere, it's going to be pissed. They aren't that easy to kill."

"My friend, I think you're confusing rattlesnakes with the hard-boiled hard-bitten intractable Boston debutantes you remember from your youth."

Jergen is spared the need to engage in witless tit for tat when Dubose's smartphone rings. It's on the seat, between his thighs, and the pride of West Virginia rubs it against his crotch, as though for luck, before taking the call.

Tarantulas, vultures, intolerable heat, rattlesnakes, and now the most disturbing thing yet: a thirty-year-old rust-bucket Dodge pickup broken down at the side of the road and, standing next to it, one of those lifelong desert dwellers, a sunbaked sun-withered old woman in red athletic shoes and cargo-pocket khakis and tan-linen shirt and straw hat, with snow-white tangles of hair and a wrinkled face reminiscent of the pinched countenance of a desert tortoise. She vigorously waves a handkerchief to signal a need for assistance. After at least eight decades in the Anza-Borrego, she's most likely a half-crazed package of bad attitude, stubbornness, and crackpot opinions that she'll insist on sharing ad nauseam.

In such circumstances, not reliably but occasionally, Radley Dubose experiences a welling up of down-home neighborliness and backwoods charm, which most of the time exists in him only to the extent that water exists in a stone. He is then capable of spending an hour to help a lost three-legged dog cross a busy street, take it to the address on its collar, and chat with the grateful owner.

With the phone to one ear, muttering solemn one- and two-word responses to whatever the caller is telling him, Dubose fortunately is not in a she-reminds-me-of-my-granny mood. He increases speed as they approach the disabled pickup, although as they flash past the old woman, he toots the horn twice as if to say that he's rooting for her not to end up as a vulture's dinner.

When the big man terminates the call and returns the smartphone to his crotch, his eyes remain unreadable behind the lenses of his sunglasses, but otherwise his expression is somber. "Here it is party time, and someone pissed in the punch bowl."

Jergen supposes that must be a Princeton expression. "Give me a translation."

"We got a really bad crocodile incident over at the Corrigan place."

"Crocodiles are tropical, not desert reptiles," Jergen says.

"It's not that kind of crocodile. It's the kind Bertold Shenneck worried about."

Shenneck was the scientist who'd developed the nanomachine brain implants. With the assistance of several financial backers of his research, he also evolved the strategy and tactics for imposing the Arcadian utopia on a troubled, disordered world.

Dubose says, "You'll see soon enough, when we get to Rooney Corrigan's place."

"Who's he?" Jergen asks.

"Third-generation Borrego Valley. Knows a lot of people around here, who's who, what's what. He's ideal for the search party."

"Sandsucker high society."

"He, his wife, two sons—all were brain-screwed last night."

"The approved term is *adjusted*. They were adjusted last night, and they're now adjusted people."

Dubose makes a dismissive sound between a sigh and a snort. "I say potato, you say *po-tah-to*."

2

Cornell woke early. On the ipod, mr. paul Simon was softly singing an ultra infectious song: "*Some people say a lie's a lie's a lie, but I say why, why deny the obvious child, why deny the obvious child. . . .*"

When Cornell had awakened hours earlier, he'd been scared and needed music. The iPod was programmed with different playlists of Mr. Paul Simon's songs that he found suitable for the dead of night.

The boy was still snoozing on the other big sofa. Both dogs were curled up there with him, and right now they didn't look like they had ever bitten anyone or ever would.

Cornell went into the bathroom, where he stopped just inside the door, abruptly in the grip of dread, though he didn't know why. Oh, yes. The toothbrush. But the toothbrush wasn't here now, and the boy hadn't meant to terrorize him. It wouldn't happen again.

Cornell brushed his teeth without fear, showered, dressed for the day, and returned to the sofas. The boy still slept, but the dogs were alert.

Mr. Paul Simon was singing: "*Losing love is like a window in your heart, everybody sees you're blown apart. . . .*"

The German shepherds got off the sofa without disturbing the boy. They were very considerate dogs.

Cornell fed them kibble and took them out to toilet.

While he stood waiting, he heard an airplane. It was louder than usual for air traffic in this remote valley. He searched the sky. When he found the plane, it was passing over at less than two thousand feet, heading south.

The dogs peed first but then they wandered around, sniffing the ground, sniffing the weeds, and took their time deciding whether and where to poop.

Just as the dogs finished their business, the sound of the airplane, which had faded, grew louder once more.

Duke and Queenie scampered over toward the little blue house, not running away, just playing with each other.

Cornell watched the sky, and this time the plane appeared on a northward course. He was pretty sure this was the same aircraft and that it was a twin-engine model, not a light single-engine Piper or the like that came and went from the Anza Air Park.

After all these years of living with himself, Cornell Jasperson still didn't know why he was the way he was. He probably never would understand himself, because each time he seemed on an even keel, his day shaped by routines and rituals that kept him nicely balanced and content, something that never disturbed him before suddenly caused him great anxiety. Like a toothbrush. Or this airplane.

Previously, the sounds made by airplanes—or by trucks, cars, motorcycles, machinery—had not once concerned him. But for some reason, this plane . . . *this plane* now threw off a sound that he *felt* as well as heard, that crawled on his skin like thousands of ants, spiraled up his nostrils, squirmed in his ears, prickled across his eyes on tens of thousands of invisible-ant legs.

For years, Cornell had worn dreadlocks. Just ten days earlier, he'd learned that Mr. Bob Marley, the reggae star, had been dead for decades. So then he began waking up at night and thinking about Mr. Bob Marley in a coffin. He felt as if he was wearing a dead man's hair. Although he never liked reggae, Cornell became so disturbed that he shaved his head as smooth as a misshapen egg.

The dreadlocks incident was a minor disturbance compared to his reaction to the airplane. The noise again slowly faded, this time as the craft flew north, but its effect on Cornell didn't diminish with its volume. Invisible ants were crawling over him and all through his insides, even through the chambers of his heart. The sound was *touching* him, touching him in the invasive, demanding way that people touched him, and he *knew* the airplane was going to drain his mind and soul from him, so that he would not be anybody anymore, just a *thing* without memories and purpose.

He shouted at the dogs, calling them to him. He turned from them and hunched his dinosaur shoulder blades and ducked his head and ran in his shambling fashion toward the barn that was a secret library, surprised at how far he had moved away from it.

The electronic key in a pocket of his jeans signaled the lock to disengage. He stumbled into the vestibule.

The dogs exploded into it behind him, excited by his anxiety, or maybe thinking he wanted to play, panting and whining with what sounded like delight, tongues lolling, claws clicking on the floor, spanking each other with their tails, dancing around in the small space, thumping against the walls. The door fell shut behind them.

From this side, the inner door of the vestibule would open only to Cornell's touch. In his fright, he reached for the lever-style handle and thought of the boy inside and stayed his hand and stood trembling, confused, torn between an urgent need for the refuge of the library and a desire not to alarm the child.

A crawly feeling head to foot, blood flukes swimming through his veins and arteries and nibbling at his heart from within its auricles and ventricles, spiders swarming across the walls of his stomach, centipedes squirming into his bones to lay eggs in his marrow: Pestilence in great variety infested him, consuming his soul and mind in millions of microscopic bites. . . .

The airplane had passed to the north, and although a little of the engine noise might still be scratching at the morning beyond the outer door, none penetrated to the vestibule. However, the absence of the offending sound didn't at once relieve his reaction to it. Sometimes, after such an episode, he was distraught for hours, needed to lie down in the quiet dark to imagine that he floated in a cooling pool of water.

But he couldn't turn off the light in the vestibule and stand here for hours until the heebie-jeebies passed. The boy might wake and wonder where he had gone. Cornell was responsible for the boy until his mother came for him, until his mother came, until his mother came. Besides, even if the foyer was entirely dark, the dogs would not be perfectly quiet. And while he was standing instead of lying down, he couldn't easily pretend that he was floating in a soothing pool of water.

"Cornell," said Cornell aloud, impatient with himself, "you can do this thing here. You can calm yourself and be responsible about the little boy. You're responsible about designing good apps that make millions of people happy, and you're responsible with managing your scary amount of money, keeping it safe and making it grow, so you can be responsible about the boy."

Of course he never saw the millions who used his apps, and he communicated with his bankers and investment advisers only by phone and email. There was no chance that they would have an opportunity to touch him. But the boy might do that, even though he knew that he shouldn't, might touch Cornell by accident.

The dogs whined, wondering why they were delayed here.

Cornell thought, *The boy is going to be at risk because of me, the boy is going to die because of me.*

Horrified, he said, "No, no, no. The boy won't die. The boy will live and grow old, live and grow old, live and grow very old."

He gripped the door handle, and the electronic lock disengaged with a soft *thunk.*

With the memory of airplane sounds crawling every inch of his skin and squirming through his bones, Cornell didn't return to the library so much as arrive there in a crash landing. Violently shaking his head and flailing his arms to cast off the offending noise, staggering forward on wobbly legs, he dropped to his knees as the jubilant dogs raced past him to greet their young master.

The boy had awakened and gotten up. He stood maybe eight feet away, holding a glass of chocolate milk, regarding Cornell with what looked like fear but might have been concern, because he said, "Are you all right? Can I do something? Are you okay?"

Gasping for breath, Cornell said, "Dogs, the dogs, me and the dogs, we were playing, they peed and pooped and then wanted to play, and we were running around under the airplane, running and running, and they wore me out."

This was a lie, but it wasn't a terrible mortal lie, just a little fib so that the boy wouldn't be afraid for Cornell or for himself.

"Do you want some chocolate milk?" the boy asked.

"Not right now." Cornell stretched out on his back. "I'm just going to lie here and calm down, calm down, calm down."

"I already got a muffin and took it to my chair. But I can get it and sit here with you."

"No, no." Cornell pretended to be breathing harder than he really needed to, because gasping helped hide the fact he shook with fear. "I just want to lie here on the cool floor, like it's a fool of water. Pool. Pool of water. Float here on the floor and close my eyes and get my death. My breath. Get my breath."

"Okay then," the boy said, and he went to his chair.

The dogs came sniffing around, and Cornell feared they would touch him with their noses, but they didn't, and then they went away to be with Travis.

The hateful, unwanted, terrifying thought came to Cornell again: *The boy is going to die because of me.*

3

HAVING TRAVELED NINETY-TWO MILES FROM HOUS-
ton, Egon Gottfrey in his Rhino GX, followed by the competent-if-
methamphetamine-popping Rupert Baldwin and the impossible
Vince Penn in their bespoke Jeep Wrangler, arrives at the bus station
in Beaumont, Texas, shortly before 7:00 A.M.

They haven't been able to view the video of Ancel and Clare in
advance of their arrival. According to the Unknown Playwright,
who evidently thinks it makes for good drama to keep putting obstacles in their way, the NSA archives the traffic-cam and public-
facility video from all major cities, but not yet from every city and
town with a population lower than 150,000, though they're working on it.

The population of Beaumont is approximately 120,000, so if the
locals want to be part of the Great Orwellian future, they better get
busy having babies.

Waiting for Gottfrey and his men is an FBI agent named Leon
Fettwiler, who is as memorable as a dish of vanilla ice cream. To the
best of Gottfrey's knowledge, Fettwiler is not an Arcadian; but he
was in the area and dispatched to view the bus-terminal video.

With Fettwiler is the bus-station manager, so nondescript that
she makes Fettwiler look flamboyant. Gottfrey doesn't even bother
to listen to her name, for it's obvious that this woman is a walk-on
and will not reappear, less a real character than a thin concept.

The video can be viewed on a monitor in the nameless manager's
office. The terminal's video recorder is old and oddly configured, so
the disc that contains the images preserves them only for seven
days, cannot be tapped to transfer its data to another device, and
can be viewed only here. Enduring the manager's convoluted explanation for this inconvenience is as boring as listening to someone read aloud from a health-insurance policy.

When the video finally runs—a four-second snippet from 5:05 P.M. the previous day—it's the quality of a 1950s porno film shot with an 8 mm camera in a motel room, using only available lamp-light. Gottfrey, Rupert, and Vince crowd together to watch a woman of Clare's height and build step out of a bus. She wears a headscarf. Following her is a Stetson-wearing man of Ancel's height and build.

"Who are they, anyway?" the station manager asks.

Viewing the brief video again, Gottfrey says, "Criminals."

"What have they done?"

"Committed crimes."

"We're not at liberty to say," Fettwiler tells the station manager, as if Gottfrey hasn't made that clear.

Video from a different camera shows the same man and woman meeting an Uber driver in front of the terminal. Since they are leaving the station, the camera catches them mostly from the back.

"Is it them?" Gottfrey asks Rupert Baldwin.

Fingering his bolo tie, shifting his weight back and forth from one of his Hush Puppies to the other, Rupert squints at a third and fourth playing of the first video segment. "Damn if I know."

Vince speaks up. "Me neither. They might be, they might not. It's hard to say. The video isn't good. The lighting isn't—"

"Oh, it's them, sure enough," says Fettwiler, mercifully putting an end to Vince Penn's analysis. "The Uber driver will confirm without hesitation."

"Where is he?" Gottfrey asks.

"He wouldn't come in here. Insists we meet him out in the parking lot."

The Uber guy is waiting beside his car, a white GMC Terrain SLE. The Unknown Playwright has found the energy to paint this character with somewhat more detail than the station manager and Fettwiler. His name is Tucker Treadmont. He's maybe thirty, stands about five feet six, weighs maybe 240 pounds. He is wearing pointy-toed boots, baggy jeans, and a pale blue polo shirt that shapes itself to his unfortunately large man breasts. His brown hair is slicked back, his round face appears so smooth as to be beardless, and his greenish gray eyes assess Gottfrey with the calculation of a card mechanic sizing up a mark.

Fettwiler produces 8 × 10 photos of Ancel and Clare from a manila envelope.

Tucker Treadmont says, "Yeah, that's the dude and his squeeze. They booked the ride an hour earlier, and I got the call."

"Where did you take them?" Gottfrey asks.

"What works best for me is I drive you there and show you."

"We have vehicles of our own."

"I could be workin' now. I'm not some stinkin' millionaire."

"We haven't booked you through Uber."

"I also drive my own time. Uber don't own my ass."

This back-and-forth continues for a half minute before Gottfrey warns Treadmont that he's obstructing justice, when what he wants to do instead is use his collapsible baton to reshape the guy's head.

The charge of obstruction is of no concern to the driver, and after yet a few more exchanges, Gottfrey decides that it doesn't matter if he breaks the rules and pays. The guy isn't real, anyway, and neither is the money. Only Gottfrey is real, and this is just the Playwright trying to make him crazy. So get on with it.

"How much if you drive and we follow?"

Treadmont says, "One hundred twenty-one dollars, fifty cents."

"You're not serious."

"The place I took them, it's not just around the corner."

Determined not to round it up with a tip, Gottfrey takes six twenties from his wallet, but he has no one-dollar bills. Rupert provides a dollar, and Vince has two quarters.

"We're fine from here," Gottfrey tells Fettwiler. "Thanks for all your help."

"I was planning to stay with you on this next part."

"Unnecessary. We've got it."

Fettwiler is gone as if he never existed.

In his Rhino GX, with Rupert and Vince in the Jeep Wrangler

behind him, Gottfrey follows the GMC Terrain out of the parking lot.

They haven't gone a block when his smartphone rings. The call is from the leader of his cell, Judge Sheila Draper-Cruxton.

The conversation that Gottfrey had with her the previous night, during his cab ride to the Hyatt Regency in Houston, was so pleasant that he looks forward to speaking with her again. Until she starts to chew him out for the screwup at the Longrin place. Janis Dern clearly had psychological problems. Gottfrey should have recognized her instability. He never should have included her in the operation. In fact, considering that she represented a grave potential risk to the revolution, he should have taken her someplace quiet and put a bullet in her head long before this. *Yada, yada, yada.* The judge assures him that his failure in this matter will have consequences and warns him not to fail to capture Ancel and Clare Hawk, because if he doesn't get his hands on them pronto, the consequences will be serious, indeed. "Were you *shtupping* the bitch?" she asks.

"What bitch?"

The judge is incensed. "What bitch are we talking about? Janis! Is that why you couldn't see she had a screw loose—because you were so busy putting new screws to her?"

"No, sir. No, ma'am, judge. I'm not like that."

"You better stop wasting your testosterone, Gottfrey. Keep your pants zipped, man up, start breaking heads, and get the job done."

Judge Sheila Draper-Cruxton terminates the call.

Following Tucker Treadmont to whatever unpleasant surprise will come next, Egon Gottfrey sourly wonders what the Unknown Playwright intends by layering on all these frustrations, what Gottfrey is meant to intuit about the direction his role should take.

He has so badly wanted to bludgeon so many people recently, not least of all Vince Penn and Tucker Treadmont. Judge Draper-Cruxton's tirade suggests that in this regard if in no other, Gottfrey intuits what the Playwright wants of him. Maybe it's time to be ruthless. If someone frustrates him, maybe he should answer them with violence. The previous night, he dreamed of shooting Ancel Hawk and slitting Clare's throat. Now that he thinks about it, the Unknown Playwright has spoken to him in dreams before when Gottfrey has been floundering in his role, and thereafter everything was all right again.

4

Palm SPRINGS TO RANCHO MIRAGE, THROUGH IN-dian Wells, past La Quinta, Jane Hawk in a world of sand traps and water hazards, more than one hundred world-class golf courses in the six up-valley towns, but with no time for leisure, living now for one purpose, with one task at which she must not fail . . .

Indio was less about leisure, a center of industry and farm-servicing companies. Much of it looked dusty, weathered, and weary here on the edge of the San Andreas Fault.

Ferrante Escobar, nephew of Enrique de Soto, operated his legit business—customizing limousines, high-end SUVs, and other vehicles for wealthy clients—out of a four-acre fenced-and-gated property in an industrial area. The manned guardhouse and the tight security had less to do with the value of the vehicle inventory than with the illegal weapons business conducted from a secret basement under one of the three large concrete-block-and-corrugated-metal buildings in which vehicles were being rebuilt.

The workers started at seven o'clock. Jane arrived shortly there-after in the pixie-cut chestnut-brown wig and the stage-prop glasses with black frames, her blue eyes made brown by contact lenses. She told the guard, "Elinor Dashwood to see Mr. Escobar," and pre-sented a California driver's license.

The guard directed her to the third building. By the time she parked the Explorer, Ferrante had come out to greet her.

Slim, good-looking, well barbered, he had the lithe movements and erect posture of a matador. He stood where the shadow of the building and the morning sun together scribed a territorial boundary on the pavement. His soft, musical voice matched his smile: "I'm so pleased to meet you. So very pleased."

He had a boyish quality, a fresh-scrubbed wide-eyed innocence that didn't comport with his second career as an arms dealer. South of thirty, he was young to have created such a successful business. But of course his Uncle Ricky had floated him the start-up money.

He knew who she really was. There were no secrets between him and Enrique.

Jane said, "I appreciate the risk you're taking by letting me put this thing together here. I'm grateful."

He nodded. There was something shy about the nod, a kind of deference in the way he stood, a coyness in his stare that seemed simultaneously to engage her and retreat from her.

His handshake was firm. But when she met his eyes, he looked away. "The vehicles from my uncle will be here by eleven. Meanwhile, we have a comfortable client lounge. Coffee. Doughnuts. TV."

"Ricky told you I'm also in need of a handgun?" She preferred to have two at all times. She'd disposed of the gun she had used to defend herself in Tahoe on Sunday, because it could be tied to the death of a major Arcadian. "A Heckler and Koch Compact .45?"

"Yes. Yes, of course. Do you want to arrange that now?"

"Best get it out of the way. I'll have a lot to do later."

"Then, please, follow me."

She got her tote from the car. It now contained the package of $120,000 for Enrique de Soto and $90,000 additional.

Ferrante led her out of sunlight into shadow.

As they stepped into a hallway, he said, "This building is devoted to the storage of vehicle parts, supplies, and my office."

Ferrante's sanctum was perhaps thirty feet square, with a fourteen-foot ceiling. The frosted-glass windows were ten feet off the floor, as if to ensure privacy even from drones. When he closed the door, an electronic lock shot home a deadbolt with a loud *clack*.

Jane saw two other doors, perhaps one to a bathroom and the other an exit directly to the outside.

The room featured sleek modern furniture—teak, steel, glass, black leather upholstery—all spotless, gleaming. Everything was of the same style except for an unusual bristling sculpture on his desk, presented on an acrylic plinth, and four disturbing four-foot-square paintings that formed a giant art block on one wall.

Each painting depicted a human heart in realistic detail: the glistening muscle so lovingly rendered that Jane could almost see it contract and expand. Blood dripped from three hearts, squirted in a rich stream from the fourth. Each organ was festooned with different severed veins and arteries: aorta, superior vena cava, descending aorta, pulmonary artery, inferior vena cava. . . . Every heart was bound and cruelly pierced by a woven cincture of thorny brambles.

Enrique said his nephew was devout. These images were the sacred heart of Christ, but not as usually portrayed. The over-the-top details and lavish gore seemed to mock the subject, though if Ferrante was truly devout, mockery was out of the question.

"What do you think of the artist's work?" Ferrante asked.

She said, "Striking."

"Yes. Exactly."

"Bold."

"Some people don't get it."

"Colorful," she said.

"If they don't get it, I never preach at them."

"That's wise."

Shyly, as before, he looked at her sideways, nodded, and then turned his attention to the paintings. "Every time I look at them, I'm deeply moved, inspired, justified."

The last word in the series was peculiar and therefore the most significant. Jane couldn't imagine any other meaning than that, to his way of thinking, his devotion justified or excused his criminal activity. His uncle Ricky wasn't the only relative who operated on the wrong side of the law. The kid was born into a crime family of sorts; so maybe he felt compelled to uphold the tradition.

As she watched Ferrante smiling and nodding and gazing at the gruesome hearts, another possibility occurred to her. Ricky claimed his nephew attended Mass every day and "says his rosary like some old *abuela* who wears a mantilla even in the shower." If Ferrante thought that being devout was adequate penance that allowed him to profit from the illegal sale of weapons, he might believe it also justified worse crimes.

Like rape and murder.

That thought wasn't evidence of rampant paranoia. It was merely a consequence of her experience.

In her time at the Bureau, Jane had captured a serial killer, J. J. Crutchfield, who insisted that he was doing the Lord's work, killing oversexed teenage girls who would corrupt teenage boys if he didn't stop them. Thus he was saving both the boys and the girls from damnation. He preserved his victims' eyes in jars, convinced—or so he claimed—that in each girl's moment of death, she'd seen God. To J.J., the eyes were sacred relics. He found it difficult, however, to explain why God wanted him to rape the women before killing them to save their souls.

While Jane pretended to admire the paintings, she was aware of her host watching her more directly than he seemed able to do when she was facing him.

As a last word on the art, she said, "Unforgettable."

When she turned to him, his smile was of a peculiar character that disturbed her, although she couldn't define the quality of it that she found unsettling.

She remembered what Enrique de Soto had told her on the phone the previous day: *But I have to say he's a weird duck . . . got this blood obsession.*

He seemed about to speak but then broke eye contact again. He went around the desk, opened a drawer, and withdrew a Heckler & Koch Compact .45 still in its original sealed box.

New weapon, no history, no waiting period, no background check, no formal or de facto registration. The guns Ferrante sold probably came from his uncle Ricky, which meant they were stolen and provided a terrific profit margin.

"How much?" Jane asked.

He met her eyes directly and for the first time did not quickly look away. "I won't accept money from you. There's something else I want, something better than money."

She put down the tote to have both hands free.

5

CARTER JERGEN FINDS THE PLACE ABHORRENT ON first sight. In the passenger seat of the VelociRaptor, he shivers with cold disgust.

Rooney Corrigan, pooh-bah of sandsucker society, maintains a small carbon footprint by generating his own electricity. The most prominent structures on his property are two sixty- or seventy-foot-tall windmills. They aren't the picturesque stone windmills with huge cloth sails seen in Holland, but ugly steel constructs, tripods reminiscent of the Martian death machines in *The War of the Worlds*.

The single-story green-stucco house—where the "crocodile incident" has occurred, whatever that might be—boasts a roof entirely of solar panels and stands on several acres of pale and sandy dirt, lacking even stones-and-cactus landscaping. The only evidence that the planet produces flora is three struggling king palms with more brown than green fronds and a misshapen olive tree lifeless for so long that its bleached, leafless limbs and weather-shredded bark might be an avant-garde sculpture wired together from the bones and brittle hair of dead men.

The long, unpaved driveway is defined only by parallel lines of stones arranged to mark its borders.

Parked near the house are two black Jeep Cherokees.

As Dubose brakes to a stop fifty yards from those vehicles and stares at the house with a dour expression, he says, "I call it a croco-dile incident. He called it 'the possible assertion and triumph of the reptile consciousness.' There's like a one-in-ten-thousand chance an adjusted person might have a catastrophic psychological collapse after the control mechanism activates."

Jergen frowns. "I never heard such a thing. Says who?"

"The genius who invented the nanoimplants."

"Bertold Shenneck is dead."

"I'm not claiming he spoke to me at a séance. He worried about this from day one. He foresaw two kinds of psychotic breakdowns."

"How do you know this, and I don't?"

"I knew someone who knew the great man. Inga Shenneck."

"His wife?"

"Before Shenneck and then for a while after she married him, she and I had this thing going."

Jergen wants to deny the obvious intended meaning of the words *this thing*. "But she . . . she was a stunner."

"Hot," Dubose says. "A lot younger than Shenneck and so hot she was thermonuclear. And insatiable. She wore me out."

Carter Jergen is not naïve. He doesn't believe life has some grand meaning. He doesn't believe in good and evil. He doesn't see any issue in black-and-white, only in innumerable shades of gray. He doesn't believe that life, society, and justice are fair or ever can be. He doesn't believe they *should* be fair. Fairness is unnatural; it's seen nowhere in nature. He believes in power. Those with the desire and the will to seize power are those best qualified to shape the future.

But it is so *unfair* that a backwoods cretin who surely got into Princeton on a fraudulently obtained scholarship, *who at breakfast folds two strips of bacon into a thick bonbon of pig fat and pops them into his mouth with his fingers,* who wouldn't know which fork to use for the fish appetizer if the butler snatched it off the table in frustration and stabbed him in the face with it, *so* unfair that *this* kind of man could have had a woman like Inga Shenneck.

Jergen says, "I admired her grace, her style, her taste. . . ."

Dubose nods. "Exactly why she was drawn to me."

"You never told me about this."

"I don't talk about my ladies. A gentleman is always discreet."

"Discreet? You just said she was insatiable."

Dubose looked puzzled. "She's dead. So what's to be discreet about after she's packed off in a coffin?"

For a moment, Jergen stares in silence at the windmills looming behind the house, their enormous blades carving the air and probably a significant number of birds in any twenty-four-hour period. The sun flares off the solar panels. The stucco is a bilious shade of green. A ragged dog of numerous heritages wanders into the driveway in front of them, squats, and takes a dump.

"I'm in Hell," Jergen says. "I don't believe in Hell, but what is this"—he sweeps one hand across the vista before them, where the dog craps in front of a house that by all appearances is built from the animal's previous defecations—"what is this if it isn't Hell?"

Dubose cocks his head and raises one eyebrow. "Are you going all dramatic on me? We can't afford existential angst in our line of work. My advice is don't watch those historical dramas on PBS, they just get your panties in a wad. Don't watch, and you'll be happier. I want you to be happy, my friend."

"Comme vous êtes gentil!" Jergen butters the flattery and thank-yous with sarcasm. *"Vous êtes trop aimable! Merci infiniment!"*

Dubose sighs and shakes his head. *"De rien, mademoiselle."*

Astonished by this revelation, Jergen says, "You speak French?"

"Do bears shit in the woods?" He places a hand on Jergen's

shoulder. "Buddy, calm yourself. If just the outside of this place freaks you, then you won't be able to handle what's inside."

Enduring the hand on his shoulder because it will be there only a moment, Carter Jergen says, "Yeah? What's inside?"

"Dead people."

"I've seen plenty of dead people. Made a few of them myself."

"Yeah, but these didn't die pretty."

6

As THOUGH HE READ DISAPPROVAL IN JANE'S FACE, Ferrante Escobar said, "We sell only to wealthy, reputable clients needing protection in an increasingly dangerous world. They don't want to risk having their weapons known and confiscated if some crisis leads to martial law. Many of them have large security staffs, and they buy in bulk, but we don't sell to anyone who might intend to resell."

His self-justifications were self-delusions, but Jane couldn't afford to alienate Ferrante Escobar. She must be in Borrego Valley this afternoon. She'd already needed more time to put together this operation than she would have liked. Further delay was unthinkable.

Nevertheless, instead of responding to his declaration that he would not accept money from her, that he wanted something else in return for the pistol, she said again, "How much?"

Anxiety molded his face. "This is a world of lies and always has been. We live in a time of even greater deceptions than in centuries past. So much of what we're told, what we see on TV, what we read in the newspapers or on the Internet, is invented to conceal the truth, protect the wicked, increase the power of those who already have more power than all the kings of history combined."

"I don't disagree," she said. "But what does that have to do with the price of a pistol?"

He became more excited, speaking fast. Earlier he'd been unable to endure her stare for more than a moment. Now he was unable to look away.

"They claim you're a true monster. No redeeming qualities. So dangerous, vicious, hateful. But all they've done is make you as unreal as the supervillain in some bad Batman movie. All over the Internet, they're talking about what you really might be. They think you know something that could bring down a lot of powerful people."

Ferrante continued to meet her eyes, but his demeanor changed. He pressed his right hand over his heart, his left over the right, as if his heart must be pounding so hard and fast that pressure needed to be applied to quiet it. With this strange posture came a change in his voice. He spoke neither as fast nor as loud as before, and there was a new tone that she could not at first name.

"They say maybe you have proof of something big. But you can't find a way to use it or get it out to the public. Because everything is so corrupt these days. Because you have to run as fast as you can just to stay alive."

When he fell silent, Jane said, "And what do *you* think?"

Anxiety faded from his face, and a tenderness replaced it. "I think you're the truth in a sea of lies. There is a painting in the Louvre in Paris. I own a print of it. She's shown in armor when Charles the Seventh was crowned the king of France."

"No," Jane said.

"You look nothing like her, but you're armored, too."

Disturbed by what she now realized was Ferrante's reverence, she said, "I *am* nothing like her. God talked to Joan of Arc, or she thought He did. He's never talked to me. I got into this for selfish reasons, to restore my husband's good name, to save my son's life. If it's grown into something larger than that, it's not anything I ever wanted. I'm not made to carry that kind of weight. I can't save an entire freaking nation. I could be dead tomorrow. Chances are I will be dead. I'm tired and lonely and scared, and I'm under no illusion that God or some guardian angel will spare me from a bullet in the head if the bastard who pulls the trigger knows how to aim."

Ferrante's hands pressed over his heart looked melodramatic and foolish, but the esteem in which he held her was genuine, not at all diminished by her refusal to be what he imagined her to be. He said, "If I had been there in the fifteenth century, at the coronation of Charles the Seventh, I would have asked her for what I'm asking of you, the only thing I want from you."

"Ferrante, listen, I can't play something I'm not. I'm no saint in the making. *The things I've done.* Damn it, listen, I'm no good at make-believe. I've got both feet in the mud of reality. I slog from here to there. I don't fly. I screw up. Both feet in mud *and blood.*"

He would not be deterred. "All I want is your blessing. Touch my head and bless my life."

If she did as he asked, just as a kindness, with no illusion that her blessing had any power, Ferrante would nonetheless receive it as a sanctification of his heart, as a hallowing of his life. Knowing what false value he would place on it, if she still did as he wanted, she would to some degree be a fraud. She should do it anyway, do it for Travis, to avoid risking this man's displeasure. After all, she would kill for Travis, lie for him, commit any sin to save him. So she should be able, just for a moment, to pretend to be a conduit for divine grace. Yet she couldn't move toward him or bring herself to speak a benediction. She didn't understand her reluctance, nor was she able to put a name to the particular fault in herself that brought her to this impasse.

She looked beyond Ferrante to the four grotesque paintings, and she thought about what Enrique had said. *He's a weird duck. . . . He's got this blood obsession. You meet him, you'll see.*

Yes, but it turned out not to be the blood of violence and vengeance and hatred that enthralled Ferrante Escobar, but instead the blood of sacrifice, the concept of redemption through suffering. To some extent, that was an obsession that Jane, with both feet in the mud of life, could understand.

Her gaze traveled from the paintings to the acrylic plinth on the desk, on which rested the bristling sculpture that had seemed strange and abstract when she'd first noticed it. She realized it was intricately braided brambles fashioned into a crown of thorns.

If for whatever reason she could not bring herself to give him what he wanted, she could give him an alternative that might not leave him alienated. She stepped to the desk and, not with her gun hand but with her left, firmly gripped the sculpture and lifted it from the display pedestal, clutched it. She clenched her teeth to bite off any expression of pain and met his eyes for a moment before returning the sculpture to the acrylic.

The thorns had dimpled her flesh in a dozen places, but blood bloomed only in tiny blossoms from three points on two fingers and from four punctures in her palm.

Ferrante Escobar stared at her hand for a long moment, his face solemn, his dark eyes unreadable. Without another word, he picked up the box containing the pistol, went to the door, led her down the hallway to the client lounge, and left her there with the new gun.

An adjacent restroom served the lounge. She cranked on the water and pumped soap from the dispenser and washed her hands. After she dried off, she clenched her left fist around a wad of paper towels, applying pressure to stop the thorn pricks from bleeding.

She wondered if Ferrante would blot the drops of blood from the floors of his office and the hallway—and what he might do with the rag that absorbed them. She decided that she would rather not know.

In the client lounge once more, she sat on a sofa. She looked at the box containing the pistol. She raised her head and stared at the frosted windows, which were set as high as those in Ferrante's office, and she thought about how strange her life had become and about how many moments of it were resonant with cryptic meaning that would remain forever beyond her powers of interpretation.

7

A WARM BREEZE, BLADE SHADOWS SCALPING THE barren earth, the ceaseless *slish-slish-slish* of carved air, perhaps one of the two windmills pumping water from a well in addition to cleaving energy from the breath of Nature . . .

As Jergen and Dubose step out of their truck and approach the Corrigan house, the front door opens, and an Arcadian named Damon Ainsley descends two steps to a concrete pad that serves as a stoop. He is a robust man with a rosy complexion that has, in this case, paled from ear to ear and gone a little gray around the eyes.

"We've got a situation," Ainsley says. A thin and bitter laugh escapes him. "*Situation.* Hell's bells, I've become a jackass, more bureaucrat than lawman, politically correct and full of newspeak. The situation, gentlemen, is a shitstorm."

According to Dubose, Dr. Bertold Shenneck, cuckolded husband of the fabulous Inga, had foreseen two types of sudden psychological collapse that might rarely ensue following the activation of a brain implant, the least dramatic being the disintegration of the ego and the id upon the recognition of being possessed and enslaved. In this case, the subject's sense of self dissolves. He loses all identity, all memory. He ceases to understand the environment around him and has no capacity for ordered thought. His mind becomes a shrieking bedlam. This is the more benign of the two possibilities.

In the worse scenario, the ego disintegrates but not the id, leaving the latter in charge. What remains in this case is a sense of self, a kind of situational and pattern-recognition memory rather than recollection of personal experience, and a capacity for ordered but primitive thought. However, the id is the aspect of the mind that seeks pleasure at any cost. Without the moderating influence of the ego, which mediates between the primal desires of the id and the social environment in which we live, there is no Dr. Jekyll anymore, nor even Mr. Hyde—but only a pleasure-seeking *thing*.

Damon Ainsley heads toward one of the Jeep Cherokees. "Got to smoke some weed to float away the nausea. Better prepare yourselves before you go in there."

"I was born prepared," Dubose says.

As Carter Jergen learned during his years at Harvard, there are two explanations for what is called the *reptile consciousness* within the human id, supposing that it exists. A scientist might say human beings are not evolved from apes so much as from all the species that constitute the history of life on Earth's land masses, which means that the first lizard to venture from sea to shore has left its genetic trace in us. On the other hand, a priest might say our reptilian impulses are the curse bestowed by the father of serpents in the Garden of Eden. In either case, the reptile consciousness has no capacity for love, compassion, mercy, or any other virtues prized by civil societies. It is driven solely by its hunger for pleasure, and one of those pleasures is the thrill of violence.

As Dubose opens the door of the Corrigan house, he pauses and pretends to be profound, a pose he finds appealing now and then. "This is a moment to remember, my friend. Dr. Shenneck thought there was a one-in-ten-thousand chance of a psychological collapse. More than sixteen thousand have been adjusted with implants, and this is the first instance of what he predicted. For you and me, it's like being there when Edison tested the first successful light bulb."

Such grandiose declarations, coming from the hillbilly sage, grate on Jergen. "How the hell is it like Edison's light bulb?"

"It's an historic moment."

"Damon Ainsley just called it a shitstorm. A shitstorm isn't my idea of an historic moment."

The big man favors Jergen with an expression like that of a patient adult speaking to an amusing but clueless child. "History isn't just an endless series of triumphs, Carter. History is about the ups *and* downs. It was an historic moment when the *Titanic* sank."

They step into the house.

8

THE RAT-COAT-GRAY TORN-RAG SKY OVER THE GULF of Mexico creeping across blackening waters, the morning sun steadily retreating from the shore, the coastal plain just twenty feet above sea level, the maze of oil refineries looking flat in the shadowless light of an oncoming storm, like a pencil drawing hung on a wall . . .

To Egon Gottfrey, on the trail of Ancel and Clare Hawk, the city of Beaumont, Texas, appears to be more detailed than Worstead, where all this began. But the Unknown Playwright is still sketching the locale rather than painting it in fullest depth and color.

Behind the wheel of his Rhino GX, Gottfrey follows Tucker Treadmont's GMC Terrain through the outskirts of the city into open country, Rupert and Vince close behind in their Jeep Wrangler. This solemn train of black vehicles feels like a funeral procession sans corpse, though it's easy enough to make a corpse if one is needed.

Along a two-lane blacktop, they come into fields of coarse matted grass and tortured weeds from some of which depend clusters of pale bladders the size of thumbs. At certain times of the year, perhaps portions of this land become marshes from which, at dusk, clouds of mosquitoes rise in such great numbers that they blacken the sky even before the last light has gone from it.

The GMC Terrain slows, signals a right turn, leaves the pavement for the wide shoulder of the road, and comes to a stop. Gottfrey parks behind it, Rupert Baldwin behind Gottfrey.

Treadmont waits in front of his vehicle, frowning at the grim sky, drawing deep breaths and snorting them out, as though he is part hound and can assess the potential of the storm by the scent that it imparts to the air. For whatever reason, the nipples of his man breasts have stiffened against his pale-blue polo shirt, a sight about as erotic as a squashed cockroach.

"Why have we stopped?" Gottfrey asks.

"This is where I left them, the cowboy dude and his woman. This is where they wanted to go."

Gottfrey and his men survey their surroundings with puzzlement.

Vince Penn says, "This is like the middle of nowhere. There's nothing. There's no place they could go. It's just fields. Just empty fields is all it is."

Pointing ahead and to the right, toward a narrow dirt lane that branches off the blacktop, Treadmont says, "The last I saw them, they were walkin' that way."

In the distance, what might be a house and two outbuildings—or a mirage—imprint their small dark shapes on the landscape.

"Did they say who lives there?" Gottfrey asks.

"I didn't ask, they didn't say, and I don't care."

"Why didn't they want you to drive them over there? Didn't that seem odd to you?"

"Mister, maybe half of everythin' that happens in life seems odd as hell to me, most of it stranger than this. Now I got a livin' to make."

When Treadmont drives away, Rupert Baldwin squints at the distant buildings. "If we drive in, they'll for sure hear us coming. What do you say we walk it?"

Like Rupert and Vince, Gottfrey is carrying a pistol on his right hip. He also has a snub-nosed revolver in an ankle holster. The three of them set out on foot.

9

THE LIVING ROOM AT THE CORRIGAN HOUSE IS FUR-
nished for comfort, with a deep sofa of no particular style and three
massive recliners, everything aimed at a big-screen television. Otherwise, the theme of the décor is nautical. The reproduced paintings
of sailing ships in calm and stormy seas are the quality that big
hotel chains purchase by the thousands. One lamp base is sheathed
in artfully arranged seashells; another features a porcelain mermaid
topped by a painted shade on which porpoises cavort.

Someone in this desert home yearns for the romance of the sea.

A young DHS agent whose name Carter Jergen doesn't know—
one of the Arcadian backup brigade that streamed into the valley
during the past thirty-six hours—sits on the edge of one of the recliners. He smokes a cigarette, tapping the ashes into a conch shell,
his hands shaking as if he's a palsied retiree.

Radley Dubose says, "Harry, is it?"

"Yeah," the agent says. "Harry Oliver."

"On the phone, you called it a slaughterhouse. To me it looks like
Mayberry, U.S.A."

A tremor ages Harry's voice to match his trembling hands. "The
kitchen, the back porch. That's where . . ."

Filtered through the roof and walls of the house, the sound of the
windmills is not as it is outside, not like giant swords slicing the air,
but rather a low, rhythmic hum. To Jergen it sounds as if some hive
fills the attic, a teeming population busy wax-laying and honey-
making and brewing a potent venom to ensure a lethal sting.

He follows Dubose into a shadowy hallway where one of two
bulbs is burned out in the ceiling light. Beyond open doors to each
side, rooms are little revealed by sunshine leaking around the edges
of closed draperies. On the walls between the doors, rough seas roll
without motion, and tumultuous skies storm without sound.

The first victim is just past the kitchen threshold. Homeland Security ID clipped to the breast pocket of his suit coat. On his back. Face torn and puckered and hollowed by several bite marks. As eyeless as Samson in Gaza.

The father, Rooney Corrigan, lies to the right of a chrome-legged dining table with a yellow Formica top. He's also faceup, though head and body are not joined.

Dubose steps cautiously to avoid the biological debris that slathers the floor, and Jergen follows with equal care.

Rooney's younger of two teenage sons is sprawled beyond the table. The condition of the corpse is so appalling that Jergen must look away.

"It's the remaining son," Dubose says, "who's suffered the psychological collapse. His name's Ramsey. From the Old English, meaning 'male sheep.' Ironic, huh? He might have been a lamb once, but not anymore."

The mother had tried to flee. She'd made it out the back door and onto the screened porch.

Blouse ripped away. Bra torn off. Face wrenched in terror. Lips cruelly bitten, mouth agape in a silent scream. The wide-open eyes suggest that the last thing she'd seen was an abomination worse than her oncoming death. Her neck is broken.

Here on the screened porch, the sound of the windmills has yet a different character. The fine mesh that bars flying insects also seines the crisp edges from the slashing-sword noise, so that the porch seems to be a way station between life and afterlife, where a host of spirit voices softly whisper secrets about what lies beyond death.

Dubose says, "Let's go have a look at Ramsey."

10

THE DIRT LANE IS ELEVATED A FOOT OR TWO ABOVE the flanking fields. It is hardpan in which Egon Gottfrey and his men leave no tracks, nor are there any bootprints impressed by Ancel and Clare Hawk the previous day.

Seen closer than from the paved road, the flourishing weeds are even stranger than they had seemed before, riotous thickets in great variety, many of the species unknown to Gottfrey. His attention is drawn to certain gnarled bushes with needled leaves and wiry stems from which are suspended clusters of pale sacs. From the highway, he'd thought the sacs were thumbsize, bladderlike. But they are larger and more like cocoons than bladders, but not cocoons, either, vaguely reminiscent of something that eludes him.

Perhaps because the eerie fields appear to be hostile, like some alien landscape that harbors unknown lethal life forms, Gottfrey thinks of Judge Sheila Draper-Cruxton and the angry dressing-down she meted out to him in their most recent phone conversation. *You better stop wasting your testosterone, Gottfrey. Keep your pants zipped, man up, start breaking heads, and get the job done.*

The dark clouds race north, harried by some high-altitude wind not felt at ground level. The sky lowers, and birds shriek overhead as they flee toward what few roosts of refuge this flat territory contains.

As Gottfrey and his men continue along the hardpan, they come to a place where the creepy bushes grow within a foot of the lane. He stops to peer more closely at them. The clustered and slightly wrinkled sacs are moist and milky but not opaque. In fact, they are semitranslucent, and dark shapes are coddled within them, as if things wait therein to be born. But these are definitely not cocoons.

"What is it, what're you doing?" Rupert Baldwin asks.

Rupert and Vince have halted twenty feet ahead of him and are watching him inspect the plant.

"I just thought . . ." Gottfrey shakes his head. "Nothing. It's nothing."

As they continue toward the buildings, he stares at the bushes, fascinated beyond all reason. He wonders if the sacs are actually part of the plant. Although they aren't spun-silk cocoons, perhaps they're extruded in another fashion by an insect unknown to him, the fields infested by some pestilence. Abruptly he stops again when he realizes of what the sacs remind him. Pale, yes. Semitranslucent, yes. But they nonetheless resemble testicles.

"Egon?" Rupert says.

"Yes, all right," he responds, and again he proceeds with them toward the buildings.

He has no doubt now that the Unknown Playwright is endorsing Judge Draper-Cruxton's instructions to break heads and get the job done. Recently, the author of all this has set the scenes with too little detail. These fields, however, are so vividly and intricately presented that they are meant to be a sign to guide him back to the proper performance of his role. *Fields* of testicle-bearing plants never seen before, they are put here to remind him of what Judge Draper-Cruxton has demanded—and of what she has threatened should he fail to perform as expected.

He has been under great stress, and this revelation has not relieved any of the pressure on him. But at least he now knows what he must do to avoid suffering the pain that the Unknown Playwright is so capable of doling out. Fulfill the dream he's had of Jane's in-laws. Shoot Ancel. Slit Clare's throat.

Yes, they must first be captured, injected, and interrogated after being enslaved. But once they reveal the whereabouts of young Travis, they will be Gottfrey's to dispose of as he wishes.

He and his men have drawn close to the buildings and now better understand their nature. The house is old, weathered, offering more bare wood than paint. Swaybacked steps. Some porch-railing balusters broken, others missing. Most windows are shattered, and the few that remain intact stare blindly from behind cataracts of dust. The yard is weeds and crawling vines that climb the rotting walls of the abandoned residence. The darkest of the structures is a sun-scorched barn with a rusted-metal roof and concave walls. What appears to be a small stable is in no better condition.

Jane's in-laws are not likely to have hidden away in such ruins. Yet the lane ends here, and no other dwellings are in sight. Maybe the scene is not only what it appears to be.

Guns drawn, Gottfrey, Rupert, and Vince begin the search.

11

THE HUMBLE DESERT HOME NOW SEEMING ALMOST to groan under the weight of an incidental, terrible grandeur bestowed by horror and tragedy, its rooms given a new dimension by a threat to the future of humanity that is here made manifest . . .

Carter Jergen is in the presence of the beast. The smell of blood and urine. The study window covered by draperies. Only the desk lamp aglow. Ordinary shadows seem to pulse with threat.

The master bedroom and Rooney Corrigan's home office are served by a different hallway from the one that connects the living room to the kitchen. In the office, DHS agents Solomon and Taratucci keep guard over seventeen-year-old Ramsey, who is in the desk chair.

The teenager's wrists are zip-tied to the arms of the chair, his ankles to the center post from which radiate five legs with wheels. In light of what the kid has done, the zip-ties have been deemed insufficient restraint. A length of rope twice encircles his chest and is knotted tightly behind the back of the chair. Likewise, rope crosses his thighs twice and secures him to the seat.

Ramsey slumps in his bonds, eyes closed, chin on his chest. He appears to be sleeping, as if four savage murders have exhausted him. He's a sizable specimen, football-linebacker material.

His blond hair is discolored by the spilled life of others, stiff and matted and spiked. Spattered face. Streaked clothes. Resting on the chair arms, his strong hands are gore-mottled, the creases of the knuckles dark with encrusted blood.

Taratucci, who looks as though he changed careers from Mafia muscle, sits in a chair about five feet from Ramsey. His pistol rests on his thigh and ready in his hand.

Solomon wears a better suit than Taratucci's, a tailored white shirt, and a club tie. His receding hair is white at the temples, his features patrician, his posture ramrod when he rises from a chair, his manner like that of a cultured attorney for a mainline law firm in business since the 1800s.

"Why is this haywire piece of meat still alive?" Radley Dubose asks. "Why didn't you make him as dead as the four in the kitchen?"

Solomon does his best to present the facts in a dispassionate, lawyerly recitation.

"For injection, we strapped the Corrigan family in the kitchen chairs. The newest iteration of the nanoweb was established in Mrs. Corrigan in three hours forty minutes. The final implant established in about four hours ten minutes. That last one was Ramsey Corrigan." Solomon glances at the young man in the office chair. "They all responded to the phrase—'Do you see the red queen?' We ran the usual control tests. They were fully adjusted people."

Originally, the sentence that accessed the mind of an adjusted person and compelled him to follow commands was "Play Manchurian with me," a reference to the classic novel of mind control, *The Manchurian Candidate* by Richard Condon, published in 1959. After Jane Hawk learned the power of those four words and could make an adjusted person obey her, the sentence was changed to

"Uncle Ira is not Uncle Ira," a line from Jack Finney's 1955 novel *Invasion of the Body Snatchers*. Hawk, the troublesome bitch, learned that one, too, necessitating the reprogramming of sixteen thousand adjusted people with yet another sentence: *Do you see the red queen?* This one, like the first, was from the Richard Condon novel, in which a brainwashed assassin, Raymond Shaw, was activated by the sight of the queen of diamonds whenever told to play a game of solitaire.

"We removed the restraints from all four," Solomon continued. "We instructed them how to search for Travis Hawk, what their role was. We're almost finished when—" He looks at the teenager, this time with obvious dread. "Ramsey puts his fists to his head and screams. I never heard such a scream, as if he was slammed by pain, rage, and terror all at once. He began to shake violently and scream louder. Something was wrong with the brain implant."

Solomon isn't able to maintain his detachment. A slight tremor comes and goes in his voice. Sometimes he pauses before he can continue.

"Kirk Granger, one of ours . . . the one dead in the kitchen. He rushes to restrain Ramsey before the kid hurts himself, bends over him with fresh zip-ties. Ramsey shrieks a long stream of obscenities worse than you'd hear in the most-violent ward of a prison for the criminally insane, not coherent, just vicious, rank. He comes out of his chair. He bites . . . bites Kirk's face . . . bites it hard. So damn fast, snake-quick. He tears into Kirk's face, his throat. He rips a carotid, maybe a jugular. Didn't see how he took the eyes. Kirk is a martial-arts guy . . . but he's blinded then dead, taken down in five seconds. Ramsey scrambles across the table, knocks his dad out of a chair, tramps his throat, snatches a cleaver from a rack, swings it. *Such power*. It's just ten seconds after he first went nuts."

Dubose returns to his unanswered question. "Why doesn't the sonofabitch have five bullets in his head?"

From his chair, without taking his eyes off Ramsey, Taratucci says, "Don't be a jerk. You notice all the bullet holes in the kitchen cabinets, the walls? He's like some bat out of Hell, how fast he moves. You can't hit what won't be a target."

Solomon says, "Brother's dead, mother runs for it. He wants her more than us, maybe to rape before he kills her. His own *mother*. It's chaos. But when we inject an entire household, we bring a Taser XREP twelve-gauge, in case there's effective resistance. So I put a round in his back while he's on the porch tearing at her clothes."

"He was so gone," Taratucci says, "he didn't know who she was."

Solomon says, "She was already dead. When he caught her and dragged her down, she broke her neck."

Staring at Ramsey Corrigan, Dubose speculates. "He knew—he could *feel*—something was deep inside his head, enslaving him. The control program tried to repress his fear, maybe applied too much pressure, burnt out some neurons, maybe the nanoweb itself badly malfunctioned, whatever, and just kicked his terror into hyperdrive, triggered a rapid-fire psychological meltdown. His psyche came apart like sugar lace. Personality dissolved. Shenneck said this might rarely happen, but he hoped a collapse would end in a catatonic state or in a condition of feeble physical and mental incoherence. He didn't think an adjusted person, damaged like this, would instead plunge all the way down through the forbidden door."

"Well," Jergen says, "damn if that's not another thing you never shared. What door? Why forbidden?"

"Shenneck said Nature is all about change, *progressive* change, always refining its creatures. Of course it's impossible for one of us to revert, through some genetic cataclysm, to an earlier physical form in the evolutionary chain. You can't go to bed human and wake up an ape. Shenneck said the same is true about our psychological state. If the history of all life from the first lizard onward is like a series of ghosts in our genome, Nature won't allow us to be haunted backward to a primitive consciousness because of *any* trauma. Nature will have built into our psyche a forbidden door forever locked against the past of the species, and no event can open it."

"Or Shenneck was wrong," Jergen says. "So then . . . hello, reptile consciousness."

"I needed all five rounds in the Taser XREP," Solomon reveals, "just to keep Ramsey disabled long enough for Taratucci and Damon Ainsley to restrain him again."

Dubose shakes his head. "You should have killed him. Let's roll the freak outside and do some target practice."

"Can't," Solomon declares. "The main lab in Menlo Park wants to study him, see if they can understand why the breakdown."

"Bring the monster in for a chat," Jergen says. "What could possibly go wrong?"

Solomon says, "They're sending in a Medevac helicopter and a team of CIA black-ops tough guys to load him and get him there."

"Sedated?"

"They don't want a sedative used in case it causes further disintegration. They want to study him just as he is."

"How many black-ops guys?"

"They said four. I want six. They think even four is too many."

If Ramsey Corrigan has been asleep, now he wakes. He raises his head, which turns slowly left to right, right to left, like a turret on a tank as the gunner seeks a target. He focuses on Jergen.

Although there is nothing inhuman about the man's eyes, the ferocity of his attention makes his stare more intense than any Jergen has previously encountered. Perhaps because of the horrific carnage in the kitchen, because Ramsey sits here in the blood of others and in his own urine, appearing eerily unconcerned and even confident in spite of being securely bound, his gaze imparts a chill to Jergen. Although his shackles constrain him, he projects an impression of being tightly coiled and ready to strike.

"Kill him now," Jergen warns.

"I agree," Solomon says. "I wish I had. But now . . . the order transferring him to Menlo Park comes from the central committee, through the regional commander, from our cell leader. Anyone who pulls the trigger on Ramsey will be considered a traitor to the revolution. The consequences . . . well, you know the consequences."

12

THE ABANDONED HOUSE IS A SANCTUARY FOR things that crawl and skitter and squirm, that produce a chrysalis in which to transform from something that creeps to something that flies, that find in wood both a home and a meal. Mold thrives and rot has its way and mushrooms sprout in the darker corners. There are the bones of dead rats, the feathers of birds that came in through broken windows and found their way out again, but no sign of Jane Hawk's in-laws.

What was thought to have been a stable is in fact a chicken coop with ramps to elevated laying boxes for the hens, a crumbling structure where the muck-soil floor is thatched with wet and moldy feathers that stick in clumps to Egon Gottfrey's shoes. Nothing lives here now but a fat and hideous pale-faced possum that hisses at him and sends him scurrying out of the building, to the barely suppressed amusement of Rupert Baldwin and Vince Penn.

The spavined barn, its rib studs cracked and termite riddled, its wall slats warped and its doors sagging, has lost two panels of the metal roof, perhaps to a high wind. On a bright day, rectangles of sunshine would slowly lengthen and then shrink across its floor, and shadows would relent. But on this occasion, with a pending storm curdling the sky, the light is gray and diffuse and in league with shadows to conceal the loft and every corner.

The poor light doesn't matter. The loft ladder might once have had twenty rungs, but just four haven't rotted away. Ancel and Clare can't have climbed there to hide.

Anyway, Gottfrey has no need of more light to know that no one has taken refuge in the barn. From crumbling concrete footings to splintering walls to the metal roof rattling now in the stiffening wind, the structure is as devoid of human habitation as any crater on Mars.

Wandering in search of clues, Vince Penn studies the floor that Gottfrey has already studied. "Nope. No recent tire tracks. None at all. No oil or grease. Not a drop. Doesn't seem like anyone kept a vehicle here recently or even back in the day."

Worstead to Hawk Ranch, Hawk Ranch to Longrin Stables, Longrin to Killeen, Killeen to Houston, Houston to Beaumont, Beaumont to this ass-end of nowhere . . .

"Dust on the floor," says Vince Penn. "Dust and like a million teeny-tiny pieces of straw. We're leaving prints. Leaving prints and disturbing all the chaff. But no tire tracks. Zero, zip, nada."

Judge Sheila Draper-Cruxton has given Gottfrey a disturbing ultimatum. And the Unknown Playwright is evidently displeased with how he has been intuiting the author's intent.

While Rupert watches Vince much as he might watch, with pity and contempt, the hopeless progress of a crippled frog dragging itself laboriously toward its pond, the inimitable Agent Penn says, "Looks like Ancel and Clare never came here. Not to the barn or coop or house. They walked to the end of the lane and kept walking. Went off through the field. Went somewhere else. Hard to say where."

None of this is real, nothing but Gottfrey's mind, the rest illusion. Only radical philosophical nihilism makes sense of this otherwise chaotic world. None of it matters. Go with the flow.

"Yeah, it's a dead end," says Vince. "Blind alley. Blank wall. Dead end." He looks at Gottfrey's feet. "Hey, Egon, your shoes look funny. Rupert, don't his shoes look funny?"

Gottfrey's shoes are caked in muck-soil from the chicken coop.

Stuck in that gluey mass are hundreds of feathers. The feathers were initially wet; but they have been drying out since he acquired them. Now, in spite of being deteriorated, they are rather fluffy.

With sudden enlightenment, Vince says, "Hey, bunny slippers. Egon, looks like you're wearing dirty bunny slippers. Don't they look like bunny slippers, Rupert?"

"Bunny slippers from Hell," says Rupert.

Gottfrey pulls his pistol, kills Vince with one round, and expends two on Rupert Baldwin, who was never a fast draw.

He does not intuit any disapproval on the part of the Unknown Playwright. Violence is wanted. The script requires bloodshed. A more aggressive Egon Gottfrey now comes onstage.

"The bolo tie is stupid," he says to Rupert's corpse.

After holstering his weapon, he wipes his shoes on the dead men's clothes as best he can.

When he steps out of the barn, the lowering gray sky reminds him of the cerebral cortex of the human brain, fissured and softly folded. In the fissures, the clouds are blackening, as though the sky is the brain of the world and contemplating darker intentions.

He follows the hardpan lane between the fields of weeds that have had significant influence on the changes in his character, to the vehicles parked alongside the highway.

From the customized Jeep Wrangler, he removes Rupert Baldwin's laptop and transfers it to the Rhino GX.

As he is getting behind the wheel of his luxury SUV, the first thunder rolls through the clotted sky, not a hard crash but instead a soft, protracted rumble that isn't preceded by visible lightning. The storm hasn't yet begun, but it is imminent.

Gottfrey starts the engine. He hangs a U-turn and heads back toward distant Beaumont.

There are still ways to find Jane Hawk's in-laws. After all, they are not ghosts, though he would like to make them so.

A new understanding comes to him, a realization that he was never meant to plod through his scenes with an entourage consist-

ing of the likes of Janis Dern and Chris Roberts and the Lobo broth-
ers and Rupert Baldwin, and certainly not with a ludicrous specimen
like Vince Penn. He is meant to be an iconic loner, which makes
sense when he is the only *real* person in this story, and which therefore puts him at the center of it. He is expected to be a hero who
stands tall and strong like Dirty Harry or Shane, a resolute cham-
pion of the revolution, who takes no shit and no prisoners. For the
first time in a while, he feels in sync with the author of the play.

He suspects that in the frantic chase from Worstead to Beaumont
and beyond, distracted more than assisted by his so-called team, he
overlooked some clue. Now that he is a loner, he will be able to see
events clearly, blow away the fog of war, so to speak, and convert
Jane's arrogant in-laws into either adjusted people or dead people.

13

EARLY TUESDAY MORNING, MINETTE BUTTERWORTH,
an English teacher, called her principal to say that she was taking a
sick day and that her husband, Robert, who taught history, was also
under the weather. Neither Minette nor Bob had missed work due
to illness in six years.

Neither of them was in the habit of lying to their employer, either. Minette felt guilty about this deception, but Bob insisted it was
for a good cause. They had been asked to assist in the search for the
kidnapped boy, and the right thing to do was cooperate with the
desperate authorities.

As Bob reassured Minette, a still, small voice within her confirmed that this was the right thing to do.

The deputies in the sheriff's department dared not go looking for the boy wearing their uniforms, in their police cars, because the kid-nappers had said they would kill the poor child at the first sign of law enforcement closing in on them. Besides, there weren't enough deputies to do the job. They needed to deputize trustworthy locals and send them out into Borrego Valley to conduct the search with-out alarming the people who had snatched the precious child.

The kidnappers were dangerous and surely armed. Minette was surprised that she didn't fear joining the hunt and was excited by the task ahead. The nice African American, Deputy Kingman, had told her there was nothing to fear, because she and Bob didn't have to confront the bad guys, only find them and then call in the depu-ties.

She loved children. She'd not yet been able to have her own. A child being harmed . . . the thought sickened and outraged her.

After a shower, when she stepped out of the stall and saw Bob naked and ready for his turn under the hot water, she was over-come by a sudden desire for him. Sex was best in the morning, be-fore the day wore them down. She put her arms around him and kissed him.

But then she realized how inappropriate it was to be making love when a five-year-old child's life depended on them. She thought of herself as a flawed but basically good person whose experience of tragedy had fine-tuned her conscience. Until this morning, how-ever, her conscience hadn't actually spoken to her, as it did now in a faint voice to confirm Bob's insistence that participating in the search was the right thing: *You know what you need to do. Get on with what you need to do, and you will be useful and happy.*

As if Bob heard that same voice, he went to the shower without comment.

Useful. At eighteen, Minette had been a frivolous girl, but she had become a serious adult almost overnight. For the past fifteen years, her happiness had depended on doing penance in one way or another. She needed to be *useful.* She earned a living as a teacher but spent nearly as much time in volunteer activities—counseling troubled children and working with organizations that served people with disabilities.

Her freshman year in college, on her own for the first time, she had slipped the belaying lines of family. She dated a guy named Mace Mackey, who was in the first year of the master's program. Mace fancied himself bad to the bone, although in truth he possessed no moral substance, either bad or good, deeper than his skin. She found him so exciting that she didn't go home for the three-month break before her sophomore year, but told her parents that she'd landed a good summer job with the university. There was no job; there was Mace, who came from a wealthy family and took care of Minette's finances, while she took care of his even more basic needs.

Minette and her younger sister, Glynis, had always been close. Glynis missed Minette. Sixteen that summer, she wanted to come visit for a week. Minette, who thought of herself as sophisticated, looked forward to showing off her cute apartment and older boyfriend. The second night of the visit, the three were returning from a death-metal concert when unearned sophistication proved to have a high price. Behind the wheel of his Maserati, Mace was flying on some pills he'd been popping all day. Minette didn't insist on driving because that would annoy him; he was no fun when annoyed. Anyway, she had a bit of a buzz on herself, from a joint and from sipping chocolate-flavored vodka. Mace totaled the Maserati. Fate proved to have a cruel sense of humor when he walked away without a scratch, Minette broke a finger—and Glynis, the only innocent among them, suffered a spinal injury that left her a paraplegic for life.

Minette, who had felt enchained by her parents' old-fashioned middle-class ways, discovered that the chain of deserved guilt came with an immense anchor at the end and couldn't be cast off as easily as bourgeois values. Fifteen years later it still encumbered her.

Useful. After the accident, she'd found happiness again only when she was useful, helping Glynis and then others, always giving more than she received. Now she could be *useful* by helping the authorities find the endangered boy.

In the bedroom, after Minette pulled on a pair of panties, as she was shrugging into a bra, she saw the bruise in the crook of her right arm. The diameter of a bottle cap. Somewhat red, too, inflamed and swollen. When touched, the spot proved tender. She looked closer and saw a puncture centered in the discoloration, directly over a vein, as if she'd had blood drawn, which she hadn't.

Maybe a spider bite. A spider or some other insect. Nothing serious. Nothing to worry about. Nothing at all. Forget about it.

After she dressed and went into the kitchen and fired up the coffeemaker, while she waited for Bob, she walked down the hall to the guest room to make the bed. At the threshold, as she began to open the door, she realized no guest was in residence at the moment.

Puzzled by her confusion, she pulled the door shut and turned away from it—and felt the terrible pull of that enduring anchor chain of guilt. Something was wrong. Something awful had happened. She must do the right thing. She must be useful. And somehow . . . being useful in this case required her to go into the guest room.

She turned to the door. Opened it. The room lay in darkness except for a few thin blades of light with which the sharp sun of the desert pierced the venetian blinds.

She stepped across the threshold and stood tense and blinkless in the gloom, listening. Then she flipped up the wall switch, and a nightstand lamp brightened the space.

To her left, the bedclothes were in disarray. Someone had spent the night here, after all.

Perplexed, she took another step into the room, turned to her right, and saw a dead woman in a wheelchair. *Oh God, her face.* It was less a face than a wound, ravaged flesh and shattered bone, her skull misshapen. But . . . not just a woman, not a stranger, *Glynis.*

Minette's heart—

As Minette took a mug from a kitchen cabinet, her heart was suddenly thudding as if she had run a race. She put the mug on the counter, pressed a hand to her breast, and felt the systole of that vital pump. She detected no irregularity, only a healthy rhythm.

Frowning, she raised her eyes from the mug to the cabinet door. She could not remember opening it.

The kitchen was richly scented with the aroma of a fine Jamaica blend.

Minette turned her attention to the burbling coffeemaker. It was nearly finished brewing, having filled the Pyrex pot almost to the eight-cup line.

Disquieted but unsure why, she crossed the kitchen to the swinging door, which stood open.

She went into the dining room, from there into the living room, and the house was less than entirely familiar to her, as though its angles and dimensions had subtly changed.

On the brink of the hallway, she stared at the farther end.

Her racing heart still could not find a calmer rhythm.

As she moved along the hallway, she felt almost weightless, drawn inexorably toward the room at the end, which seemed to have the gravity of an entire planet contained within its walls.

Halfway to the guest bedroom, Minette was halted by a vivid memory: *the Maserati fishtailing at high speed, the back end jumping a curb, the car airborne, slamming into the oak, rebounding with the violence of the impact. Shaken, she tries the front passenger door, surprised to find it still works. She gets out, stumbles a few feet from the vehicle before regaining her balance, and turns. . . . The rear passenger-side door is crumpled like cardboard, jammed into the backseat; beyond the cocked and glassless window, Glynis's face rises moon-white, and blood sprays on her breath when she screams.*

Minette stands trembling in the hallway, wondering why this horrendous memory should recur to her now in such graphic detail.

Something was wrong with her. She wasn't herself, moving past perplexity toward a frightening bewilderment.

She was also moving along the hall again. The guest-room door. She opened it. Stepped into the room. She flipped the light switch.

The bedclothes were tangled and spilling off the mattress. Someone had slept here last night.

Other signs of a visitor were to the right of the door: carpet stains and small pieces of debris. In the deep-pile forest-green carpet, the stains appeared black. Although the debris resisted identification, Minette became queasy at the sight of it, and she looked away.

The door to the walk-in closet stood ajar. She stepped around the stains, crossed the room, opened the closet door, and discovered a wheelchair. The woman in the chair faced away from Minette, into the closet, her head tipped to the right. The back of the woman's head was broken open. A dangling chunk of skull bone was suspended by a flap of skin and strands of hair.

Minette remembered this, remembered seeing the face now turned away from her. In fact, she herself had moved the wheelchair into the closet.

Minette's heart—

Sitting at the kitchen table, hands clasped around a mug of hot coffee, Minette Butterworth felt her heartbeat subside from a gallop to a more ordinary pace, and it no longer knocked against her breastbone. Paroxysmal supraventricular tachycardia, an acceleration of the heart when no cause was evident, had troubled her grandmother, and perhaps she had inherited a propensity for it. The condition wasn't life-threatening. *Ventricular* tachycardia, on the other hand, could lead to a sudden cessation of the heartbeat and was far more serious than the supraventricular form, requiring a pacemaker. But her grandmother hadn't needed one, and neither would Minette.

She didn't worry about the episode, because an inner voice said she had nothing to fear. Nothing whatsoever. Nothing. Nothing. All would be well if she made herself useful.

When Bob came into the kitchen, showered and shaved and dressed for the day, he drank his coffee while standing. "We've got to get moving, Min. We have our assignment, places to look, people to see. A helluva lot of them."

Getting up from the table, Minette said, "That poor little boy must be terrified. What kind of people kidnap a helpless child?"

"We have more damn crime in this country than the big shots in Washington will ever admit," Bob grumbled. "It's only going to get worse."

He drove their Toyota Tacoma pickup. She didn't need to give him directions. He'd memorized the assignment, which was unusual. Minette had a facility for memorization, especially when it came to poetry, but not her Bobby. He was an excellent teacher, but if she didn't give him a written list, if she just rattled off five items for him to pick up at the market, he would forget one or two. Yet he remembered every detail of their complicated assignment as if he were programmed.

Happily, they didn't need to check on any of the folks in the other three residences on their little lane. Those people, too, had volunteered to assist in the search. They were darn good neighbors, and they were darn good people. Thinking about all of them wanting to help save that precious little boy, Minette was filled with a warm sense of community. She almost wanted to cry.

14

At 10:38, AHEAD OF SCHEDULE, ENRIQUE DE SOTO'S deliveryman, Tio, arrived with the Tiffin Allegro motor home, towing a white Chevrolet Suburban. The gate guard instructed him to park at the back of Ferrante Escobar's fenced four-acre property and summoned Elinor Dashwood—Jane—from the client lounge.

Tio was maybe thirty, the ideal height and weight to be a

Thoroughbred-racing jockey. A white welt of scar tissue across his throat suggested an encounter in which his adversary had failed either to kill him or rob him of his voice.

The man who would drive Tio back to Nogales, Arizona, followed in a Porsche 911 Turbo S. He parked near the motor home with the engine running and the air-conditioning on, and he never got out of the car.

The repainted Allegro was a sparkly midnight blue, not a color in the Tiffin catalog. The company decorated their vehicles with bold multicolor wind-stream stripes flaring along the flanks. Ricky had refined this motif so that there were fewer and smaller stripes of lower contrast with the base color, rendered in a single shade of high-gloss ruby red. The vehicle was so eye-catching that no one would imagine that it was on a clandestine mission.

Carrying her tote bag, Jane followed Tio into the motor home. Except for the windshield, the windows were tinted, and the vehicle carried a cargo of shadows.

She and Tio settled into the dinette booth, facing each other across the table.

She gave him the plastic-wrapped brick of money. "A hundred twenty K, as agreed."

Tio put the cash in a tote bag of his own. "Enrique, he tells me don't check is it funny money and don't do a count. He wants you should know he trusts you like no one else. You should trust him the same once you're over this widow thing."

Jane smiled. "He's one hell of a romantic guy, my Ricky."

"Yeah, all the ladies love him, and that's no shit. Plates on both vehicles, registration and proof of insurance in the consoles. Special plates for the Suburban and the other stuff you wanted"—he gestured toward the rear of the motor home—"it's all there in the bedroom."

Sliding out of the booth, she said, "Wait here."

"You really gonna look it's all there?"

"I really am."

When nervous, Tio fingered the scar on his throat. "I tell Ricky you don't take it on faith, it's gonna break the man's heart."

"I'm sure it's all there. But before I'm in the middle of this business deal I'm setting up, I want to be certain I've got exactly what I need, that there's been no misunderstanding about what I asked Ricky for. Anyway, let's not tell him I had to do inventory, spare him the heartbreak."

"That's good with me. I hate to see the man sad." He stopped fingering the scar. "You never know what crazy shit he's gonna do when he's sad."

When she returned from the bedroom, Jane said, "Everything's just as it should be."

Tio gestured to the booth she had vacated. "Park yourself and let me say some shit."

She sat but said, "I'm expecting my partners very soon."

"I'll keep it quick. I want you should know some important truths about the man."

"Ricky?"

"What other man we been talkin' about?"

"Go on."

"First, he's hung like a horse. *Un enorme garañón.*"

Jane said, "I'm willing to believe that—but how do you know?"

"I stood beside him at urinals a hundred times. Understand, I don't look on purpose. I mean, I don't have no interest. But you take a piss with a guy often enough, you notice sooner or later."

"Understood."

"The first couple times with a new girl, maybe he goes off too quick. But after that, she's not so fresh to him, then he can last longer than any stud you ever knew. Twice as long."

"And how would you know that? Not saying I doubt you."

Tio held out his right hand, so she could see the tattoo on the back. A red heart was enwrapped with a rippling blue ribbon on which red letters declared in Spanish, MAYA OWNS TIO FOREVER. "She's my girl."

"She made you put her brand on you?"

He regarded Jane with an expression of pity. "Maybe you don't read guys too good. No bitch makes Tio do nothin'. I did it myself for love."

"That's very moving."

Tio ducked his head, embarrassed by his sentimentality. "Maya, she was Ricky's best girl, but he moved on. So then me and Maya, we found this special thing together, like destiny or somethin'. She's hotter than hot."

"And that's how you know Ricky has staying power. Pillow talk between you and Maya."

Tio shrugged. "You know how it goes. You get off together, it's so great, and then after, while you're layin' there, you gotta talk about *somethin'*." He realized Jane might infer the wrong thing from what he'd said. "Just so you know, I'm a marathon guy in the sack, just like Ricky. *Lo puedo hacer por horas.*"

"I can tell just by looking at you," Jane said.

"Yeah, but I'm not talkin' me here. I'm talkin' Enrique, what you need to know."

Jane felt as though she had been swept into the role of Roxane in a grotesque parody of *Cyrano de Bergerac*, with Tio as a less than eloquent Cyrano, Enrique offstage as the even less verbally gifted Christian de Neuvillette.

Smiling, Tio put his hands together in prayer mode as if to suggest that God was witness to the truth of his words. "Ricky, he never hit no bitch in his life. He never would hit no bitch. He treats them all like ladies."

"If he ever hit me," Jane said, "he'd have one less hand."

Tio's smile froze.

"I'm just sayin'," Jane added.

Tio's prayerful hands separated, and he nervously fingered his scarred throat. "I don't see no reason to share that with Ricky."

Jane smiled and nodded. "We don't want to make him sad. You just tell Ricky that I said nothing you told me about him was news to me. I've always admired him from a distance, first as a married woman with vows to respect and now as a widow in mourning."

When Jane rose to her feet, Tio said, "I also gotta tell how Ricky is crazy about music, you bein' a piano player and all."

"Come along now. I've got work to do before I, like Roxane, take myself off to a nunnery."

As Jane was speaking, Tio got out of the booth with the tote full of money. When she got to the word *nunnery*, he flinched as if he'd been slapped. "*No, usted no puede!* You cannot! I tell you Maya is hotter than hot, and you're so very hotter than her. This is a crazy thing for you. For my sister, yes, but never for you."

Of course he did not get the reference and therefore did not get the joke, but Jane saw value in his lack of understanding, a way to keep Enrique at bay if she should need another vehicle from him in the future. With great solemnity, she said, "If I survive this business I'm caught up in, considering all the violence to which I've been a party, I'll be most at peace if my in-laws raise my son and I withdraw from the world. There is an order at a monastery in Arizona, the Poor Clares of Perpetual Adoration. I believe I would be happy there. After all, Audrey Hepburn became a nun."

Tio was doubly nonplussed. "Audrey *who*?"

"She was the most gorgeous movie star of her time, the Jennifer Lawrence of her day, but even more beautiful, and she became a nun, Sister Luke. She served the poor in the Congo, where she contracted tuberculosis." Jane neglected to add that this occurred in a movie, *The Nun's Story*.

Clearly distressed, Tio said, "I am broken to hear you'll do this."

She squeezed his shoulder as if with affection and moved him toward the front door of the motor home. "Just be happy for me, Tio. Be happy for me and go back home to Maya. After all, you are hers forever."

15

Minette and Robert Butterworth were assigned to pay surprise visits to the homes of their students, who would now be in school. In the case of well-behaved and studious kids, Min and Bob would represent to the parents that the child was being evaluated as a possible recipient for a full college scholarship under a program sponsored by a wealthy philanthropist. As regarded ill-behaved or underperforming kids, the visit supposedly would be about evaluating them for possible placement in a program funded by a philanthropist who developed new high-tech methods of instruction for struggling students.

While in the residence, they would be alert for any indication that something was not right. They had been provided with a list of clues that might indicate sympathy for Jane Hawk and the presence of her son. Min and Bob had memorized that list, though she couldn't recall exactly when she had studied it.

If no one was home when they came calling—quite likely to be the case, because most families needed two incomes these days—then she and Bob would enter and search the place. They had been provided with a police lock-release gun, a nifty device that could open any deadbolt.

Two German shepherds had disappeared with the boy. Minette didn't understand why kidnappers would take dogs or why the dogs would allow themselves to be taken. But that's the way it was. No point in puzzling over it. No point at all. Just accept the facts and move on. Do what you're told. Be useful. The dogs weren't dangerous. She and Bob didn't have to worry about being bitten. No need to worry at all. In fact, if they found two German shepherds that responded to the names Duke and Queenie, then the boy would be somewhere nearby. However, there was a chance that the kidnappers found the dogs to be too much trouble and killed them.

Therefore, it was necessary to search outside each residence, too, for any signs that something had recently been buried on the property.

Minette thought she would be nervous about entering other people's homes uninvited and poking around in their things. But at the second, fourth, and fifth of the first five houses, when no one answered the bell or knock, she breezed through those places with no sense that what she was doing might be improper or dangerous.

After all, they were working with the authorities as part of a new citizen's support team for the police. They were doing the right thing. It wasn't dangerous, really. Heck, it wasn't dangerous at all. There was nothing to be concerned about. Nothing. Nothing at all. Besides, it felt so darn good to be *useful*.

The fifth house belonged to Walter and Louise Atlee, parents of Minette's student Colter Atlee. Colter was a nice kid, good student, and Minette thought it unlikely that his mom and dad would be mixed up with kidnappers. But a little boy's life was in jeopardy, and it was like that nice African American policeman, Deputy Kingman, had said—these days, you just couldn't be sure who anyone was or what they might do. You couldn't risk a little boy's life by giving a pass to people like Walter and Louise Atlee just because you *thought* you could be sure they were good people.

As Minette pored through the papers taken from the desk in Walter Atlee's study, a weird thing happened. Speaking in a stage whisper and yet bell-clear, a man's angry voice spewed out a long stream of obscene and blasphemous words, dozens and dozens of them, like the ravings of a madman, as disgusting as they were meaningless. She had never heard anything so raw and vicious. The whisperer sounded as though he must be there in the study with her, but she was alone.

When the voice fell silent after perhaps half a minute, Bob entered the study. "Min, what the hell? You hear that?"

"Yeah. I did. Someone's in the house."

"No one's here but us."

The cursing resumed, still a stage whisper but louder than before, and Minette realized the voice wasn't in the study, after all. It was in her head.

"The whispering room," she said.

She'd never heard that term before, but she knew immediately what it meant, and it neither surprised nor frightened her. The whispering room allowed microwave communication between others like her and Bob, others who had been made useful. When you had something important to share in the whispering room, it went out to everyone else who had a whispering room within a radius of twenty miles, so they could be coordinated for a purpose and function well together. Functioning smoothly together was essential in this increasingly dysfunctional world. The whispering room was a tool that made a person more useful.

Unfortunately, the angry and incoherent man grossly misused this wonderful new service, this internal Twitter system. Rather than communicating something helpful to others, he broadcast an insane, vitriolic rant. And now with the words came sharp attitude, fierce emotion. Minette could not only hear the sender's fury, but also *feel* it, his lust and bloodlust, carried on the words, woven through the obscenities, so that she felt unclean and assaulted. Those vile words came in repetitious, rhythmic rushes like some ferocious canticle, building in intensity, building and building until it had the power of a Gregorian chant, suddenly louder, more insistent, and Minette had no way to disconnect from it, his fury *exploding* into her head.

Shaken, she sat in the office chair to wait out the onslaught, but soon needed to grip the desk with both hands, as if it were a wave-tossed fragment of a sunken ship, her one desperate hope of staying above water on a storm-racked and rolling sea. The vulgar salvos of hate and threat grew in volume and velocity, became a constant cannonade of malevolent words twined with caustic emotions that were alien to her, emotions hot with cruel desire but that howled through her like an arctic wind. In the progress of the storm, she realized that no longer were all the sounds in the sender's rant words, but now also shrieks and hisses and shrill cries like the keening of coyotes chasing down prey, and with this difference came a change in the nature of the emotions flooding into her whispering room, a new coarseness, a primitive bludgeoning-shredding power that was both terrifying and alluring. The sender's transmission swelled into a fierce declaration of freedom from all obligations and all consequences, a celebration of the thrill of violent rape, killing, and the savage destruction of all that is the Other. As this river of alien emotion sluiced through the channels of her brain, Minette became mildly apprehensive as she felt something slowly eroding within her, as if this influx from the sender were a solvent.

Near the door to the hallway, Bob had dropped to his knees and then fallen onto his side. He lay with his hands clasped to his head, but otherwise in the fetal position, with his back bent and knees drawn toward his chest, as though preparing to be born again.

Minette lost all ability to judge the pace of the passage of time. Whether the invasion of her whispering room and, therefore, her mind lasted minutes or hours, she couldn't say. But the sense that something essential was eroding from her continued, although the disquiet that initially troubled her soon passed, and in its place arose an agreeable anticipation.

Moments after her apprehension was rinsed from Minette, her Bobby came out of the fetal position, whereupon he did something unexpected and exciting.

PART FOUR

Whispering
Armageddon

1

LUTHER TILLMAN, FOUR TIMES ELECTED SHERIFF OF
a mostly rural county in Minnesota, was tall and solidly built, yet he
moved with catlike quiet. When he opened the door of the motor
home and stepped inside, Jane knew at once that he'd arrived, not
because the vehicle softly protested when it took his weight, but
because the man had presence.

She'd last seen him twelve days earlier, when he and his daughter Jolie had gone to ground in Texas with friends of hers, Leland
and Nadine Sacket, entrepreneurs and now philanthropists, opera-
tors of the Sacket Home and School for orphaned children. At Jane's
request, Leland had flown Luther to Palm Springs in the Sackets'
Learjet this morning and had driven him to Indio in a rental car.

Because he had been tied to Jane by the authorities and the press,
he had shaved his head since she'd last seen him, and his face was
beginning to disappear behind a flourishing salt-and-pepper beard.
He had spent most of his life in uniforms and suits, a pillar of the
community; now he wore red sneakers, black jeans, a killer T-shirt
featuring the face of the singer and actress Janelle Monáe, a loose

black-denim jacket cut to mid-thigh, the better to carry a concealed weapon, and a bling necklace of silver chain links. He looked like Dennis Haysbert might have looked in the role of a fiftysomething gang leader in the hood, a godfather of street crime, if Haysbert had ever been given a chance to play such a character.

Jane slid out of the dinette booth, where she'd been checking out various items she had purchased from her forged-documents source in Reseda, and got to her feet. "You're not as pretty as Janelle Monáe, but you look damn good to me."

As they hugged each other, he said, "I doubt I can kick ass like Janelle, but I'm ready to do my best."

They had been through a lot together in the two days between when they met in Iron Furnace, Kentucky, and parted in Texas. Jane not only trusted him with her own life but with that of her child.

He said, "I don't know how you don't look tired, all you've been through."

"I'm tired enough," she said, "and scared. Travis is safe for the moment, hidden away. But they know he's somewhere in Borrego Valley, and if we don't get to him soon, these sonsofbitches will."

She led him to the dinette booth, and they sat facing each other across the table.

Luther had picked up the trail of the Arcadian conspiracy when a friend of his, a schoolteacher named Cora Gundersun, had committed suicide in a flamboyant fashion, taking forty-six other people with her, including a governor and congressman. He had not believed she was capable of such an atrocity. His reward for dogged and brilliant detective work had been the loss of his wife, Rebecca, and his older daughter, Twyla, who had been injected with control mechanisms and were now enslaved. His younger daughter, seventeen-year-old Jolie, remained in hiding with the Sackets in Texas.

"How did Jolie take it when you told her you were coming here?"

"Pretty much how a Marine wife like you takes bad news. Jolie doesn't swoon and get the vapors. She thinks I can single-handedly break these bastards, so she's all for us taking them down to get your boy. For such a smart girl, she has too much faith in me."

"Only what's been earned," Jane said. "You're not carrying any ID, are you?"

"No."

"Now you are."

She slid a driver's license across the table. The photo was the one he had emailed to the house of the dancing gnomes in Reseda.

"It's on file with the DMV in Sacramento," she said. "So it'll pass any police check. You're now Wilson Ellington from Burbank. The street address is real, and it's an apartment complex, but there's no apartment twenty-five. They stop at twenty-four."

"You know the best sources. Incredible quality," Luther said, studying the hologram of the Great Seal of the State of California that appeared and disappeared as the license was viewed from different angles.

"Maybe I've always belonged on the dark side of the law."

"In this topsy-turvy time, your side is the right side. I imagine you have a plan."

"I'll go over it with you. You ever fired an automatic assault shotgun?"

He raised his eyebrows. "I've never even seen one."

"You'll like it."

"What do we need it for?"

"Insurance. Just in case."

2

THE RANT WAS A RIVER RACING, CURRENTS OF words rippled through with wordless expressions of rage and need and hatred, a tireless primal scream as nuanced as Nature herself, a corrosive erosive flood tide surging through Minette, so loud now that no sound in the world around her could compete. . . .

Such a great volume poured into her and nothing poured out, for she had been struck dumb by the power of this tsunami of sound and primitive emotion. She sat behind the desk with her mouth agape but issuing only silence. To make room for the incoming dark deluge, structures within her dissolved.

The fear evoked by the assault faded. A tentative excitement rose in her and soon grew into a thrill born from a sense of wild possibilities, feral freedom.

Bob, Bobby, her man, he let go, *let loose*, went for it, tore a picture off the wall and smashed it repeatedly against an armchair, glass shattering-flying, frame splintering. He dropped the ruined picture and picked up the chair, the big chair—such strength, such *power*—and threw it, just threw the chair into a freestanding set of bookshelves, and the shelves toppled and the books spilled across the floor. He snatched up a book and tore it apart and threw it away and snatched up another, ripped off the dust jacket, ripped off the boards, ripped with the animal glee of a predator rending its prey. His face wrenched with rage, yet she thought he might be laughing, delighting in both his fury and the destruction.

She understood, she did, how all this clutter of humanity could infuriate, the way they lived, their pretension, so many *things* all around, too many *things*. The voice screaming in her whispering room was calling her to something better, to something pure, calling her to break free of this humdrum existence, to shuck off the bonds of bullshit civilization, admit to her true essence, which was animal, to stop striving for the sake of striving, to cast off the burden that millions of years of change had layered on her kind until it *crushed* her animal spirit.

He, the man, he ripped the shade off a floor lamp, picked the lamp up by its pole, swung it like a hammer, the heavy base smashing several porcelain figures, ladies in fine gowns. It was so *exciting* to see the fancy bitches' hands torn from their glossy arms, their arms from their bodies, exhilarating to see their bodies shattered and headless on the floor. The man sweating and red-faced and so *powerful*. She couldn't remember his name. Her own name eluded her, didn't matter, any name was a burden, like a brand on cattle, the hateful slave mark society burned onto you.

He looked at her, the man, the male, he looked. She could feel his wild delight, joy, *rapture* in throwing off all restraints. There was a thing on the desk before her—the word *computer* passed through her mind but meant nothing to her—and she picked it up, raised it high, threw it. Tethered to the wall by cords of some kind, it took brief flight, came to a sudden stop in midair, and ripped free of the wall with a spurt of sparks. It crashed to the floor, and the sound of the impact shivered through her, untying knots that she'd never known existed. She began to come loose and free.

3

EGON GOTTFREY CHECKS INTO A HOTEL IN BEAU-mont to take time to discern what the script expects of him. The hotel is so lacking in character that he feels as though he has taken a room in the mere *concept* of a hotel—which, given his radical philosophical nihilism, is exactly what he's done.

Nevertheless, because food and drink have taste and effect even if they are unreal, he goes downstairs for lunch, to have a sandwich and a drink or two at the hotel bar. A pressed-copper ceiling, walls and floor and booths and tables and chairs of dark wood, and red-vinyl upholstery are reflected in a long back-bar mirror, so the place seems immense and even lonelier than it is.

The bartender is a tall guy with big hair and a bigger gut. But with a cold stare and a grim expression, Gottfrey turns the man from a hearty-Texas-howdy type into a quiet, efficient server.

He is sipping his second Scotch when his bacon cheeseburger is served, and he's two bites into the sandwich when a fussy-looking professorial type sits at the bar with one stool between them.

This obvious walk-on character has unkempt white hair and white eyebrows that haven't been trimmed since the turn of the millennium. He's wearing a black onyx stud in one ear, wire-rimmed half-lens glasses, a bow tie, a plaid shirt, a classic tweed sport coat, brown wool pants, and white athletic socks with moccasin-style loafers. The man is so *detailed* and so not Texan that Gottfrey realizes the Unknown Playwright is using the professor as an avatar, stepping into the play to deliver a message that must not be ignored.

The professor orders the same Scotch that Gottfrey is drinking, which is another sign of his importance to the story. While the man waits for his drink, he opens a thick paperback and sits reading, as if unaware that another customer watches from one stool removed.

Gottfrey understands the Playwright's narrative structure well enough to know that the book matters. In fact, it seems to glow in the faux professor's hands. *In the Garden of Beasts* by Erik Larson. Judging by the cover, it's a work of nonfiction set in Nazi Germany.

Gottfrey finishes half his burger before he says, "Good book?"

Pretending to be surprised that anyone shares the bar with him, the professor pulls his reading glasses farther down his nose and peers over them at Gottfrey. "It's brilliant, actually. A chilling depiction of an entire society descending from normalcy into almost universal madness in just a year or so. I feel a disturbing parallel to our own times and that long-ago Nazi ascendancy."

Gottfrey says, "The National Socialist German Workers' Party. Hitler and that ragtag crew around him—they seemed to be such a bunch of clowns, though I guess they couldn't have been just that."

This observation inspires a sense of intellectual brotherhood in the professor. He swivels on his barstool to more directly face Gottfrey, puts aside the book, and grips his Scotch glass in an age-spotted fist. "They were precisely what you say—a cabal of clowns, foolish misfits and geeks and thugs, pretenders to philosophical depth, ignorant know-nothings who fancied themselves intellectuals."

Gottfrey nods thoughtfully. "Yet they led an entire nation into a war and genocide that killed tens of millions."

"Our own time, sir, is infested with their ilk."

"But *how*," Gottfrey wonders. "How could they so easily lead a rational nation into ruin?"

"Yes, how? Look at them. Goering had a soft baby face. Horst Wessel was a chinless wonder. Had he been an actor, Martin Bormann would've been typecast as a gangster. Himmler, a sexless nebbish. Hess really looked like a Neanderthal! But they understood the power of symbols—swastika, Nazi flag—the power of rituals and costumes. Those Nazi uniforms, the SS especially. Hitler in trench coats and battle jackets! A bunch of dishrags made glamorous with *costumes*. They were pretenders, actors, assigning to themselves leadership roles and giving stellar performances . . . for a while. Beware actors who can become anyone they wish to be; they are in fact no one at all, cold and empty, though they can be pied pipers to the masses."

The professor drains his Scotch. The bartender delivers a fresh glass of whisky even as his customer finishes the first.

Thinking about Vince Penn and Rupert Baldwin and Janis Dern, and so many others, Gottfrey says, "But for a conspiracy of clowns to take power and crush all adversaries, they must have something more than an understanding of symbols, rituals, and costumes."

"Passion!" the professor declares. "They had more passion than those who resisted them. A passion to rule, to tear down society and remake it more to their liking, a passion to silence all dissent and to make a world in which they wouldn't have to hear an opinion at variance with their own. The passion for destruction always has more appeal to more people than does the passion to preserve and build. It's an ugly truth of human nature. Passion, sir. The kind of raw passion that breeds ruthlessness."

Gottfrey nods. "They so believed in the rightness of their cause that they could kill without compunction. If you can kill without remorse, then you can slaughter your way to absolute power."

"Sad to say, but yes."

"If you want to be a leader," Gottfrey continues, "embrace the role. Don't just go along for the ride. Symbols, costumes, glamour, and passion can make even clowns appear to be godlike. The least likely among us can triumph."

"How true," says the professor. "How dismal but how true."

Although his companion has not finished the second Scotch, Egon Gottfrey says, "I was depressed when I sat down here, but you have so lifted my spirits that I want to buy you a drink, if I may."

"Sir, I never decline the kindness of strangers. But how peculiar that such a dark subject should lift your spirits."

"Not at all," says Egon Gottfrey. "You have helped me with a personal dilemma, and I am in your debt."

4

WEARING WHITE SNEAKERS, BREEZY-CUT WHITE chinos, and a bright pink-and-blue Hawaiian shirt with a flamingo pattern, eighty-one-year-old Bernie Riggowitz stood five feet seven, weighed at most 140 pounds, and didn't look like anyone's image of ideal backup in a crisis. A little over a week earlier, urgently in need of new wheels, Jane had forced Bernie at gunpoint to give her a ride in his Mercedes E350 from Middle of Nowhere, Texas, all the way to Nogales, Arizona. He had proved not only to have the right stuff, but also to *be* the right stuff—unflappable, quick-witted, and game. Somehow, the kidnapping had turned into an agreeable road trip at the end of which they were *mishpokhe*.

Now, in the Tiffin Allegro, Bernie sat in a dinette booth with Jane, across the table from Luther Tillman, listening to their story of Techno Arcadians and injectable brain-tropic self-assembling nanoparticle control mechanisms. He exhibited none of the amazement or fear that might be expected. He asked no questions. His face revealed nothing of his thoughts, and although he listened intently, there was a faraway look in his eyes.

Concerned that she couldn't read his reaction, Jane said, "Bernie, what's wrong? It sounds too cockamamie or something?"

"Dear, you should excuse the expression, but it sounds so *not* cockamamie that my *kishkes* turned to jelly."

"Listen, if you feel this is more than you bargained for, if you want to back out—"

Putting a hand on her arm, Bernie said, "Darling, stop already. You should live so long that I'd ever back out on you." To Luther, he said, "I am so sorry about your wife and daughter. The pain . . ." He grimaced in sympathy and could say no more.

Luther loomed across the table like a version of Thor, and there was a rumble as of distant thunder in his voice. "We're not going to let the bastards take Travis from Jane."

"Your lips to God's ear." Bernie squeezed Jane's arm. "I don't put much stock in the cabala, but I'm told in *Sepher Yetzirah* it says something about making a golem from clay and using it for vengeance. What these Arcadian *momzers* are doing is a reverse golem. They take precious human beings and mold them into obedient clay. It's not possible to back away from this and still have any self-respect. So when do I get a gun?"

"You won't need one," Jane said.

"Maybe I will. I know from guns. Back in the day, the wig business was not all bagels and cream cheese."

To Luther, Jane said, "Bernie and his wife owned a wig company. Elegant Weave. They sold wigs up and down the eastern seaboard."

"Fourteen states and D.C.," Bernie said. "It was mostly a city business, so there were the usual wiseguys wanted their cut. Better you should declare bankruptcy the day you open your doors. We didn't give them *bupkis*. I had a gun; Miriam, too. We could make hard-boiled like Bogart and Bacall when we had to convince the *khazers* we were tough." He turned his hands palms-up. "I'm embarrassed to admit, Sheriff, our guns weren't legal. But we never did shoot anybody."

Jane stared at Bernie in silence for a moment. "You think you know someone, then you find out he's a tough guy."

"That was a long time ago. I'm eighty-one now. I'm about as tough as a cheese *kreplakh*."

Luther said, "God knows what we're going into. You should have a gun, Mr. Riggowitz. You cool with that, Jane?"

"How long has it been since you fired one?" she asked Bernie.

"About three weeks. Wherever I am, I find a shooting range once a month and do some target practice."

"You mean you have a gun?"

"An old man who likes to drive mostly at night and through some lonely wide-open spaces, he shouldn't have a gun? It's there in my suitcase. I just wanted to feel you out, did you think me having a gun was kosher."

She said, "The night in Texas I jacked your car, you had a gun then?"

He smiled and nodded. "In a special holder under the driver's seat, muzzle backward, grip forward, so I could just reach under and snap open the sleeve and have it in hand."

"Why didn't you pull it on me?"

He looked aghast. "Pull a pistol on a girl as pretty as you? Enough already!"

"They call me a monster. What if I had been?"

"*Bubeleh*, I needed about a minute to know your heart is maybe half your body weight. Am I right, Sheriff?"

"Never more so, Mr. Riggowitz. And call me Luther."

"Mr. Riggowitz was my father. Call me Bernie."

Luther's smile was the first that Jane had seen since he'd boarded the motor home. He said, "We have a dream team here."

She put an arm around Bernie and kissed his cheek and said, "Okay, Eliot Ness. You drive the motor home, sneak Luther and me into Borrego Valley, then be ready to sneak us out. If you need the gun, use it. But if you have to start shooting, it'll mean we're over the cliff."

5

SHE RAGED WITH HER MATE THROUGH THE HOUSE— overturning, tearing, smashing—driven by the rapid rant inside her head, a fierce voice in a language half remembered both by the unknown raver and she who received his tirade, not just words but also hatreds that were not her own but became hers, too, upon receipt. Vivid images were transmitted into her mind's eye from elsewhere: *enormous overhead blades whisking the wind; a savagely bitten, eyeless face; a cleaver raised in a clenched fist; again the huge blades whirling faster, faster, flashing with reflections of silvery sunshine; a human head rolling as if toward an array of tenpins; dolphins leaping on a lampshade; storm-tossed ships hung on a wall; a burst of fragile bones and feathers as a winging bird encounters the bright, spinning blades and disintegrates like a clay target shotgunned from the sky. . . .* Those continuing visions thrilled her as she wrenched open the door of a display cabinet with enough force to tear it from its hinges. She flung the cabinet door, and the misshapen discus clattered against a wall with a shattering of glass. Within the cabinet were cups and saucers, plates and bowls. From a shelf, she scooped up gold-rimmed china chargers and threw the stack onto the dining table. She grabbed a gravy boat in her left hand, a small cream pitcher in her right, and smashed them together as if they were a pair of cymbals; as the porcelain disintegrated, she cut the ball of her thumb. Blood welled, and with something like vampiric need, she put her mouth to the cut, sucked, and drank of herself. Having seen this, her mate relented in his rampage and took her hand and brought it to his mouth and sampled the essence of her. The taste inflamed in them a fierce desire, a rutting frenzy, which the ranting voice in her head encouraged, so that she found herself upon a table from which most of the broken china had been swept away, half their clothes somehow gone, and he upon her. They rocked the table with carnal rhythm, copulation without tenderness or love, so ferocious that it was both thrilling and terrifying. They were incapable of language, their animal voices resounding from the walls of the ravaged room. At the peak of her excitement, an image came into her mind's eye that was not from the ranting Other, that arose from her own experience, a remnant of her faded memory: *a dead woman slouched in a wheelchair, her once-pretty face grossly distorted.* With that memory, a dark wave of grief washed through her, and in the throes of coitus she suddenly spoke: "I am . . . I am . . . Minette." But she could not sustain the grief, nor the memory. In the wake of the grief rose a tide of rage that swept away the name forever, and with the name went the last of her memories, all human purpose, all hope, all promise of transcendence. The male finished and rolled off her, off the dining table, stood sweating and swaying and satiated. Among the few shards of broken china still on the table, she gripped a pointed sharp-edged chunk of porcelain ware and, with pleasure greater than that of copulation, used it to attack and kill the male.

6

AS CARTER JERGEN AND RADLEY DUBOSE CRUISE the town of Borrego Springs, alert for telltale stains on the fabric of normalcy that might be a clue to the whereabouts of the Hawk boy, many pedestrians do a double take at the sight of the formidable black VelociRaptor. Jergen reads envy in the faces of many of the men, who would no doubt forfeit a year of their stunted desert lives to drive such a thrilling vehicle. He knows how they feel.

A Sphinx in sunglasses, his stony face carved by solemnity, Dubose says, "I don't like what I'm feeling."

"Then keep your hand off your crotch," Jergen replies.

"This is no time for frivolity, my friend. I possess a highly developed intuition, almost a sixth sense, if you will, especially regarding trouble pending. At this very moment, I feel something portentous imminent. Something momentous and ominous. I can feel it in the ether, see it in the slant of sunlight, smell it in the dry desert air."

In Carter Jergen's mind, the hills of West Virginia, from which Dubose hails, are populated with rustic soothsayers and grizzled old men who, with a forked stick, can divine what they claim is the best place to drill for water, toothless old women who call themselves haruspices and foretell the future from the entrails of slaughtered animals, bible-thumping prophets of Apocalypse, and other backwoods Cassandras in great variety. Growing up among such occult-oriented hayseeds, Radley Dubose's mind, such as it is, must be woven through with so many threads of superstition that the dons of Princeton had no chance of instilling in him the secular superstitions that they prefer.

"So will it be a plague of locusts, frogs, flies, boils?" Jergen asks.

After a thoughtful silence, Dubose says, "It's something about Ramsey Corrigan. . . ."

"The one in ten thousand. Reptile consciousness. What about him?"

"Something . . ."

"So you said."

"We overlooked something."

"Something?"

"Yeah, something." Dubose pulls to the curb and stops. As still as stone, the beefy lion-bodied man stares through his wraparound shades, through the tinted windshield, gazing at the Anza-Borrego wasteland as if it is an Egyptian desert in which some ancient truth lies buried in a sea of sand.

After a minute, Jergen says, "Okay if I turn on some music?"

Just then, a siren wails. A county sheriff's patrol car turns the corner ahead, its lightbar flashing, and accelerates, heading south.

Dubose pulls the steering wheel hard to the left, arcs across two lanes, and follows the black-and-white, riding its tail as if it's a police escort sent specifically for him.

"This is it," he says.

"This is what?"

"The something."

"How can you know that?" Jergen asks.

With evident pity, Dubose says, "How can you *not* know, my friend? How can you not?"

7

THE LOW BARRENS, A WILDERNESS OF SAND, WHERE in summer there will be no surcease from heat, as there sometimes can be in high deserts, the sun already merciless here on the brink of spring, quivery thermals rising from the blacktop, like spirits liberated from graves beneath the pavement . . .

Out of Indio, cruising south on State Highway 86, boosted on his doughnut-shaped prostate-friendly foam pillow, Bernie Riggowitz handled the big motor home with confidence. Sitting high above the roadway seemed to empower him. When other motorists displeased him, he expressed his frustration colorfully. "Look at that schmo, going twenty miles over the limit. From the way he drives, a person could think he wears his buttocks for earmuffs."

In the copilot's seat beside him, Jane said, "Twenty-seven more miles to Salton City, then west on County Highway 22 for about thirty miles."

Behind Jane, in the free-standing Euro recliner between her seat and the door, Luther said, "I'm looking at the sofa. You sure it's the right fit?"

"I wouldn't want to spend the night there, but maybe it'll get me through a roadblock if there is one."

Another speeder, faster than the first, inspired Bernie to say, "That schmo shouldn't wreck himself and wind up with wheels for legs, but it'll be a regular miracle if he doesn't."

Jane felt safe with Bernie at the wheel and Luther at her back, but the world beyond the windshield seemed more hostile than ever. The Salton Sea came into view on the left, a reminder that the land on this side of the Santa Rosa Mountains was depressed, the water surface more than two hundred feet below sea level. The sun made quicksilver of the salt water, which glimmered less like a mirror than like some toxic lake in a dream peopled by drowning victims who, breathless and salt-blinded, swam forever through the depths, searching for living swimmers to drag down and suffocate.

8

THE TWO-STORY CLAPBOARD HOUSE IS SUR-
rounded by a mantle of real grass, shaded by four tall, flourishing
phoenix palms. The property must have a deep-drilled well that
allows the owners to pretend that they are living in a more hospi-
table climate than is the case.

A Buick Encore is parked alongside the road, twenty feet short of
the driveway and north of the house. The sheriff's-department
Dodge Charger passes the Buick and parks just the other side of the
entrance to the property, directly in front of the residence.

Dubose turns boldly between those vehicles, into the driveway,
past a mailbox surmounted by a plaque bearing the name ATLEE. As
he sets the brake and switches off the engine, he says, "Do you smell
the something now, my friend? Do you smell it, see it, feel it in the
very air?"

"Smell, see, feel what?"

"Looming crisis," says Dubose and gets out of the VelociRaptor.

Jergen is relieved to see that the two sheriff's deputies were
among those at the market on Sunday, following the shooting of
Gavin and Jessica Washington. They know Jergen and Dubose carry
National Security Agency credentials. The locals forfeited jurisdiction on the Washington killings, superseded by federal authorities;
and they are likely to relent without argument in this case as well, if
that's what Dubose wants.

"That's Mrs. Atlee," one of the deputies says, "Louise Atlee," as
a fortyish woman gets out of the Buick and approaches them. "She
called nine-one-one to report a four-sixty."

"Burglary?" Dubose says.

"Yes, sir."

Agitated and distressed, Mrs. Atlee arrives. "Thank the Lord
you're here. Something's gotta be done. I'm afraid maybe it's too

late, but *something's gotta be done*. I turn in the driveway, a living room window shatters, just *shatters*! And . . . and . . ." Her mouth softens, her lips tremble, tears brim in her eyes. "And then my beautiful, beloved Wilkinson longcase is heaved into the yard like garbage to be hauled away. It was horrible, *horrible*."

"Who is Wilkinson Longcase?" one of the deputies asks, his right hand resting on the grip of his service revolver now that burglary seems to have escalated to murder.

"It's not a who," Dubose informs him. "It's a what. A George the Third longcase clock, what you might call a grandfather clock, made by Thomas Wilkinson, mid-to-late eighteenth century."

With mixed emotions, none of them good, Carter Jergen regards his partner, the heretofore unrevealed antique-clock expert. Jergen is glad *he* wasn't the one to ask who Wilkinson Longcase was.

Mrs. Atlee says, "My one antique, handed down through five generations, and now . . . now probably wrecked beyond repair."

She extends one arm, one trembling finger, and Jergen looks where she points. The longcase lies on a side yard, canted against the bole of a phoenix palm.

"The clock crashes through the window, so I back fast out of the driveway, park along the road, call nine-one-one. I get out of the car, there's this hellacious noise, just *hellacious*, inside my pretty little house, like someone smashing everything in my house." Tears spill down her cheeks. "There's shouting, too, cursing, two voices, a man and a woman. So I get back in my car, keep the engine running, ready to go. But then you're here, and now it's quiet, all quiet in there. Whoever it was, they must've escaped out the back."

The concern that the perpetrators have fled the scene is at once allayed when the front door of the house opens and a naked woman steps onto the porch. Her hair is a wild, tangled mane. Her hands appear to be gloved in blood. She is Minette Butterworth, one of the adjusted people, whose wheelchair-bound sister Dubose shot three times the previous night.

9

THUNDER AVALANCHES DOWN THE SKY, SHUDDER-
ing the bones of the hotel in Beaumont, and shatters of rain break
against the windows, near one of which Egon Gottfrey sits at a
small table in the living room of his suite, working on the late Rupert Baldwin's laptop.

He begins with a list of names. Jim Lee Cassidy, the Realtor in
Killeen, who saw Ancel and Clare Hawk heading on foot toward
the bus station. Sue Ann McMaster, the clerk at the bus station who
ticketed them through to Houston. Lonnie John Bricker, the driver
behind the wheel of the bus from Killeen to Houston. Tucker Treadmont, the discourteous Uber driver in Beaumont, who for $121.50
led them to an isolated rural property containing an abandoned
house, reeking chicken coop, and ramshackle barn.

The one name Gottfrey needs and doesn't have is that of the bus-
station manager in Beaumont, such a nondescript character in an
obvious walk-on role that, at the time, there seemed to be no reason
to remember her. Using the NSA's bottomless data troves and back-
door connections to thousands of government and private-industry
computer systems nationwide, he requires six minutes to discover
that the station manager's name is Mary Lou Spencer.

Assuming that Ancel and Clare Hawk indeed borrowed the Mercury Mountaineer belonging to the Longrins, and assuming that in
fact they drove it to Killeen, where they abandoned it, the question
then becomes: Did they really go from Killeen to Houston?

The Unknown Playwright has thrown Gottfrey into a puzzle pit,
and if he doesn't figure his way out of it, there is inevitably going to
be pain.

Gottfrey is as sure as he can be about anything that the portly
Tucker Treadmont, with his pointy-toed boots and man breasts and

calculating greenish-gray eyes, never took the Hawks anywhere, let alone to that rotting house, stinking chicken coop, and tumbledown barn.

The easiest course of action is to track down Treadmont and torture the truth out of him. But that might be a mistake. If it's expected he will take such action, he could be walking into a trap.

The Unknown Playwright wants him to be an iconic loner and a violent force. But the U.P. also doesn't want anything to be easy for Gottfrey; otherwise, he wouldn't have been sent chasing across half of Texas.

Apocalyptic, multifigured bolts of lightning flare and flare over Beaumont, as if some giant otherworldly spider is skittering through the city on white-hot electric legs. Runnels of rain on the window glass quiver with mercurial reflections.

Egon Gottfrey starts with Jim Lee Cassidy, the white-haired Realtor in Killeen, and rapidly builds a profile. Cassidy is sixty-six. Born in Waco, Texas. Served twenty years in the Army before retiring and taking up a career in real estate at the age of thirty-nine. Married to Bonnie Cassidy, maiden name Norton. Two children: Clint, thirty-three; Coraline, thirty-five.

Because Clint is approximately the age of the late Nick Hawk and because of his father's military record, Gottfrey is keen to learn if the son volunteered with the Marine Corps, where he might have served with Nick. But Clint has no military history. He was born with *talipes equinovarus*, the worst kind of clubfoot. Early surgery corrected the condition but not enough to make him soldier material. Coraline has not been in any of the services, either.

Egon Gottfrey is patient. He is certain a connection exists between one of these people and the Hawks that will reveal where Jane's in-laws went between Killeen and Beaumont. He will find it.

He likes being a loner. No chattering fools. No bolo ties.

Soon he moves on to the second name on his list. Sue Ann McMaster, the bus station clerk in Killeen.

To Gottfrey, the battlefield sky full of flash and flame and can-nonade is not merely a storm, but also a celebration of his reinter-pretation of his role. The Unknown Playwright is pleased. From time to time, Gottfrey turns from the laptop screen to the window and stares at the weather-racked day, which seems so *real*, but is painted in thrilling detail just for him.

10

A HOLLOWNESS IN CARTER JERGEN'S CHEST, AS though something has fallen out of him . . . The oppressive heat, the sun glare, the deep strangeness of the situation together inspiring alarm, a sense of mortal peril impending . . .

Minette Butterworth stands tall and naked on the porch, staring not at the five people riveted by her sudden appearance, but at her hands, which she raises before her face as though bewildered to find them slick with blood.

To Carter Jergen, Radley Dubose murmurs, "He is one lucky guy."

"Who?"

"Old Bob Butterworth, of course. The way she was dressed last night, who could know a body like *that* was under her clothes? Purely delicious."

Although some effort is required to look away from the goddess of death on the porch, although Dubose should long ago have ceased to have the power to astonish and appall, Jergen stares at him in disbelief. "You can't be serious."

"My friend, when it comes to making the beast with two backs, I'm always serious."

"Where *is* Bob?" Jergen suddenly wonders.

"I suspect his luck ran out."

Minette lowers her crimson hands and moves off the shaded porch, slowly descending the steps with the measured grace of a high-fashion model, and even the hard desert sunshine flatters her. She stops on the walkway and at last directs her attention to those who have been transfixed by her.

The younger of the deputies declares, "She's hurt," and starts forward to render assistance.

Dubose seizes him by one shoulder, halts him. "Whoa, not your jurisdiction, son. This is part of what happened at the market Sunday afternoon. This is our turf now."

"But she's hurt."

"I don't think so."

As if to confirm what Dubose says, Minette Butterworth lets out a full-voiced shriek as eerie and chilling as the cry of a coyote with blood on its breath celebrating the rending of prey. Then from her issues a vicious stream of obscenities braided through with hisses and guttural sounds, a rant as furious as it is incoherent.

This is a female voice, but otherwise Jergen feels as though he's listening to Ramsey Corrigan, who slaughtered his parents, his brother, and an Arcadian who was also a Homeland Security agent.

As if conjured, a phone appears in Dubose's hand. He's already into his contacts directory. With one touch, he calls the Desert Flora Study Group that occupies the tent and the cluster of trucks along Borrego Springs Road. "Kill Ramsey Corrigan. *Kill him now!* He's transmitting psychological disintegration through the whispering room."

Minette falls silent, staring as if she expects a response.

Carter draws his pistol.

One of the deputies says, "What's happening?"

Mrs. Atlee starts backing away, toward her Buick.

To the on-duty officer at the Desert Flora Study Group, Dubose says, "Roadblocks. Fast. Every highway leaving the valley."

They have not established traditional roadblocks because, if possible, they *want* Jane Hawk to enter Borrego Valley by whatever deception she devises, perhaps let her feel a little cocky before closing the exits behind her.

As Jergen reminds the big man of this, Dubose cuts him off. "It's not just about Hawk now. We injected fifty people last night."

The hollow feeling in Carter Jergen's chest expands to his gut. His alarm escalates into fright, but he dares not succumb to fear. "Maybe they're not all as far gone as this crazy bitch."

"Maybe not. Maybe nanowebs aren't in every case facilitating the breakdown and repurposing of highly complex neural pathways. But the human brain has a high plasticity, which makes it vulnerable as hell to this. Maybe the fifty we brain-screwed are in a variety of psychotic states, some of them still able to pass for normal. But none of the freaks will play nice just because we say, 'Do you see the red queen?' Gotta contain this fast, take 'em down."

"Contain it? Fifty dead isn't containment."

"Not just fifty. Fifty plus collateral damage."

Collateral damage. Jergen realizes that *he* is potentially collateral damage.

"Let them out of the valley," Dubose says, "it'll be harder to impose a news blackout on whatever they do. And if we have to check every vehicle going out, we're revealing our hand to the Hawk bitch, so we might as well check everyone coming in, nail her if we can."

"Maybe she's already here."

"I'd bet on it," Dubose says.

Although it seems as if Minette Butterworth will at any moment charge them in a fit of savage fury, instead she turns and leaps up the porch steps and disappears into the house, gone in two seconds.

11

A FADED BLUE SKY. SUN-BLASTED SAND AND ROCK. Sparse, seared vegetation in scraggly configurations that suggested the mutant consequence of some long-ago incident involving a devastating release of deadly radiation . . .

The land seemed to speak, seemed to say, *The boy is mine now and forever.*

They were on County Highway S22, the Salton Sea behind them, maybe twenty-seven miles from the heart of Borrego Springs, when Jane spotted the big highway department truck parked ten feet off the road, about fifty yards ahead of them. No pavement repairs were under way. No workers were attendant to the vehicle.

"Slow down," she told Bernie, "but don't stop."

As they drifted toward the truck, she saw what she expected: the lens hood of a camera in a motion-detector-activated video-and-transmitter package mounted under the bumper of the truck. Their license plate was scanned and instantly sent to whatever special operations post the Arcadians had set up in Borrego Valley.

She had no concern that Enrique de Soto had let her down this time. A check of the DMV would show that the Tiffin Allegro was registered to Albert Rudolph Neary.

"Okay, up to speed." As Bernie accelerated, she said, "What's your name again?"

Instead of answering simply, he elaborated. "Well, Mama named me Albert Rudolph, and she called me Al, but I never did much like Al, even though I loved Mama. So ever since she died when I was just seventeen, I've gone by Rudy."

Still perched on the Euro recliner behind Jane, Luther Tillman said, "So where you from, Rudy?"

"Born in Topeka, left Kansas after Mama died. My dad passed from a heart attack when I was a baby. Came west and been here ever since. Right now I live in Carpinteria, a pretty town, a true little slice of Heaven. Penny, my wife—Jesus bless her soul—she died four years ago. Penny loved the desert, so I spread her ashes there, like she wanted, and I come back every April to visit with her."

Jane was impressed that Bernie had changed his speech patterns and vernacular, which required a sustained conscious effort. "All that detail—where'd that come from?"

He smiled. "In the wig business, a person has to be something of—you should excuse the expression—a bullshit artist."

12

BEAUMONT FLOATING IN THE FLUX OF THE STORM and Egon Gottfrey swimming in an ocean of data, fingers stroking the laptop keys . . .

Sue Ann McMaster, Killeen bus-station clerk, twenty-nine years old, born in Vidor, Texas, is married to Kevin Eugene McMaster, who is the manager of a landscaping company. Sue Ann is the mother of two children, eight-year-old Jack and six-year-old Nancy. Nothing in her life suggests she is connected in any way to the Hawk family.

Gottfrey almost misses a fact that links her not to the Hawks but to at least another person in the chain of deceit that resulted in his being led to that desolate property where Baldwin and Penn now lie dead—assuming one believes they ever existed. Sue Ann McMaster was born Sue Ann Luckman. But following her marriage to Kevin nine years earlier, when she applied for a revised driver's license to reflect her married name, her previous license was not in the name Luckman, but in the name Spencer. Further digging reveals that a first marriage, at the age of seventeen, to one Roger John

Spencer, of Beaumont, ended after eight months, when he was killed in a traffic accident.

Spencer. The fifth name on Gottfrey's list is Mary Lou Spencer, the bus-station manager here in Beaumont. He needs only five minutes to learn that she is the mother of three, that one of her children was Roger John Spencer, the very same who died in a traffic accident eleven years ago.

If Gottfrey didn't understand that the world and everything in it is illusionary, he might think it unremarkable that this link between Sue Ann and Mary Lou exists.

Obviously, if Mary is working in the bus business in Beaumont and Sue is, back in the day, perhaps employed at the same station, it is the most natural thing for Roger to encounter his mother's young coworker, be smitten by her, and eventually marry her. Two years after Roger's death, when Sue meets Kevin McMaster and marries him and moves to Killeen, it is also logical that she would seek employment at the bus station, perhaps even arrange for a transfer from Beaumont.

If you believe the world is real, intricately detailed, and infinitely layered, you might expect an endless series of minor coincidences of this nature and find nothing suspicious in them.

Because Gottfrey is aware that the world is an exceptionally clever conceit, not as complex and deep as it seems, but merely a narrative spun by the Unknown Playwright for his/her/its enjoyment, he knows at once that this link between Sue and Mary is evidence of a nefarious conspiracy.

In addition, he is certain that the three other names on his list are also players in an elaborate campaign of misdirection with the intention of concealing the true whereabouts of Ancel and Clare. All he needs to do is find their connections and, upon reviewing the material he gathers on them, determine which of them is most likely to know where Jane Hawk's in-laws have gone. Then he can cut the truth out of the deceitful bastard or bitch, whichever proves to be the case.

Because Gottfrey enjoys back-door access to the NSA's Utah Data Center and all its myriad connections across the country, he expects to wrap this up in an hour or less.

A prolonged nova of lightning explodes across the day, as if the illusion of a storm sky and a universe beyond has in an instant been ripped away and the searing truth of existence revealed. The thunder, crashing close in the wake of the first flare, rocks the foundations of this world.

The Unknown Playwright approves. The fun will soon begin.

13

BERNIE SLOWED FOR A SUDDEN BACKUP IN TRAFFIC.

The vehicles in line were mostly cars and SUVs. From the high cockpit of the motor home, Jane Hawk had a clear enough view of the obstruction to identify it. She said, "Police roadblock."

As the motor home came to a halt, she disconnected her safety harness, swiveled the copilot's chair, and thrust to her feet.

Luther was on the move, heading toward the bedroom at the back of the Tiffin Allegro.

Jane stepped past the dinette booth to a sofa that doubled as a pull-out bed, opposite the fridge and cooktop.

"Give a shout, you need help," said Bernie.

"I can take care of this. You just be the best Albert Rudolph Neary you can be."

The sofa bed was on a platform that Enrique de Soto had raised from thirteen inches to fifteen. He had taken the folding bed and its mechanism out of the platform, so that it was now hollow. In its original condition, thick sofa cushions had to be removed to access the pull-out bed and unfold it. Now that it had been remade, the seat cushions were glued to a slab of inch-thick particleboard, the edge of which was concealed with welting.

When she pushed on the welted edge of the particleboard, she released a pressure latch that freed the entire slab to which the pillows were glued. It glided forward on hidden roller tracks, exposing the hiding place beneath.

Jane stepped over the cushions and sat in the cavity. She stretched out flat on her back, head against one sidewall of the sofa, feet against the other.

In the bedroom, in similar fashion, Luther would be secreting himself within the larger platform of the queen-size bed, the box springs having been removed by Enrique and replaced by particleboard that supported the mattress.

With one hand, Jane slid the pillowed platform shut, and the pressure latch clicked. She would be able to release the latch from this position when the time came to climb out. In the confining darkness, she listened to the low rumble of the engine as, in fits and starts, the vehicle moved forward toward the roadblock.

If the motor home had been transporting illegal drugs and if this had been a border crossing with experienced DEA agents, they would have found the secret stashes in about three minutes, even without the assistance of dogs. But the men manning the roadblock were FBI or Homeland Security, or maybe NSA, not drug-enforcement types, and they were probably not familiar with human-trafficking techniques, either. With Bernie Riggowitz behind the wheel, the least likely getaway driver in the annals of crime, any search of the Tiffin Allegro was likely to be perfunctory.

14

Having taken refuge in the driver's seat of her Buick, doors locked and engine running, Mrs. Atlee stares out at Carter Jergen and the others as though she is in a deep-sea submersible, watching the strange marine creatures in an oceanic crevasse as they go about their watery business unaware that they are about to be torn apart and swallowed by some approaching leviathan.

Perhaps because they are baffled and frightened by the behavior of the naked, bloody Minette, the two deputies acquiesce to Radley Dubose's assumption of authority. As directed, Deputy Utley goes to the northeast corner of the house, from which he can see two sides of the residence, and Deputy Parkwood goes to the southwest corner to maintain surveillance of the other two sides. They will sound an alarm if the woman attempts to flee the house by door or window.

A de Havilland DHC-6 Twin Otter passes overhead, ceaselessly netting transmissions from those carrier waves that are assigned to disposable cellphones, hoping Jane Hawk will make a call, allowing them to get a fix on her. In this debilitating heat, the airplane's turboprop engines sound like the lazy droning of a giant bumblebee.

Dubose intends to go into the house through the front door. He expects Jergen to go with him.

"We should wait for backup," Jergen counsels as he proceeds across the yard with the big man.

"There is no backup, my friend. Backup is busy manning those roadblocks and tracking zombies."

"Zombies? What're you talking about zombies?"

"Zombies like Minette Butterworth."

As Dubose reaches the porch steps, Jergen halts short of them. The sun is a torch. The air is as dry as that in a blast furnace. Each inhalation sears his throat. "She's not a zombie. She's fallen through the forbidden door. Psychological retrogression, like you said. Reptile consciousness."

Turning to Jergen, Dubose speaks with a degree of impatience meant to shame Jergen for being thickheaded. "If she has any memory of her life to date, it's minimal. If there's a natural law that tells us right from wrong, she's no longer aware of it. She has no Tao, no conscience, no inhibitions, maybe not even any fear. She lives entirely for pleasure, and one of her greatest pleasures is the thrill of violence. She is fearless of consequences because she no longer has the intellectual capacity to imagine what they might be or even that there are such things as consequences. To her, the world is a rats' warren, and she's a serpent with no other purpose than to hunt. Like a snake, she'll kill to eat and defend herself, but unlike a snake, she'll also kill in an orgasmic frenzy, just for the excitement of it, for the rush of emotion, because it makes her clitoris throb like nothing else can. In that viperous brain of hers, in that black hole of collapsed psychology, there's no longer a taboo of any kind, certainly not one against cannibalism. From her perspective, meat is meat, and you're no more sacred than a rat. Now do you want to debate whether the term *zombie* applies, as if we're having tea in Cambridge?"

Jergen's mouth has filled with saliva, as if he is about to vomit. He swallows hard and swallows again. "You saw what Ramsey Corrigan did to his parents, his brother, that Homeland agent who was a martial-arts specialist—*what he did in seconds*."

"He's seventeen, bigger than an NFL linebacker. Minette is thirty-four, seventeen years older, less than half his weight, just a damn girl, a *gash*, and she doesn't have the advantage of surprise like Ramsey Corrigan did. Are you gonna help me get this done, or are you gonna wimp out on me?"

While Dubose turns away and climbs the porch steps, Carter Jergen doesn't bother to catalogue the advantages of wimping out, which are countless, but tries unsuccessfully to think of a single convincing benefit to manning up and accompanying his partner.

Dubose reaches the porch.

Dismayed but not entirely surprised, Jergen ascends the steps in his partner's wake. He is loath to admit to the truth of his own psychology, which is not reptilian but which is certainly screwed up. As much as Radley Dubose frustrates, appalls, and disgusts him, Jergen wants the big man's approval. Maybe that is because Jergen's mother loves only her political and charitable causes, and because his father is remote, incapable of affection, and disapproving of everything short of perfection. Self-analysis was a key fascination of the perpetual juveniles with whom he matriculated at Harvard; but Jergen, who found that practice puerile then, finds it no less so now. He doesn't know why anyone does anything, least of all himself.

Dubose is an inbred backwoods rustic from a squalid family, poorly educated at Princeton, crude, often mannerless. But he is also an indomitable force free of self-doubt, ruthless, brutal, in love with power and its many privileges, a confirmed elitist in spite of his origins, a rapist and murderer without any capacity for guilt or even regret, because he knows that the only "natural law" is the law of the blade and the gun, that conscience and virtue are fictions, merely inventions of those who wish to rule others by self-righteous moral intimidation; so there is much about him to admire. Perhaps Dubose is not an ideal surrogate big brother, but Jergen follows him across the porch and, warily, into the house.

15

NONE OF THE OFFICERS AT THE ROADBLOCK WORE a uniform, but a Homeland Security photo ID hung on a lanyard around the neck of the one seeking Bernie's attention.

The Tiffin Allegro was equipped with a driver's door, optional on that model. Bernie put down the window and looked as solemn as his aging, Muppet face would allow. "Wow. Homeland Security must mean big trouble."

The agent had to peer up at him in the high driver's seat. The man had a *gurnisht* face, an unfortunate nothing from brow to chin that you would remember for maybe thirty seconds after he turned away.

He said, "We're just seeking a fugitive, sir. No crisis. May I see your license?"

"Got it ready. Thought you'd need it," Bernie said, passing the license through the open window.

The agent scanned it with a device that resembled a small flashlight and returned it to him.

Jane's document source in Reseda had digitally massaged the photo that Bernie emailed them, so that it still resembled him as much as the average DMV portrait resembled anyone, while altering certain features enough to ensure that photo-recognition software would never match the picture on Albert Rudolph Neary's license with any photograph of Bernie Riggowitz.

Returning the license to Bernie, the agent said, "Mr. Neary, I am respectfully requesting your permission to have Homeland Security agents board your motor home in order to search it. You have the right to refuse this request, whereupon I will ask you please to pull off the highway and wait while we seek a search warrant."

"No need for any of that, sir. Rudy Neary is as damn proud to be an American as anyone, maybe more proud than most these days. Have a look, have a look."

Two agents came aboard through the starboard-side passenger door, the first one young and lean with buzz-cut hair and eyes like wet slate. He wasn't wearing a sport coat, and a pistol was ready in his belt holster. "Is anyone traveling with you, Mr. Neary?"

"Nope. Just lonesome me."

"This will only take a couple minutes," he said as he moved into the living space behind the cockpit.

Bernie thought, *Adoshem, Adoshem, make these men stupid and blind and careless.* He felt reasonably confident they wouldn't find Jane or Luther, or the weapons and other gear that were secreted in the hollow bases of the dinette booth benches.

The second agent was older, his brown hair threaded with white, pure snow at the temples. He was about twenty pounds overweight, with a pleasant rubbery face and an avuncular manner. No coat. Another belt holster. He sighed wearily as he sat in the copilot's chair and smiled warmly enough to toast a slice of challah. The ID on his lanyard said he was Walter Hackett.

"Quite a vehicle you have here, Mr. Neary, a real beauty. I dream about getting one of these when I finally hang up the shield."

"My son-in-law says it's too big for me. I guess he thinks the only thing just my size is either a La-Z-Boy recliner or a coffin."

"My daughter married one of those," Hackett commiserated. "What brings you to Borrego Springs, aside from escaping the son-in-law?"

"I hope you won't arrest me when I tell you, but my wife's last wish was to have her ashes spread on the desert here, where all the wildflowers bloom in the spring. I'm pretty damn sure it breaks one crazy damn environmental law or another."

"Sorry to hear about your loss. But no reason to worry. I don't work for the EPA." Hackett's eyes were the gray of iron with specks of rust. "You have them with you now—her ashes?"

"Oh, no. That was four years ago. I just come back to visit on every wedding anniversary."

"She was a lucky woman, married to such a romantic. What was your wife's name?"

Bernie made no effort to summon tears. They welled in him naturally at the thought of Miriam, even though he'd never spread her ashes here or anywhere. "Penelope. But nobody ever called her anything but Penny."

"I lost my wife nine years ago," said Hackett, "but a divorce doesn't hurt as much, even when you never saw it coming."

"Either way, it's hard, I think," said Bernie. "It's a lonely world, either way."

"True enough. How long do you intend to stay here in the valley?"

"I'm booked three days at the RV park. But with all this here commotion, I'm nervous about staying. Grim reaper's gonna get to me soon enough. Don't want some damn terrorist doing his job for him."

"Relax, Mr. Neary. There's no terrorist threat here. Just a man on the run we need to find."

16

JANE HAWK CASKETED IN THE STIFLING DARK, LIS-tening to muffled voices, footfalls on thinly carpeted floorboards, doors being opened and closed . . .

The motor home was convincingly staged. Bernie had brought two suitcases of clothes and had hung them in the closet, folded them in dresser drawers. He had laid out his toiletries in the bathroom. A couple of magazines and a book lay on his nightstand, another book and half a cup of cold coffee were on a side table next to the sofa in which Jane hid. He was an old man traveling alone, and no detail had been overlooked that might betray her and Luther's presence.

Yet the search seemed to be taking too long.

Her arms were resting full-length at her sides. When something crawled onto the back of her left hand, she twitched involuntarily to fling it off, and her hand bumped against the inner face of the front board of the sofa platform.

The sound was soft, a muffled thump, that surely couldn't be heard above the grumble of the idling engine. But the voices fell silent, as if in reaction to the noise she'd made.

The crawling thing found her again. Its feelers, legs, and busy questing suggested that it must be a sizable cockroach that had come all the way from Nogales. She allowed it to explore her fingers, the back of her hand, her wrist.

17

ROOM BY ROOM, HERE IS AN URGENT PROPHECY OF a post-Armageddon landscape, a future of mindless destruction and inescapable ruin, condensed into symbolic wreckage and presented like an elaborate installation by an artist driven mad by his vision. Ripped and tangled draperies torn down from bent rods. Lovely paintings gouged and slashed in broken frames, as though beauty itself so offended the destroyers that they could not abide it. Upholstery slashed, entrails of stuffing spilling out of gutted furniture, deconstructed chairs. A large-screen LED television unracked from the wall and cast down and hammered with a brass lamp, its electronic window to a world of wonders now crazed like the blinded eye of a beaten corpse. Porcelain figurines beheaded and dismembered, likewise a collection of antique dolls violated with such apparent ferocity that Jergen could only assume that those who rampaged here found the human form, in civilized depiction, an intolerable affront. Damp yellowish arcs of urine sprayed across panels of wallpaper. Books thrown down from shelves and urinated on, and in one open volume a deposit of feces. Glassware reduced to sparkling splinters, shattered plates and cups. In the demolished dining room, the half-naked remains of a ravaged man, the husband, hideously disfigured, his mouth gaping in a silent cry of havoc, genitals missing. Room by room, here is a vision of an apocalypse without revelation, without meaning, a scorched-earth war of all against all, when time past will be obliterated and neither will there be time future, only the perpetual storm of time present, the nights long and cold, the horror unremitting.

Each with his pistol drawn and in a firm two-hand grip, arms extended, Jergen and Dubose proceed with utmost caution, without comment, quick and low through archways and doorways, every closet door a potential lid to a lethal jack-in-the-box. Jergen is aware that the front sight of his weapon jumps on target, while Dubose's remains steady, but he can't settle his hands without stilling his heart, which booms as it never has from mere physical exertion. Failing to find Minette on the first floor, they ascend the stairs.

The upper floor is untouched. No one has come here in thrall to a destructive fury. Although downstairs there were bloody prints of a woman's bare feet, there are none here. Nevertheless, they clear the rooms and attendant spaces one by one, until they can say with certainty that she is gone.

Lowering his pistol, Dubose says, "She must have run straight through the house and out the back door before we even posted the deputies to watch for her."

"Gone where?"

"There's that resort and golf course not far from here, a lot of houses around it, but mostly just the desert."

Dubose uses his smartphone to call the Desert Flora Study Group and order the Airbus H120 helicopter into the air. He wants it to conduct an ultra-low-altitude search—to hell with whether it puzzles and annoys the locals—not just for a naked woman on foot but also for signs of any outbreak of chaos related to the other forty-five people who were brain-screwed the previous night. It's forty-five, rather than forty-nine, because the four members of the Corrigan family are already dead.

The term should be *adjusted* rather than *brain-screwed*. But in these circumstances, Jergen would feel like an idiot if he corrected Dubose.

Outside in the yard again, Radley Dubose conferences with Deputies Utley and Parkwood, whose uniform shirts are stained with sweat. He explains that the woman escaped, that he and Jergen will be searching for her, and that they should return to the sheriff's substation in Borrego Springs to await a visit by Homeland Security personnel who will explain to them and their brethren the nature of the threat that has arisen on their turf.

"All I can tell you now," Dubose lies, "is maybe terrorists contaminated some local wells with a drug similar to—but far more powerful than—phencyclidine, which is called 'angel dust' on the street, an animal tranquilizer. If you ever tried to subdue a PCP user, you know they're as crazy as shithouse rats, with the strength of ten. The crap these terrorists have brewed up makes angel dust seem as harmless as a packet of Splenda."

Not for the first time, Carter Jergen is amazed that Dubose can sell bullshit as if it were candy. His intimidating size, practiced solemnity, and Olympian confidence seem to mesmerize people, like these deputies, who should be able to see through his claptrap as easily as through a recently squeegeed window.

Faces pale, eyes haunted, Utley and Parkwood buy the fake news and head back toward the black-and-white Dodge Charger parked along the county highway.

The day is hotter than ever and bright enough to give Jergen a headache, as if he's perpetually staring into a spotlight no matter where he looks. He needs a cold drink and two aspirin and a month at a fine southern resort hotel shaded by ancient magnolias, but he's only going to get two of the three.

He says, "You better get some of our crew over to the sheriff's substation before the local cops start acting on your crazy story."

Dubose holds up the smartphone in his hand. "The line's been open to the Desert Flora guys." He puts the phone to his face. "You heard all that? Good. Corral the locals before they bring media down on us." He terminates the call.

"I'm a little surprised," says Jergen, "that instead you didn't just shoot them, drag them in the house, and set the place on fire."

"It was an option, my friend. But Mrs. Atlee, sitting there in her Buick with the engine running, might have peeled out as Utley and Parkwood were going down before either of us could get to her."

En route to the Charger, Deputy Utley detours to have a word with Mrs. Atlee. When Utley gets in the patrol car and they head back toward Borrego Springs, Mrs. Atlee follows them.

"Good thing the VelociRaptor has six-wheel drive," Dubose says as he moves toward the vehicle. "We'll probably have to go off-road to find our zombie hottie."

There's a cooler behind the front seats, from which they take two cold cans of Red Bull. Without complaint, Jergen climbs into the front passenger seat and shakes two aspirin from a bottle stowed in the console box. Dubose gets behind the steering wheel with the air of a king for whom the vehicle was expressly designed and built.

As the big man puts on his sunglasses and starts the engine, Jergen says, "I half think you'd do her if you had the chance."

"Do who?"

"The zombie hottie. Minette Butterworth."

"The former Minette Butterworth," Dubose corrects. "If I was sure I wouldn't have my package torn off like Lucky Bob, damn right I'd do her."

"No offense, but that's insane."

"It's not insane, my friend. I just have a more adventurous spirit than you have. As feral and fierce as the bitch is now, she'd be a unique experience, unforgettable, like every boy's best-ever wet dream."

"Not *every* boy's," Jergen demurs.

As he drives slowly past the house, between the palm trees and toward the open land beyond, Dubose says, "You know what I wish for you, Cubby?"

"What's with the 'Cubby'?"

"It's a little private nickname I have for you."

"Yeah, well, keep it private. I don't like it."

"You will," Dubose assures him. "What I wish for you, Cubby, is that one day you'll get past your uptight Boston Brahmin background and finally start to *live*, really live unchained."

"I already live unchained," Jergen says.

"The sad thing is that you *think* you do. But you're knotted up with inhibitions. You're a thousand Gordian knots of inhibitions. Repressed, suppressed, yearning after forbidden fruit, tabooridden, your emotions embargoed, your desires proscribed."

After a swig of Red Bull, Jergen says, "I've committed every felony known to man. I've *murdered* people, all kinds of people, women as well as men. If I could get my hands on this Hawk brat, this Travis kid, I'd kill him, too."

"Yes," Dubose acknowledges, "but not with *verve*, Cubby. Not with the pure delight and the conviction of righteousness that comes with the total inner freedom of a true revolutionary. That's what I wish for you. Total inner freedom."

In spite of himself, Jergen is moved by his partner's concern, though he's not prepared to admit it. "That's you, is it?" he asks. "Total inner freedom."

"Total."

"How long did it take you to get this total inner freedom?"

"I think I was seven years old," Radley Dubose says. "Though maybe six."

18

THE VOICES FELL SILENT. JANE HEARD THE DISTINC-
tive sound of the vehicle's front door slamming shut. After a moment, the motor home began to move again, slowly at first, but then
accelerating.

She pressed the interior latch release and slid open the seat of the
sofa, admitting light to her hiding place.

As she rose into a crouch, Bernie called back to her from the driver's seat. "I'm so smooth at this, I could make a fool of a lie detector—
kayn ayn hore."

From her previous road trip with him, she knew that *kayn ayn
hore* was sort of like "knock wood," words meant to ward off the
evil eye.

She stepped over the slab of particleboard to which the sofa cushions were glued, and she stood considering the cockroach. It had
crawled under the sleeve of her sport coat, up her bare arm, under
the sleeve of her T-shirt, into her armpit, between her breasts.

Sliding a hand into the left cup of her bra, she captured the bug
and withdrew it. The creature twitched and quivered against the
palm of her closed hand.

Although she could easily have crushed it, she did not.

She thought of Ivan Petro, the man she had killed two days ago
in self-defense, in an oak grove north of Los Angeles, and thinking
of him brought back to her the faces of others.

The cockroach was a pest, a feeder on filth and a carrier of disease, but it wasn't a mortal threat to her.

If she respected this humble creature, perhaps she would be able
to reach Travis and convey him to a safe place—*kayn ayn hore.*

She opened her hand and dropped the insect into the hollow
under the sofa, watched it scurry into a corner of that space, and
slid shut the trick seat.

As Jane crossed to the kitchen sink to wash her hands, Luther Tillman stepped out of the door to the master bedroom at the back of the motor home. "So we're in," he said as he moved forward, swaying slightly with the motion of the moving vehicle.

"We're in," she said. "Next stop, the RV park."

19

HOT LIGHT FALLING GOOD ON YOUR SKIN. SOFT earth warm underfoot.

Running, running. Don't know where, don't know why. Just free and running, running, running.

Trees. Shade. Stop in shade. Drop to your knees. Kneel panting in shade. Sweating and panting.

Wound in your hand not bleeding much. Lick carefully.

Warmth between your legs reminds you of male. Shiver with thrill of his agony, how he broke, how he bled.

Thirst. Mouth dry. Throat raw. No smell of water here.

Find water. Food. But where?

Overhead, things unseen flutter in trees, alive and fluttering, sheltering from heat.

Your thirst and hunger breed fear. Fear makes thirst greater, hunger sharper. Fear feeds fear. Fluttering in trees suddenly seems sinister.

No more voice in your head. But something crawling inside your head. Crawling, crawling. Flickers of lightning inside your head, bright lines of tattered webbing.

Fear of things unseen, fear of aloneness, fear of being alone with things unseen.

Running again. Urgently, urgently. Out of trees. Harder earth. Grass whipping your legs, pricking, stinging.

Hot light falling burns now. Burns the skin, stings the eyes. Earth hurts underfoot. Pain. Pain sharpens fear, breeds desperation.

Shapes ahead. Shapes blue like the blue above where light falls from. Different trees, shade but less shade from different trees. A blue place in the shade.

Alone. Thirst. Hunger. Confusion. Who am I, what am I, where am I, why? Danger, danger, danger. Alone. *Hide.*

In the big blue shape, a tall white shape with clear shapes. Words come and go, familiar but only half understood—*door* and *windows.* You look through.

A place beyond. Shaded place out of falling, burning light.

Water place? Food place? Safe place for hiding? Something there that needs killing?

Crawling inside your head. Crawling things seeking one another. *Stone.* Means what? *Stone.* Means nothing, nothing.

Again into hot falling light. Urgent, urgent. Looking for something. What? *Rock.* Yes, this. This rock.

Clear-shape window breaks. Reach through. Find thing that turns. Door thing opens, closes.

Hot inside but shade everywhere.

Listen, listen. Any sound a threat. Silence a threat. Sound and silence both feed fear. Fear fuels more fear.

Smell water. A drop falls from shiny curve, falls into white hollow space. Another drop. Another.

Fumble with shiny things. One turns. Water comes. You drink. Cool, wet, good. Make water stop.

Moving through shaded spaces, threat at every turn, unbearable threat, unbearable.

Sit in a corner, back to the corner, shaded spaces in front, listening, wondering, fearing. Threatened and alone.

Fear breeds fear, breeds anger, breeds rage.

Bright broken web threads glimmering inside your head.

Crawling things seeking inside your head. Crawling and faintly whispering far away. Many threatening whispers far away.

Icy fear, blistering rage. You shake with both. No cure for fear except rage, and rage seething into fury.

Threatening whispers beget enraged whispering of your own. You whisper a challenge, an invitation to come here, come find you, come be killed, kill or be killed, come to the different trees, the blue place. *Kill, kill, kill.*

20

CORNELL JASPERSON KNOWS MORE ABOUT DOGS now than he did a few days earlier, and one thing he knows is that they don't necessarily pee a lot, but they pee to a pretty rigid schedule.

The last time Cornell took Duke and Queenie out to pee, first thing that morning, the sound of a low-flying twin-engine airplane in this usually quiet valley had for some reason triggered an intense anxiety attack from which he had needed hours to fully recover.

He didn't want to take the dogs out again, because maybe the plane was still up there. If he had another anxiety attack, it might be even worse than the first one. Maybe he would collapse outside and be unable to get back into his library, leaving the boy alone and frightened. When he collapsed, maybe he would lose control of the dogs and never see them again and have to tell the heartbroken boy that the dogs had run away, and the boy would hate him and would never eat sandwiches with him again and would never ask him to read aloud again, so then Cornell would have to live alone like before, which was what he had always thought he preferred until recently.

Although he didn't want to risk walking the dogs, the dogs insisted on being walked. There was no getting out of it.

He wouldn't take them without leashes, as he had done before, just in case the unusual airplane was passing inexplicably low and the imaginary ants started crawling all over him and he had to get inside quickly.

The boy clipped the leashes to their collars, so that Cornell wouldn't have to chance the dogs touching his bare skin.

"I could take them out," the boy said.

"No. You're a lot safer here. I'll be back soon. I'll make a new kind of sandwich. Little bags of potato chips. Good muffins for dessert."

"Sandwiches with sweet pickles on the side?" the boy asked.

"Yes. Precisely. And cola 'canned under the authority of the Coca-Cola Company, Atlanta, Georgia, 30313, by a member of the Coca-Cola Bottlers Association, Atlanta, George, 30327.'"

The boy laughed softly. "I like you."

"I like me, too, though I'm a walking nutbar. Umm. Umm. And I like you, Travis Hawk."

Cornell let the dogs take him outside, and he held the leashes tightly while they smelled the ground and the weeds and each other and then more ground and weeds before taking turns peeing.

The day was too hot and too bright, everything flat in the hard light. Quiet. At the moment no airplane was growling through the sky immediately overhead.

But then the scream shrilled through the day. He had never heard anything like it. Maybe the dogs hadn't heard anything like it, either, because they raised their heads and pricked their ears and stood very still.

The scream came again, a little muffled, half like a person screaming and half like an animal. The first time, the screamer had sounded miserable and frightened. But the second time there was rage in the cry, too, a scary ferocity.

It seemed to come from the little blue house in which Cornell had lived while building his library for the end of the world.

The dogs were focused on the house, and they started to pull Cornell toward it. He struggled to hold them back. When the third scream cleaved the day, it was so chilling that the dogs changed their minds about wanting to investigate the source.

Cornell wasn't seized by anxiety. He cautioned himself not to be his worst self, to be his better and calmer self. Not that he always listened to himself at times like this, though sometimes he did. He turned the dogs away from the house and walked them back to the barn that wasn't a barn.

No further screams issued from the little blue house during the time that Cornell took to get into his library and out of the too-hot too-bright day, which had suddenly become also too strange.

Cornell had been expecting the boy's mother to come today, and he had been hoping she would not get here until late, until after lunch and reading-aloud time, maybe not until after dinner. But now he wished she were here already.

21

TORRENTIAL WIND-DRIVEN RAIN RUSHES IN FROM the Gulf of Mexico as if that entire body of water will be drawn into the thunderheads and purified of its salt and thrown down onto the lowlands of Texas in some dire judgment that will require an enormous ark and animals boarded two by two.

Egon Gottfrey in the Rhino GX, westbound from Beaumont to Houston, powers through flooded swales in the pavement, the tires casting up dark wings of dirty water. The wipers can't always cope with the downpour. Frequently the windshield presents the world as cataracted eyes might see it: misty, bleary, the buildings distorted into the grotesque structures of some alternate universe.

Nevertheless, Gottfrey drives fast, exceeding the posted limits, not in the least concerned about a collision, considering that the traffic with which he shares the road is as much an illusion as is the highway itself. Anyway, he can see clearly what he most needs to see: the truth of the conspiracy that misled him, who helped Ancel and Clare Hawk, and where Jane's in-laws have taken refuge.

He has a long drive ahead of him, especially in this weather, but triumph awaits him at the end. Maybe he will get to Ancel and Clare too late to wrench from them young Travis's location while it still matters, but it will never be too late to inject and enslave them.

PART FIVE

Plain Jane

1

MOST OF THE LONG-EXISTING CAMPGROUNDS IN Borrego Valley were open in season only, and not all were motor-home friendly. A new facility, Hammersmith Family RV Park, had booked the Tiffin Allegro by phone, with the promise of a three-day cash deposit on arrival.

The white Chevy Suburban, which the motor home was towing, had to be unhitched and left in a lot immediately outside the campground prior to check-in, because the spaces allotted to RVs weren't large enough to accommodate additional vehicles. In that blacktop parking lot, where thermals rising off the pavement smelled faintly of tar, Jane and Luther transferred their weapons and other gear from the Tiffin Allegro to the Suburban.

Bernie hadn't slept well since getting Jane's call on Monday, not because he feared for himself, and not just because he feared that she would be killed. He also dreaded that he might even *see her being killed*, whereupon he would be so emptied of all hope for this world that he might curse Adonai, the sacred name of God, which was never a good idea. He said, "The longer I don't get a call from you, the more I'm going *meshugge*."

"You'll be fine," she said. "You always are."

"You take care of each other."

"That's the plan," Luther said, as he climbed in the driver's seat of the Suburban. He pulled the door shut, started the engine.

Jane said, "Did you put it on? You don't look like you did."

"It's silly. I'm not in the action, but I'll put it on."

"There's nothing silly about it. These bastards have quietly locked down this valley. Before we're out of here, it might be something worse than a street fight. It might be even more intimate than that, the equivalent of a cage fight."

"I'll wear it already. But it's heavy."

"It's not heavy. It's level two, not level four, not hard plates of Dyneema polyethylene or ceramic like on a battlefield. It's fine-weave chainmail and Kevlar, very light, light enough. Under a roomy Hawaiian shirt, nobody knows. And you promised me."

"So I'll wear it! Now make like a real granddaughter and give me a hug."

Hugging him, she said, "You better wear it."

"You're such a noodge. A promise is a promise with me."

"If I don't call in two hours, be ready to split. If I don't call in two and a half, get the hell out of here."

Bernie felt a tightness in his chest, as if he might have a cardiac episode, which he wouldn't because he had no heart problems and because this wasn't the time or place for a responsible person to drop dead. "It's not like I spent my life abandoning people, so why should you think it'll be easy for me?"

"You won't be abandoning anyone," she assured him. "If I don't call, we'll be dead."

"It won't turn out that way. You'll get your boy."

She didn't smile when she said, "Your lips to God's ear."

As she got into the Suburban, Bernie said, "Don't forget." She looked back at him. "Always and forever—*mishpokhe*."

"*Mishpokhe*," she said, letting the *kh* rattle against the roof of her mouth just right. She pulled the door shut, and Luther drove the Suburban out of the parking lot.

Bernie Riggowitz, being Albert Rudolph Neary, checked into the Hammersmith Family RV Park.

They assigned him to a nice, quiet space near the back of the campground. He hooked up only to their electric service.

With the air-conditioning full blast, he sat in the copilot's chair and sipped from a cold can of 7-Up and took an acid-reducing pill and stared through the windshield.

There were palm trees so recently planted and fresh that they didn't look the least bit sun withered. There was a big swimming pool with a wide deck around it. There were lounge chairs on the deck for people who wanted to tan. There were big red umbrellas shielding tables where you could play cards or whatever. The water in the pool was pale blue with a reflection of the sky and rippled with silver reflections of the sun. Everything was very pretty.

The scene turned his stomach, as if he'd eaten a pound or two of the sweetest prune-jam *homantash* anyone had ever baked. He knew he shouldn't take a second acid-reducing pill. He chewed a pair of Tums instead.

He didn't know why all this prettiness should sicken him.

Okay, not true. He knew why, all right. Much as he tried not to be negative, he couldn't help but think that the afternoon might not turn out pretty in the end.

2

HENRY LORIMAR AND HIS PARTNER, NELSON LUFT, neighbors of Robert and Minette Butterworth, had been helping authorities in the search for the kidnapped little boy when the obscene ranting had begun. For a moment, Henry thought it came from the sound system of their Lexus SUV, which he was driving; but then somehow he understood that it issued instead from deep inside his head. He was briefly frightened by this realization, until a still, small voice assured him this was the new normal, that all was well, that he should accept and move on with his work. This was nothing more than the whispering room, a high-tech communications system that linked the civilian volunteers who were searching for the missing child. Yes, whoever the ranting person might be, he was misusing the technology, but this was just the whispering room, one of the many advantages of the new normal.

Evidently, Nelson received the ferocious rant at greater volume or on a more penetrating wavelength than did Henry. While the rapid gush of vicious obscenities was offensive and distracting to Henry, it proved at once painful to Nelson, and soon became *excruciating*. Within the safety harness that secured him to the front passenger seat, Nelson writhed in torment, his hands alternately clamped to his head or pounding on the door, on the window, as though he was desperate to escape but had forgotten how to get out of the vehicle.

Each time fear rose in Henry Lorimar, a voice separate from that of the ranter counseled him to remain calm. There was nothing to be concerned about. If he just did what was expected of him, if he searched for the missing boy according to his instructions, all would be well. He would be happy, content, at peace.

Nevertheless, unable to concentrate on his driving, he pulled off the road. Shifted into park. Engaged the emergency brake. He left the engine running to maintain the air-conditioning.

The one voice ranted, loud and increasingly animalistic, but the other voice spoke so softly that it wasn't a voice as much as it was like a conscience, an inner source of moral guidance telling him that he needed to do what he had been tasked to do, that if he did the right thing, he would be happy, content, and at peace. This conscience-like counselor was authoritative, irresistible, therefore not at all like a conscience, which could be ignored, but more like a . . . controller. Yet as much as Henry wanted to obey, he remained paralyzed because the louder voice bored into him, tore at him, though in a strangely thrilling way, drilling down until it struck nerves in him that didn't flash with pain when touched but instead flared with pleasure, desires so deeply buried and so beyond his experience that he didn't have words to describe them.

For a while, the outer world did not press upon his senses, and he lived entirely in his head, in the assault of words and wordless cries counterpointed by the quiet but insistent instruction of his controller. Soon, the ranter's vocal transmissions were accompanied by fierce emotions—hatred, fury, lust—so scalding that they seemed to peel away layers of Henry's identity, as superheated steam might peel away skin. With the sounds and emotions came images of extreme violence that seemed beautiful to him and sexual congress so intense that, in its way, it was another kind of violence.

At one point, Henry Lorimar became aware of the sound of the idling car engine, the cold air blowing from the dashboard vents, and the stink of human waste. The last of those sensations turned his head to the right, where his partner, Nelson Luft, no longer writhed in agony.

White-faced and frail, Nelson slumped in his safety harness, head turned toward Henry, mouth agape, blood dripping from the cups of his ears. He had soiled himself. He was alive, softly inhaling and exhaling, his gaze moving slowly over the interior of the Lexus, as if everything on which his eyes alighted was mysterious to him. When he met Henry's stare, Nelson appeared not to recognize his partner of fifteen years, regarding him with the same puzzlement inspired by the steering wheel, the radio, and the cup holders in the console.

Cold horror and grief iced Henry's heart, and he began to surface from the thrall of the hateful rant. But the conscience that was not a conscience pressed him to put the Lexus in gear and get on with the search for the kidnapped boy, as he had agreed to do, *as he had been instructed.* Everything else meant nothing. Nelson Luft meant nothing. Nelson could be dealt with later. Nelson could wait. Nelson would be fine. Henry needed only to do what he had been told to do, what urgently needed to be done, and then he would be very happy, content, and at peace.

As horror and grief melted out of him, however, Henry didn't release the emergency brake or put the car in gear. Like the sea to the moon, he succumbed to the tidal pull of the rant. The interior of the Lexus faded from his awareness as the exquisite images of violence and thrilling fornication flooded in upon him, accompanied by raw emotions and the tsunami of words that darkled his mind.

How much time passed, Henry could not say, but eventually the ranter stopped transmitting. Gradually, Henry became aware of the vehicle in which he sat, although at first he could not identify it or recall its purpose.

The whispering room was quiet, no communications incoming, but another strange sound in his head troubled him: sputtering-sizzling, subtle but persistent. When his eyes were closed, he could see—or perhaps he imagined—a darkness in his head across which the radials and spirals of a web pulsed irregularly with light, as if a current of varying power coursed through those filaments.

Degree by degree, knowledge and functionality returned to him. He sat up straighter. He adjusted his shirt collar. He remembered the remaining places he and Nelson needed to visit in their low-key search for the kidnapped boy, and he realized that he had better get on with the task.

In the passenger seat, Nelson Luft no longer breathed. His stare was as fixed as that of a mannequin. Blood had stopped seeping from his ears.

This was nothing to be concerned about. Nothing important. Nothing that mattered at all. Nelson could be dealt with later.

The important thing was to get on with the urgent hunt for the missing and endangered boy. It was misguided and selfish to think that anything mattered other than finding the boy.

The vehicle reeked of feces, but that was a mere inconvenience. Henry could get used to it. He was already getting used to it. Soon he wouldn't smell it at all.

He released the emergency brake and put the Lexus in gear and drove back onto the highway. He could drive, but he wasn't at ease behind the wheel like he'd been before. Everything seemed unfamiliar to him, almost as if he were a young teenager again, just learning to handle a motor vehicle.

Something had changed in him. He couldn't focus on what he was doing as well as he once had. His mind kept drifting. Fear without cause came and went, as did sharp spasms of anger. Dramatic images of violence and brutal sex, none from Henry's personal experience, quivered through his mind as vividly as if they were things that he had done.

He'd driven only a mile when a new voice rose in the whispering room, this one female. Simultaneously furious and frightened, ridden by hungers she could name and others for which she knew no words, she transmitted incoherent chains of words, hatred and desire, a threat and a challenge. Images, too. A blue stucco house with a white metal roof. Shaded by shabby palm trees. She wanted sex and blood, wanted to quell her fear by instilling terror in others, wanted the thrill of exercising her power and inflicting pain, wanted to scream into the void that she sensed yawning beneath her and, by sheer ferocity, prevent it from enfolding her into oblivion.

She was like a siren on night reefs, singing ships to their wreckage, and her enticing song appealed to some part of Henry that he didn't understand, to a secret second heart that beat a tempo different from his first and that held within its throbbing chambers a blackness darker than death.

He knew the blue stucco house with the white metal roof. And even in his current condition, he knew how to get there.

For now, he had forgotten the boy, and the conscience that wasn't a conscience could no longer control him.

The female voice was irresistibly alluring, calling to some self-

destructive aspect of Henry Lorimar, but it was also savage and so
venomous that he might need a weapon. He pulled the car off the
road long enough to get a combination long-handled lug wrench/
pry bar from the SUV's tool kit.

3

Two DIRT RUTS, STUBBLED WITH DEAD WEEDS, LED
past the abandoned blue stucco house and the ragged queen palms,
past the yard of pea gravel and specimen cacti. Luther drove around
behind the place and parked beside the attached one-car garage,
which shielded the Chevy Suburban from the sight of anyone passing on the county highway.

"Come civilian, leave official," Luther said. "Still the plan?"

"I don't see any reason to change it. It's been smooth so far, but
maybe not much longer. You know what to do."

"I know what to do," he agreed. "Go to your boy."

She walked along the weedy driveway for about seventy or
eighty yards, to a turnaround in front of the dilapidated barn, which
she knew was not only what it appeared to be.

The hot desert air vibrated with the sawing of insects that busied
their bowstring legs, cars buzzing past on the distant county road,
and an airplane whisking the day with turboprop blades. An aircraft had droned past when they were unhitching the Suburban
from the motor home. Maybe this was the same one, seeking to
seine her voice and location from the sky when she used a burner
phone.

She stood before the weathered man-size door with its worm-
eaten sun-split boards and rusted hinges, looking up where Gavin

Washington had told her a concealed camera would be focused on her.

Hidden motion detectors had alerted Cornell Jasperson to her presence. The electronic lock opened with a buzz and a clunk.

Jane stepped into a white-walled vestibule where a camera surmounted a metal door. The door behind her closed automatically, and the one before her opened.

Lamplit in jewel tones, shadowy in places, lined with thousands of colorful spines, before her lay the fabled library for the end of the world, as magical as Gavin had described it.

At some distance stood Cornell: almost seven feet tall, knobjointed like a mechanical construct, misshapen, a figure of fright on a dark street, but with the face of an angel, awkward and clearly shy.

Nearer stood Travis, utterly still, as if he thirsted for the sight of her and could not move until his thirst was slaked.

She saw in this precious boy not just her child, but the best of herself and the best of her beloved husband. She saw the most cherished part of her past, too, all the years of happiness with Nick, and her future in its entirety, for there could be no future worth having if Travis wasn't in it. When they weren't together, she thought of him as bigger than he was, perhaps because she had all of her heart and hope invested in this boy, and in spite of her dire situation, her hope was no little thing. Now he seemed so much smaller and more fragile than she remembered, vulnerable and as easily taken from her as Nick had been, as her mother had been.

She approached him and dropped to her knees, and he flew into her arms, clutching her with something like desperation.

The dogs whined, seemed to debate the proper protocol, and settled on the floor to comfort each other.

Just then, neither Jane nor Travis felt a need to speak. The substance of him, the warmth of him, the sweetness of his breath, the rabbit thump of his heart as he pressed against her were worth more than all the words in this vast library. She kissed the top of his head, kissed his brow, and when he put one small hand to her face, she kissed the fingers, the palm.

The words *love you* passed between them, the only words that seemed important enough to speak, though by speaking them, Travis lost his composure. Tears flooded his eyes, and he revealed that, even at his age, he held no illusions about the fate of his former guardians, the Washingtons, though he had concealed his certainty until now. "They're gone. Aunt Jess and Uncle Gavin, we're never gonna see them again. They woulda come back by now. They're dead, aren't they dead, Mommy?"

When they had gone on the run from their house in Virginia, he'd begun calling her Mom, as if aware that he needed to grow up faster than nature intended. Sunday night, when she took a call from him on her burner phone, he'd reverted to Mommy. Now again.

She had many reasons to hate the people aligned against her, these arrogant self-named Techno Arcadians, not least of all because they took her boy's father from him, but also because they stole his innocence. They forced on him an awareness of the darkness of this world that he otherwise would have discovered slowly over the years, with his parents' guidance, in a manner that would have made it easier for him to come to terms with the harder truths of life.

On Sunday, speaking with him on the phone, she'd thought Travis feared that Jessie and Gavin had been killed, but she had seen no compelling reason to confirm his fear. Not while he was feeling so vulnerable. Not while she was hundreds of miles away from him and could not take him in her arms.

He was in her arms now, and among the many things she owed him was the truth. She knew from hard experience that too little truth in any family led to enduring pain. If her mother had not concealed the serious marital problems between her and Jane's father, if the great pianist Martin Duroc had known his daughter was aware of his affair and might testify to her mother's distress, perhaps he would not have dared to kill one wife to get another.

"Yes, sweetie, Jessie and Gavin are gone. They were very brave. They were very brave all their lives. And they loved you as if you were their own child."

His voice was thick, tremulous, choked with tears. "What can we do? What can we *do*?"

She held him tight and rocked with him there on the floor. "We can remember them always, sweetheart, never forget how brave they were, how wonderful and kind and giving and funny. We can love them always, and every night in our prayers we can say thanks for having had them in our lives."

He spoke into her throat, which was wet with his tears. "It's not enough. They won't know."

"But they will know, honey. They will know every night. They will hear you every night, and they will know you loved them as much as they loved you."

Her grief was now doubled by his grief. She wondered how many heartbreaks a child so young could endure.

4

CORNELL STOOD BY ONE OF HIS FAVORITE ARM-chairs, in the warm golden light of his prettiest stained-glass floor lamp, surrounded by the consolation of his books, and he knew no comfort, only misery.

He could not bear the boy's grief, the tears. He wanted to do something to soothe this child, comfort him, but there was nothing he could do. He dared not hug Travis as the mother did. A mere hug would plummet Cornell into an anxiety attack, and he would be no good to anyone, a big strange ugly man curled in the fetal position and shaking with fear, unable to stand, hardly able to speak, a burden to them, not a comfort.

He stood wringing his large hands, ceaselessly shifting his weight from one foot to the other, as if he needed to go someplace at once but didn't know where. He had long been at peace with his limitations, at peace with the hard road that was his only route through life, but he was not at peace now. He did not remember ever having wept before, but he was weeping.

5

THE DESERT WAS NEW TO LUTHER TILLMAN, AND HE liked it about as much as he might like being forked onto a barbecue and broiled over charcoal. He had known hotter days than this, even in his home state of Minnesota, but there was something about the pale sky and the dry air and the dusty trees and the mostly barren earth that intensified the effect of the heat and, for him anyway, made ninety degrees significantly more oppressive here than it would have been in a different landscape.

He shrugged out of his black-denim jacket. He considered taking off his shoulder rig, but under the current circumstances, he would feel more naked without the pistol than if he stripped out of all his clothes.

The gear in the back of the Chevy Suburban included a forty-foot garden hose with a special nozzle and two identical one-quart bottle-like attachments, each filled with a custom-mixed solvent, that fed their contents into the water stream in a continuous measured flow.

He found the hose bib at the corner of the garage where Jane had been told it would be, tested the water pressure, and hooked up the hose.

The white paint was a special blend that Enrique de Soto had concocted and applied in Nogales. The solvent turned the paint to something like chalk, and the water washed it off, leaving the factory-applied black paint intact. There were also three large, white block letters on the roof of the vehicle, the same three repeated on the front doors—FBI—and these letters likewise were impervious to the solvent.

Come civilian, leave official. Once they had the boy, they didn't want to risk being stopped by authorities between here and the motor home in the RV park. If a roadblock was encountered, an FBI vehicle could more likely be driven around it without being forced to stop.

Like some alchemist of ages long past, Luther washed the white Suburban to black while the sun, in a far less magical fashion, beat on his shaved head and glazed his face with sweat.

6

IN THE CORNER WHERE SHADOWS DRIFT AROUND and over you, there is no passage of time, for you know not time, but only the eternal now.

There is hunger in the now. Fear. Hatred. Hatred of all that is not you. Anything that is not you is a potential threat.

You are awake, eyes open, but dreaming. Dark dreams darkle down into ever deeper darkness.

In the now is desire, but only of the most primitive kind. For food. For prey. For violence that conquers threat and fills your mouth with the nourishing blood of the Other.

Within your head, whispers come, whispers go, words as *meaningless as wind in dry grass or rats' feet over broken glass.*

Emotions come, sent by Others. Their fear and hatred inspire greater fear and hatred of your own.

Images of violence occurring elsewhere in the now, prey being slashed, beheaded, gutted. The rutting frenzy of Others mounting their prey before they kill it.

Such images stir passions of your own, passions as cold as they are intense, but always fear endures even in passion. *I will show you fear in a handful of dust.*

A sudden sound injects new fear into the now. A familiar sound, yet you cannot name it or imagine its source. The word *engine* passes repeatedly through your mind but means nothing to you, and by its very meaninglessness further irritates.

You uncoil from the corner, weave upright in shadows, stand listening.

Move through shadowy spaces into a space with more light. To a clear shape through which light falls.

Others are here. A female moves away through dead weeds, toward a big place shaped dark against the day.

Nearer is a large white object that stirs in you a memory of moving effortlessly fast—fast, faster—through varied landscapes.

These memories are confusing, disturbing, but fragile. They dissolve in a fog of forgetfulness.

What remains is a certainty that this white object is the source of the sound that drew you from the corner where you coiled.

A male Other is busy at this source of the sound. The male is not aware of you.

You stand to one side of this clear shape through which light falls, so you can't be easily seen. You watch the male. You watch.

A thing happens that excites you. Water gushes, arcs, and the white object becomes black.

Like day becomes night, white becomes black. But no one *makes* day into night. Day makes itself into night.

This male Other frightens you. Can he make day into night? Can he wash away the light forever? Such power terrifies you.

No cure for fear except rage, and rage seething into fury.

You look around in growing desperation.

Urgent, urgent.

Things you grip pull open other things, revealing spaces within. Spaces full of familiar items, but you have no names for them, can imagine no purpose for them.

Until you find the space full of sharp things. A row of sharp things. You know what to do with one of these. Yes, you know just what to do.

7

CARTER JERGEN IS CERTAIN THAT HE AND DUBOSE will find Minette Butterworth, wild and naked, within five minutes of driving into the barrens behind the Atlee family's wrecked house. That expectation is not fulfilled.

These sun-hammered wastes don't offer many places to hide. Here and there a zigzagging declivity has been cracked into the land by an earthquake. A few shallow washes mark the paths of flash floods that on rare occasions overwhelm the Anza-Borrego with tarantula-drowning downpours. The desert scrub is too sparse to provide cover. An occasional cluster of trees, perhaps sustained by an artesian well within reach of their roots, might conceal a woman who'd gone through the forbidden door and fallen into a psychological abyss; but none of them does.

In this part of the valley, houses are far apart. In her new incarnation, however, the former Minette Butterworth seems to be as fast as an instinctive predator. She might have homed in on another residence and made it to that cover in a few minutes.

When Jergen pictures her—and others like her—bursting in on an unsuspecting family, the catastrophe under way abruptly expands to terrifying dimensions in his imagination.

Unable to find any sign of the feral woman in the open desert, they now need to move from house to house, seeking the place—and the people—she might at this moment be destroying.

As he returns to the county highway and pilots the VelociRaptor down-valley, Dubose holds forth as though for a rapt audience. "Like the girls whose pasts and personalities are flushed out of them so they can be remade into eager sex toys for the Aspasia clubs, those men transformed into rayshaws for security duty have no more inner life than machines."

Raymond Shaw is the brainwashed assassin in *The Manchurian Candidate*. When the late Bertold Shenneck created brain-screwed and programmed men to serve as obedient and fearless security agents at his gated estate in Napa, the great scientist thought it was amusing to call them rayshaws. Except for their expressionless faces and a disturbing deadness in the eyes, they are able to pass for normal: neatly dressed, quiet, eerily polite. They are more focused on their duties than even the most highly trained, dedicated, and fearless bodyguards could ever be. When a threat to their master manifests, they are swift and brutal in response, for they harbor no slightest compunction about killing any trespasser.

As Dubose waxes on about the viciousness of rayshaws and their incapacity for doubt or remorse, Jergen finally interrupts. "And your point is what?"

"My point, Cubby, is that I've thought the last thing I would ever want would be to have a gladiator moment with a rayshaw as my opponent. But having seen what Ramsey Corrigan did to his family and what our fair Minette did to her husband, old Lucky Bob, I'd go toe to toe with any rayshaw before I'd want to be locked in a room with that bitch and no weapon but my bare hands. A rayshaw is just a meat machine with sophisticated programming, but she's something else altogether. She's a slaughtering zombie, purely demonic."

Jergen suspects that Dubose is playing some stupid Princeton sport with him, some psychological game intended to maneuver him into a panic room of the mind, so that he will say something that can be mocked.

Nevertheless, he asks, "If she's a purely demonic, slaughtering zombie, then why are we being so dumb that we're chasing her?"

"Because such is our fate, Cubby. A man can't escape his fate, especially not men like us, dedicated revolutionaries who have bound over our fortunes to the cause, reaching for the brass ring of total power, knowing that if we miss it, we will be destroyed, crushed and thrown away as if we never lived. Such is the hard bargain we made with destiny, a bargain few men have the courage to make."

Exasperated by this grandiose speechifying, Jergen says, "Well, I don't see myself at all that way."

Dubose turns upon Jergen a smile of genteel pity. "I know you don't, Cubby. That's why from time to time I give you these little pep talks. To encourage you to better understand yourself and the heroic enterprise on which you're embarked."

8

TRAVIS HAD HIS BAGS PACKED AND STANDING BY, but as it turned out, Cornell Jasperson had packed a bag, too.

Like a benign gargoyle that had come alive and climbed down from its high perch on some Gothic building, the big man stood before Jane in a beseeching posture. He swayed from side to side, scuffing the floor with his shoes, holding his hands against his chest as though to contain the hope in his heart for fear it would escape him. "I need to go with the boy, please and thank you. I need to go with the boy. I need to go with him. The boy."

Jane had known that Travis could not be asked to abandon the dogs in spite of the difficulty they would pose during any escape from Borrego Valley. He had lost too much already. He no doubt felt guilty about Gavin and Jessie, though he had no responsibility for the sacrifice they had willingly made. Even though he had known Duke and Queenie for only a few months, the bonds between a boy and his dogs were such that, after what he had already been through, forcing him to leave the German shepherds behind would break something in him that might never be repaired. She'd made preparations for the dogs, but not for a gentle giant with a personality disorder, who couldn't be touched without suffering a disabling anxiety attack.

"Umm. Umm. I'm pretty sure I can be a better burden," said Cornell. "Umm. What I meant to say is a better *person*. If you take me with you, I'm pretty sure I'll betray well. *Behave* well."

Whether they had conspired in this beforehand or not, Travis was instantly on board with Cornell's request. "We have to take him with us, Mom. Me and Mr. Jasperson, we're going to Atlanta someday to see them bottle Coca-Cola."

"The last couple days," said Cornell, "the dogs touched me, but I always pretended like they didn't, pretended really hard, and so I didn't have an attack. Then after a while, I didn't need to pretend anymore." He reached down to touch one of the shepherds, and the big dog wagged its tail.

"You gotta let him come," Travis pleaded. "He makes really good sandwiches and the best muffins ever. He's got a fipaleen recipe for pineapple-coconut muffins, and he made them all millionaires."

"Not the muffins," Cornell explained. "I made the Filipino workers all millionaires. I can't touch people because I'm a full-on Planters nutbar that way. Umm. Umm. But I can take good care of the dogs." He looked down at his feet, as shy as a child, then raised his eyes to Jane once more. "Besides, if I stay here, sooner or later the bad people will come for me. Won't they come for me?"

He was right. They would figure out where Travis had been kept, and they would take Cornell into custody if for no other reason than to bleed him of his fortune.

She said, "We don't leave the wounded behind. Somehow we'll fit you in."

"He reads aloud better than anyone," Travis assured her with a note of desperation, "and he was real nice about the toothbrush."

"Relax, cowboy," she said. "It's already decided. You two wait here with the dogs. I'll go see how Luther's doing, and we'll bring the Suburban over here to load up."

9

IT WAS A SLOW DAY IN THE CONVENIENCE STORE. Bipin Gaitonde, born in Bombay but a proud citizen of the desert for seventeen years, husband of Zoya, father of three, enterprising entrepreneur, attended the cash register in his store when customers were present, and when he was alone, he busied himself replenishing the candy racks.

He had just come out of the stockroom with a carton of PayDay bars when the Cadillac XT5 exploded through the big front window. A fierce horizontal rain of glittering bits of glass sleeted through the store, followed by a storm of Cheez Doodles shot from bursting bags. Potato chips expelled from their ruptured packages were cast through the air like a barrage of martial-arts throwing stars.

Insanely, the motorist accelerated upon entrance. The first row of displays came apart and toppled noisily into aisle two, and the Cadillac began to surmount the broken shelves and all the scattered merchandise.

Bipin dropped the PayDays. He leaped out of the way, scrambled onto the cashier's counter.

The vehicle came to a halt mid-store, canted on rubble, two tires punctured, its windshield dissolved. Veils of steam rose around the edges of its buckled hood.

The driver forced open his door and bulled his way out of the Caddy, pressing aside parts of a shattered display, kicking angrily at obstructing packages of national-brand cupcakes and cream-filled baked goods that Bipin found tasteless but that sold well.

He knew this man. Buckley Tolbert. Founder of Heart of Home, the oldest restaurant in Borrego Springs. Sixtysomething white-haired sweet-faced soft-spoken Bucky Tolbert was a friend to every-one, generous and amusing.

Getting out of the Cadillac, Bucky fired off a fusillade of unchar-acteristic vulgarities and obscenities, filth exploding from him like bullets from a machine gun.

Crouched atop the cashier's counter, Bipin Gaitonde was shocked by those indecencies. Although he sold certain risqué magazines in his store, he displayed them in plain-paper sleeves that revealed only the name of the publication and prevented the magazine from being opened until it was purchased and removed from the prem-ises.

"Mr. Tolbert," Bipin admonished, "do you not hear yourself?"

As though he became aware of Bipin only then, the restaurateur began peppering his salty language with vicious threats, primarily involving Bipin's emasculation. In spite of his age, and though as a hazard of his occupation he weighed perhaps forty pounds too much, Buckley Tolbert clambered over the wreckage, crossing the store and coming toward Bipin, with the alacrity and grace of a mountain lion.

Once an ardent hiker, Bipin had been high in the San Bernardino

Mountains five years earlier when, late in the afternoon, he turned a bend in the trail and saw a four-hundred-pound mountain lion leap from an upslope stand of pines onto the back of an unsuspecting deer. The big cat drove its prey to the ground and tore out its throat before Bipin had the presence of mind to start shaking with terror. He had not gone hiking since that day.

Now it seemed as if some god of lions had descended to the earth and had come to Bipin in an avatar that had once been Buckley Tolbert. Reflections of the store's flickering lights flashed in Tolbert's eyes. The man's face flushed and twisted with such insane fury that it seemed his rage alone ought to pop a cerebral artery or torture his aging heart into cardiac arrest. Bipin realized—almost too late—that he was the deer in this scenario, not entirely unsuspecting but paralyzed by disbelief.

As Buckley Tolbert approached the cashier's station, shrieking now like some venomous spirit liberated from Hell, Bipin dropped from the counter into the space behind. He could hardly believe it was necessary to reach for the pistol that he kept on a shelf under the cash register, for he had obtained it to defend against total strangers who might enter the store with armed robbery in mind, which had not yet once happened in quiet Borrego Springs. He had definitely *not* purchased the gun with the expectation that he would need it to shoot a neighbor and friend, but he grabbed it anyway.

Buckley Tolbert vaulted onto the counter and stood up, and Bipin turned with the pistol in hand as his former friend towered over him. Tolbert's white hair stood out from his scalp as if he'd received an electric shock. His eyes were pools of malice. A thick string of snot hung from his nose, quivering like an extruded worm. Blood slicked his chin, encircled his mouth, glistened on his lips, and misted on his exhalation when he hissed fiercely between his clenched and bloodstained teeth.

Somehow Bipin Gaitonde knew that this blood was not Tolbert's, that it was evidence of an unthinkable attack on someone else before he had crashed his Cadillac into the convenience store. In the same instant, Tolbert plunged from the counter and Bipin fired. The big man fell past him, snaring a fistful of Bipin's hair and pulling him off his feet.

They landed with Bipin on top. Although the space behind the counter was narrow, Tolbert rolled them and achieved the superior position, maybe wounded or maybe not.

Bipin still gripped the pistol in his right hand, but that arm was under him, crushed between him and the floor. Pain coursed from shoulder to wrist. Under his attacker's bulk, he could draw only shallow breaths into his compressed lungs.

With inhuman strength, Tolbert—this *thing* that had been Tolbert—pinned Bipin's left arm to the floor, incapacitating him. He lowered his florid face close to Bipin's face, spraying him with spittle and blood. His left hand scraped at his captive's brow, the fingers curved into a claw, and Bipin had no doubt that Tolbert was going to take his eyes.

He thought of his wife, Zoya, and their children being left alone in this dark world. The horror of failing them gave him the strength to heave up, not violently enough to throw Tolbert off, but enough to free his trapped right arm, in which the nerves were hot wires conducting a disabling pain through muscle and bone.

Maybe his arm was broken. Maybe he couldn't grip the gun. But it was not broken. As he brought up the weapon, he fired, and the shot took off a piece of his attacker's left ear.

Howling, Tolbert flinched back, clamping his hands over both ears, as though for an instant he couldn't tell which of them was bullet-torn.

Recoil almost denied Bipin the pistol, but he held the weapon now in a two-hand grip. At a range of mere inches, he shot Tolbert in the face once, twice.

The attacker fell to the right, mouth open in a silent scream, the architecture of his face remodeled by the double blast, his hair on fire from the muzzle flash.

Bipin sat up and frantically scooted backward on the vinyl-tile floor until a wall of the wraparound cashier's station prevented further retreat. He struggled to his feet and stood with the pistol in both hands, arms fully extended, as though Tolbert's resurrection and a renewed assault were a matter not of *if*, but *when*.

At thirty-five, Bipin Gaitonde had never before raised a hand against another human being. When he bought the pistol, Zoya had smiled and said that he was too gentle ever to use it, so empathetic that he would sympathize with a robber in need and not only give him all the cash in the register but also offer to write a check.

Weeping quietly, he stood over the dead restaurateur and did not look up from the corpse until a siren shrilled. It was a rare sound in Borrego Springs.

He turned his attention toward the shattered front window, but he didn't expect the imminent arrival of the police. Intuitively, he knew this: The madness that had burst into his store was something new in the world, hydra-headed and already manifesting elsewhere.

10

THE DAY WAS THE SAME AS IT HAD BEEN BEFORE JANE went into the library for the end of the world: hot, dry, still, with the faintest alkaline smell to the air, the signature scent of a true desert. Unseen insects were engaged in a monotone celebration of life, and in the distance a low-flying twin-engine airplane sought cellphone revelations that she was not foolish enough to provide.

In spite of the sameness of the day then and the day now, she'd gone only a few steps from the dilapidated barn when that intuitive perception of things seen and unseen told her change had come, the degree of risk had risen, time was running out.

She halted, alert for threats, scanning the day more carefully. Luther was finishing the transformation of the Suburban from white to black. The solvent provided by Ricky de Soto appeared to be worth the outrageous price he placed on it.

If something had gone wrong, if a crisis was impending, Luther seemed unaware. His years in law enforcement and his intelligence had left him with intuition no less sharp than hers, so if he was unconcerned, perhaps she was just jumpy, more worried mother now than calculating cop.

Yes, but . . . Luther was handling the hose, and the water that sluiced the white paint from the Suburban drummed loudly enough to mask other sounds from him. Intuition was in part subconscious perception. What the busy surface of the mind might be too occupied to notice, the quiet inner mind perceived, interpreted; then it tried to pass along its concern by raising the hairs on the back of your neck or sending a faux centipede down the ladder of your spine.

If one of the five senses was compromised—in this case Luther's hearing—intuition was to that degree crippled.

A few steps after leaving the barn, perhaps Jane perceived the merest suggestion of the figure in the doorway of the blue stucco house. In any case, she saw it more clearly when she had closed from seventy yards to fifty, its full nature undefined in those shadows but somehow peculiar—and beyond Luther's awareness.

She didn't call out to him at once, because he might not hear her. Besides, if the individual on the porch was focused on Luther and not yet aware of Jane, no need to shout and precipitate action.

No one lived in the house. Jessie and Gavin would have stayed there with Travis; but they were dead. They must be dead.

Jane walked fast but didn't run. The faster she moved, the more she would call attention to herself in the stranger's peripheral vision. She was thirty or forty yards from the house when the figure moved out of the doorway, farther onto the porch, and she saw that it was a woman. Not Jessie Washington. A naked woman.

The presence of the woman was itself a spanner in the works, but her nudity was so bizarre that she represented some greater crisis the nature of which Jane couldn't comprehend.

Jane was less than twenty yards from the house when the naked woman saw her, which was also when Luther finished washing off the Suburban, killed the water, and dropped the hose. Running now, Jane saw something bright in the woman's hand, maybe a knife, and she drew her pistol and called out, "Luther, the porch!"

Surprised, he turned first to Jane, then pivoted toward the unclothed woman.

The stranger was indeed holding a butcher knife in her right hand. She backed into the house and closed the door.

Luther had drawn his pistol by the time Jane reached him. "Who the hell—"

"I don't know," she said. "But this means we have to get out of here fast. Change the plates. I'll go inside."

"Shit, no. Not alone."

"There's no time to tag-team her. Change the plates."

Ricky de Soto had supplied them with government license plates. Federal departments wore special plates with prefix codes specific to each—EPA for the Environmental Protection Agency, OEO for Office of Economic Opportunity, SAA for the United States Senate—and an FBI vehicle should be wearing the prefix J because the Bureau was under the purview of the Department of Justice. Some Bureau vehicles had FBI emblazoned on doors and roofs, though many did not. Calling attention to the Suburban by block-lettering it ought to let them slide around roadblocks and through chokepoints more easily, but the wrong plates would betray them as surely as would bumper stickers proclaiming COPS SUCK.

"What if she's not alone in there?" Luther worried.

"Seconds count. We don't just have Travis and the dogs now. We're taking Cornell."

"Holy shit."

"Change the plates, but watch your back. Then drive to the barn and load up."

She hurried toward the porch steps.

11

CARTER JERGEN FEELS THAT THE DESERT—everything and everyone in it—is so alien to normal human experience that it might as well be on a planet in another galaxy. This feeling is further distilled when he and Dubose come across the wrecked vehicles littering the county highway.

The first is a cherry-red Honda sedan, turned on its starboard flank, its roof smashed against a roadside retaining wall built to prevent an eroding bluff from washing across the road in a flash flood. For maybe sixty feet leading to the Honda, the pavement is littered with pieces of the vehicle and wads of safety glass. The blacktop is scarred and imprinted with red paint, as if something impacted the car, overturned it, and then shoved it sixty feet before ramming it hard into the wall.

Jergen gets out of the VelociRaptor and goes to have a look at the Honda and comes back and gets into the passenger seat and says, "Dead woman in there."

"What kind of dead woman?" Dubose asks.

"What do you mean, 'what kind'?"

"Ethnicity, age, appearance, clothing, nature of injuries. In an investigation as complex as the one we've undertaken, Cubby, you just never know what detail may prove to be the little piece of the puzzle that makes sense of the entire picture."

"Caucasian, maybe thirty, brunette, shorts and a halter top, all busted up."

"Attractive?"

"What—you're going to hump a corpse now?"

"Get real, my friend. If this is a crime scene and if the girl is attractive, her looks could have something to do with why she was murdered. A former husband. A jealous boyfriend."

"Who is this jealous boyfriend—King Kong? He grabs a Honda and shuffleboards it sixty feet into a wall?"

"Sarcasm does not become you, Cubby."

"Anyway, we're not here to investigate murders."

"She might have information we need. Are you sure she's dead?"

"If she isn't, she ought to be."

"Good enough," says Dubose.

They cruise not quite one mile before coming upon a Mini Cooper that has somehow been boosted off the pavement and slammed into an oak with such terrific force that its mangled undercarriage is locked tight around the massive, cracked tree trunk, so that the petite vehicle is suspended about four feet off the ground.

Although he doesn't offer a reason, Dubose will not take his turn getting out of the VelociRaptor to have a closer look at the Mini Cooper. Of course he doesn't want to give Jergen an opportunity to occupy the driver's seat in his absence.

Jergen returns from the oak tree. "Mexican, about twenty-five, jeans and a T-shirt. Broken arm, at least one broken leg, probably a major spinal injury. Exceedingly attractive, I think you'd say."

"I can read through your pathetic deception, my friend. You didn't use a pronoun because you're trying to avoid saying it's a man, as though I'll run to have a look based on 'exceedingly attractive.'"

"Maybe you *are* a reincarnation of Sherlock Holmes after all."

"This Mexican is alive?"

"Probably not for long. Unconscious and fading."

Dubose sighs. "So we can't question him. And even if he does live and it's with a major spinal injury, it won't be a high quality of life. Shall we operate by triage rules and hope the next one, if there is a next, will be more useful to us?"

"Works for me."

Half a mile later, around a turn, they discover a Big Dog Bulldog Bagger, a motorcycle with wide-swept fairing and saddlebags, once a sweet machine with a 111-cubic-inch V-twin motor but now just wrack and ruin. Eighty or a hundred feet beyond the Big Dog, the man who'd been riding it now lies squashed on the pavement as if he's been put through a giant sandwich press. He's obviously been run over several times by a persistent motorist.

The tire tracks of the vehicle used in this homicide are imprinted on the pavement in the victim's bodily fluids. Although the sun has already mostly dried the tracks, the pattern is clear enough to allow Radley Dubose to declare portentously, "Damn big truck."

12

JANE IN THE KITCHEN. NO COOLER HERE THAN OUT-side. The old house vaguely scented with dry-rot fungus. Pale panes of porch-door glass. One pane broken out, shards on the floor.

Hard sunshine slanted through the window above the sink, so precisely defined by the shape of the pane that the light had sharp edges and sliced the shadows at the cut lines so that they were sharp-edged, too. Dust motes turning slowly in the illumining shaft. Shadows billowing in the corners as if monks had here discarded their robes. Black-and-white patterns laid out as though delivering a profound message in geometric forms. The scene reminded her of some old pre-color movie, the title forgotten, in which protagonist and antagonist had faced off in a war-ravaged church. She couldn't remember who died, who lived, or if perhaps no one survived.

She stood listening, but there was nothing to hear until she moved, whereupon the old vinyl-tile flooring crackled underfoot. Floorboards creaked beneath the vinyl.

On the farther side of the kitchen, an open door led to what might be the living room.

To her right, a door probably connected the kitchen to the single-car garage. It stood maybe eight inches ajar.

Jane needed her left hand for tasks. Her right arm, the gun arm, was straight out in front of her.

She picked up a shard of glass from the floor, a crescent-moon-shaped fragment about four inches across, and she stood it on its points, the curve propped against the back door.

Now the nearer of the other two doors. Hinged to swing away from her. Stand on the side opposite the hinges. Through the eight-inch gap, there was gloom beyond. One dirt-glazed window, like a TV turned to a dead channel, admitted barely enough light to suggest the shape of a vehicle, an SUV. It must be Gavin and Jessie's Range Rover. They'd left it here when they drove Cornell's Honda to the market in town—and died there. Quiet in the little garage. She held her breath and listened and didn't know if the silence she heard was perhaps the woman with the knife holding *her* breath.

She threw the door open. Its corroded hinges rasped. It slammed against the wall in there, and no one responded. Doorways were bad, the worst. She went through low and fast, head and pistol first, from the half-lit kitchen to the darker garage, moving at once to the right, pressing her back against the wall. There was no good way to die, but she had a particular aversion to being stabbed, to the cold intrusion of steel and the vicious twist of the blade. Her heart knocked hard against her breastbone as she reached up and felt the wall and found the switch near the doorframe and clicked on the overhead fluorescent fixtures.

No sign of the woman with the knife. A row of cabinets along the front wall, none large enough to be a hiding place for an adult. Drop low for a quick look under the Range Rover. Nothing. No one inside, either. The only exterior door in the garage was the big one that accommodated a vehicle.

After entering the kitchen with no less caution than she'd left it, she closed the connecting door. She snatched up another fragment of glass, and used it as a telltale; when she returned, if the shards weren't as she'd left them, she'd know someone had entered the house and waited in the garage for a chance to surprise her.

Beyond the kitchen lay a living room where the front door was secured with a deadbolt. There were as well two small bedrooms, one bath, and a study. The rooms contained mismatched discount-warehouse furniture that Cornell had left behind when he moved to his library and bunker—and all were deserted.

The woman couldn't have gone out the front door and engaged the deadbolt behind her. None of the windows were broken or open, and in fact they all appeared to be painted shut, inoperable.

The heat was stifling. Even breathing through her mouth, Jane wasn't as quiet as she wanted to be.

In a corner of the study, one door remained to be investigated. Maybe a closet. She sheltered against the frame, put her left hand on the knob—and hesitated.

Her memory worked the image of the naked woman. Medusa mass of hair. Face at once lovely and horrific, empty of everything except ferocity. A face strangely reminiscent of that Goya painting *Saturn Devouring His Children*, which contained no loveliness whatsoever. The bold nudity, the bloody hands, the knife.

This was something new in the world. It was surely related to the work of the Arcadians—but how?

Gun arm across her waist. Muzzle toward whatever might burst out of this last unknown space. Keeping pressure on the trigger. She twisted the doorknob, cast open the door. No response.

She dared the doorway and saw splintered boards swaybacked with the weight of time: steps leading down into darkness that seemed impenetrable and final. In houses of this age, in country vulnerable to earthquakes, basements were rare.

Studying the dust on the wide landing for signs that someone had recently descended, Jane startled when a loud crash issued from elsewhere in the house, demanding her immediate attention.

But there was no lock on the cellar door. And because it opened onto the landing, it couldn't be braced shut from this side.

Another crash from the front of the house, the splintering of wood.

Maybe the woman with the knife wasn't down there in the dark. *Like hell she's not.* Maybe she wouldn't come up when Jane was busy elsewhere. *Like hell she won't.*

Jane hurried out of the study as a third crash reverberated through the walls of the small house.

13

CARTER JERGEN IS NOT ONE TO REGRET HIS LIFE choices, although now that the revolution has brought him to this desolate ass-end of nowhere, he wonders if he should have taken longer than three minutes to join the Techno Arcadians when his aunt Deirdre had given him an invitation. Charming Aunt Deirdre is his favorite relative, a dazzling intellectual, a self-made business-woman worth $700 million, childless, and certain to have included him in her will. Now it seems as if he would have been wiser if he had declined her invitation and instead had killed her in some manner that would not have incriminated him.

Through the windshield, Jergen regards the lightweight Toyota pickup that is on its roof beside the highway, crushed, tires blown, and on fire—although the flames are subsiding. A blackened, partly fleshed skeleton hangs upside down in the driver's seat like a large, charred, melted campfire marshmallow.

Radley Dubose places a call to the Desert Flora Study Group. He asks about the Airbus H120 that he earlier ordered into the air to search for Minette Butterworth and for signs of chaos related to the people who were brain-screwed the previous night. He inquires if the flight crew of that aircraft might have noticed anything unusual on this length of county highway.

Apparently, the helo pilot and copilot have reported in excess of a single disturbance, because Dubose does more listening than talking for perhaps four minutes. He punctuates the Desert Flora Study Group agent's report with "Huh" and "Really" and "Shit," and "Not good, compadre, not good."

When Dubose terminates the call, Jergen says, "If together we can devise an accidental death for my aunt Deirdre, I would split with you what's likely to be a minimum hundred-million-dollar inheritance. Maybe a great deal more."

Dubose is disapproving, though not of homicide. "Let's avoid being distracted by such mundane concerns as money. Not with the revolution at stake. Do you recall that one of the fifty people injected last night was a Mr. Arlen Hosteen?"

"I've got enough on my mind without having to remember the names of fifty losers."

"Arlen Hosteen," Dubose says, "is the owner of Valleywide Waste Management, the local trash-collection firm. He sometimes services one of his company's routes himself when a driver is sick. He seemed a good enlistee in the hunt for the Hawk brat. No one thinks twice about a garbage truck pulling up to house after house, so he has a chance to give each place a lookover, check trash cans at curbside to see if any contents suggest the presence of a small child in a family that doesn't have kids."

"Brilliant," Jergen says sarcastically.

"Not as it has turned out, I'm afraid. Hosteen is driving an immense trash-collection truck with front-loading arms that can lift the heaviest dumpster with ease. It's like a tank."

"So he's gone through the forbidden door, has he? Just like Minette."

"He has obviously deteriorated mentally, but evidently not as much as she has. And by all reports, he's not naked."

"That's something to be thankful for."

Dubose drives onto the highway once more. "The Airbus crew saw Hosteen rampaging, but they haven't stayed on him because other more disturbing incidents require their attention."

"More disturbing than Hosteen? How many other incidents?"

"Six. Not to worry. We'll find Hosteen and shut him down."

"In his garbage-truck tank? That won't be easy."

"You may remember, I met your aunt Deirdre. Killing Hosteen in his truck will be a lot easier than killing that ballbuster."

14

JANE ON THE MOVE. HECKLER IN A TWO-HAND GRIP, just under her line of vision. A short, narrow hall served the bedrooms and study.

When she stepped into the living room, she saw that the old, weathered, desiccated front door had cracked loose of its hinges; it hung askew, fixed to the frame only by its deadbolt. Having kicked in the door, a fortyish man, pale and disheveled and sweating profusely, looking both angry and bewildered, stood just inside the room, maybe fifteen feet from her, holding an iron pry bar that had an angled neck and lug wrench at one end.

Keeping the Heckler's front sight on the intruder, positioned so that peripheral vision might alert her to movement in the hallway to her left, Jane said, "Put it down."

He was costumed neither in black leather nor in a vest made from human nipples, nor with a necklace fashioned from the teeth of his victims, in neither a leather mask nor a hood imprinted with the face from Edvard Munch's painting *The Scream*, as movies routinely portrayed existential threats like this. He wore a blue-and-yellow-striped polo shirt, white slacks, and white topsiders without socks, a mundane monster for an insipid age when imagination had gone digital and the true horrors of the world were so disturbing that a lot of people found it easier to fear imaginary threats.

Ignoring Jane's command, he said, "Was you? Was you, is you the bitch, bitch? The bitch in my head, you?"

He must be on one drug or another, maybe an entire apothecary. His blue eyes were wide and lunatic, yet as clear and alert as the eyes of a hunting owl. Anger contorted his face; not anger alone, but also perhaps some neurological disorder. Every muscle from hairline to chin and ear to ear moved not in concert but in disjunctive arrangements, producing a shifting kaleidoscope of grotesque expressions. Although every look was unnatural in the extreme, they all conveyed rage, hatred, and demented lust.

"Put down the crowbar," she repeated.

He took one step toward her and raised his voice, loud and menacing. "Is you? Is you? Is you whisper sex me, sex me, kill me, kill you, kill you, sex me, kill, kill, whisper inside head?"

The whispering room.

He was one of the adjusted people, and something was very damn wrong with his program.

Maybe because the pry bar looked almost as long as a Taser XREP 12-gauge shotgun, she thought of Ivan Petro on Monday, coming for her from out of the oak trees. She thought of the hammer with which she'd been pounding the burner phone, of how she hadn't dropped it before drawing her gun but instead had thrown it. Life was raveled through with inexplicable patterns that could never be understood but could be recognized by anyone who acknowledged their existence, so Jane knew what this creature was about to do even before *he* knew. Insane as he might be, he still wasn't going to charge into a pistol pointed at him; he would throw the pry bar.

Whoever this man might have been, he was no longer that person. He was enslaved by a nanoweb, but also coming apart psychologically under the control mechanism's influence. What she had to do next was an act of mercy, not murder; and if she hesitated to grant him that mercy, he would smash her face, crack her skull.

He drew back the iron bar. She shot him in the chest. The bullet convulsed him, but he threw the weapon. Half a second after the first round, the second didn't just tear through his throat. The .45 hollow-point *removed* his throat, took out the spine, so his head wobbled like one of those bobble-head figures that people put on the dashboards of their cars. His empty body collapsed with so little sound that it seemed as if the greater part of his substance had been the mind and soul no longer contained in the package of flesh and bone. His pitch was feeble. The pry bar went wide of her and bounced along the floor—just as the naked woman erupted from the hallway and slashed hard with the butcher knife to cut deep.

15

IMMEDIATELY BEFORE THE CRAZY PERSON CAME OUT of nowhere and the waking nightmare started, Bernie Riggowitz was thinking about the three Ls—life, loss, and love.

Life is finding people you love and then losing them, sometimes after sixty years, sometimes after a few months or even a week, all the loss meant to keep you humble and remind you that your life is likewise stamped with an expiration date, so that you'll use your days to the best of your ability, in the service of what is good. Bernie understood the grand strategy of life's design, and he didn't presume to think that he knew better how it should have been done, but—*shit, shit, shit!*—he was fed up with all the losing of people.

Bernie in the Tiffin Allegro cockpit, behind the wheel, was too nervous to do anything other than stare out at the grounds of the RV park, hoping to absorb some of the tranquillity from the sun, the majestic palm trees, the glimmering water in the pool.

It didn't work. He anxiously checked his wristwatch every five or six minutes, thinking an hour had gone by.

Only three times in his life had he come to love someone in mere hours or less. Miriam had always said that she fell in love with him at first sight, and he said he did, too, but the truth was that he needed maybe an hour to fall in love with her, but then he fell all the way and hard. He fell in love with Nasia, his only child, in less than half a minute after his first look at her. What kind of monster didn't love his own baby with every fiber of his being? He'd needed maybe two hours to fall in love with Jane, who'd called herself Alice at the time. His love for Miriam involved heart and mind and body, but his love for Jane was a heart-and-mind thing. In truth, if he'd been thirty-one instead of eighty-one, and if he'd never met Miriam, this would have been a heart-mind-body thing, but he didn't have it in him to be a dirty old man.

If Jane died, Bernie's life of optimism was going to end as a life of despair. And if she lost her *boychik*, Bernie was damn well after all going to assume that he knew better how the world and life should have been designed.

He checked his watch yet again, having expected to hear from Jane by now, certain that two hours had passed, that something had gone wrong. But she and Luther had set out from the RV park only a little more than an hour earlier.

That was when the crazy person appeared on the deck surrounding the big pool and began to pitch the lounge chairs into the water.

16

JANE PIVOTED TOWARD THE THREAT, BUT THE NAKED woman was too close, coming in as low and fast as a striking snake unraveling from its coils, *so damn fast*, already past the pistol. The knife slashed right to left across Jane's abdomen, slicing open her T-shirt as if the fabric were gossamer, making a zipperlike sound as it scored the SafeGuard vest underneath. The body armor featured fine chainmail to protect against edge weapons, plus an underlying Kevlar layer that provided ballistic protection.

The vest didn't fail. Would never fail. But it was only a vest, leaving points of vulnerability—face, throat, hands. The attacker had ferocious energy, feral quickness, uncanny strength. Even as the knife sliced across the armor, she body-slammed Jane, driving her back into a wall. A hard shock to the spine. A moment when darkness encroached at the edges of vision. A transient right-side weakness. Jane's right hand opened involuntarily, and the Heckler fell with a soft thump on the carpet.

Full-body contact now, hand-to-hand, a death struggle. Jane seized the other's right wrist in her left hand as the woman raised the knife to stab.

Her foul breath a thick tide, the stink of sour sweat and urine and blood steaming off her, the woman didn't cycle through a panoply of tortured expressions, as had the man before her. Her face seemed forged of iron, every bone beneath the skin and every muscle in that rigid countenance fired into hard angles of fury and hate. In her eyes an icy void attested to a mind pitiless and purged of empathy. She growled low in her throat and hissed and spat, but said not a word, not one obscenity or curse, as though in her depravity she wasn't human any longer, but an animal, a predator at least as vicious as any in nature.

She clutched Jane's throat, trying to choke her, but that hand was slick with blood from a wound in the palm, and the woman didn't have full strength in it.

Martial arts had their uses, but they seldom worked on the street the way they did in a dojo. When you were pinned against a wall by a zombified psychopath who pressed closer in her frenzy, trying to bite your face, judo and karate were strictly action-movie choreography. You needed to resort to plain techniques, plain old everyday brutality, plain-Jane stuff.

Caused by the shock of impact, Jane's brief right-side weakness passed. With her left hand, she continued to stiff-arm the insistent attacker's raised knife. With her right, she now clutched the wrist of the hand at her throat and used her thumb to apply crippling pressure on the radial nerve, maintaining eye contact because animals could sometimes be intimidated by an unrelenting stare. She planted her right foot flat against the wall, tensed the calf and thigh, and drove her knee hard between her assailant's spread legs, did it again, and a third time. A woman wouldn't be incapacitated by such a blow, as a man might be, but the vulva was richly endowed with nerves; the pain should make her relent or even drop the knife.

Didn't happen. In her killing fury, the woman was beyond pain, an engine of destruction fueled and armored by epinephrine.

They were deep in the extreme cage fight of which Jane had warned Bernie, mean and dirty, no rules, no compassion, a contest that allowed only one survivor. As the pinched radial nerve failed the tendons and muscles that it served, the attacker suffered wrist-drop, her grip strength gone. Jane punched her assailant's throat, hoping to tear the cartilage around the larynx. The woman's head snapped back. Jane punched again, harder than before. A third punch, aimed higher, broke the nose. She clawed at an eye. Gagging, gasping, the attacker dropped the knife, stumbled backward. Jane stooped and grabbed the pistol from the carpet and rose and fired once point-blank. She would have fired again, but that was when the blast came and the house rocked on its foundation and part of the front wall collapsed into the living room.

17

THE TUBULAR-FRAME NYLON-WEBBING LOUNGE chairs floating in the sun-sparkled pool, bobbing and yawing, turning in circles, knocking together, as if invisible sunbathers were frolicking together in some water game . . .

On the farther side of the pool from Bernie Riggowitz, the raging person wasn't only tossing lounge chairs into the swimming pool. He was also overturning tables with their big center-fixed red umbrellas and kicking over the other chairs.

At first it didn't occur to Bernie, watching from the cockpit of the motor home, that the man might be homicidal, only that he must have a grudge against the RV park management or maybe a crazy hatred of outdoor furniture. And surely he must be very drunk. At the moment there were no vacationers in the pool or on the deck around it, no one whom the *shikker* might attack.

Then Holden Hammersmith, patriarch of the clan that operated Hammersmith Family RV Park, the man who registered Albert Rudolph Neary and took his cash and escorted the Tiffin Allegro to its current campground space, hurried into view from the direction of the park office and convenience store. He was accompanied by his sixteen-year-old son, Sammy, who had assisted Bernie, alias Rudy, with the electrical hookup. Holden was about six feet one, maybe 220 pounds. A neck that could never be encompassed by the collar of an off-the-rack shirt. Shoulders like the Hulk. Popeye forearms.

The boy was still growing, a few inches shorter than his dad, forty pounds lighter.

The elder Hammersmith shouted at the vandal, though Bernie couldn't hear what he was saying. The *shikker*, if in fact he was a drunk, at first ignored father and son, moving to the next lounger and pitching it into the pool.

Holden caught up with the guy and seized him by one shoulder, which was when things took a turn Bernie couldn't have foreseen.

The vandal stood about five feet eight, weighed like 150. He was little Paddington Bear to Holden's full-size grizzly. Even if the guy wanted a fight and was something of a scrapper, he would likely wind up with two broken arms and *kishkes* scrambled like eggs.

Except when the guy turned on Holden Hammersmith, he didn't do anything that a drunken brawler would do. Didn't throw a wild punch. Didn't kick or pull a knife. With startling swiftness, as bold as a tiger and as lithe as a monkey, he scrambled up the bigger man as if scampering up a tree. From this distance, Bernie couldn't be sure, but it looked as though, as Holden staggered backward in surprise, the vandal seized his ears or his hair and bit his face.

Whatever was happening over there, it seemed too weird to be only a common occurrence in another sunny day in beautiful Borrego Valley. Somehow it had to do with this cabal Jane had squared off against, these shmucks who thought people were just tools that they could use and break and discard.

From under the driver's seat, Bernie withdrew a Springfield TRP-Pro chambered for .45 ACP. He threw open the door and got out of the motor home and hurried out from under the palm trees, across the blacktop loop that served the campground, onto the pool decking, and around the long rectangle of water toward the men struggling on the farther side.

18

THE HOUSE ROCKED WITH THE BLAST, WHICH SUB-
sumed the crack of the Heckler & Koch, and the naked attacker fell
backward with a third eye weeping in her forehead.

Jane thought, *Bomb*.

Window glass cascaded into the room. Wallboard bowed inward
and fissured and expelled clouds of plaster dust, followed by shattered wall studs and exterior sheathing and blue stucco and elements of the front porch. Ultimately, in another half second, there
followed the bumper, grille, and hydraulic rams of an immense
front-loaded garbage truck.

The huge vehicle exploded into the house, shoving a dry tide of
ruins ahead of it, engine howling, blazing headlights burning away
shadows, the billowing dust motes glittering like minute droplets
in a fog of pesticide. The ceiling sagged. The rotting carpet split, the
wood flooring gave way, and the truck lurched to a halt as its front
wheels dropped between floor joists and through the ceiling of the
basement, stranding it in the living room.

The wiper blades began to sweep across the windshield, whisking off the dust. Up there in the driver's seat loomed a macabre
figure out of *A Clockwork Orange,* a man who shrieked with a kind
of fierce and wrathful delight—part madhouse laugh, part scream,
all threat. His lewd, goatish face was distorted by lust and by hatred
of the lusted-after Other, for in a savage and deranged mind, sex
and murder were two sides of the same thrill, neither as satisfying
as when they were combined in one violent act.

The sagging ceiling began to collapse. As wallboard buckled and
split overhead, Jane turned and sprinted into the kitchen, toward
the back door. The floor shuddered and rolled underfoot, staggering her, as though the garbage truck might plunge through the joists

and into the basement, pulling with it the entire back half of the small house.

19

Luther Tillman loaded the boy's luggage, Cornell's bag, and the two German shepherds into the back of the Suburban. As he closed the tailgate, he heard the first loud noise from the distant residence, maybe like a door being broken down. After a minute or so came the first and second gunshots.

He stood for a moment, staring at the house, wanting to go to Jane's side.

In the world as it had been when he'd grown up, a man went to a woman's aid, always and without excuse. Rebecca, his wife, lost now to a controlling nanoimplant, had called him chivalrous, and he had always liked to hear her say it.

But it wasn't chivalry, not that formal and flowery and self-aware code of knightly behavior from times medieval. It was simpler than that. There was wrong; there was right. You knew in your blood and bones which was which. If you *knew* what was right but you didn't try to *do* what was right regardless of the risk, then you weren't just a bad man, you weren't even any kind of man at all.

The world in which he'd grown up had faded around him as he lived; it was now as ancient in its way as that of the pharaohs buried in the Egyptian pyramids. This darker reality had replaced it. He didn't want this world. He wanted the one before it, the one of his youth, a mere twenty or twenty-five years ago, but if he could not turn back time, he could at least live by the values of that lost place.

While the right thing was usually the hardest thing to do, sometimes it seemed the easiest, like now, when the right thing was to avoid abandoning the urgent task at hand, get Travis and Cornell into the Suburban, and only then drive over to the house and pick up Jane. He'd been an officer of the law, four times elected county sheriff, and although he'd been through some hair-raising moments on the job, Jane had undoubtedly fought her way out of more tight spots than he had. If he'd ever known anyone, woman or man, who didn't need to have a knight ride to the rescue, it was Jane Hawk.

Travis and Cornell were waiting in the vestibule, and when he called to them, they stepped outside.

The boy ran to the black Suburban and climbed in through the port side. Travis sat on the floor, not on the backseat, below window level, and Luther closed the door.

Cornell shambled after Travis, not bothering to make certain that his library for the end of the world was locked behind him. He had said he didn't expect ever to return: *I don't want to live half dead anymore, please and thank you. All alive or all dead—either way is better.* Now he got in the back starboard door.

Careful not to touch Cornell, Luther slipped doctored zip-ties around his wrists and his ankles, so he might pass for a prisoner.

As Luther opened the driver's door, he heard a truck engine on the highway, rapidly accelerating and drawing nearer. He looked out there and saw the behemoth swing off the blacktop, roar across the pea-gravel landscape, shred through specimen cacti, plow through the front porch, and slam into the house.

20

HOURS OF LIGHT REMAIN, BUT THE THUNDER-heads allow nothing more than an enduring dusk except when lightning alchemizes the falling rain into torrents of molten silver.

The wet highway flickers as if fitfully lit from underneath, and Egon Gottfrey passes vehicles with steamed windows further blurred by streaming rain, the ill-defined figures within like condemned spirits who have elected to forgo a downbound train in favor of taking the road to damnation.

Outbound from Beaumont in the Rhino GX, he is approaching Houston, in which he has no interest anymore. Beaumont, Houston, Killeen—every one is a false lead, nothing more than the Unknown Playwright's version of a wild-goose chase. Although Ancel and Clare Hawk borrowed the Longrins' Mercury Mountaineer, they never drove it as far as Killeen, and they never boarded a bus to anywhere.

Earlier, Gottfrey had switched on the radio, which happened to be tuned to an NPR program featuring an interview with Elon Musk, the billionaire entrepreneur and hot-tub philosopher invented by the Unknown Playwright to spice this world with humor. Musk says, among other curious things, that there is only a one in a billion chance that this world is base reality; he says it's almost certainly true that we exist in a computer simulation. If Musk were a real person, as Gottfrey is, instead of a character in this cosmic drama, and if Musk studied radical philosophical nihilism, he'd know, as Gottfrey knows beyond doubt, that there is no computer simulation because the existence of computers, like the existence of everything else, can't be proved. They are imaginary magical devices.

It's no coincidence that Gottfrey was inspired to turn on the radio, that it was tuned to an NPR station, and that the interview with Musk was under way; the U.P. wants to poke a little fun at him and remind him that all his efforts on the computer, which have led to the discovery of Ancel and Clare's whereabouts, were really the work of the U.P., who will be responsible for his triumph.

Ahead repeated lightning shapes the city out of the gloom, the buildings shivering in the storm flares, light running liquidly along the superstructure of a bridge. An ominous red beacon swivels high atop what might be a radio-station transmission tower, like some lighthouse marking the place where the world finally will end.

The Unknown Playwright is investing the scene with so much dramatic weather that Gottfrey is certain that the climax of this episode will occur soon.

In Houston, he turns north on Interstate 45, the midafternoon traffic crawling through the drumming downpour, so thick that he can no longer exceed the speed limit. He is not troubled by the delay.

Conroe is only forty miles away, a thriving city of a little over eighty thousand, on the southern edge of Sam Houston National Forest. In Conroe, Jane Hawk's in-laws have taken refuge, certain that their sanctuary cannot be discovered.

PART SIX

Tragedy

1

THE LITTLE HOUSE GROANED IN DISTRESS, AS IF awakening from a long sleep and realizing how very old it was, how arthritic its joints, how brittle its bones. When Jane tried to leave, the back door stuck as though swollen and warped, but the problem was that the entire rear wall of the structure had tweaked. In the now misaligned frame, the encased door was wedged tight.

She holstered her pistol and gripped the knob with both hands and put everything she had into a hard sustained pull, but the door wouldn't budge.

The four-pane window in the top half wasn't big enough to get through, even if she broke out the muntins along with the remaining glass.

The bigger window above the sink was painted shut, with thicker muntins. She would need too long to clear it and clamber out.

She tried the door again, wrenching it from side to side even as she pulled on it.

Although the living room ceiling had collapsed onto the truck, the driver remained in control. Insanely, he pumped the accelerator, as if he foolishly believed that the front wheels could be forced out of the spaces between the floor joists into which they had crashed. The powerful engine screamed. The floor of the house shuddered, creaked, and cracked as the wheels strove to force the vehicle forward.

With the sleeve of her sport coat, Jane wiped sweat off her brow, out of her salt-stung eyes. She was trained, conditioned, *born* to deal with lethal threats, to outthink and outmaneuver whatever villainous sonofabitch—or bitch—wanted to take her down. But this was *chaos*, bedlam wrought by a self-destructive, unpredictable lunatic. Reason and wit wouldn't necessarily carry the day. Anyway, the immediate enemy was the house; guns and hand-to-hand combat skills were of no use against an inanimate adversary.

She considered returning to the living room, trying to pop the driver through the windshield. However, the ceiling and the attic structure had crashed down on him, burying the truck, and she wasn't likely to have a clear shot. Besides, things were continuing to come apart, especially toward the front of the house, and returning there might be the death of her.

The garage. There would be no electric power, because surely the circuit breakers had all been tripped when the truck rammed into the residence. But the big tilt-up garage door could be manually operated.

As Jane turned toward the connecting door where her telltale shard of glass was undisturbed, the maniacal driver tramped the accelerator all the way down and didn't let up this time. The truck's voice escalated until it sounded less like a machine and more like some denizen of a Jurassic swamp, expressing its mindless fury in a world where intelligence and reason counted for nothing, where the only guarantors of life were brute strength and ferocity. A reeking pale-blue cloud of exhaust fumes flooded out of the living room, into the kitchen. Under Jane's feet, under the vinyl tiles, slabs of plywood began to shift and stress against one another like those tectonic plates in the earth that could crack open the faults in continents and shove mountain ranges from the bowels of the planet, creating towering alps where once there were flat plains.

She moved toward the door between kitchen and garage, and a more profound shudder passed through the house, a thunderous quaking, followed by tortured sounds of structure deconstructing. She thought the immense truck was about to plunge entirely into the basement, but instead the garage broke loose of the residence and collapsed. The connecting door burst inward, debris—including a large rafter—erupting toward Jane. She leaped sideways and jumped back, and the four-by-six came to a stop where she had been standing, gouging a wide ribbon of vinyl skin off the sub-flooring. The door to the garage was blocked now by lumber and sharp-edged sheets of corrugated-metal roofing and masses of pink fiberglass insulation acrawl with highly agitated silverfish.

The house tweaked again. Windows shattered. The valve stem in the ancient sink faucet must have failed; the handle and spindle and packing nut and faucet guts blew loose, and a high-pressure stream of water shot into the air. The truck screamed. The air thickened with fumes. Frosted-plastic panels buckled and cracked and fell out of the ceiling light box, the floor sagged, and the back door rattled violently in its frame.

If it's still wedged tight, it wouldn't rattle. Rattling means loose.

She stepped across the intruding garage rafter and yanked on the door, yanked again, and it opened. Rushing onto the back porch, down the steps, onto the pea gravel, she exhaled the bitter exhaust fumes and sucked in fresh air and heard herself saying, *"Thank you, thank you, thank you."*

Wheeling along the weedy ruts that served as the driveway, the Chevy Suburban approached from the barn.

As Jane hurried to the vehicle, a black helicopter clattered past at an altitude of no more than two hundred feet. She looked up, visoring her eyes with one hand, and watched it turn east and then circle west.

Luther braked to a stop.

Jane opened the passenger door but didn't get aboard. She stood watching the helo as it executed a 180.

An Airbus H120. Manufactured in Canada. Seating for the pilot and four passengers. Used by various agencies of the United States government.

The Airbus was coming back for another look.

"Luther, get out of the car," she said urgently.

"What's happening?"

"*Get out, hurry!* Just Luther. Not you, Cornell, not Travis."

Inside the house, the garbage truck shrieked, and the building continued to come apart.

The helicopter had almost executed its turn. It was perhaps a quarter mile directly south of their position.

Luther opened his door and got out of the Suburban and regarded Jane across the roof. "What're we doing?"

The helicopter had completed its turn. Heading for them now.

"Wave," she said.

Luther looked toward the approaching aircraft.

"Wave at them. Remember the white FBI on our roof. We aren't leaving here. Just arrived. We have this covered, checking it out."

2

Bernie rounded the end of the pool, which blazed with reflected sunshine. The bobbling lounge chairs looked as if they were being smelted down so that their aluminum could be recycled.

In spite of the fact that the monkey-quick maniac was smaller than his victim, he had dragged Holden Hammersmith down. He now straddled his prey's chest like the conjured demon out of that fearsome painting *The Nightmare*, by Henry Fuseli, which had haunted Miriam after they had seen it in a museum. Hammersmith couldn't seem to throw the guy off. The attacker endured the bigger man's blows as if he no longer had the capacity to feel pain, and he struck blows of his own. Like a vulture pecking at carrion, he darted his head between the flying fists to bite Holden's face.

The boy, Sammy, hovered close, shouting, in great distress, but he'd suffered bites on a hand and forearm, and he was too terrified to throw himself on the assailant and try to drag him off.

Bernie realized at once that this wasn't a cease-and-desist stop-or-I'll-shoot situation, like he hoped it might be. Whether the crazed man might be one of the misfortunes who had been injected with a nanomachine brain implant or was something else altogether, he was for sure a *meshugener*—insane, obsessed, bizarre. He wasn't going to respond to either reason or threat.

Back in the day when Bernie pretended to be a hard-boiled hard-ass to prevent the mob pigs from taking a slice of his business, he had never needed to shoot anyone, *baruch ha-Shem*. He didn't want to shoot anyone now. But he couldn't stand by and watch Hammersmith be murdered.

When Sammy dared to grab at the would-be killer, Bernie said, "No, stay back," and he quickly acted in the boy's stead. He could not hope to inflict just an arm or leg wound, because he was likely to shoot the struggling victim as well as the attacker. With his left hand, he seized a fistful of the crazed person's thick dark hair. Twisted. Pulled hard. Forced the madman's head up, back, away from Hammersmith. "Enough already, enough." Entreaty proved useless. The demon glared, its twisted mouth wet with blood, its blue eyes as empty of humanity as the eyes of those who long ago operated gas chambers in which millions died and furnaces in which others were burned alive. The thing snapped at him, teeth like chisels. Bernie jammed the muzzle of the Springfield TRP-Pro against the side of its head—"*Sholem aleichem*, peace unto you"—

and with horror but without remorse, he squeezed the trigger. The hollow-point .45 round went clear through the head and struck the thick bole of a palm tree, from which it tore a chunk the size of a fist.

3

Having descended to about a hundred feet, the helicopter approached for a second look. Both front seats were occupied behind the cockpit glass.

"Walk with me, Luther. We're checking the place out, doing our job, just two Bureau grunts."

"We're not dressed FBI, especially me."

As they hurried toward the house, Jane said, "Yeah, but they know this shit going down today isn't a legit Bureau operation. It's an occasion to dress street."

Inside the house, the truck still screamed like some behemoth floundering in quicksand and raging at its inevitable descent.

As the helo passed over, its fleet shadow shading them for an instant, the back porch collapsed. Sheets of metal roofing sprang loose and were caught in the chopper's downblast, twanging as they flexed like the great wings of a flock borne out of a dream about bodiless robot birds.

Still the truck engine raced.

Arriving at the front of the house, as the helo arced back to follow them, Jane and Luther surveyed the scene as if they were first responders. She drew her pistol so this might look real. Luther did the same. Together they stepped tentatively into the ruins of the porch, which was still overhung by a damaged roof.

When the front wheels had broken through the living room floorboards, the joists blocked the axle, at least temporarily stopping the truck from diving into the basement. But the vehicle had tipped forward, and the rear wheels, which remained this side of the breech in the wall, had lifted off the rubble; they spun without effect.

Luther raised his voice over the engine roar and the clatter of the hovering Airbus. "What if they put down?"

"They're not backup," Jane said. "Just chopper jockeys, search and surveillance."

They had flown over the house twice, so they must have seen something of the truck through the hole where part of the main roof had fallen in on it. However, because a couple of strategic posts still supported the torn and sagging front-porch roof, the men in the helo were not at an angle to be able to see the rear wheels spinning uselessly. The noise made by the Airbus would, for those aboard it, mask the noise of the truck, and they might also be wearing headphones. If Jane and Luther acted as though whatever crazy thing had happened here was over except for the cleanup, the helo boys would have every reason to believe it.

"Better get out there," Luther said, "before they decide to call backup *for* us."

"Let them see you put away the gun."

Jane kicked through the ruins and back to the pea-gravel lawn. She holstered her pistol and gave the Airbus guys two thumbs up.

Luther thumbed them, too, and waved them off.

The chopper hovered for a moment, but then it turned in place and faced north and buzzed away.

They watched it until it was no bigger than a fat housefly. Then they sprinted for the Suburban.

4

With one hand, the father held his bitten chin together. That was the worst of it. Lesser bites in his left trapezius muscle, left cheek, left brow at the arc of the eye socket, right thumb, right forearm. None of the wounds was mortal. Only the reconstruction of the chin might leave him disfigured. But the pain must have been severe.

Holden was beefy, self-confident, unaccustomed to being afraid, but he was scared now, and angry. On his feet, swaying, he muttered curses at his attacker, even though the man lay dead on the pool deck, his bullet-deformed head half empty.

The son kept trying to call 911 with an iPhone. "They don't answer." He was shaken, shaking, frightened by the very fact that his father was afraid. "There's nobody there. We need an ambulance. *Why isn't anyone there?*"

Bernie took the phone from the teenager and wiped the blood-spotted screen on his shirt and entered the three digits. Two rings. An automatic pickup was followed not by a 911 operator's voice or any version of *please hold*, but by an electronic twitter and a series of clicks. And then silence.

"Is there someone who can drive you?" Bernie asked the boy.

"My mom."

The mother was already running toward them from the office.

To the father, Bernie said, "Hold the chin, apply pressure, but with an ice pack if you have one. You want to minimize the bleeding *and* the swelling. You understand?"

"Yes."

The boy shouted at his mother to bring the car. "The hospital! We gotta get Dad to the hospital!"

Bernie realized that he didn't have the burner phone on which

Jane would call him. He'd left it in the motor home. He turned away from the Hammersmiths and shoved the pistol under his waistband and concealed it with his Hawaiian shirt and hurried along the pool decking.

He was almost to the end of the pool when the full importance of what had happened abruptly settled upon him, and his heart began to pound. He had intervened in a violent assault and shot a man—a *thing*, something like a golem but not made of mud, a golem *without* a soul that had once been a man *with* a soul. He had shot him *to death*. Yet somehow he'd remained calm throughout the confrontation. He had not been afraid, only concerned about doing what needed to be done.

Now his heart knocked hard, though not because he was worried about the consequences of what he'd done, which he wasn't. These events—the insane attack, the shooting, the failure of the 911 system—had something to do with Jane and her boy. She'd said her enemies would be here in force and seal off the valley as best they could. But suddenly it seemed they hadn't just sealed it off. They had also transported the valley out of the world as Bernie had always known it, out of the real world into the darkest corner of the Twilight Zone where anything could happen but nothing good could be expected.

As Bernie approached a large Winnebago, one of the other motor homes currently in the park, a deeply tanned barrel-chested man in sandals and khaki shorts stepped out of it. He gestured toward the farther side of the pool. "What's going on? What the hell happened over there?"

"Crazy man," Bernie replied. He kept moving. "Big fight. Somebody shot somebody."

"Oh shit."

Before boarding the Tiffin, Bernie disconnected it from the park's power supply. By the time he took the .45 from his waistband and put it on the console box and got behind the wheel and started the engine, the Winnebago was roaring past on its way out of the park. A minute later a Thor Motor Coach decamped, and behind it a Fleetwood.

Shivering in the outflow of air-conditioning, which wasn't very cold, Bernie picked up the burner phone and stared at it, hoping.

5

PASSENGER AS ALWAYS, CARTER JERGEN IS BEING driven through the quivering thermals that rise from the sun-scorched blacktop, the wasteland flat and sere and daunting to all sides, like a dreamscape in which emaciated horses bearing dead riders will appear in a long, ghastly procession, as they do sometimes in his sleep.

The four-door six-wheel VelociRaptor is a big vehicle, but it's a subcompact compared to the Valleywide Waste Management über-truck, which could demolish it in the equivalent of a head-butting contest. The V-Raptor is the very essence of cool, yes, but driving cool wheels when you go off a cliff won't buy you a soft landing.

Having conceived of his mortality while touring the scene of slaughter in the kitchen of the Corrigan house, Carter Jergen is hour by hour becoming more obsessed with the prospect of his death, which previously had seemed no more likely than going to bed here in California and waking up on the moon.

He doesn't want to find the dumpster-lifting truck and endure the demolition derby that might ensue. He doesn't want to come face-to-face with Arlen Hosteen, because Hosteen has gone through the forbidden door and fallen down the forbidden stairs and is just an older version of Ramsey Corrigan, the teenage mutant death machine. After having been enthusiastically in the hunt for Jane Hawk,

Jergen does not any longer want to find her, either. Now that he's able to conceive of his death, he's increasingly concerned that Jane Hawk will deliver it to him. He's surprised by the transformation he's undergoing, but he's pretty close to embracing a live-and-let-live attitude, and it doesn't feel half bad.

"Maybe we need to step back and rethink," he says.

"Step back from what?" Dubose asks.

"The brink."

"What brink?"

"Jane Hawk."

"She's a brink? She's not a brink. She's a dumb bitch who's been damn lucky."

"She could be a brink," Jergen insists. "We've been racing after her full tilt for so long, we could suddenly find ourselves airborne with a long drop and nothing below but rocks."

Radley Dubose doesn't bother to reduce speed when he looks away from the road and pulls his sunglasses down his nose with one finger and peers at Jergen over the frames. "You're too young to be going through a midlife crisis, Cubby."

"I have a bad feeling."

"Well, I have a good feeling."

"I've never had a bad feeling like this before."

Dubose repositions his sunglasses and looks at the road again and says, "Maybe you need testosterone shots."

This is when Dubose receives a call from the Desert Flora Study Group. The Valleywide Waste Management truck—and probably Arlen Hosteen with it—has been spotted by the Airbus crew conducting low-altitude surveillance. The truck plowed into a house approximately one and a half miles from the VelociRaptor's current position. FBI agents—Arcadians, of course—are already on the scene.

6

Travis had been huddled on the floor behind the driver's seat, below window level. At his mother's instruction, he now sat on the seat long enough to thrust his legs into a roomy gray duffel bag she provided, pulled it up to his shoulders as if it were a sleeping bag, and then returned to the floor, where he curled in the fetal position. Head toward the front of the vehicle, back to the port-side door, he faced the transmission hump that separated his half of the backseat from Cornell's. He was small enough to fit nicely in that footwell.

Jane leaned through the open door and kissed his cheek. She pulled the duffel bag over his head and partly closed the drawcords at the top, leaving a large enough opening for air to enter.

"Are you okay, sweetie?"

"I'm good."

The gray bag was emblazoned with a red cross in a white circle.

"Now, you're just bandages, honey, lots of bandages and medical supplies. If we're stopped, you don't move."

From within the duffel, he said, "Not a finger."

"You're a brave boy."

"I'm an FBI kid."

When Jane looked up from the Red Cross bag, she met Cornell Jasperson's stare. His eyes glistened with torment.

He whispered too softly for Travis to hear, "*I won't let him die, won't let him, won't let him.*"

The white plastic zip-ties around his wrists and ankles had been cut and mended with white tape. They looked secure, but they could be pulled apart with ease.

"Just play it like I explained," she whispered, "and we'll all make it."

When she closed the door, she realized that, in the imploded house, still alive in the cab of the truck, the driver continued to pump the accelerator with demonic insistence. The engine roared and an underlying shrill grinding noise might have been the front axle spinning relentlessly against the joists that had not yet given way. If he was one of the adjusted people, something had gone so wrong with his nanoweb control mechanism that he was now perhaps as much of a machine as was the truck he had once commanded, stuck in gear and unable to shift himself into neutral.

She hurried around to the front passenger seat, where Luther had propped the fully automatic 12-gauge shotgun on its butt plate, barrel against the dashboard. She stood it between her legs, keeping it upright by pincering it with her knees, and pulled the door shut.

As they drove past the destroyed residence, the mounded wreckage abruptly cratered as apparently the joists succumbed. The basement swallowed the truck along with a few tons of debris, and the ruins disgorged a thick gray plume. The only portion of the structure remaining upright was a six-foot-wide section of stuccoed wall with a glassless centered window offering a view of churning dust, like a cenotaph standing as a memorial to a lost civilization.

In the backseat, Cornell said, "Good-bye, little blue house."

Twenty yards north of the ruins, a Lexus SUV was parked aslant the shoulder of the road, its back end on the pavement, the driver's door standing open. There appeared to be a dead man slumped in the front passenger seat.

"What's this?" Luther wondered.

Jane figured that the man who had broken down the front door, before the arrival of the garbage truck, had driven the Lexus. *Is you whisper sex me, sex me, kill me, kill you . . . whisper inside head?*

To Luther, she said, "I'll explain later. If I can. Just get us the hell out of here."

They headed north on the leg of County Highway S3 that was called Borrego Springs Road.

7

ALTHOUGH HE WAS EXPECTING THE CALL, BERNIE Riggowitz startled and almost dropped the phone when it rang. He said only, "Yes."

To allow for an array of scenarios, they had prearranged four possible sites for a rendezvous, each identified only by a number.

Jane said, "One," which meant she and Luther and Travis were en route in the Suburban with no one wounded and with every reason to believe they could get back to the parking lot, just outside of the campground gate, where they had parted earlier.

Because of the bizarre attack on Holden Hammersmith and the shooting that had left a dead man on the pool deck, Bernie was nervous about remaining at this facility for the fifteen or twenty minutes Luther might require for the drive from the southern end of the valley.

On the other hand, no one was answering 911 calls, suggesting local law enforcement must be either overwhelmed by events that Bernie could only imagine or compromised by the marshaled forces searching for Jane. If no one was dispatching ambulances or patrol cars, the RV park most likely wouldn't be acrawl with police anytime soon.

In answer to her "One," he said, "One," and pressed END.

The call had been so short that the carrier-wave fishermen aboard the trolling airplane could not have had time to lock on either phone's signal and track it to source.

Nevertheless, Bernie got out of the driver's seat and stepped into the living room and put the burner on the floor and used a hammer to smash it, as Jane had instructed.

On terminating the call, she would have thrown her phone out the window of the Suburban.

They could no longer communicate. But come good luck or bad, they would not need to speak again until they were face-to-face.

8

DUBOSE DRIVES NORTH ON THE LEG OF COUNTY Highway S3 called Yanqui Pass Road, turns south on Borrego Springs Road, and after half a mile slows to look at the Lexus in which a corpse slumps in the passenger seat. He parks in front of the abandoned SUV.

Carter Jergen doesn't want to join in his partner's inspection of the Lexus. He wants to live and let live, or rather live and let the dead be dead. However, he doesn't want to be told again that he needs testosterone shots.

Even with his newfound awareness of his mortality, he *still* needs Radley Dubose's approval. This need is sick, and Jergen knows it's sick, but it's powerful. Dubose is a West Virginia hillbilly with the thinnest patina of sophistication acquired at a second-rate Ivy League school, a lousy dresser, a noisy eater, a mannerless rube who speaks competent French, yes, but with embarrassing pretension. Nonetheless, Dubose is cool. There's no getting around it. He's a self-possessed, imperturbable, totally cool dude. Cool has been a goal of Carter Jergen's since middle school, but he's made little progress toward coolness. Here he sits in an outfit that would meet with the approval of the best fashion magazine in the world, *GQ*, a few thousand dollars' worth of clothes. He also wears a GraffStar Eclipse ultra-slim lightweight titanium wristwatch, and yet he knows in his heart that he is not in the least cool. In fact, when he looks at the GraffStar Eclipse to see what hour it is, as this might be the hour when he dies, he is mortified that he can't tell the time. The watch has an entirely black face, black hands, and black check marks instead of numbers, and at the moment, anyway, he might as well be looking into a collapsed star, into a black hole, strapped to his wrist. Dubose wears a Timex, or something even cheesier, with a plain white face and numbers, but Jergen is too embarrassed to ask him the time.

At the Lexus, Dubose opens the passenger door to have a closer look at the deceased, while Jergen stands at the driver's door, pinching his nose against the stench. The dead man has voided his bowels and bladder, and his ears are full of blood.

"One of the fifty we brain-screwed last night," Dubose says. "Name's Nelson Luft."

Dubose is at all times au courant with details like the names of the plebs, the rabble, the nobodies with whom they are currently involved. To Carter Jergen, this has always seemed to be proof that the big man lacks a well-honed mind that can focus on what's most important. But now even this seems cool, evidence that Dubose can take in the whole picture while remaining focused on salient issues.

"His partner is Henry Lorimar. Henry must be somewhere near." Moving toward the house, Dubose draws his pistol, suggesting that Henry is another Ramsey Corrigan. "Hackles up, Cubby."

9

Travis in the duffel. Cornell playing prisoner. Luther pushing the Suburban past the speed limit, relying on the lettered doors and roof to grant them safe passage, the pale desert burning away toward stark mountains in every direction, and an eerie sense of something unseen falling toward them at high speed . . .

Never in her life had Jane bought a lottery ticket or put a coin in a slot machine. She possessed an intuitive awareness of the odds of success and failure in any undertaking, and the odds for a gambler were terrible. If she had to be in the game, she wanted to be the one who stacked the deck or replaced the regulation ivories with a pair of loaded dice. For any operation like this, she thought it out ahead, went over it at least a hundred times in her mind. Once she was on the ground and everyone was in play, she relied equally on training and intuition, and she remained keen for any advantage that might present itself.

Yet she never dared to be certain of the plan's efficacy while it was unfolding. The more distance they put between themselves and Cornell's property and the closer they drew to Bernie and the motor home, the greater her tension grew.

She wasn't superstitious. A broken mirror, a black cat crossing her path, spilled salt—nothing of that nature could ever disquiet her. However, although this world was beautiful beyond reckoning, it was also a dark world. Evil conspired in every corner, in sunshine and in shadow, and only a fool thought otherwise.

So much was at stake for her now, not only her own life but that of her child and those of her friends. For the moment, the personal took priority over the mere fate of humanity and the loss of its free will. She wished that she'd taken an acid reducer. Her hands were cold. Icy. Her chest felt tight. She had lost so much. Luther had lost more. Cornell was rich, but he'd lost the greater part of an ordinary life even before he'd been born. They were not going to lose anything more. This was a dark world, yes, but they were not going to allow the darkness to swallow them. Screw that.

As they approached a crossroad, Luther braked for three black Jeep Grand Cherokees, all arrayed with rooftop lightbars, all with sirens wailing, as they raced from east to west, one behind the other.

Jane read the shields on the doors of the Cherokees: "Homeland Security."

Luther drove through the intersection in the wake of the Jeeps, and less than half a mile later they came upon an overturned Toyota pickup blackened by a recent fire. The driver had not gotten out alive. Two minutes later, they arrived at a deconstructed motorcycle and the grisly remains of its rider. And then a battered Mini Cooper hung up on the trunk of a cleaved but still standing oak tree.

"WTF?" Luther wondered.

When they discovered a red Honda lying on its flank and smashed roof-first into a retaining wall, as if it had been squashed by an army tank, Jane put both hands on the automatic shotgun that was braced between her knees.

Provided by her source in Reseda, the weapon was a slick knock-off of the Auto Assault-12 that had been developed in the United States. This one had been manufactured without license in Iran. Thirty-eight inches long, including a thirteen-inch barrel. The thirty-two-round drum magazine would empty in six seconds on full auto. Heavy. About fifteen pounds when fully loaded with 12-gauge shells. This one was loaded with slugs instead of buckshot. It fired from a locked breech and looked like a hard gun to manage, though it was in fact sweet. The weapon's gas-operated system absorbed 80 percent of the recoil, and a spring pared off another 10 percent, so the kickback was a small fraction of that from an ordinary 12-gauge.

They were maybe ten minutes from the RV park where Bernie waited.

10

MAYBE HENRY LORIMAR IS PROWLING AROUND, alive and demented, reduced to a reptile consciousness, but Jergen hopes the brain-screwed pleb is dead in the demolished house.

He and Dubose circle the structure, looking for indications, signs, manifestations, stains on the fabric of normalcy—the usual bullshit stuff. But it seems to Jergen that there is no smallest swatch of clean normalcy, that the fabric is stained from end to end, that everything they see is a sign. And what every sign seems to portend is death.

"Where's the FBI?" Dubose wonders. "According to the pilot, he overflew an FBI Suburban here just minutes ago."

"Maybe they weren't ready to dig through the ruins. Dangerous work. What for, anyway? Who cares if Arlen Hosteen is dead in his garbage truck?"

In such situations, it is never clear if Dubose is considering anything Jergen says. The big man affects that profound-pondering expression that suggests Jergen is a feeble version of Dr. Watson with little to offer.

"And why," Dubose broods, "did Hosteen come here of all places? What drew him?"

"Maybe he just didn't like the color of the stucco."

"What drew Henry Lorimar here?"

Behind the imploded garage, Dubose becomes fascinated with a garden hose. Between the threaded fitting at the end of the hose and the nozzle is one of those one-quart-bottle attachments that allows the water spray to be mixed with lawn fertilizer, pesticide, or other substances. Another bottle lies discarded and empty. The pea gravel is wet in places, not yet dried by the fierce afternoon sun.

"What the hell were they doing here?" Dubose wonders, pinching his chin with thumb and forefinger to convey a meditative mood.

Vague impressions in the thick carpet of pea gravel lead Jergen to risk an observation that might be worthy of mockery. "They aren't clear, but aren't these tire tracks?"

Studying the pebbled desert landscaping, Dubose says, "Could these be tire tracks? But from what vehicle? The FBI's? What were they doing with the hose?"

"Washing the Suburban?" Jergen ventures.

"The entire valley's descending into chaos, these brain-screwed freaks on a killing spree everywhere, and a couple agents decide to wash their wheels? I don't think so, my friend, though I understand how deeply you Harvard men are into waxed and shiny transportation."

Frowning, Dubose crouches and plucks from the gravel a lump of pasty-white substance that he works between thumb and forefinger. He sniffs the material.

Carter Jergen surveys their surroundings for any sign of Henry Lorimar or some other hapless specimen exemplifying the heretofore unanticipated dangers of the direct interfacing of the human brain with a computer.

"Chalky," Dubose says of the pasty white stuff. "Smells maybe a little like paint."

11

WITH ITS MASSES OF WITCHY GRAY HAIR AND ITS wet breath, the storm seems to pursue the Rhino GX north from the Gulf of Mexico, blasting bedevilments of wind-driven rain against the tailgate, howling curses at the side windows.

By now the average tropical depression would have exhausted its pyrotechnics; but this is weather as stage setting, and the Unknown Playwright employs it lavishly. As Egon Gottfrey at last arrives in Conroe and wends his way to the northeast perimeter of the city, the storm stabs the darkening day with dagger after dagger, and all the works of man and nature leap, leap, leap in stroboscopic terror.

This neighborhood of handsome houses features multi-acre lots on low rolling hills. In the eerie rapture of lashing silvery rain beribboned with serpentine fog and flickering with the goblin light of the tortured heavens, tall pine trees stand in groups as though they are sentinels on the watch for otherworldly threats that the storm might blow in from some parallel universe.

Egon Gottfrey drives past the target house, circles the block. He parks three doors south and across the street from the residence. A two-story brick beauty painted white. Set well back from the quiet street. Black shutters framing the windows. Four broad front steps leading up to a portico with six columns. In the dismal day, warm amber light is welcoming in several windows.

The wind fails, and now the downpour continues strictly on the vertical.

The Rhino stands under the boughs of an enormous pine, in front of vacant acreage. Gottfrey douses the headlights and switches off the wipers. But to maintain the air-conditioning, he doesn't kill the engine. The vehicle's windows are darkly tinted, and the day is too warm for his presence to be betrayed by exhaust vapor. In such a fierce storm, perhaps not even a single soul will be out walking and curious enough to wonder if the idling engine might suggest that someone is conducting surveillance.

On the passenger seat is the Medexpress carrier. The digital read-out shows the interior temperature is forty-five degrees, more than cool enough to ensure that the ampules containing the control mechanisms will be effective when injected.

Gottfrey intends to wait for darkness. Ancel and Clare think they are clever. They fail to understand, however, that their roles are not central to this drama, while *he* is the iconic loner around whom every scene is structured. Their fate shall be enslavement.

12

As RADLEY DUBOSE PROWLS THE SCENE BESIDE THE ruined garage, the white, wet substance clings to his shoes, and pea gravel sticks to the pasty stuff.

This is reason enough for Carter Jergen to remain a few steps back from the site of the investigation. He is wearing gray suede seven-eye lace-up ankle-fit trainers by Axel Arigato. In both the Corrigan and Atlee houses, he barely avoided getting blood on the exquisitely finished suede. He is damn well not going to soil the shoes irrevocably by competing with Dubose in a pointless game of Name the Mysterious Crap.

The big man tramps across the layer of gravel—which seems to average four or five inches in depth—scowling as he considers the subtleties of texture and distribution. With one shoe, he scrapes away the little stones to reveal bare earth.

"It's mud underneath. Someone recently used a lot of water with an urgent purpose," he observes solemnly, as though he will shortly retire to his rooms on Baker Street, there to fill his favorite pipe with black tobacco and play his violin while pondering this clue.

Dubose walks in widening circles, scanning the ground. He halts when, in addition to the crunching noise, there arises a metallic sound like an empty soft-drink can crumpling under his weight. He scrapes aside several inches of little stones to reveal a buried California license plate. A *pair* of plates. Not rusted and long out of date. The current design.

Frowning, he holds the plates between thumb and forefinger of his right hand, as if they are the first two cards in a poker hand played with a giant deck.

From his safe-for-the-shoes position, Carter Jergen feels his oppressive sense of impending doom relieved somewhat by the mixed emotions that Dubose stirs in him: contempt for the man's boobish pretension, grudging admiration for the way he often resolves a mystery in spite of being born with a hillbilly brain that has been further stupefied by the faculty of Princeton, and an embarrassing but undeniable adolescent veneration of the big man's total cool-ness and—*admit it*—his genuine charisma.

Suddenly Dubose casts aside the license plates and withdraws his smartphone from a pocket. "No time to relay this through the Desert Flora Study Group. Got to call him direct."

"Call who?" Jergen asks.

"Whom. The helo pilot. Live and learn, Cubby." When the pilot answers, Dubose says, "Hawk somehow brought a white Suburban through roadblocks. Washed off the special-formula paint with a solvent. Put on federal tags. It's that black FBI Suburban you scoped out where the truck took down a house. *Find it, and we'll have the bitch.*"

Jergen stands awestruck, his hope renewed.

13

THEY WERE TWO MINUTES FROM BERNIE. JANE wasn't superstitious, but her many experiences of desperate situa-tions had taught her that sometimes the closer your destination, the more you might slip-slide away. Which only made sense. When your adversaries were formidable—whether they were two socio-pathic serial killers on an isolated farm or multiple law-enforcement agencies of the United States government—the longer you took to wrap up a piece of business, the greater the chances that you would lose momentum and the other side would gain it. In such circum-stances, time was seldom a friend.

She called out to Travis where he curled in the duffel bag on the floor behind the driver's seat. "How're you doing, Travis?" When he didn't answer, she raised her voice. "Travis, are you okay?"

This time he said something, but too softly for her to hear.

Cornell relayed the boy's reply. "Umm. Umm. He says bandages don't talk."

Luther laughed, and after a hesitation, Jane laughed as well, though at the moment laughter made her nervous. Even though she didn't believe in fate, she wanted to avoid taunting it.

Luther turned off the highway onto the approach road to the RV campground. Bernie had moved the motor home to the overflow parking lot outside the main gate. He stood beside it in the sun. In white sneakers and white chinos and a pink-and-blue Hawaiian shirt, slight and white-haired, with a face that would have gotten him role after role as a kindly grandfather if the movies still told stories in which kindly grandfathers were relevant, just the sight of him would have given her hope. Except the uncharacteristic angularity and tension of his posture signaled that something was wrong.

14

JERGEN HEARS A CAR STOP IN FRONT OF THE HOUSE, and a door slams. Already additional investigators are swarming to the property.

Looking around wonderingly at the garden hose and the license plates and the pea gravel and the chalky, pasty white stuff, he is able to put some of the pieces together, but the puzzle is far from complete.

"How can you be sure it was Hawk?"

"Helo pilot reported one agent was a woman."

"We have several in the valley right now."

"The other was a black guy."

"We got black guys."

"That Minnesota sheriff she teamed up with before was black."

"You think the boy was hiding in the house?" Jergen asks.

"Maybe in the house." Dubose's attention shifts to the distant ramshackle barn. "The house or somewhere on the property."

"But why did Hosteen drive his truck into this place?"

"I don't know *everything*, Cubby." He picks up the license plates he previously discarded. "Gotta call Desert Flora, have them run a search of plates scanned on incoming traffic, see where the Suburban came from when it was white."

Just then an outlandish yet somehow familiar figure appears from around the ruins of the house and says, "Hey now, boys, that there's some ass-kickin' truck you got. I'd get myself one if I had more than a pot to pee in, which is about all I got after four lazy squanderin' husbands and what with the pathetic check I get from the thievin' embezzlers at Social Security."

She looks as old as the desert, centuries of hot sun baked into her wrinkled face, long tangles of brittle white hair frizzling from under her wide-brimmed straw hat. Dressed in a red neckerchief, a tan-linen shirt almost as wrinkled as she is, cargo-pocket khakis, and red athletic shoes, she carries a big shoulder-slung purse from which peers a small dog, a Pomeranian that regards Jergen and Dubose with keen interest.

"I figured a fancy-ass truck like yours couldn't stay hid for long in the Anza-Borrego. A dandy like that'n, must take years of profitable sinnin' to pay for it. What's the sticker price on that there sucker?"

Dubose smiles, though not warmly, and says, "We're FBI and this is a crime scene, ma'am. You need to leave the property."

She cocks her head and squints at them, and the Pomeranian does the same, as if it mimics her gestures as a parrot might mimic her colorful language.

"You boys 'member me broke down by the side of the road in killer heat, you went blowin' by like a wind out of Hell?"

"Ah," Jergen says, "yes, that rust-bucket Dodge pickup."

The old woman says, "I come here to tell you a thing or damn two about manners and courtesy, seein' as how your worthless parents never done their job."

"Granny," Dubose says, "you could get yourself in a world of trouble if you don't vamoose."

Ignoring the implication that she risks arrest for interfering with an investigation, the old woman says, "Maybe some didn't stop 'cause they were on their way to comfort a dyin' child. But you're not that kind. What blisters my butt is you not only go flyin' past, but you just got to mock me with a toot-toot. Wasn't me alone might wither and blow away in that killer heat, was Larry, too." At the mention of his name, Larry the Pomeranian looks adoringly at his guardian. "This here precious pup is the light of my life, the only one who's loved me in ninety years. You toot-toot me, you toot-toot him."

Dubose has had enough. When the big man has had enough, he is a wonder to watch. "Listen, you stupid dried-up old twat, you get your skinny ass out of here, or I'll break more bones than you can count, make you watch me crush Larry's head, and then bury you alive in the rubble of this house."

She sighs. "Idiot." She draws a Sig Sauer P245 from her monster purse and shoots Dubose twice point-blank. She shoots Jergen as he goes for his pistol, shoots him again as the weapon falls from his hand.

He collapses to the pea gravel.

Suffering pain far greater than anything he's ever known or imagined, Jergen looks up at the old woman as she stares down with disdain. "Rattlesnakes," she declares. "Shit, I musta killed a thousand of 'em."

From Jergen's perspective, when the shooter turns and walks away, she is not a diminutive old woman any longer, but a towering figure with a mystical aura. His entire life now seems to have been a wandering without purpose, incoherent until she walked in to say, *Hey now, boys, that's some ass-kickin' truck you got,* whereafter she has defined his life as he's never been able to do, has drawn a red circle around his thirty-seven years and penciled in the margin one word: *meaningless.*

15

IN CASE THE AUTHORITIES WERE STOPPING ALL INcoming and outgoing traffic at the roadblocks, as they had done little more than two and a half hours earlier, Cornell Jasperson would leave Borrego Valley in the motor home, tucked under the platform bed, where Luther Tillman had hidden earlier. Travis would occupy the smaller space under the built-in sofa, where Jane had been concealed.

She helped the boy extricate himself from the duffel bag, and she knelt beside the Suburban to hold him close, to feel the beating of his heart and look into his eyes. They were his father's eyes in every striation, in their crystalline clarity, in the directness with which they met her eyes.

"Good so far," she said. "Not much farther to go. Mr. Riggowitz will show you where to hide. He's a lovely man. Do exactly what he tells you to do."

"I will."

"Listen, in there where you're going to hide, there might be this cockroach. Don't let it scare you at the wrong moment."

"Cock-a-roaches don't scare me, Mom."

"I should have said don't let it startle you. Be very quiet and still, and everything will be all right."

"Why can't you hide in the motor home with us?"

"There aren't enough spaces to hide, sweetie. Besides, Luther and I are going to be Bernie's escort. Like a police escort."

She hugged him very tight again and kissed his cheek, his brow.

"Hurry now. Mr. Riggowitz is waiting."

As Luther led the boy to meet Bernie at the starboard door of the Tiffin Allegro, into which Cornell had already climbed, as Jane got to her feet, she heard the helicopter.

16

CARTER JERGEN LYING HELPLESS ON A CATAFALQUE of pea gravel, under a searing sun as fierce as the eye of some merciless monocular judge, a chorus of crickets singing a monotonous dirge . . .

The agony first squeezes from him screams more terrible than those to which any of the people he's executed have ever given voice. But either his nervous system short-circuits from an overload of pain or his brain is pumping out a flood of endorphins, for the torment soon subsides to mere misery. He doesn't know exactly where he's been shot and lacks the courage to assess his wounds. He is too weak to move and growing weaker by the moment. Bleeding out. He can smell the blood.

He is lying on his side, facing Radley Dubose, whom he believes is dead. The big man is sprawled flat on his back, arms out to his sides.

Then Dubose speaks. "An historic moment, my friend."

"Call nine-one-one," says Jergen as a flicker of hope fires through his unadjusted brain.

"No can do, Cubby. I'm paralyzed from the neck down. No feeling at all. Wish I'd called Desert Flora about the bitch Hawk before I called the pilot. Now only the pilot knows."

Jergen begins to weep.

"No tears are warranted," Dubose counsels. "This is a great and noble death."

"Noble?" Carter Jergen is still capable of astonishment and a small flame of anger. "Noble? Tell me what the hell is noble about it?"

"We're dying for the revolution."

Jergen's words come in a rhythm of exhaustion. "We're dying 'cause you tooted at a creepy old, crazy old skank demented from a lifetime of vicious heat, tarantulas, snakes, flying bats eating flying beetles in the night, and four useless desert-rat husbands, who she probably deserved, the hateful bitch."

"Whom, not who," Dubose corrects. "Love the revolution, my friend. It is our monument."

Jergen's vision is fading. He can draw only shallow breaths. "It's bullshit. The revolution. Just bullshit."

"All revolutions are bullshit, Cubby. That is . . . until you win one. Then you rule like gods and take what you want, who you want. Meanwhile . . . man, what a ride."

Jergen's hearing is fading, too. Dubose sounds distant. He can hardly hear the big man. He whispers an expression of love, such as he knows it: "You were always so cool. How could this happen to you when you were always so cool?"

If Dubose answers, Jergen does not hear him.

17

THE POSSIBLE EVIL INTENTIONS OF THOSE WHO FLY the Airbus H120 imparted to the aircraft a monstrous quality, so that as it streaked across the desert scrub toward the RV campground, it appeared less like a machine than like a huge wasp with lethal venom to deliver. The helo's approach was so direct and fast, Jane could only assume that in the half hour since the pilot left them unmolested at the ruined house, he had found a reason to reconsider their legitimacy and to seek them out.

Now he and his crewmate had seen Travis being led to the motor home, a boy approximately the size of the one they were hunting.

Jane pulled open the front passenger door and grabbed the Auto Assault-12 as the chopper racketed over the car, over the Tiffin Allegro, and executed an arc of return.

She hated this. She was trained for the street, not for the battlefield. In the Bureau, and even since, when she'd been forced to kill, the enemy had been a person, dimensional and detailed; she had seen his face, had known beyond all doubt that he was malicious and an immediate threat to her life or the life of an innocent. But *this* confrontation was of the nature of war, not law enforcement. She couldn't see the faces of the men in the chopper, didn't know their names, didn't with certainty understand their intentions. In war you needed to kill at a distance, at the earliest opportunity. Otherwise you could be overwhelmed and lose your advantage—and then the fight. But the need to do this made her feel . . . not wicked, not even unclean, but in part responsible because it might not have come to this if she had been a little smarter, quicker.

There was no time for self-examination. She existed only for her boy, to give him a chance at life and perhaps yet a world worth living in. What laws Jane broke and what sins she committed in his defense were a cancer on no one else's soul but her own, and she alone would bear the consequences all the way to the grave and perhaps beyond.

The pilot used the Airbus H120 as a weapon of intimidation, clearing the roof of the motor home by no more than twenty feet. Maybe the copilot was also a shooter. Jane couldn't know if they were strictly on a surveillance run or might be combat ready. When the chopper crossed the Suburban and turned its flank to her, the starboard door might be open to facilitate automatic fire.

Loaded with slugs, the Auto Assault-12 had an effective range of one hundred meters. As the helo passed over the Suburban far lower than that, Jane moved boldly under it and emptied the drum magazine. With a muzzle velocity of eleven hundred feet per second, the shotgun pumped out thirty-two slugs in six seconds. The auto-fire reports stuttered loud across the parking lot, but the recoil-reduction system was as effective as claimed, the butt plate of the stock bumping against her shoulder not with jarring violence, but as if giving her a rapid series of attaboys to encourage her attack.

At such close range, the slugs ripped holes in the aircraft's undercarriage. Wrecked one of the skids. Rattled hard through the whirling rotor blades to no good effect. Tore up the tail pylon. Blew out the tail rotor. Disintegrated the horizontal stabilizer.

Seventy or eighty feet past Jane, the Airbus wobbled into an uncontrolled death spin. It came back toward her, and a thrill of terror fired her heart as if it were a drum magazine in her breast. Then the chopper spun away from her, drawing a gray spiral of smoke on the bright air. The engine quit, and the helo tipped, and a blade of the rotary wing gouged the blacktop. The Airbus flipped, tumbled, exploded, vanishing in a beautiful bright flower of infinite petals that for a moment seemed to grant pilot and copilot absolution in death, but then the broken craft reappeared as a scorched carcass, and the petals of flame became mere tongues of fire that licked through the wreckage with fiendish hunger.

Jane turned toward the Suburban.

The two dogs were at the side window of the cargo area, neither of them barking. They seemed not to have been frightened by either the gunfire or the crashing Airbus. Their dark liquid eyes regarded Jane with grave interest, as though in their veins flowed the blood of seers, as if they intended, by the intensity of their stares, to convey to her the nature of some oncoming calamity.

Luther stood on the farther side of the vehicle. "Shit."

"An avalanche of it," she agreed.

"You think they had time to report finding us?"

"Maybe."

"They'd be excited, overconfident, caught up in the moment."

They were both aboard the Suburban. The engine of the motor home turned over, started.

Jane said, "We're too deep in for a change of plans. It's this or nothing. Let's roll."

18

In THE BEDROOM OF THE TIFFIN ALLEGRO, CORNELL Jasperson found the secret space under the queen-size bed to be comfortable and even pleasant. He was not having an anxiety attack, but darkness always calmed him in the throes of such an event, and it calmed him now. As when he was burning with anxiety, Cornell imagined himself floating in a soothing pool of cool water. Under the bed platform, where no one could touch him, he wouldn't go nutbar and make a spectacle of himself at the very worst moment, which might have happened if he had remained in the Suburban.

The motor home began to move, slowly at first and then faster. Engine rumble and road noise filtered up into the secret space where Cornell lay. It wasn't pleasant to the ear, but he could endure it. This wasn't like the sound of the airplane that had touched him all over like thousands of crawling ants and spooked him into an anxiety attack. He would be all right. He really would. Nobody could touch him here.

Mr. Riggowitz seemed like a good person. Very old, but gentle and concerned. A nice smile. When he'd shown Cornell the space under the bed, Mr. Riggowitz said he'd driven from one end of the country to the other, over and over again, so he knew what he was doing behind the wheel of the motor home. He would do a fine job. They were safe in his hands.

Nevertheless, Cornell wished that their driver was Mr. Paul Simon, the songwriter and singer. He knew it wasn't realistic to wish for this. Mr. Paul Simon was too famous and probably too rich to drive a bus for anyone, though a constant kindness in his music suggested he would be a person of humility and understanding who would do anything that he could to assist someone in distress.

A disturbing thought occurred to Cornell. Until recently, he had worn his hair in dreadlocks like Mr. Bob Marley, the singer, but he cut them off when he learned that the reggae star had been dead for decades. Although he loved Mr. Paul Simon's music, he did not closely follow the singer's life, and now he realized that he didn't know if Mr. Paul Simon was alive or had passed away.

If Mr. Paul Simon had passed away, Cornell shouldn't be wishing that the singer-songwriter was driving the motor home. Mr. Riggowitz was very old, but alive, which made him better suited to the task.

Thinking about all this, Cornell became nervous. The darkness and the imaginary pool of cool and soothing water were helpful, but to further calm himself, he began to sing aloud softly, "Diamonds on the soles of my shoes."

19

Jane Hawk knew the desert offered unique beauty, but under the current circumstances, this stark realm seemed to have been salted and otherwise poisoned. What little grew across the pale surrounding plain appeared misshapen and threatening, as though the roots of all the local flora extended far down into infernal regions, originating in the tortured souls of the citizens of that deep darkness.

When they had first arrived here, the land had seemed to speak to her, and now she felt that it repeated what it had said then: *The boy is mine now and forever.*

They had arrived on County Highway S22, but they were leaving on State Highway 78 to avoid encountering the same agents at the same roadblock. Bernie had entered the valley as ordinary Albert Neary, but he was leaving with an FBI escort, which couldn't be easily explained to those who remembered him from a few hours earlier.

Luther drove five miles below the speed limit. They didn't want to appear to be fleeing and thereby draw undue interest. In the motor home, Bernie remained only three car lengths behind them.

Traffic seemed heavier than normal, nearly all of it outbound from the valley. The motorists who passed the Tiffin and Suburban were traveling much faster than the speed limit. Although nothing about the people glimpsed in those vehicles confirmed their panic, Jane suspected an urgent exodus was under way, inspired by extreme, bizarre violence witnessed and rumored.

She had a second thirty-two-round drum for the Auto Assault-12. The barrel of the shotgun was still warm when she changed out the depleted magazine.

Whether the search operation had learned that she was in an FBI Suburban or whether that discovery died with the crew of the

Airbus, security at all the roadblocks had surely tightened in the hours since she arrived. The professionals hunting her possessed intuition no less keen than hers. They would feel in their bones that this was the day when she would come, that she was among them, and in fact that she might already have her boy and be on the way out.

Furthermore, they evidently had augmented their searchers with a cadre of adjusted people, and something had gone terribly wrong. The ensuing chaos gave them another reason to conduct tighter searches of every outbound and inbound vehicle. They might even seal off the valley for the duration and allow no one to enter or leave.

She couldn't risk the motor home being subjected to a closer inspection than it had received earlier in the day. She and Luther would try to bluff their way through the roadblock with Bureau ID and badges that she'd gotten on Monday from her source in Reseda.

Duke and Queenie might give them away; however, the dogs might as likely add credibility to their story of escorting a VIP Arcadian out of the chaos zone. Yes, it was known that Gavin and Jessica Washington owned a pair of German shepherds. But Jane suspected most of these elitist Arcadian creeps would be unable to imagine that she might risk rescuing the dogs along with her boy. Their ethics, such as any existed, were utilitarian ethics. Were their roles and hers reversed, they would abandon the dogs or even kill them rather than bring them along. Fortunately, Duke and Queenie were of the breed most often trained to assist law-enforcement officers, and the Bureau employed a kennel's worth of them.

After certain events in Iron Furnace, Kentucky, Luther had been publicly connected to Jane. However, he hadn't been at her side during subsequent hits she made on Arcadians in Orange County, California, and Lake Tahoe. They might think he had died or gone to ground in grief over the nanoweb enslavement of his wife and older daughter, unwilling to risk his remaining child, Jolie, by further helping America's most-wanted fugitive. Luther could not disguise his race or his size, but his shaved head, beard, and new wardrobe might be enough to avoid suspicion.

As for Jane, she was being Elinor Dashwood. Shoulder-length blond hair long gone. Pixie-cut chestnut-brown wig. Colored contact lenses to turn her blue eyes brown. Stage-prop glasses. A simple disguise was nearly always successful if worn with confidence. Never avoid eye contact. When stared at, stare back. When flirted with, flirt in return. Don't evade casual conversations with strangers; in fact, initiate them. Know who Elinor Dashwood is, and then *be* her.

They were approaching the crest of a low rise when Luther said, "Something's on fire."

A dark column churned high into the faded-blue sky. Three vultures circled the smoke as though it bore the scent of charred carrion that whet their appetite.

The Suburban topped the rise. Half a mile ahead, lightbars flashed on the barricading vehicles, one of which burned furiously.

20

THE WATER SURGING IN THE GUTTERS BEARS UPON it phosphorescent laces of foam. Deprived of wind, the rain falls hard in plumb lines. Thin scarves of fog do not race like the rain, but instead wander through the day to a different tempo, like lost spirits seeking some final resting place, glowing with the lightning as if each bolt is a welcoming call that lures them toward some far shore.

The scene is beautiful, and it is crafted solely to enhance the drama of what Egon Gottfrey will soon do. Yet he's weary of it.

Here in eastern Texas, in the central time zone, perhaps half an hour of daylight remains, but the dark-gray overcast is so thick that the sun seems already to be setting behind the swollen clouds. He is eager to proceed and would approach the target house now if only the storm would relent.

A moment later, the volume of rain diminishes. Becomes a light drizzle. The drizzle becomes sprinkles. The arsenal of Heaven seems to have fired its last thunderbolt. In the gathering gloom, the rain entirely stops.

21

Luther said, "This doesn't look good."

Vehicles had been ordered off the road and were parked on the flanking desert, three long parallel rows beside the outbound lane, many fewer along the inbound side. Agents wearing FBI T-shirts and baseball caps were carrying riot guns and watching over the restive motorists in their cars and trucks. The Bureau boys looked pissed, as though they wouldn't hesitate to shoot out tires—maybe even a windshield—if one of the drivers they'd ordered into limbo decided to tramp on the accelerator and take off.

Jane said, "If we are who we say we are, we'll play it bold. Drive straight into it but slow."

In the eastbound lane, a disabled Dodge Charger, which perhaps had been serving as a barricade, had been T-boned at high speed by a Cadillac Escalade. The Charger was on its side, afire. The front doors stood open on the Caddy.

Evidently run down by the Escalade, two mangled corpses—one male, one female—lay in the eastbound lane.

As Luther pulled around the dead to proceed slowly eastbound in the westbound lane, an armed agent waved him vigorously toward the shoulder of the highway.

"We're coming straight at them, so they can't see the FBI on the roof and doors," Luther said.

"Or maybe the Airbus pilot got the word out, and these guys are on to our game."

Jane put down the window in her door as Luther lowered his. She held out the badge in her right hand, raised high for all to see, as Luther offered his in his left hand.

The agent still waved them insistently to the side of the road, and two other men warily moved forward with their shotguns raised, one to each flank of the Suburban.

With the motor home close behind, Luther braked to a stop, but didn't leave the pavement.

The Auto Assault-12 stood between Jane's knees, butt on the floor, muzzle aimed toward the ceiling. Under the circumstances, it availed her nothing. Any attempt to use it would draw instant fire from the two approaching agents.

The man who came to the driver's side saw FBI on the door, but he didn't lower his weapon. Blood spattered his face, maybe not his own blood. From a distance, Jane had thought these men looked angry, and they did, but they were also terrified, wide-eyed and as pale as soap, wound so tight that if a neural spring failed, there could be unintended shotgun fire.

"What's happened here?" Luther asked.

Staying three steps back from the driver's door, the agent spoke as if Luther's simple question was an affront. "What *happened* here? What do you *think* happened here? What's it look like happened here. Freakin' zombies happened, like they're happening everywhere."

The agent on Jane's side said, "In like ten seconds one of our guys *had his face chewed apart, torn off.* What kind of crazy bastard can do that, can even *think* of doing it?"

Luther said, "That's why we've been ordered to escort the man in the motor home the hell out of here."

The bloodied agent looked toward the Tiffin Allegro. "Who's he, he gets an escort?"

"Better you don't know a name. There's no revolution without him. He's from the central committee."

Jane leaned toward the console and looked through the driver's door window at the agent. She didn't have to fake anxiety; her voice was shot through with fear for her boy. "Hey, listen, the guy in the RV is a mean ballbuster. You want to know who *really* runs the DOJ and the Bureau, pulls the strings—it's not the attorney general or the director, it's that sonofabitch back there. If we don't get him out of here fast and then something goes wrong, we'll wind up with needles in our arms. Maybe you have bigger worries right now, but number one with me is being injected and brain-fucked. So can you just, damn it, please cut us some slack?"

The agent glanced at the Tiffin again, then quickly away, as if the man up there behind the wheel might curse him with the evil eye. He was harried, shaken, thrown off his game by recent weird events. "All right. Go on through. But slow. It's a mess."

Although Luther and Jane had been granted permission to proceed, the other agents watched them with sharp suspicion as they passed. Beyond the wrecked Cadillac and the burning Dodge Charger, four more bodies were splayed on the pavement, two perhaps cut down by gunfire, at least one of the others butchered in a manner that Jane could not discern.

Small flying insects of a species unknown to her had ventured forth from their shadowed havens into the desert heat, enticed by the feast of fresh blood. Wings silvered by sunlight, they swarmed in shimmering hysteria above the dead, and the burning car smoked into a sky as pale and dry as the land below. Beyond the windows of the impounded vehicles alongside the highway could be seen stricken faces, drivers and passengers who seemed as patient as spectral voyagers waiting on the bank of that final, black river for the ferry that forever conveyed travelers in only one direction.

As the scene of horror and chilling portent receded, Jane felt no relief. The junction of State Highways 78 and 86 lay about twenty miles ahead, and the town of Indio—where they would return to the comparative safety of Ferrante Escobar's fenced property—was almost another fifty miles farther. In seventy miles, in this new wicked world aborning, anything could happen.

22

IN ALL LIKELIHOOD, THE DOWNPOUR CEASES ONLY temporarily, to facilitate Egon Gottfrey's approach to the target house. Once he gains entrance to the residence, no doubt the Unknown Playwright will cue the lightning and thunder, crank on the spigot, and flood the scene with storm effects once more, as this act of the drama moves toward its violent, Wagnerian conclusion.

Carrying the Medexpress container and a tote bag, he crosses the quiet street to the house that stands three doors south of the one where Ancel and Clare Hawk abide in a false sense of security. He turns north.

The storm in intermission clots and blackens the sky no less than during its performance. The early dusk it has brought to Conroe becomes darker with each step that Gottfrey takes.

The following is what he knows by dint of extensive use of NSA data troves and connections. Sue Ann McMaster, born Sue Ann Luckman, the clerk at the bus station in Killeen, was once married to Roger John Spencer, her first husband, for eight months prior to his death in a traffic accident. Roger's mother is Mary Ann Spencer, now the manager of the bus station in Beaumont, who presented Egon with the staged video of Ancel and Clare stand-ins arriving from Houston. Tucker Treadmont, the young Uber driver with man breasts and a snarky attitude—who led Egon, Rupert, and Vince out of Beaumont to an abandoned house in the boonies—is the son of Arnette and Cory Treadmont. Arnette's maiden name is Lemon. She is the daughter of Lisa and Carl Lemon. Carl is Lisa's second husband. Her first was one Bobby Lee Bricker. Lisa and Bobby Lee, now in their seventies, had a child all those years ago and named him Lonnie John. Lonnie John Bricker isn't only the half brother of Arnette Lemon Treadmont, but is also the driver who, during a Skype interview with Gottfrey, claimed that Ancel and Clare Hawk were passengers when, on Monday, he drove the 10:25 bus from Killeen to Houston. This leaves Jim Lee Cassidy, the tall, folksy, white-haired Realtor and lying sack of shit in Killeen, who claimed that Ancel and Clare had been getting out of the Mercury Mountaineer in front of his office when his valise fell open, spilling a lot of important papers; supposedly they helped him pick up the documents before the wind blew them away, and then they hurried off in the direction of the bus station. Jim Lee Cassidy is surely the wily bastard who worked out this chain of deception. Sue Ann McMaster and her husband live in a house in Killeen that they acquired through Cassidy, as do Lonnie John Bricker and his partner. Arnette and Cory Treadmont had lived in Beaumont, where their son Tucker still resides, but they later moved to Killeen, where they bought a house through the ever-busy Jim Lee Cassidy. The links between Cassidy and the Hawks were more difficult to uncover. Jim Lee has an older sister, Corrina June, seventy, who is married to one Preston Eugene Fletcher. Preston Fletcher has a twin sister, Posey, who is married to one Johnny Don Ackerman. Posey and Johnny Don have two daughters and a son, all grown. The son is Dr. David Ackerman, forty-two, a military historian and a civilian employee at the Corps Combat Development Command at Quantico, to which Nick Hawk had for a while been assigned. There Nick met Jane.

Those are facts known to Gottfrey, and the following are suppositions he makes from those discoveries. Nick and Jane Hawk were friends with Dr. David Ackerman at Quantico. Subsequent to Nick's death and Jane's ascension to the most-wanted-fugitive list, David Ackerman discreetly contacted the Hawks to say that he wanted to help any way he could, and Jane vouched for him to her in-laws. At some point it was decided that Ancel and Clare might one day need a bolt-hole and a plan to obscure the journey they would make to get to it. David Ackerman's parents, Posey and Johnny Don, now retired, made a lot of money in the construction industry in Conroe. They lived in a large house on three acres, but owned as well a vacation home in Florida, where they spent part of the year. Whether they were home in Conroe or not, they were pleased to allow Ancel and Clare to hide there if and when the need arose. So Ancel and Claire didn't drive the Longrins' Mercury Mountaineer to Killeen. Say they drove it as far as Austin. Say they were met in Austin by Dr. David Ackerman's sisters, Kay and Lucy. Say Kay drove them four hours to the house in Conroe, while Lucy drove the Mountaineer to Killeen and parked it in front of the real estate company owned by her uncle Jim Lee Cassidy, who then waited for the authorities to tie the Mercury Mountaineer to the Hawks and locate the vehicle by its GPS signal, so that he could send them to Sue Ann McMaster and the bus station.

Texas isn't real and neither are Texans, but Egon Gottfrey hates the state and its people nonetheless.

There's no point hating the Unknown Playwright who created Texas and Texans; because when all is said and done, this has been conceived as a dramatic vehicle in which Gottfrey will triumph and achieve greatness as an iconic loner. But though he doesn't hate the U.P., Gottfrey does sometimes wonder about his/her/its mental state.

Now the street darkles under the paused storm.

He arrives at the Ackerman property.

Posey and Johnny Don are in Florida.

Although the daughters, Kay and Lucy, will do all errands for Ancel and Clare, so that the fugitives can remain in the house and not risk being recognized, the siblings will now be at their own homes with their families.

Gottfrey follows the long driveway to the house.

The landscape lights, evidently on a timer, are not yet lit.

Immense pine trees overhang the driveway.

All is secluded, dark, and quiet except for the rainwater that drips from the branches of the pines.

The house has a security system provided by Vigilant Eagle, Inc. It no longer works.

From his hotel suite in Beaumont, using a laptop, via the NSA, Gottfrey had entered the Vigilant Eagle computer system by a back door. From there he'd accessed the computer that the alarm company had installed in the Ackerman house to monitor and ensure the proper response condition was at all times maintained by door, window, motion-detection, and glass-break sensors. He did a bit of fiddling.

The readouts that are part of the alarm keypads throughout the residence continue to show a properly functioning system. But when he forces entry, no alarm will sound and no alert will be received at Vigilant Eagle's central station.

He circles the imposing house, studying it.

A few lights brighten windows upstairs. The only lights downstairs are toward the front of the residence.

Some windows are covered with draperies or at least sheers, but others allow him views of the interior. He doesn't see anyone.

The kitchen at the back of the house is dark.

Rather than a porch, there is a large covered patio.

By the back door, he puts down the Medexpress carrier and the tote bag. From the tote, he withdraws a LockAid lock-release gun that will automatically pick any deadbolt.

This device isn't entirely silent. He will need to pull the trigger a few times to cast all the pins to the shear line. In a quiet house, the clicking noise might draw attention.

He can hear no music, no television.

When he hesitates, the storm abruptly resumes, rain hammering on the patio roof.

Gottfrey smiles.

There is no lightning or thunder at the moment, but the rataplan of rain will mask what noise the lock-release gun makes.

He uses a penlight, on and quickly off, to locate the keyway in the deadbolt. He inserts the thin pick of the gun. He needs to pull the trigger five times to disengage the lock.

He puts away the LockAid. From the tote bag he removes a Taser pistol and a spray bottle of chloroform.

Leaving the tote and the cooler of ampules on the patio, he enters the kitchen and eases the door shut behind him.

His long-building frustration is about to be relieved. To get information about Jane and her boy, he needs only to inject one of her in-laws, which will be Ancel. If Clare is still the looker that Lonnie John Bricker says she is, he will use her and then beat her to death with his collapsible baton.

His eyes are sufficiently dark adapted that he has no fear of setting a foot wrong and making noise. Besides, he is the lead of this drama, every line of every scene crafted to serve him.

On the farther side of the kitchen, a door to a hallway stands half open. Soft light beyond.

He circles the kitchen island. The susurration of the rain in the night. The hum of the refrigerator. Two glowing digital readouts mark the time on the stacked ovens.

He is two steps short of the half-open hallway door when the cold muzzle of a gun is pressed to the back of his head.

Startled, Gottfrey lets the bottle of chloroform slip from his left hand.

A man with a deep voice says, "Drop the Taser, too. Don't mind doin' my share of housework, but I don't want to be moppin' up your brains from this nice mahogany floor."

Gottfrey drops the Taser.

"How many others," the man asks.

"Other what?"

"Other pestilential specimens like you."

"There's only me," Gottfrey replies, trying to imagine how the U.P. is going to get him past this reversal of fortunes and allow his inevitable triumph by the end of this act.

"Only you?" says the gunman. "Not damn likely."

"I'm an iconic loner," Gottfrey declares with some pride. "Like Dirty Harry or Shane."

The gunman is silent for a moment but then says, "Loner, my ass. You're a creature of the hive if ever there was one."

23

THREE MINUTES AFTER LUTHER TILLMAN PARKED the black Suburban at the back of the fenced compound, Ferrante Escobar's men had pulled off the forged federal license plates identifying it as Department of Justice ordnance. One minute after that, they'd moved the vehicle into the paint shop to strip it down and repaint it neither white nor black. Maybe Sahara Sand or Grecian Blue.

In anticipation of the rescue party's success, Ferrante's uncle, Enrique de Soto, had gifted Jane and her team with a bottle of Dom Pérignon, which all along had been chilling in the Tiffin Allegro's refrigerator. There was a large bottle of root beer for Travis.

"Umm. Umm. I would prefer root beer, too," said Cornell, who did not stand with them, but sat apart in a chair that was too small for him. "Root beer, please and thank you."

A card from Ricky came with an offer to take back the Tiffin and the Suburban, for which Jane had paid $120,000 cash; he'd give her a $50,000 credit toward whatever future purchase she might make.

He proposed an alternative deal in which she would receive $90,000 in credit instead of $50,000, but the terms were onerous.

Jane was and wasn't in the mood for a brief celebration. She was inexpressibly grateful to have Travis safe with her. However, in truth, no one in her company would be safe for long; and she needed to decide on other arrangements for him.

Whether she felt like a celebration or not, she knew the value of one: the essential sense of camaraderie it generated, the hope that it inspired. They sipped the icy champagne from plastic cups, and Travis had his root beer, which he shared with Cornell, while the dogs drank water from a bowl and ate peanut-butter treats and repeatedly explored the motor home, wagging their tails and delighting in a banquet of smells that no human nose could detect.

Neither Jane nor Luther nor Bernie—nor probably Cornell—could shake the foreboding with which the events of the past few hours had left them. Their laughter was muted. What toasts they made were modest and too solemn for a celebration.

She loved these three men for their courage, their loyalty, their kindness, but she could not keep her eyes from Travis. If the sight of the boy filled her with gratitude, it also settled on her a sadness close to grief, because they would so soon need to part.

24

AFTER FLYING LUTHER TO PALM SPRINGS IN HIS Learjet and then driving him to Ferrante Escobar's place of business earlier that day, Leland Sacket had returned to Palm Springs in his rental car to wait for a call. Now he was once more en route to Indio. Before this day was done, he and Luther would fly back to the Sacket Home and School in Texas. Jolie Tillman waited there for her father, in the company of scores of orphans, wondering if she would soon be one of them.

Jane walked with Luther to the guardhouse near the entrance to Ferrante's compound and explained why Travis would not, after all, be going to Texas with him.

"I hope to God these Techno Arcadian bastards don't find you and Jolie there. I don't think they will. I think the link between the Sackets and Nick's family is too obscure for them to smell it out. But if they do . . . This is awful and selfish of me, Luther, but I've got to say it anyway. If they do smell out that connection and find you and Jolie there, they will inevitably find Travis. I've never met your Jolie, but I know I'd love her. And I love you. I can't have all three of you in one place. I can't lose all of you in one moment. Besides, there's the issue of Cornell."

He said, "I've been wondering about that."

"It's truly amazing how Travis has bonded with Cornell in such a short time. He's going to be devastated if I send him somewhere different from where Cornell goes. He's a strong little kid, but he isn't stone. He's lost so much. He can't lose Cornell, too."

"Maybe Cornell can't handle losing him, either."

She smiled. "I think you're right."

The early April afternoon began to submit to a sunset that gilded the fleecy clouds in the west, and a warm breeze issued out of the north, bearing on it something like the scent of orange blossoms.

"But, Jane, Cornell can't take care of Travis long term."

"No, he can't. Anyway, soon they're going to find his library for the end of the world, his bunker, and they're going to know he harbored Travis, and after that he'll be almost as wanted as I am. Do you realize how much they'll torture him just by touching? Poor Cornell has no defenses against people like them."

"But where . . . ?"

"Bernie had a talk with me. He says his daughter, Nasia, and her husband, Segev, have a big house on a double lot in Scottsdale. The property is very private. No one has to know there's two new residents. Travis and Cornell will each have his own room. And Bernie says they love dogs, they have one of their own, so Duke and Queenie are welcome. Nasia and Segev—they've been wanting Bernie to give up driving from one end of the country to the other, and now he has even more reasons to stay in Scottsdale. They'll like that."

"But do they know what they're getting into, who you are, the risks of taking in Travis and Cornell?"

"Bernie told them about the little adventure we had together a couple of weeks ago, the night I carjacked him—and the next day at Ricky de Soto's place in Nogales. He didn't know who I was then, but later he saw me on TV, and he put it all together. They know where he went today and why. He says they're half expecting they might have . . . visitors."

Luther stood amazed. "How extraordinary."

"More than you know. Bernie was a child in Auschwitz. He lost his parents there."

"My God."

"He told me a little while ago. It's a miracle he survived, thrived, became the sweet and optimistic man he is. He understands what totalitarianism is, from the right, from the left. He knows the evil of these Arcadians and knows this is war, there's no retreating from it. He says not to take in Travis and Cornell would be to shame himself forever and soil the names of his mother and father. He says that Nasia and Segev feel the same and, if they didn't, he couldn't abide them, even though Nasia is his only child. If I can't trust Bernie, then this is a world where no one can be trusted."

Just then, Leland Sacket pulled up to the guardhouse in his rental car.

Jane felt as though everything was slipping away from her: all those she loved, the past, the future, the light of the day and all other light that it represented. She put her arms around Luther and held him very tight, and his arms were strong around her as they said their good-byes.

She waved at Leland Sacket and stood watching the two men drive away, stood watching the highway even after they were out of sight, stood watching as the gilded clouds grew as red as blood in the west, and then she walked back to the motor home before the night came all the way down.

25

IN THE TIFFIN ALLEGRO, SHE SETTLED WITH TRAVIS on the queen-size bed and held him and listened to him talk of Cornell's good sandwiches and coconut-pineapple muffins and Coca-Cola in Atlanta and Mr. Paul Simon and the problem with leaving your toothbrush on the bathroom sink.

He was trying to buy time with his stories, keep her with him by the power of his voice. He'd known they wouldn't yet be together permanently again as they had been in Virginia, before his dad died, but he had hoped to have a few days with her, not just a few hours.

When it was time for him to join Bernie and Cornell in Bernie's Mercedes E350, they moved from the bed to the front door in stages, parting in baby steps, pausing for him to ask questions.

"Will you come visit us?"

"You know I will."

"When?"

"As soon as I can."

"Will you get the bad guys, they killed my dad."

"Am I FBI or what?"

"You're major FBI," he said.

He didn't know the depth of the ocean of trouble in which she swam, didn't know that she was America's most-wanted fugitive, the beautiful monster of ten thousand newscasts, hunted by legions.

"Do you think Hannah's okay?" he asked.

Hannah was the pony that Gavin and Jessie had gotten him soon before they'd had to go on the run with the boy. The pony had been left behind.

"Hannah's being well taken care of, honey."

"Will I see her again one day?"

"I'm sure of it," Jane lied.

"I was getting real good, riding her. Uncle Gavin said I was gonna be a real horseman."

"Which you will be. I've no doubt about it."

"Even rodeos, you think?"

In Nick's youth, he had competed in rodeos.

"Even rodeos," Jane said.

At the car, he held fast to her. She didn't know if she could get him to let go. She didn't know if she could make *herself* let go.

In the end, because she was who she was and because he was his mother's son, they did let go.

She watched the Mercedes drive away into the night, as she had watched Luther and Leland drive away in the light of sunset, watched until there was nothing to see.

Then she loaded all her gear from the motor home into her Ford Explorer Sport.

26

EGON GOTTFREY SITS AT A DESK IN A BOOK-LINED study.

Six men stand at various points in the room, watching him. None of them is Ancel Hawk.

They say that one of their friends is already driving the Rhino GX to Austin, where he will strip out the GPS and then abandon the vehicle.

This does not concern Gottfrey. After all, the Rhino cannot be proven to exist, and neither can Austin. The room in which he sits is also an illusion.

He needs only to think of what must be done to put him in sync once more with the intentions of the Unknown Playwright, and all will be well.

From time to time, one of the men questions Gottfrey, and they remain half convinced there are others in the night with whom they must deal.

His answer is always the same, the five words he knows that the U.P. wants to hear from him. "I am an iconic loner."

Almost an hour after Gottfrey was taken captive, Ancel Hawk finally appears. He carries the Medexpress cooler that contains the control mechanisms in ampules of amber fluid.

As Ancel places the cooler on the desk, lightning rips the fabric of the night, and thunder speaks against the window glass.

One of the other men says, "Ben can do that, Ancel. You keep Clare company, hold her hand."

Clare Hawk appears in the doorway. "I don't need my hand held. And we can't ask any of you to do a thing like this."

"The bastard deserves it," another man declares.

"He no doubt does," Clare says. "But this is going to be on no one's conscience but mine and Ancel's."

The readout on the Medexpress cooler reports a temperature of forty-seven degrees. The control mechanisms are still viable.

An uneasiness arises in Egon Gottfrey. Ever since he shot Rupert Baldwin and Vince Penn, he has assumed that this drama is a stirring story of his dedication to the revolution, his genius for sleuthing, and his skill at violent action. As he watches Ancel Hawk open the cooler and as dry-ice vapor steams from it, a dark thought crosses Gottfrey's mind. Could it be that the U.P. has taken a detour into Shakespeare territory, the land of Macbeth and Lear and Hamlet? Could this be not at all what Gottfrey has thought? Could this be a tragedy?

27

JANE SAT IN THE EXPLORER, NEAR THE TIFFIN ALLE-gro, in the dark, with the engine running and the air-conditioning blowing hard. She needed to leave this place, but she could not drive.

She had wept as profoundly as this when she found her mother dead, when she lost Nick, but never otherwise in nearly twenty-eight years of life. Those first two times, she wept from mortal cause—her mother lost, her husband gone forever. But her precious child was not lost, and she despised this sobbing, not because it revealed a fatal weakness in her, but because it seemed to tempt fate. Even though she didn't believe in fate, she felt that crying this hard, letting grief so rack her, might somehow ensure that this weeping was for Travis in advance of his certain death, that she was losing him by crying so hard for him.

When Ferrante Escobar knocked on the window in the driver's door, she told him to go away, but he would not go. He bent down, staring in at her, until at last she lowered the window. "I'm all right, Ferrante. I don't need anyone to talk to. Just a minute. A minute or two, and then I'll go."

"I have nothing to say to you, Jane Hawk. I'm not a man of words. I just thought . . . you might need a hand to hold."

Because of the disturbing paintings in his office and what his uncle, Enrique, had called his "obsession with blood," she thought the moment would be creepy when she gave him her hand, but it was instead surprisingly tender. He stood there for a few minutes, his grip gentle, though hers was fierce. And her tears passed.

When she let go of him, he walked away into the dark.

She put up the window and shifted the car into gear and drove out of Indio into Palm Springs. She found a motel and paid cash for a room and took a long shower as hot as she could tolerate. When she dressed, she assumed the identity of Leslie Anderson, using an ash-blond wig, lenses that turned her blue eyes gray, and a fake mole the size of a pea, which attached to her upper lip with spirit gum. Leslie wore too much makeup and Smashbox lipstick.

Before she went out for dinner, she turned on the television and checked a cable-news network. There had been a terrorist attack in, of all places, rural Borrego Valley. It was believed that the area's water supply had been contaminated with a powerful animal tranquilizer—related to phencyclidine, angel dust, but a hundred times more powerful—that had inspired acts of extreme violence.

Yeah, right.

In a corner booth in a quiet restaurant with low lighting, she ate a filet mignon with sliced fresh tomatoes, asparagus, haricot verts. She drank two glasses of good cabernet.

She was too exhausted to sleep. She walked residential streets for two hours, under the benediction of the infinite and eternal stars. Minute by minute and step by lonely step, as surely as her lungs drew life from the air, her mind drew from the night and all its wonder, drew from it the increasing conviction that she was born for this fight and that she would not lose it. She had compiled and secreted away a lot of evidence. She knew what she needed next. She didn't know how to get it; but she would figure that out. Bernie Riggowitz had survived Auschwitz, and in spite of all his losses, he stood now with her. *Mishpokhe.* He was proof that though evil could win in the short term, it could be defeated in time.

She had no illusions. Her life hung by a thread. She was no more special than anyone else. Over the millennia, billions upon billions of people had died, been remembered briefly, been forgotten; and they were now gone as if they'd never existed. She was merely another among those billions. But just as she had no illusions, so in this matter she had no choices. She could be only who she was, could do only what she had always done, and one thing she had *never* done was surrender.

Author's Note

In the previous Jane Hawk novel, *The Crooked Staircase*, and again in *The Forbidden Door* I have rescheduled the annual blooming of the Anza-Borrego Desert to a later date in the spring. Thousands of tourists come to Borrego Springs to see this spectacular display; they would have been a serious complication to Jane's rescue operation, which was already difficult enough.

Carter Jergen, a character in this novel, has an acerbic view of Borrego Springs and environs that I do not share. I would like to visit again someday without having to don a disguise.

To keep the story moving, I have taken certain liberties with vehicle maintenance and other procedures at the bus stations in Houston and Beaumont, Texas.

In part 5, chapter 6, Minette Butterworth, an English teacher, is reduced to a subhuman condition. During this scene, through her mind pass words that mean nothing to her, though once they had meant a great deal: first, "meaningless as wind in dry grass or rat's feet over broken glass"; then "I will show you fear in a handful of dust." These are lines from "The Hollow Men" and "The Wasteland" by T. S. Eliot.

Please turn the page for a preview of

the next Jane Hawk novel

by #1 *New York Times* bestselling author

DEAN KOONTZ

THE NIGHT WINDOW

1

THE TRIPLE-PANE FLOOR-TO-CEILING WINDOWS OF Hollister's study frame the rising plain to the west, the foothills, and the distant Rocky Mountains that were long ago born from the earth in cataclysm, now dark and majestic against a sullen sky. It is a view to match the man who stands at this wall of glass. The word *cataclysm* is a synonym for *disaster* or *upheaval* but also for *revolution*, and he is the leader of the greatest revolution in history. The greatest and the last. The end of history is near, after which his vision of a pacified world will endure forever.

Meanwhile, there are mundane tasks to perform, obligations to address. For one thing, there is someone who needs to be killed.

In about two hours, when a late-season storm descends on these high plains east of Denver, the hunt will begin, and one of two men will die at the hand of the other, a fact that Wainwright Warwick Hollister finds neither exhilarating nor frightening. Of profound importance to Hollister is that he avoid the character weaknesses of his father, Orenthal Hollister, and at all times comport himself in a more formidable and responsible manner than had his old man.

Among other things, this means that when someone needs to be eliminated, the killing can't always be done by a hireling. If a man is too finicky to get blood on his hands once in a while, or if he lacks the courage to put himself at physical risk, then he can't claim to be a leader in this world of wolves, nor even a member of the pack, but is instead only a sheep in wolf's clothing.

The hunt will occur here, on Crystal Creek Ranch, Hollister's nine-thousand-acre spread, unto itself a world of pine forests and rolling meadows. The chase will not be fair, because Hollister does not believe in fairness, which exists nowhere either in nature or in the human sphere. Fairness is an illusion of the weak and ignorant; it is the insincere promise made by those who manipulate the masses for gain.

The quarry, however, will have a chance to survive. A very slim one, but a chance. Although Hollister's father, Orenthal, had been a powerful man physically as well as financially, his heart had been that of a coward. If ever he had decided that he couldn't farm out *all* the violence required for the furtherance of his business, if he'd seen the moral need for every prince to be also a warrior, he wouldn't have given the quarry any chance whatsoever. The hunt would have been an empty ritual with only one possible end: the triumph of Orenthal and the death of his prey.

Now the security system, which always knows Hollister's location in this forty-six-thousand-square-foot residence, speaks in a soft, feminine voice. *"Mr. Thomas Buckle has arrived in the library."*

Thomas Buckle is a houseguest from Los Angeles. The sole passenger on Hollister's Gulfstream V, he had landed at 10:00 this morning on the Crystal Creek Ranch's six-thousand-foot airstrip, had been driven 1.6 miles from the hangar to the main house in a Rolls Royce Phantom, and had been settled in a guest suite on the main floor.

He will most likely be dead by dawn.

The house is a sleek, ultramodern masterpiece of native stone, glass, and stainless steel, with floors of limestone on which ornately figured antique Persian carpets float like lush warm islands on a cold pale sea.

The library contains twenty-five thousand volumes that Hollister inherited from his father. The old man was a lifelong reader of novels. But his son has no use for fiction. Wainwright Warwick Hollister is a realist from his epidermis to his marrow. Orenthal also read many works of philosophy, forever searching for the meaning of life. His son has no use for philosophy because he already knows the two words that give life its meaning: *money* and *power*. Only money and power can defend against the chaos of this world and ensure a life of pleasure. Those people whom he can't buy, Hollister can destroy. People are tools, unless they decline to be used, whereupon they become merely obstructions that must be broken and quickly swept aside—or eliminated entirely.

With no need for his father's books, he had considered donating the collection to a charity or university but instead moved them to this place as a reminder of the old man's fatal weakness.

Now, as Hollister enters the library, Thomas Buckle turns from the shelves and says, "What a magnificent collection. First editions of everything from Bradbury to Wolfe. Hammett and Hemingway. Stark and Steinbeck. Such eclectic taste."

Buckle is twenty-six, handsome enough to be an actor, though he dreams of a career as a famous film director. He has already made two low-budget movies acclaimed by some critics, but box-office success has eluded him. He is at a crucial juncture, an ambitious young man of considerable talent whose philosophy and vision are at odds with the common wisdom that currently prevails in Hollywood, which he has begun to discover will limit his opportunities.

He has come here in response to a personal phone call from Wainwright Hollister, who expressed admiration for the young man's work and a desire to discuss a business proposal involving film production. This is a lie. However, as people are tools, so lies are nothing more than the various grips that one must apply to make them perform as wanted.

Upon the director's arrival, Hollister had briefly greeted him, so that now there is no need for the formalities of introduction. A smile is all he requires when he says, "Perhaps you would like to select one of these novels that's never been filmed and make it our first project together."

Although he is the least sentimental of men and has no capacity for the more tender emotions, Wainwright Hollister is graced with a broad, almost supernaturally pleasant face that can produce a smile with as many charming permutations as that of any courtesan in history, and he can use it to bewitch both women and men. They see compassion when in fact he regards them with icy contempt, see mercy when they should see cruelty, see humility when he views them with condescension. He is universally thought to be a most amiable man with a singular capacity for friendship, though in his heart he views everyone as a stranger too unknowable ever to be a friend. He uses his supple, glorious smile as if it is a farmer's seeding machine, planting kernels of deceit deep in everyone he meets.

Having been flown to Colorado in high style and having been treated like a prodigal son, Thomas Buckle takes seriously the offer to select any book in this library to translate to film. He looks around wonderingly at the shelves of material. "Oh, well, I sure wouldn't want to make that choice lightly, sir. I'd want to have a better idea of what's here."

"You'll have plenty of time to pore through the collection later," Hollister lies. "Let's have lunch. And please dispense with the 'sir.' I haven't been knighted. Just call me Wayne. Wainwright is a mouthful, and Warwick sounds like the villain in some superhero movie."

Thomas Buckle is an honest young man. His father is a tailor, a salaried employee of a dry-cleaning shop, and his mother works as a department-store seamstress. Although his parents struggled to contribute to his film-school tuition, Thomas paid for most of it, having worked part-time jobs since his freshman year in high school. On his two movies, he cut his fees for writing, directing, and co-producing in order to add to the budget for better actors and more scene setups. He is too naïve to realize that his producing partner on those projects didn't share his scruples and cleverly siphoned off some of the studio's money, which Hollister discovered from the exhaustive investigation he commissioned of Buckle's affairs. As the honest child of honest people, as an earnest artist and a striver in the all-American tradition, the young man has an abundance of hope and determination, but a serious deficit of street smarts; much to learn and no time left to learn it.

As they make their way from the library to the dining room, Tom Buckle can't restrain himself from commenting on the grandeur of the house and the high pedigree of the paintings on the walls—Jackson Pollock, Jasper Johns, Robert Rauschenberg, Andy Warhol, Damien Hirst. . . . He is a poor boy enchanted by Hollister's great wealth, much as the sorcerer's apprentice might be captivated by the mystery of his master during the first day on the job.

There is no envy in his manner, no evidence of greed. Rather, as a filmmaker, he is besotted with the visuals. The drama of the house appeals to him as a story setting, and he is spinning some private narrative in his mind. Perhaps he imagines a biographical film of his own life, with this scene as the turning point between failure and phenomenal success.

Hollister enjoys answering questions about the architecture and the art, telling anecdotes of construction and acquisition. Only when he senses that Tom Buckle has been drawn into his host's orbit, and then with great calculation, does Wainwright Hollister put one arm around the young director's shoulders in the manner of a doting uncle.

This familiarity is received without the slightest stiffening or surprise. Honest men from honest families are at a disadvantage in this world of lies. The poor fool is as good as dead already.

2

THE WISDOM OF MILLENNIA AND NUMEROUS CUL-
tures was stacked on a grid maze of shelves flanking dimly lighted
aisles in which no one searched for knowledge, all as quiet as an
undiscovered pharaoh's tomb in a pyramid drifted over by a thousand feet of sand.

That first Wednesday morning in April, Jane Hawk was en-
sconced in a library in the San Fernando Valley, north of Los Angeles, using one of the public-access workstations nestled in a
computer alcove, which at the moment offered the only action in
the building. Because every computer featured a GPS locater—as
did every smartphone, electronic tablet, and laptop—she carried
none of those things. Although the authorities searching for her
knew she used library computers, on this occasion she avoided
websites they might expect to be of interest to her. Consequently,
she was relatively secure in the conviction that none of her probes
would trigger a track-to-source security program and pinpoint her
location.

Many people using a computer or smartphone became so distracted that they ceased to be aware of what happened in the world
around them and were in Condition White, one of the four Cooper
Color Codes describing levels of situational awareness. After earn-
ing a college degree in forensic psychology in three years, after
twelve weeks of training at Quantico, and after having served as an
FBI agent for six years before going rogue, Jane was perpetually in
Condition Yellow: relaxed but alert, aware, not in expectation of an
attack, but never oblivious of significant events around her.

Continuous situational awareness was necessary to avoid being
cast abruptly into Condition Red, with a genuine threat imminent.

Between yellow and red was Condition Orange, when an aware
and alert person recognized something strange or wrong in a situa-

tion, a potential threat looming. In this case, through peripheral vision, she realized that a man who'd entered after her and settled at one of the other computers was spending considerably more time watching her than the screen before him.

Maybe he was staring at her just because he liked the way she looked. She had considerable experience of men's admiration.

Her own hair concealed by an excellent shaggy-cut ash-blond wig, blue eyes made gray by contact lenses, a fake mole the size of a pea attached to her upper lip with spirit gum, wearing a little too much makeup and Smashbox lipstick, she was deep in her Leslie Anderson identity. Because she looked younger than she was and wore a pair of stage-prop glasses with bright red frames, she could be mistaken for a studious college girl. She never behaved in a furtive or nervous manner, as the most-wanted fugitive on the FBI list might be expected to do, but called attention to herself in subtle ways—yawning, stretching, muttering at the computer screen— and chatted up anyone who spoke to her. She was confident that no average citizen would easily see through Leslie Anderson and recognize the wanted woman whom the media called the "beautiful monster."

However, the guy kept staring at her. Twice when she casually glanced in his direction, he quickly looked away, pretending to be absorbed in the data on his screen.

His genetic roots were in the subcontinent of India. Caramel skin, black hair, large dark eyes. Perhaps thirty pounds overweight. A pleasant, round face. Maybe twenty-five. Dressed in khakis and a yellow pullover.

He didn't fit the profile of law enforcement or that of an intelligence-agency spook. Nevertheless, he made her uneasy. More than uneasy. She never dismissed the still, small voice of intuition that had so often kept her alive.

So, Condition Orange. Two options: engage or evade. The second was nearly always the better choice, as the first was more likely to lead to Condition Red and a violent confrontation.

Jane backed out of the website she had been exploring, clicked off the computer, picked up her tote, and walked out of the alcove.

As she moved toward the front desk, she glanced back. The plump man was standing, holding something in his left hand, at his side, so she couldn't identify it, and watching her intently as he spoke into his phone.

When she opened the door at the main entrance, she saw another man standing by her metallic-gray Ford Explorer Scout in the public parking lot, talking on *his* phone. Tall, lean, dressed all in black, he was too distant for her to see his face. But on this mild sunny day, his knee-length raincoat might have been worn to conceal a sawed-off shotgun or maybe a Taser XREP 12-gauge that could deliver an electronic projectile and a disabling shock from a distance of a hundred feet. He looked as real as death and yet phantasmal, like an assassin who had slipped through a rent in the cosmic fabric between this world and another, on some mystical mission.

The Explorer, a stolen vehicle, had been scrubbed of its former identity in Mexico, given a purpose-built 700-horsepower 502 Chevy engine, and purchased from a reliable black-market dealer in Nogales, Arizona, who didn't keep records. There seemed to be no way it could have been tied to her.

Instead of stepping outside, she closed the door and turned to her right and made her way through the shelves of books. The aisles weren't a maze to her, because she had scouted the place when she arrived, before settling at the computer.

An EXIT sign marked a door to a back hallway that was fragrant with fresh-brewed coffee. Offices. Storerooms. An open refreshments niche with a refrigerator. A short hall intersected the longer one, and at the end, another door opened out to a small staff-parking area with an alleyway beyond.

Three cars and a Chevy Tahoe had occupied this back lot when she checked it earlier.

Now in addition to those vehicles, a white Cadillac Escalade stood in the fifth of seven spaces, to the west of the library's back door. The woman in the driver's seat of the Caddy had the same caramel complexion and black hair as the man at the computer. She had a phone to her ear and was speaking to someone, which didn't prove complicity in a plot, though her eyes fixed on Jane like a shooter's eyes on a target.

In any crisis situation, the most important thing to do was get off the X, move, because if you weren't moving away from the threat, someone with bad intentions was for damn sure moving closer to you.

Avoiding the Escalade, Jane went east. Along the north side of the alley, shadows of two-, three-, and four-story buildings painted a pattern like castle crenellations on the pavement, and she stayed in that shade for what little cover it provided, moving quickly past dumpsters standing sentinel. To the south, past the library, there was a park and beyond that a kindergarten with a fenced playground.

She was opposite the park, where phoenix palms rustled in a light breeze and swayed their shadows on the grass, when the tall man in the raincoat appeared as if conjured, coming toward her, not running, in no hurry, as though it was ordained that she was his to take at will.

The structures to her left housed businesses, the names of which were emblazoned on the back doors: a gift shop, a restaurant, a stationery store, another restaurant. The buildings in that block shared walls, so there were no service passages between enterprises.

When a sedan pulled into the east end of the alley and angled to a stop, serving as a barricade, Jane didn't bother to look behind herself, because she had no doubt the Escalade had likewise blocked the west end of the alleyway.

As she hurried along, she tried doors, and the third one—CLASSIC PORTRAIT PHOTOGRAPHY—wasn't locked. She went inside, where a series of small windows near the ceiling admitted enough light to reveal a combination receiving area and storage room.

The shelves were empty. When she turned to the alley door to engage the deadbolt, the lock was broken.

She'd been skillfully herded to this place. The previous tenant had moved out. She had walked into a trap.

3

THE FORMAL DINING ROOM, WHICH SEATS TWENTY, isn't intimate enough for the conversation that Wainwright Hollister intends to have with Thomas Buckle. They are served in the breakfast room, which is separated from the immense kitchen by a butler's pantry.

A large Francis Bacon painting of smudges, whorls, and jagged lines is the only painting in the twenty-foot-square chamber, a work of alarming dislocations that hangs opposite the ordered vista of nature—groves of evergreens and undulant meadows—visible beyond the floor-to-ceiling windows.

They sit at the stainless-steel and cast-glass table. Buckle faces the windows, so the immense and lonely nature of the ranch will have been impressed upon him by the time he learns that he is to be hunted to the death in that cold vastness. Hollister faces the young director and the painting behind him, for the art of Francis Bacon reflects his view of human society as chaotic and confirms his belief in the necessity of imposing order by brute power and extreme violence.

The chef, Andre, is busy in the kitchen. Lovely Mai-Mai serves them, beginning with an icy glass of pinot grigio and small plates of Andre's Parmesan crisps.

Tom Buckle is clearly charmed by the girl's beauty and grace.

However, the almost comic awkwardness with which he tries to engage her in conversation as she performs her duties has less to do with sexual attraction than with the fact that he is out of his element, the son of a tailor and a seamstress, abashed by the splendor of the wealth all around him and uncertain how to behave with the staff of such a great house. He chats up Mai-Mai as if she is a waitress in a restaurant.

Because she's well trained, the very ideal of a servant, Mai-Mai is polite but not familiar, at all times smiling but properly distant.

When the two men are alone, Hollister raises his glass in a toast. "To a great adventure together."

He is amused to see that Buckle rises an inch or two off his chair, intending to get up and lean across the table in order to clink glasses with his host. But at once the director realizes that the width of the table will make this maneuver awkward and that he should take his cue from Hollister and remain seated. He pretends to have been merely adjusting his position in the chair as he says, "To a great adventure."

After they taste the superb wine, Wainwright Hollister says, "I am prepared to invest six hundred million in a slate of films, but not in a partnership with a traditional studio, where I'm certain the bookkeeping would leave me with a return far under one percent or no return at all." He is lying, but his singular smile could sell ice to Eskimos or apostasy to the pope.

Although Buckle surely knows that he's in the presence of a man who thinks big and is worth twenty billion dollars, he is all but struck speechless by the figure his lunch companion has mentioned. "Well . . . that is . . . you could . . . a very valuable catalog of films could be created for that much money."

Hollister nods agreement. "Exactly—if we avoid the outrageous budgets of the mindless special-effects extravaganzas that Hollywood churns out these days. What I have in mind, Tom, are exciting and intense and *meaningful* films of the kind you make, with budgets between twenty and sixty million per picture. Timeless stories that will speak to people as powerfully fifty years from now as they will on their initial release."

Hollister raises his glass again in an unexpressed endorsement of his initial toast, and Buckle takes the cue, raising his glass as well and then drinking with his host, a vision of cinematic glory shining in his eyes.

Leaning forward in his chair, with a genial warmth that he is able to summon as easily as a man with chronic bronchitis can cough up phlegm, Hollister says, "May I tell you a story, Tom, one that I think will make a wonderful motion picture?"

"Of course. Yes. I'd love to hear it."

"Now, if you find it clichéd or jejune, you must be honest with me. Honesty between partners is essential."

The word *partners* visibly heartens Buckle. "I couldn't agree more, Wayne. But I want to hear it out to the end before I comment. I've got to understand the roundness of the concept."

"Of course you know who Jane Hawk is."

"Everyone knows who she is—top of the news for weeks."

"Indicted for espionage, treason, murder," Hollister recaps.

Buckle nods. "They now say she even murdered her husband, the hero Marine, that he didn't commit suicide."

Leaning forward a little more, cocking his head, Hollister speaks in a stage whisper. "What if it's all lies?"

Buckle looks perplexed. "How can it all be lies? I mean—"

Holding up one hand to stop the young man, Hollister says, "Wait for the roundness of the concept."

He leans back in his chair, pausing to enjoy one of the Parmesan crisps.

Buckle tries one as well. "These are delicious. I've never had anything quite like them. Perfect with this wine."

"Andre, my chef," Hollister says, "is an adjusted person. He is obsessed with food. He lives only to cook."

If the term "adjusted person" strikes Thomas Buckle as odd, he gives no indication of puzzlement.

After a sip of wine, Hollister continues. "According to friends of hers, Jane became obsessed with proving her husband, Nick, didn't commit suicide, that he was murdered, and when she took a leave of absence from the FBI, she devoted herself to investigating Nick's death. On the other hand, authorities and media say she was merely putting up a good front to divert suspicion from her role in his death. We're told she drugged him and got him into the bathtub and slit his throat, cutting his carotid artery with his Marine Ka-Bar knife in such a way that it looked to the coroner as if he'd taken his own life. *But what if that's all a lie?*"

Buckle is intrigued. "*What if* is the essence of storytelling. So what if?"

Hollister continues with relish. "Jane told friends that in her research she found a fifteen percent increase in suicides during the past few years, that all of it involved well-liked, stable people successful in their professions, happy in their relationships, none with a history of depression, people like her husband."

"A few nights ago," Tom Buckle says, "on that TV show *Sunday Magazine*, they did an hour about Hawk. They included experts who said the rate of suicide isn't constant. It goes up, goes down. And all this about happy people killing themselves isn't the case."

"Remember my 'what if,' Tom. What if it's all a lie, and some in the media are part of it? What if Jane Hawk is on to something, and they need to demonize her with false charges, silence her?"

"You see this as a conspiracy story."

"Exactly."

"Well, then it would sure be a conspiracy of unprecedented proportions."

"Unprecedented," Hollister agrees. "Heroic. Involving thousands of powerful people in government and the private sector. Let's say these conspirators called themselves . . . Techno Arcadians."

"Arcadia. From ancient Greece. A place of peace, innocence, prosperity. Essentially Utopia."

Hollister beams and claps his hands twice. "You are just the young man to understand my story."

"But why 'techno'?"

"Do you know what nanotechnology is, Tom?"

"Very tiny machines made up of a handful of atoms, or maybe molecules. They say it's the future, with unlimited medical and industrial applications."

"You are so cutting-edge," Hollister declares and pushes a call button on the table leg. "When I saw your films, I said 'This is a guy on the cutting edge,' and I'm delighted to see I was right."

In answer to the silent summons, Mai-Mai returns to freshen their wine and remove the empty plates that held the Parmesan crisps.

Thomas Buckle smiles at her and thanks her, but he seems to have intuited that the proper behavior in these circumstances is to treat her with reserve, not as if she were working at Olive Garden.

The entertainment business hasn't coarsened him yet, for though Mai-Mai fascinates and attracts him, he watches her not with evident lust, but with an almost adolescent wistfulness and yearning.

When the two men are alone once more, Hollister says, "Let's suppose these conspirators, these Techno Arcadians, have developed a nanomachine brain implant, a control mechanism, that makes complete puppets of the people in whom it's installed. And the puppets don't know what's been done to them, don't know they're now . . . property."

The director blinks, blinks, and a certain quiet excitement comes over him that has nothing to do with six hundred million dollars, that arises from his passion for filmmaking.

"So . . . central to the story would be the issue of free will. A conspiracy intent on subjugating all humanity, the death of freedom, a sort of technologically imposed slavery."

Hollister grins like an amateur author thrilled that a real writer found merit in his scenario. "You like it so far?"

"I damn well do. I like it more by the minute. Even though Jane Hawk inspired the idea, we can't say this is her story, so we'd have to change the character to maybe a CIA agent or something, make her a little older. Maybe it's even a male lead. But one thing . . . why would anyone submit to having such a brain implant surgically installed?"

Leaning forward again, punctuating his revelation with a wink, Hollister speaks in a stage whisper. *"No surgery required. You drug them or otherwise overpower them when they're alone, and the implant is administered by injection."*

4

JANE HAWK HURRIED OUT OF THE STORAGE ROOM. Milky daylight spilled through a large sales area and curdled to gray in a hallway. Two doors stood open on each side of the hall, a shadowy bath and dark empty offices.

At the front of the store, two frosted-glass show windows each bore the words CLASSIC PORTRAIT PHOTOGRAPHY painted in script, reversed from her perspective. Between the windows stood a door with a frosted inlay, and as she approached it, a man shape loomed beyond like a stalker emerging out of fog in a disturbing dream.

He must be one of them. She'd have to take him down to get to the street and away, but even if he was a mortal threat, she could not risk resorting to gunfire when there were sure to be pedestrians on the sidewalk.

The tall man in the raincoat might already be entering the back of the place from the alleyway.

Jane's attention swung toward an interior door to her right, four panels of solid wood, no glass. If it was only a closet, she was cornered.

Instead, beyond lay stairs ascending into gloom. In nearly blinding darkness, she used the handrail to guard against a fall until she arrived at a landing. Another flight led up to a second landing where pale light issued from an open door.

Perhaps the photographer who had once run a business out of the ground floor had lived above his studio.

Considering that the people closing in on her seemed to have herded her into this building, one of them might be waiting in the second-floor apartment.

Her heart labored but didn't race, for she was in the grip of dread rather than full-blown fright. If these were Arcadians—and who else could they be?—they were not going to kill her here. They were going to corner her, Taser her, chloroform her, and convey her to a secure facility where she could scream herself hoarse without being heard by anyone sympathetic to her plight.

Ultimately they were going to inject her with the neural lace that would web her brain and enslave her. Then they would drain from her the names of everyone who had been of assistance to her in this crusade and would insist upon knowing the whereabouts of her five-year-old son, Travis. When she was their obedient puppet, they would eventually instruct her to kill herself.

But not just herself. She knew these elitist creeps. She knew the icy coldness of their minds, the blackness of their hearts, the pure contempt with which they viewed those who did not share their misanthropic view of humanity and did not endorse their narcissism. They would relish cruel vengeance for the trouble she had caused them, for their comrades who had tried to murder her and had been killed instead. They would instruct her to torture her own child and slaughter him; only when he was brutally ravaged and dead would they tell her to kill herself. In the thrall of the nanoweb, with its filaments wound through her brain, she would be unable to resist even the most horrific of their commands.

Compared to injection, a quick death would be a mercy.

She put her tote beside the open door. Drew the Heckler & Koch Compact .45 from the rig under her sport coat. She hated clearing doorways in such situations, but there was no time to hesitate.

Pistol in a two-hand grip, leading with head and gun, low and fast, she crossed the threshold, stepped to the right, back against the wall, eyes on the Heckler's front sight as she swept the room left to right.

Three windows facing the street. No blinds or drapes. Morning light slanting in under scalloped fabric awnings. No furniture. No carpeting on the hardwood floor. Nothing moved except a few dust balls stirred by the slight draft she'd made on entering.

An archway connected this room to others toward the back of the building, where darkness reigned, and there was a door on the right, ajar.

She held her breath and heard only silence. Both training and intuition argued that if someone was in the apartment with her, he would have made a move by now.

The silence was broken when a sound rose from below, perhaps someone ascending the stairs.

She returned to the apartment entrance to retrieve her tote. Among other things, it contained $90,000, all of which—and more— she had taken from the stashes of wealthy Arcadians who had tried and failed to kill her. She couldn't afford to lose it; she was fighting a quiet war, but a war nonetheless, and wars cost money.

The building was old, and the stairs creaked under the weight of whoever was climbing them.

She closed the door. The deadbolt was intact. She engaged it.

5

Mai-mai serves a small chopped salad sprinkled with pine nuts and crumbles of feta cheese.

Tom Buckle smiles and thanks her and watches her lithe form as she exits through the butler's pantry.

When the girl is gone, Wainwright Hollister says, "I need to explain how an injectable brain implant might be feasible, Tom. I don't want you to think of this as a science-fiction movie. It's a thoroughly contemporary thriller."

"I know a little about nanotech, Wayne, just enough to accept the premise."

"Good. Very good. Now suppose hundreds of thousands of these microscopic constructs can be suspended in ampules of fluid and stored at temperatures between—oh, let's say thirty-six and fifty degrees, where they remain in stasis. When injected, the warmth of the blood gradually activates them. They're brain-tropic. The veins conduct them to the heart, then the carotid and vertebral arteries bring them to the brain. Do you know what the blood-brain barrier is, Tom?"

Buckle evidently finds the salad highly agreeable and pauses to swallow a mouthful before saying, "I've heard of it, but I'm no whiz when it comes to medical matters."

"Nor do you need to be. You're an artist and a damn fine one. Ideas and emotions are the stuff of your work. So . . . the blood-brain barrier is a complex biological mechanism that allows vital substances in the blood to penetrate the walls of the brain's numerous capillaries while keeping out harmful substances, such as certain drugs. Let's imagine these amazingly tiny nanoconstructs have been designed to pass through the blood-brain barrier, after which they assemble into a control mechanism in the brain."

"Could they really self-assemble? I mean, many, many thousands of them?"

"An excellent question, Tom. We wouldn't have a viable story if I didn't have an answer!" Hollister pauses to enjoy his salad.

"It's snowing." Thomas Buckle points to the windows behind his host.

Hollister turns in his chair to watch the first snowflakes, the size of quarters and half dollars, spiraling out of the low clouds like some jackpot disgorged by a celestial slot machine.

Refocusing his attention on his guest, he says, "The forecast is for twelve inches. Temperature will drop to the low twenties by nightfall. No wind yet, but it's coming. Winter lingers on these plains. Have you experienced a storm in territory such as this?"

"I'm a California boy. My experience of snow is entirely from TV and movies."

Hollister nods. "If a man were on the run from a killer on a night like the one coming, his least concern might be his would-be assassin. The weather itself could be the deadlier foe." Before Buckle might wonder at this odd statement, his host favors him with a beguiling smile. "I've got a story in mind for just such a movie. But before I bore you with a second scenario, let's see if I can make my nano tale convincing to the end. You asked how these tiny constructs could be made to self-assemble in the brain. Have you heard the term *Brownian movement*?"

6

JANE WAS AT THE MOMENT SAFE BEHIND THE LOCKED door of the second-floor apartment, although not safe for long.

This was a two-story building, and like all the buildings in this block—whether two, three, or four stories—it had a flat roof with a low parapet. There would be an exit to the roof somewhere in these rooms, probably by way of a spiral metal staircase tucked into a service closet.

But she didn't want to go up and out that way. If she got to the roof through a trapdoor or through a stairhead shed, she might discover that they had anticipated her and had stationed one of their own up there to greet her. Then she would have nowhere to go.

Even if no sonofabitch with an XREP Taser waited above, Jane didn't fancy a wild flight across rooftops as in a James Bond flick. Although the buildings varied in height, they were contiguous, and she was likely to find service ladders bolted to walls to allow roof maintenance men easy passage from one elevation to another. However, she'd already counted five agents in this operation, so there might be more. And if they had mounted a force of that size, they might also have a drone at their service.

She'd previously survived an encounter with two weaponized drones in a San Diego park, something similar to a DJI Inspire 1 Pro with a three-axis gimbaled camera. An eight- or ten-pound drone couldn't be fitted with even a miniature belt-feed loaded with .22-caliber rounds, because the recoil would destabilize the craft. But those in San Diego featured a low-recoil compressed-air weapon that fired needle-like quarrels perhaps containing a tranquilizer.

The people now closing in on her would not risk using such a drone on a busy suburban street in a commercial district, but they might keep one hovering above the roofs where, if she appeared, she could be at once dropped unconscious without much chance that anyone at street level would see the assault.

The prospect of a machine assailant gave her a deeper chill than did a thug with an XREP Taser 12-gauge, not necessarily for good reason, but because it seemed to herald a new world in which those people not enslaved by nanoweb neural lace would be policed and punished by robots incapable of empathy or mercy.

She went to the front windows of the apartment living room, which faced onto the street and offered her the best—the only— chance of escaping capture.

7

SITTING WITH HIS BACK TO THE WINDOWS, HOLLIS-ter is so attuned to the moment, so looking forward to Tom Buckle's sudden realization of his dire situation, so enthusiastic about the pending hunt, his senses so heightened that he can almost feel the huge snowflakes spiraling through the windless day behind his back, can almost hear those delicate wheels of crystal lace turning as they descend, can almost smell the blood that will form patterns in brilliant contrast across a canvas of snow.

"Brownian movement," he explains, "is progress by random motion. It's one of nature's primary mechanisms, Tom. The easiest way to explain is with the example of ribosomes, those tiny mitten-shaped organelles that exist in enormous numbers in the cytoplasm of human cells. They manufacture proteins."

When his host pauses for wine, Buckle appears to be dazzled when he says, "Man, you've really worked this story out in detail."

Hollister can feel his blue eyes twinkling with merriment, and he knows his captivating smile has never served him better. "Only because I so very much want you to be part of this, to sign on for this adventure with me. Now, ribosomes. Each one has more than fifty different components. If you break down thousands of ribosomes into their individual components and thoroughly mix them in a suspending fluid, then they ricochet off the molecules of the suspending medium and keep knocking against one another until one by one the fifty-some parts come together like puzzle pieces and, amazingly, assemble into whole ribosomes again. *That* is Brownian movement. It works with Bertold Shenneck's control mechanism because each of the components is designed to fit in only one place, so the puzzle can't assemble incorrectly."

"Shenneck?" Buckle asks.

Hollister should not have mentioned Shenneck, who had in fact invented the nanoweb implant. Now he covers his slip of the tongue. "As I was working this out, I needed to name some characters. That's just what I call the scientist who developed the nanoweb implant."

"It's a good name for the character, but . . ." The director frowns. "It sounds a little familiar. We should check it out, make sure there's not a prominent Bertold Shenneck out there anywhere."

Hollister dismisses the issue with a wave of one hand. "I'm not wedded to the name. Not at all. You're better than I am at this."

Having finished his salad, the director blots his mouth on his napkin. "So how long does it take this brain implant to assemble once it's been injected?"

"Maybe eight or ten hours with the first-generation implant, but the device will be improved, so it might be brought down to, say, four hours. The subject has no memory of being restrained and injected. Once the control mechanism is in place, his mind can be accessed with a key phrase like 'Play Manchurian with me.' Once accessed, he'll do anything he's told to do—and think he's acting of his own volition."

The key phrase delights Buckle. "That great Cold War movie about brainwashing. *The Manchurian Candidate.* John Frankenheimer directed from a Richard Condon novel. Sinatra and Laurence Harvey. Angela Lansbury as Harvey's power-mad mother. About 1962, I think."

"Shenneck liked his little jokes. The scientist character. Whatever we're going to call him."

"My head is swimming, Wayne, but in a good way. I'm really getting into the whole concept. But exactly how does this tie to Jane Hawk, where we started?"

Responding to the call button, Mai-Mai enters to remove the salad plates.

Hollister says, "Just imagine, Tom, that these Techno Arcadians are intent not only on repressing the unruly masses by injecting and controlling selected leaders in politics, religion, business, and the arts. They also want to prevent charismatic individuals with wrong ideas from influencing the culture."

Tom smiles at Mai-Mai and then responds to his host. "What wrong ideas?"

"Any ideas in disagreement with Arcadian philosophy. Let's say it's been decided that controlling these charismatic types isn't enough, that it's necessary to remove their unique genomes from society, prevent them from propagating. So they receive a brain implant and are later directed to commit suicide."

Tom Buckle nods. "Like Jane Hawk's husband. But how would these people be chosen for elimination?"

"The computer model identifies them by their public statements, beliefs, accomplishments. Then they're put on the Hamlet list."

"Hamlet? Why Hamlet?"

"The theory is that if someone had killed Hamlet in the first act, a lot more people would have been alive at the end."

Frowning, Tom Buckle says, "For the movie, we'd probably have to call it something other than the Hamlet list. Anyway, how many people would be on this list?"

"Let's imagine the computer model says that, in a country as large as ours, two hundred and ten thousand of the most charismatic potential leaders in each generation would have to be removed at the rate of eight thousand four hundred a year."

"Mass murder. This is a very dark movie, Wayne."

"To the Arcadians, it's not murder. They think of it as culling from the herd any individuals with dangerous potential, a necessary step toward peace and stability."

Lovely Mai-Mai returns with the entrée: sea bass, asparagus, and miniature buttered raviolis stuffed with mascarpone and red peppers.

Conversation throughout the main course focuses on what changes to make in the lead character and possible twists and turns in the story line. Hollister enjoys this blue-sky session far more than he would if he were actually going to finance a motion picture.

Movies are terrible investments. Perhaps one out of ten makes a profit. And there are countless ways that the distribution company can massage the box office numbers and pad the costs, so when there is a profit, much of it disappears.

However, Tom is bright and enthusiastic. Inventing this movie with him is a pleasure. The more the young man talks, the clearer it becomes that the computer model was right to put him on the Hamlet list, and it is good that he will be dead by dawn.

When Mai-Mai returns to remove their plates, Hollister says, "The time has come for you to do as we discussed."

She meets his stare, and though she is submissive, she is also afraid. Her lips part as if she will speak, but instead of words, her voluptuous mouth produces only tremors.

As she stands beside her master's chair, Hollister takes one of her hands in both of his, and he smiles reassuringly. He speaks to her as he might to a daughter. "It's all right, child. It's just a moment of performance art. You have always excelled as an artist. This is what you were born to do."

Her fear abates. The tremor fades. She answers his smile with an affectionate smile of her own. She bends down to kiss his cheek.

Tom Buckle watches with evident perplexity. When Mai-Mai leaves the room with their plates, the filmmaker is at a loss for words and covers his uncertainty by taking a sip of wine and savoring it.

"I see you're curious about Mai-Mai," Hollister says.

"No, not at all," Buckle demurs. "It's none of my business."

"In fact, Tom, it's the essence of your business here. Mai-Mai is twenty-seven, a year older than you, an exceptional woman."

Tom glances toward the swinging door through which Mai-Mai left the room. "She's quite beautiful."

"Quite," Hollister echoes. "She's also supremely talented. Her paintings redefine realism. They're stunning. By the time she was twenty-two, she'd won numerous awards. By the time she was twenty-four, her work was represented by the most prestigious galleries. She broke new ground as well by combining several of her larger paintings with a unique form of performance art that began to draw enthusiastic crowds."

"Does she still paint?"

"Oh, yes. Better than ever. Magnificent images exquisitely rendered."

"Then why . . ."

"Why is she here serving us lunch?"

"I can't help but wonder."

"She creates paintings but doesn't sell them anymore."

"You sure know how to build mystery, Wayne."

Hollister smiles. "I've intrigued you, have I?"

"Greatly. I'd love to see these paintings."

"You can't. After she finishes a new canvas, she destroys it."

Bafflement creases Tom Buckle's brow. "Whyever would she do such a thing?"

"Because she's an adjusted person. She made the list."

This incident with Mai-Mai has disoriented Tom just enough so that the word *list* has no immediate meaning for him.

"The Hamlet list," Hollister explains.

Puzzlement gives way to misunderstanding, and Tom smiles. "You give one hell of a pitch meeting, Tom. And she's quite an actress."

"She's not an actress," Hollister assures him. "She's just an obedient little bitch. She destroys them because I tell her to."

Just then Tom Buckle's gaze shifts from his host to the wall of glass behind him. "What on earth . . . ?" Tom rises from his chair.

Wainwright Hollister gets to his feet as well and turns to the window.

Mai-Mai stands naked on the terrace, in the swiftly falling snow, facing them and smiling serenely, seeming more mystical than real.

"Her body is as perfect as her face," says Hollister, "but one can grow tired even of such perfection. I've had enough of her."

A scarlet silk scarf drapes Mai-Mai's right hand. It slides to the snow-carpeted terrace, revealing a pistol.

"Performance art," Tom Buckle tells himself, for he is both confused and in denial.

Soundlessly snow falls and falls, cascades of white petals, as Mai-Mai puts the barrel of the gun in her mouth and seems to breathe out the dragon fire of muzzle flash, seems to fold to the terrace in slow motion, the flowerfall of snow settling silently on her silent corpse.

About the Type

This book was set in Palatino, a typeface designed by the German typographer Hermann Zapf (b. 1918). It was named after the Renaissance calligrapher Giovanbattista Palatino. Zapf designed it between 1948 and 1952, and it was his first typeface to be introduced in America. It is a face of unusual elegance.